PIECES FROM A SMALL BOMB

Pieces
from a Small Bomb

by George Cuomo

DOUBLEDAY & COMPANY, INC., GARDEN CITY, NEW YORK, 1976

Library of Congress Cataloging in Publication Data

Cuomo, George.
Pieces from a small bomb.

I. Title.
PZ4.C9733Pi [PS3553.U6] 813'.5'4
ISBN 0-385-11078-2
Library of Congress Catalog Card Number 75–23572

For Rita
And Joe
And John and Joseph

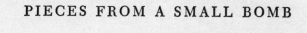

PIECES FROM A SMALL BOMB

I.

Jerome

JEROME TINNEY BELIEVED that appearances counted. No point creaking around in a moth-eaten robe, displaying your infirmities, when you could play the sport in a bow tie. Of course you paid the price, such as it was, for your vanity. First thing this morning as Jerome was on his way to the barbershop he was pounced upon as a soft touch, which he was, by a panhandler who'd spotted him from across the street. "Help out a friend, pop?" the unfortunate man croaked, stabbing forth a grimy hand. "Spare a little something to ease another's misfortune?"

Jerome arrived just as Budd was opening for the day, and took the chair near the window.

"A little closer on the sides, Mr. Tinney?"

"No," Jerome told him. "They're wearing it long."

Budd Huddleston obediently shifted to the back, ticking away.

"Trim up the beard then?" Budd would have loved to get his hands on it.

"No thanks," Jerome said. The beard was as full and white as it ought to be, and not to be fiddled with.

Another customer entered, and waited on one of the mismatched chairs under the long mirror. A young man, no more than forty-five, he'd come in quietly, nodding to Budd and picking up a *Reader's Digest*, not again so much as raising his eyes. A bespectacled, mild-looking fellow, content, it seemed, to hide behind his magazine.

Jerome settled back. Luxuriating. Beneath that perfumed sheet you naturally assumed the regal slouch. The heft and weight of the chair did it, the thick metallic base, the glossy cold arms, the curved headrest with its crinkly tissue paper. Inside that gleaming base some nifty apparatus made the chair revolve as smooth as oil, rise and descend in awesome silence. How could anyone occupy that throne without feeling some tickle of the royal grandeur? At the same time, in that huge tucked-in bib and with a sour giant brandishing his silvery weapon over you, you were also that ages-ago child, pouting and fearful, a tingle of excitement vibrating in your chest as those springy tufts fluttered down. Thus both Kid and King. But when it was over, Budd Huddleston would remove the encircling sheet with a practiced flourish and Jerome Tinney would emerge once again as the simple body he truly was, energetic, quick-eyed, still confident after all these years of a solid foothold in the world.

"Getting along pretty good, Mr. Tinney?"

"Staying out of trouble, I guess," Jerome said.

Budd Huddleston responded with a dry hard grunt. He was hardly your man of a million smiles. A large body, a burden to his feet, with a broad fleshy face and eyes that squinted at you through steel-rimmed glasses. A habit of snapping each bill counting change. At one time Budd had helpers for his three chairs, but he worked alone now. The neighborhood had gone to seed, and Budd was not one to make his own breaks. He lacked the spark, preferring to live with complaints, tension, bile. Jerome could envision him each night, asleep in his sluggish bed, grinding his teeth monotonously. . . .

"Hey!" Budd yelled.

The yell seemed to come a split second before the blast, and Jerome wanted to respond, to ask Budd what the matter was. But the shouldering wall of air that slammed through the room dumped him like a cabbage from a box.

It was all sixes and sevens then. It was rattle your brain, and swing, swing, sweet swing-a-loo.

He was sitting on the floor, blinking thoughtfully, like a child regarding the tantrum he's just had. Hair; glass; magazine covers. He placed a hand to his shirt and felt a wetness.

He flushed with embarrassment before all those people. What business was it of theirs, snuffling around like scavengers, their faces thrust into his amid all that clutter?

Your dignity was always the first thing to go, trampled by the mob. Yahoos everywhere.

He viewed it all through eyes as plastic as a doll's. *Here I am,* he kept telling himself.

Two men, three, a dozen, steered him like a drunk across the splintered lights. Out the door. Between two lines of eyes on the sun-bright sidewalk.

"I'm all right. Where are you taking me?"

"Easy now, pop."

He rose, floating, through the wide-swung doors.

"Stop it. What have I done?"

"Easy does it. Slow and easy."

They kept him strapped down. The doors, magically, reopened. Floating again, he dipped and bobbed into the sunlight, a broken piece on a wave.

Everything stopped. He kept his eyes closed. Someone pinched his arm but Jerome refused to acknowledge him. He wanted to rage against all the fuss but was drifting away to darkness like a ghost fading into a wall.

Still, he was hardly surprised, after all that clamor, to get away with nothing more than a cut over his ribs, a fat pink worm. He'd been fooled more than once before into thinking the jig was up, the first time more than fifty years ago, face down in the Ardennes mud, clamping his helmet tight with the fingers of one outspread hand.

The doctor stitched up the cut with four tiny black bows and slapped on a gauze pad, showing more concern—too much, it seemed to Jerome—about the bump on the back of his head. After you reached a certain age doctors became shamelessly possessive about those signs of damage and decay that would at last deliver you into their keep. Jerome was presented with an ice pack and made to rest on a white bed behind white curtains.

"I'd take it easy awhile," the doctor said upon his return. "A little bump like that, the shock; it takes something out of you."

He was no more than a boy. Doctors weren't the only ones; bankers, even Presidents, hardly shaving yet, telling you how to run your life. What did they know about the long haul?

"The other fellow," the doctor said, "wasn't so lucky."

"The barber?"

"No—he's all right. The other one. He's dead."

"What do you mean, dead?"

"I mean dead. Severed jugular. Ruptured trachea."

The corner of Jerome's mouth twitched. His brain felt *thin,* like some dry stretched membrane.

"It happens," the doctor said.

"What the hell kind of talk is that?"

A cop was waiting for him in the lobby but said he didn't want to bother him now with a lot of questions. Maybe tomorrow . . . ?

"What was it?" Jerome asked.

"A bomb," the cop said.

A nurse was recruited to push him through the long polished corridor in a wheel chair, to make sure he didn't trip on something and end up suing. She wheeled him like a package down a concrete ramp to the sidewalk and offered to help him into the taxi. It riled him. The whole thing riled him. Who gave anyone the right to drop a bomb in the middle of your life?

"The wound's not mortal, girl. I can manage." But he stood up too quickly and felt lightheaded. The nurse took his arm and maneuvered him through the door and onto the leathery seat. He winced; the stitches felt like cats' claws. Astonishingly, he was out of breath. "Thanks, sweetheart." Puffing like a weakling. "I'm all right now."

Jerome had always been sturdy, sound of tooth and bone, and he wasn't about to be done in by a scratch and a small bump. Staying power, after all, was his ace. He got it from his father who, although a little dotty at the end from acquiring religion, was still going strong at ninety-one, and finally lost out to pleurisy only because the doctor dosed him up for something else, measles maybe, or leg cramps. So much for the glories of modern medicine. And Jerome had played by the rules, holding up his end for too many years to give up now, after getting this far, or let his life be blown to pieces by the first fool to come along with a crazy notion. But he couldn't shake off that odd stretched slowness in his mind. Something—his balance, his sense of solid purchase—seemed to be draining downward and dissolving out like fine spray from his fingertips and toes.

A nip of sherry, he decided, would help.

He lay in bed, groggy and muted but tingling with excitement. He waited for the hourly news on the radio and finally heard it. It wasn't easy to shrug off, your own name intoned in some announcer's impartial voice. Your nerve endings fluttered like delicate hairs. He could feel then—he hadn't earlier—the glass scoring the flesh, ripping into the only body you'd ever have, your one ticket to the game. He put his fingertips to the bandage, gingerly, and heard his name again, like the banging of a gong.

I am the event they're reporting to me. I am the history I'm listening to.

That, for sure, was one tune he'd never hummed before.

All things considered, he awoke pretty chipper the next morning. The newest kid on the block, twirling a stick. It drove both his wives crazy, God rest them, but his spirits always rose with the sun. He'd spent forty years back in Boston selling grindstones, emery disks, and Carborundum wheels, starting on a borrowed sample case and ending with his own company and a nest egg for a California retirement, across the Bay from San Francisco, and that kind of luck didn't come to slugabeds.

Or to people who never responded to anything, good or bad, with more than a shrug. Jerome had an offer once for his business. A number of offers, but one in particular. It would have set him up for life, and he was no more than fifty then, just coming into his prime. He turned it down cold, and everybody said he was crazy. Why don't you want to sell? they kept asking. Because it's *mine*, he told them, that's why, and if you can't understand that you can't understand anything.

He read the story in the morning paper, read it twice, and then changed the gauze pad, studying his bare ribs soberly. The skin around the cut had turned hard and glossy beneath the tiny black crosses, producing a slight puckering itch.

He left, closing the apartment door behind him, listening for the faint click of the lock and feeling enormously relieved when the whole building didn't just blow up in his face.

He double-parked with the motor running and gazed across the street. Four wooden sawhorses barricaded the sidewalk. A policeman, chin up, arms folded with billy club dangling from one hand, stood next to the candy-stripe pole. He stared at Jerome.

Amazingly the plate-glass window was intact. Had he merely imagined the window blown out, the whole shop demolished? He could recall it perfectly: the crowd, the noise and confusion —and the front window shattered to bits. He would have sworn to it.

The three barber chairs were still standing, whitened under a layer of powdery dust, but the big mirror was gone, leaving a naked rectangle of clean paint. The back wall was ripped open, exposing laths and plaster and jagged chicken wire. The bottles and gleaming instruments had disappeared from the marble shelf. He couldn't see the floor but remembered it covered with glittering fragments. The recollection reassured him.

The policeman moved to the curb, arms at his side now, and peered across at Jerome. Briefed, no doubt, to watch for the perpetrator slinking back to admire his handiwork.

A person could plant a bomb anywhere he wanted, for whatever reason caught his fancy. Nothing so entrenched it couldn't be blasted to smithereens in a twinkling. The thought didn't do much to brighten your day. The world a pressure cooker ready to explode, even out here, along the edges of that magnificent Bay, where a few million natives of somewhere else had hoped to find the weather warmer, the sun brighter, the life more gentle. Even here violence and melodrama our daily dish. What held body and soul together anyhow? What but the grace of God and a potful of luck kept the streets from running with blood?

The policeman stepped from the curb, his eyes steady, and moved toward him. Startled, Jerome hit the gas and roared away.

Jerome had seen the picture in the paper, read the obituary. Harold Bengar, forty-four, for seventeen years a teacher of social studies, no go-getter maybe but probably decent and sincere, helpful to the pupils. Survived by his wife, one son, two daughters, a mother.

A quiet man, to judge from the way he'd hidden behind his magazine, wanting only to be inconspicuous.

Conspicuous enough now among the heavy-laden group on the grass, with all eyes on the lacquered wood box. His name in the newspapers for the last time, soon to be removed from his homeroom door, no longer scribbled on the tops of weekly quizzes.

Spades looping, the dirt rumbling upon the lowered box, that final thunder. Funerals were harsh fare for old men, and Jerome gritted his teeth, standing on the soft grass. Everybody's got the same joker in his deck and he wondered, if his card had come up amid the flying glass, whether the civics teacher would have bothered to come. Dorothy and Valerie obviously would not: he'd been there, bleak and dreary, hat in hand, to bury each in turn, and that was one social obligation that never got repaid. And the kids, and *their* kids, scattered like birdseed all over the country, making their way, paying off the mortgages; two sons and two daughters and—what was it now?—eleven grandchildren, some almost ready to start their own families; all of them too busy, understandably, to make the useless western trek just to watch some geezer, a stranger, eased into the ground.

The crowd began drifting away. Jerome gazed hard at the faces. Had the police dispatched a plainclothesman to the grave site—looking for tension, a too-studied innocence, the one person somehow specially marked?

Departing mourners approached the widow. *Dead*, they all

said. Eventually, after hearing it from all her friends, she would believe it. *Dead*, they said, that solemn chorus, that flat-footed procession, until the word reverberated for her.

Jerome struggled against the urge to go up and say, *Your husband and I, never having met, share a deep bond.* It was true. The same nameless bastard almost got both of them.

He went to her. She stared wide-eyed, waiting for him to identify himself. He took her hand. It was dry as a stick. "I'm terribly sorry," he said. "It was dreadful. No one had the right."

From that doleful setting Jerome proceeded downtown to police headquarters, hardly a more cheerful place, a begrimed fortress of slabs and narrow windows. Even the broad steps leading up to the entrance, a medium-sized city's medium-sized gesture toward civic splendor, were splotched with pigeon droppings.

Mr. Amicus
Deputy Chief, Detectives

The office was as spare and somber as its occupant, who greeted Jerome morosely from behind his ancient grainy desk. Your arrival just one more letdown in his already dreary day. He wore a dark suit, a white shirt, a tie. Too gloomy by half, with the small firm mouth of a puritan. Tenacious. Nothing you could spring—murder, mayhem, or the routing of the troops, horse, foot, and dragoon—was going to budge this fellow off dead center.

"I understand you weren't hurt too badly, Mr. Tinney," he began, still frowning.

"That's right," Jerome said. "I made it, I survived. I gave your secretary my complete statement."

"I'm sure it'll be helpful."

"The truth is, I don't even know what hit me."

"It was a bomb."

"What kind? The paper didn't say."

"We asked them not to," Amicus said. "A few sticks of dynamite in a pipe—between you and me."

"A crude explosive device, eh?"

"Not all that crude," Amicus said.

"Sophisticated then?"

"Not exactly. Small, though."

"Seems big enough when you're sitting there like Humpty Dumpty on top of it."

Amicus leaned forward to pick up his black pen. A clean desk man, the walls equally bare, no pictures, no bric-a-brac, nothing to distract him, no sign that the human race ever created anything more interesting than swivel chairs and roll-away file drawers. He twirled the black pen slowly in his right hand, observing his own performance with a critical eye. "You don't suppose anybody was out to get you, do you?"

"Me?" Jerome thought hard: an extravagant possibility, not without its temptations, but hardly credible.

Amicus stopped twirling to give him a disapproving look: *It could happen. You've got as much claim to disaster as the next guy.*

"I doubt if anyone's after me," Jerome said.

"Do you go there the same time every week?"

"No," Jerome said. "That's the worst of it. I could have been blotted out by pure chance." He paused, eying the detective for a reaction. "Who did it, do you know?"

Amicus shrugged.

"There must be suspects. You must have clues, leads."

"Nothing I'd brag about right now."

Amicus seemed to enjoy his own caginess, although to read that fellow's thoughts you had to work fine. He didn't give you much to go on. A flick of one eyelid, the hint of a smile.

"Aren't you going to ask me any more questions? I thought that's why you had me come."

"I'm sure your statement will be just fine."

Jerome had expected more deference, a greater show of interest. "I was there," he pointed out. "A sitting duck for the first wild man to come along."

Amicus remained impassive.

Jerome tried another tack. "I guess Budd and I are your two key witnesses."

"That's right. You were the lucky ones."

"The other fellow got killed," Jerome said, still awed by the thought. "While reading the *Reader's Digest*."

"I didn't know he was reading the *Reader's Digest*."

"It's all in my statement. I've just come from his funeral."

"The schoolteacher's? Did you know him?"

"I felt a bond of sorts."

Amicus seemed dubious.

"If there's any way I can help . . ." Jerome said.

"Not right at the moment. One thing: You look to me like a man who'd find a classier barber."

"I've been going there for years."

"It's practically part of the West Side now," Amicus said.

"The neighborhood's changed," Jerome said. And then, perking up: "Was somebody out to get Budd?"

"I guess it's a possibility."

"Or the schoolteacher. You're looking into all this aren't you?"

"We look into everything. We're very thorough."

You couldn't tell from that gray unwavering expression if Amicus had everything in the palm of his hand or was trying to cover up the fact that he didn't. For all his show of self-assurance, Amicus didn't necessarily strike you as a man to resolve mysteries. Not the real ones, at any rate. Not the ones that made a difference.

"Did you know," Jerome inquired, "that the Jewish people bury their dead the next day? Twenty-four hours is the outside limit."

"I know," Amicus said.

"I guess you get lots of this. Bombs, I mean."

"Not in barbershops. Hardly ever in barbershops."

"You can count on me for help. I hope you realize that."

"That's kind of you." Amicus stood up. "Thank you for coming."

Jerome stood up too. "I've plenty of free time, so that's no problem."

"Fine," Amicus said. "Very good."

Jerome retraced his path through the desolate hallways and down the broad pigeon-specked steps whereupon, when he reached the sidewalk, he was approached by a real stunner of a woman, tall and fine, and dressed to the hilt.

"I'm Olivia Cowan," she said, offering a lovely hand, and Jerome was surprised—delighted—to feel a small odd *flip* in his chest. The years melted like snow. It might have been the sheen of her long black hair, the press of bosom and leg against her dress. It could have been the subdued voice, the high cheekbones in the porcelain-fine face. The sublime aura given off by certain women. ("Horses sweat," his mother used to tell him, "men perspire, ladies glow.")

"Jerome Tinney," he replied, tipping his hat. "At your service."

"I came out just as you went in," she said. "I've been waiting for you."

"I had no inkling."

"I saw your picture in the paper. What did he say to you?"

"Mr. Amicus? Little enough, why?"

"Did he say who did it?"

"No," Jerome said. "Do you know who did it?"

"No," she said after a hesitation.

"Are you involved?"

"No," she said. "Not really." But something was gnawing at her beneath that cool reserve. "A friend of mine," she said. "I won't bore you. I was just wondering what he asked."

"He hardly did much asking, although I was more than willing to help. I feel a stake, after all, in seeing this cleared up."

She turned thoughtful.

"If there's a problem," he offered, "I've plenty of free time."

She nodded, still thoughtful.

"Citizens, after all, have a responsibility."

"You're very sweet," she said, smiling for the first time.

"You seem disturbed," Jerome said.

"Oh no," she said. "Really."

She gazed past Jerome. He turned to see a silver Jaguar with a sparkling grille moving slowly down the street toward them, ten thousand dollars worth of car with a Negro chauffeur behind the wheel. More like a houseboy, his head barely above the wheel, his eyes masked behind gigantic sunglasses. He was medium dark, with a balloon-sized crop of electric black hair and one of those mustache and goatee combinations that encircle the mouth. The fellow slowed the car and looked directly at Olivia, his glasses like black tunnels on his dark gray face. It was not the look, somehow, of a houseboy.

"Thank you," Olivia said to Jerome. She hesitated, then added, "It's been nice talking," and walked away, her head high, her long legs flashing.

It's not easy, of course, when a woman like that materializes before your eyes, pleading for help, to let her drift off with the crowd. The Jaguar had slowed again at the corner, and the boy poked out his head, the hair like a black sun, to look back at Olivia walking toward him. He turned left then, and when Olivia reached the corner she also turned left.

It was one of those sharp moments, with no time for divvying up options. But he'd sensed the depth of something troubling her.

He hopped into his car, started the motor, and pulled away, all in seconds, but calmly, with a smoothness that exhilarated him. He swung left at the corner and saw the silver Jaguar double-parked, then moving again, two heads visible through the rear window. He felt a little jump of excitement. At the same time he felt remarkably detached: some ancient sage viewing it all—tragedy, melodrama, farce—with a steady and ironic eye.

No wonder cops looked self-contained. No wonder Amicus seemed so smug behind that flat noncommittal gaze.

He followed the Jaguar through the stone pillars of the university and along the main campus drive, between wide green lawns and past the glassy student center, the stone block library. Students wandered nonchalantly in the afternoon sun, without a care in the world. The city seemed miles away.

Then they were out again, with a vengeance. You only had to cross the street from the newest building on campus to find yourself in the very bowels of the city's melancholy slums, the worst and oldest part of the West Side, long ago disfigured beyond redemption. All those stores with their weathered signs (THRIFT SHOP—2ND-HAND CLOTHS), their accordion iron gates padlocked nightly across the glass windows. Dogs sniffed at the bountiful garbage cans, one ragged kid chased another, and in the gutter lay an overturned supermarket cart—the brightest, shiniest thing around. The houses were two, three, four stories high, old and cramped, filthy, fretted with rusty fire escapes and lopsided window shades. The vacant lots were like dumps;

were dumps. Kids, women, men congregated on steps, on milk cases in front of stores, at the curbs. It used to be called Niggertown. Then it became the ghetto. Now it was the West Side. It had grown and spread, but the only thing that had changed was the name.

Not a place to make you proud of your country, nor the place, really, that you envisioned as California during those wintry Boston storms. But Jerome had not come West with any intention of disappearing into some pastel retirement community on the desert, a few thousand garden apartments complete with social directors and shuffleboard courts. Too much the city boy for that, he needed a real world around him, movement and bustle, people making their way. He wrote off Los Angeles as too brash, and San Francisco itself—although he was tempted— as a bit precious for his taste. So he found an apartment across the Bay from San Francisco, where the Southern Pacific reached its noisy western terminus, where the dock wallopers and machinists and assembly workers provided a reasonable mixture of the humankind, along with those sun-tanned Nordics you saw on the billboards. Back in the heyday of Jack London, the oyster pirates set out under cover of night from this side of the Bay; it was a place where the going had never been easy, never that gentle Golden Land. Here people always had to scrabble and claw to make their way.

The Jaguar swung to the curb and stopped. Jerome had just gone through an intersection, leaving him in a pretty dicey situation. He could either try a quick U-turn on that terribly narrow street, or brazen it out by driving right past them.

He drove past, keeping his eyes riveted ahead. But Olivia was already out of the car, flagging him down: *Here! Here we are!*

Jerome hit the brake, and the car behind him—which he hadn't noticed—screeched and honked furiously. He pulled to the curb to let the man pass: an outraged black giant, holding the wheel with one hand and gesturing obscenely with the other.

"Big galoot!" Jerome yelled out after him.

In the mirror he saw Olivia walking toward him. She looked pretty composed, all in all. Jerome admired composure in a woman. He climbed out to the sidewalk and touched his hat. "Another surprise," he said. "I'm honored."

"You almost got lost at that red light. We went as slowly as we could."

They stood in front of a vacant store, its plate-glass window covered with a coat of whitewash.

"You don't want to get the wrong idea," he told her.

"That's all right," she said. "As long as you were enjoying yourself."

The colored boy approached, his dark glasses wrapped around his face with the wide earpieces plunging into the undergrowth of hair. He couldn't have been over twenty, and walked with an odd sideways twist, his left shoulder dropping sharply. He wore black skintight trousers, polished black shoes, and one of those loose fancy-colored overshirts, straight from the heart of Africa. He was shorter than Olivia, shorter than Jerome, narrow-shouldered, narrow-hipped, frail and spindly with spidery legs and small narrow feet. A hundred pounds maybe, dripping wet.

He gave Jerome the once-over, lingering in particular over the white beard. He didn't say anything, and neither did Olivia, leaving Jerome to get the ball rolling.

"I feel like a stranger in a strange land," he said, gesturing at the houses, the streets, the people. Every black face on the block seemed turned toward them. Several men watched from in front of the grim café across the street, like enemy sentries. "And that's not right. We're all Americans. We're all in the same boat."

"This is Sylvester Childs," Olivia said.

"My pleasure. Jerome Tinney."

"I know," the boy said. The dark glasses and the mustache-goatee and that ball of electrified hair practically turned his face into a tribal mask.

"I'll leave you people now," Olivia said.

"Eh?"

"I was just dropping Sylvester off."

"I don't own a car," Sylvester said. He made it sound like a statement of principle.

"I don't want you to think I was following you," Jerome told him.

"I assumed you were following both of us," Olivia said.

"I guess not," Sylvester said. "I guess I was just the bonus."

"It's not worth quibbling over," Jerome said.

"I don't want you following me when I leave," Olivia said.

"Of course not," Jerome assured her.

"Maybe I can show him around," Sylvester said.

"That'd be nice," Olivia said. "He's gone to all this bother."

"No bother," Jerome said.

"Sure it was," Sylvester said. He had an easy drawling speech that seemed to give the lie to the masklike expression. "Trucking all over town like that, ending up way out in the jungle with all the aboriginies."

A patrol car cruised slowly past. For the first time Sylvester's face changed: teeth bared now, he grinned like a begoggled jack-o'-lantern at the two cops. Soberly, they stared back.

"Know them?" Jerome asked.

"Old friends," the boy said. "Distinguished acquaintances."

The patrol car drifted by, the cops watching the people and the people watching the cops.

Olivia nodded good-by to Sylvester, to Jerome. The kids and the men across the street watched her get into the car. When she drove off, the kids and the men, leaning their elbows on the tops of cars, slouching on stone steps, turned back to Jerome.

"You clean, mister?" Sylvester asked. "You come as a friend?"

"Of course," Jerome said, a bit sharply. He felt deserted and without, in truth, much going for him.

"The officials sometimes work out very intricate deals."

"What officials?"

Sylvester laughed it off and headed for the whitewashed glass door. He pushed it open and bowed Jerome in, placing one hand flat against his stomach. He looked like a gnome, some kind of cagey dwarf, about to wink maybe, although naturally you couldn't tell with the dark glasses.

Jerome didn't feel he could pull back and so stepped briskly inside, removing his hat and hoping for the best. It was a large high-ceilinged room, a store stripped bare, the walls covered with posters and handbills. Two long tables stood end to end along one wall; folding chairs, boxes and bundles, tin cans for ashtrays, a tilting fridge, a mostly empty case of Dr. Pepper. Books and sweaters lay scattered about, but only two people were present, a young white man and a bronze-skinned colored girl with orange hair. Both were crouched down at the back, removing pamphlets from brown cartons. They turned a heavy eye toward Jerome, their expressions about as hospitable as smoked glass. The fellow wore a bright red and white wool cap.

The room reminded Jerome of a neighborhood union hall he knew in the thirties, before he had his own business, when hard times had him running the tool crib in a machine shop. Almost forty years ago, but this place had the same feeling, the same stale emptiness. You'd think, with all the history in between, places wouldn't look the same anymore.

Sylvester closed the door but stayed behind Jerome, not moving or making a sound. No one moved or made a sound. "Hello," Jerome said, smiling, but neither the fellow nor the colored girl smiled back. The girl straightened up, though, and the fellow dropped his pamphlets to the floor and did the same. But that was it, without a word. Jerome glanced over his shoulder at Sylvester, who took this as his cue to step forward. He gestured toward the girl. "This is Louise," he said.

"Pleased to meet you," Jerome said.

"This is Ruel," Sylvester said.

"Rule?"

"R-U-E-L," Sylvester said.

"How do," Jerome said.

The fellow was maybe a couple of years older than Sylvester, and at least a foot taller. He looked like a basketball player, a real beanstalk with an elongated face and peach-basket hands and a lean hard body that gave the impression of having a lot of spring. You could see him leaping over everyone for the ball, taking off like a jumping jack. But he stood lazily, the way athletes do, and glared at Jerome, not exactly angry but with a kind of fearsome unbendingness, an expression that didn't go with the jaunty red and white cap and its jiggling pom-pom.

"This gentleman here," Sylvester said, "Mr. Jerome Tinney by name, has just come from a conversation with Mr. Amicus about the barbershop."

They observed Jerome steadily.

"I was the one," Jerome explained, "who was sitting there when the bomb went off, getting my hair cut."

They looked at his hair.

"I invited him by to say hello," Sylvester said.

"Why? Does he know something?"

"More'n we do, I figure."

"I don't even know what hit me," Jerome said. He didn't want them getting the wrong idea. They looked pretty touchy, all in all, and there was something about being blown out of a chair one day that left you disinclined to push your luck the next.

Sylvester, however, smiled genially. He seemed by all odds the friendliest of the bunch, once you got used to the dark glasses and the hair. And his manner of speaking, even though it fluctuated between sounding pretty educated and pure piney woods, never lost its easy offhand quality. "We figured you for more of an expert."

"The police seem to be the experts," Jerome said. "They have the responsibility, after all."

"They come at us, there's gonna be trouble," the girl—Louise, with the orange hair—said.

"Come at you?" Jerome said.

Louise said nothing, and neither did the two boys.

A large election poster on the wall caught Jerome's eye. He recognized the face but couldn't make out the writing without leaning forward and squinting.

The Time Is Now!
JUSTIN GAGE!

"Know our friend there?" Sylvester inquired.

"Voted for him," Jerome said.

"So did we," Sylvester said. "Only let's stick with the barber-shop, okay?"

"What do you want to know? Why did you bring me here?"

"Hey, man—we didn't bring you nowhere. You *followed* us, remember?"

"What?" Ruel said. "This guy followed you here? From talking with Amicus?"

"He ain't gonna bite," Sylvester said quietly. "He's just a regular normal senior citizen."

"What're you doing—inviting people in off the street? I thought you were supposed to be over at the clinic. What the hell were you doing at the station house?"

Sylvester paused. "I was *at* the clinic. I was over there this morning long before you ever got dragged out of bed, would be my guess. And I was down at the station house with a friend, if that's all right with you."

Ruel narrowed his eyes. "You chauffeuring her around again? I thought colored chauffeurs went out of style. What is it—you planning on bringing them back?"

Jerome glanced at Louise, thinking she'd be offended, but she didn't seem to be. Neither did Sylvester, who gazed at Ruel patiently, one shoulder low, the other high and turned in, his eyes hidden behind the glasses.

Ruel turned to Jerome. "You shouldn't come nosing around maybe. You nose around too much, you end up seeing more than you want."

Jerome couldn't tell if Ruel was angry at him too, or just at Sylvester for bringing him.

"I offered to show him around," Sylvester said. And then, to Jerome: "If you're ready now, maybe we can begin the tour."

"I thought this was it," Jerome said.

"Just the first stop," Sylvester said.

"Maybe he's seen all he wants," Ruel said.

"Nah," Sylvester said. "There's lots more. You coming, Ruel? You joining us?"

"No thanks."

"You still game?" Sylvester asked Jerome.

"I've survived so far," Jerome said.

"You a regular Tarzan, eh, for a man your age? Surviving way out here in the jungle."

He said it with a smile, and Jerome suspected he'd begun to take kindly to him.

Sylvester turned out to be surprisingly light-footed, scuttling along with his odd sideways hunch, his polished black shoes skipping with quick beats. He led Jerome into an alley, hopping a short wooden gate halfway down, aiming straight for it as if planning to crash right through, then at the last moment vaulting casually over it, his legs scissoring in mid-air and his African overshirt billowing like a parachute. He turned back then to unlatch the gate for Jerome.

They came out between two old brownstones.

"Ralston Street," Sylvester said. His gesture took in the whole block, including a jingling ice-cream truck across the street, the driver at the open refrigerator door, the kids clutching coins, unwrapping Popsicles. Sylvester stepped aside to let two colored women pass, one pushing a baby stroller. They ignored him to gaze quizzically at Jerome. He tipped his hat.

"Up there," Sylvester said, motioning to an apartment house across the street. "Third floor rear; he's in prison. White guy too. Not all black here, you know. Ratty is what it is, but some's white ratty. Anyhow this guy thought these people were helping him out, leading him right to the pay-off. The golden rainbow. Only he was being set up, if you know what I mean, for the large fall. Tough, but people figure he asked for it, being dumb. Old lady works night shift now at Arless Bakery; bread-wrapping machine. Four kids."

They stepped to the curb.

"What do you wanna see now? Pimps? Whores? Dope addicts? We got all the regular assortment. Lots of torn-up vets around too, but I don't see none out taking the air right now."

"I don't want to talk about that war."

"Better wars in your day, eh?"

"There sure were," Jerome said. "Although I could've done without the lot of them."

"Ever serve yourself?"

"Yesterday," Jerome said.

"Hey, now?"

"In France."

"World War Two?"

"One," Jerome said.

"In here now." Sylvester cut into the vestibule of an old apartment house, the floor tiles worn, the dull brass mailbox door dangling open. "No elevator," he said, heading for the dark staircase and skimming sideways up the metal-tipped steps to the first landing with Jerome in hot pursuit. They doubled back along the narrow hall and climbed to the second floor, the walls gray, the lights weak, the air rancid from last week's fry grease, then the third floor, the fourth, Jerome puffing and wheezing, and then up another flight and out through a latched metal door to the tar-paper roof. Sylvester used a two-by-four chunk to keep the door from locking them out and led Jerome past flapping shirts and TV antennas and hooded, rocket-shaped exhaust pipes to the short brick wall at the edge. The mortar was crumbling and the cement crown had cracks like a road map. Black smoke flecked with gray ash swirled up from the incinerator chimney. Beer cans. An empty whiskey bottle with the label soaked off.

"View," Sylvester said. He wasn't even breathing hard. "See it all from here, save a lot of tromping about. University. Right over there, as you can see. Very convenient for the studious types. Pendleton Street, where the bus runs, all the big stores. Hennings Street. Know what's on Hennings Street?"

"What?" Jerome said, gulping for air.

"Welfare office, man. Everybody knows that."

"I grew up in a place like this," Jerome said between breaths. "Before they had welfare offices."

"That the truth now? A real funky, rough place like this? When, back in the big depression?"

"Before. I could tell you about the depression too, if you're interested."

"But you made your way. You found yourself a niche. And now you got a nice retirement out here in the sun country."

"I sold grindstones. I sold Carborundum wheels. Fast and Exceeding Fine, that was our motto."

"Tough sledding, though? Especially at first?"

"I did without a few meals along the way."

"Hey, man—we got things in common. We can trade horror stories. Only around here, you know, the big depression never ended. Like over there, the Safeway. Sells more frozen horsemeat than any place in the world. *Pet Food,* it says on the label, but the dogs are lucky to get the leavings, if you follow me."

"Do you live around here?"

"Yes, sir, I do. I live right around here, with my mother."

"Are you at the university? Bright young fellow like yourself."

"Oh yes. I am a regular bona fidey university student."

"Hard work's what it takes. I had salesmen I never saw without a cup of coffee in their hands. At the end of the month they always wondered how come the others got the fat envelopes."

"Ain't all bad around here, you know. Some nice houses, nice blocks. Green; see the green over there? There's even a dude that got this real fantastic tree in his front yard, pomegranate tree. Man, people from the whole neighborhood tromp over there come spring and stand on the sidewalk, digging those crazy blossoms."

"More power to him," Jerome said. Four stories below, a patrol car cruised down the block, moving in from their left. "Are those the same cops?" Jerome asked.

"Same," Sylvester said. "Feel like dropping some pennies, rouse them up a bit?"

"Why would I want to do that?"

"No harm. Hit their roof, that's all, send them chomping around after us."

"What happens when we get caught?"

"Wouldn't, if you stuck with me. Really show you places then."

"I think I'll skip that part."

"We got bombardiers, just kids, that'll bong a car roof every time, practically computing wind resistance and all. And down inside the vehicle, that penny sounds like a regular Chinese gong. It's like the Big Bell of Doom. I mean, it re*verb*erates. Your *ears* ring."

The patrol car moved directly beneath them.

"For sure now? Not even one little old cent?"

"They're public servants," Jerome said. "They've got a difficult job to perform."

"Too bad, big opportunity." Sylvester ticked his tongue sadly and watched the patrol car pass. Then he looked up, his eyes hidden behind the black circles. "You doing okay? You enjoying yourself now?"

"I'm doing fine," Jerome assured him.

"We ain't giving you any excitement though. Tell you what. Let's say they're after us, okay? Really running ass. And we gotta move, man, we gotta vanish, real fast, and there's only one way. The fire escape. Okay—go!"

Sylvester broke for the iron ladder, its two hand bars arching over the brick wall in giant loops.

"Hey—"

He lunged at the ladder, grabbing the near loop with one hand and swinging out from the roof, out past the stone wall, his body horizontal, poised in mid-air four stories over the street.

Jerome's heart leaped.

Sylvester grabbed the other metal loop with his free hand and landed with his feet a few rungs down the side of the building, only his head showing over the brick wall. His head disappeared.

Jerome raced to the ladder and peered down, tingling. Sylvester was already two stories down, skimming along the slatted fire escape landing and then sliding down the perpendicular ladder to the next landing, like a fireman down a pole, his feet not touching the rungs, his body foreshortened beneath the huge black ball of hair. He dropped from the last ladder to the sidewalk, landing in a crouch, his shirt billowing.

In seconds.

Sylvester backed into the street, face upturned, hands on hips, waiting for Jerome to follow suit.

Jerome waved, a sort of salute, a sign-off, and walked back across the tar-paper roof and through the metal door, removing the two-by-four chunk to let the door lock behind him. On the second-floor landing a man with his key in a door stiffened in the dim hallway and glared over his shoulder with white bulging eyes, and for just a moment Jerome wondered if he wouldn't have been safer, all in all, diving headfirst down the ladder.

Sylvester was leaning against a parked car in front of the entrance with his arms folded across his narrow chest, his ankles crossed, his polished black shoes glistening, unscuffed. He straightened up and reached forth to feel the lapel of Jerome's jacket between his thumb and forefinger. "Fine threads, man. I really dig fine threads." Then he smiled and said, "C'mon, we'll head on back."

They returned through the alley. The show was over. Sylvester was quiet, his pace leisurely now.

"You got a problem there with your back, eh, son?"

"That's right," Sylvester said.

"Born like that, or hurt yourself?"

"Born."

"That's all right. You don't have to take a back seat to anyone, the way you get around."

They fell silent again.

"I got the impression before," Jerome said, "that you and your friends thought maybe the police were after you. Is it about the bomb?"

"Seems like it, from where we sit."

"You wouldn't do a thing like that, would you?"

"Course I wouldn't. You can tell that right away, can't you?"

"It's crazy anyhow. Who'd want to blow up a barbershop?"

"I'd sure like to find out."

"I would too, I can tell you. And I expect to. It's no fun getting blown out of a chair. The other fellow, the schoolteacher, ended up dead on the spot."

"I read about that," Sylvester said.

"I'm willing enough to go when the time comes, but not with some stranger having the whole say-so."

"I get your drift."

"I don't even like the idea of little kids in pigtails dropping pennies on my car, meaning no harm."

"Okay."

"Neighborliness at least deserves a try. Common decency."

"That's it. The eagle will fly with the dove. The lion will befriend the lamb."

"Don't sell your ideals short. Don't toss them into the gutter with the garbage."

"Hey, you're a regular patriot, man."

"The great Forty-Eight," Jerome said.

"C'mon, man. Fifty."

"I know. Everything's changing."

They emerged from the alley, back at the store front. Sylvester stopped by the whitewashed window and looked up at Jerome, his head sort of naturally tilted from the slant of his body. "I gave you the tour," he said. "First class."

"I appreciate your taking the trouble."

"Now you gotta play fair . . . what'd you come for?"

"Nothing," Jerome said. "Nothing at all."

"Just tagging the lady, then? That the kind of old man you are? Chasing the pretty skirts, grooving in on all the chicks?"

"It wasn't that."

"Maybe you're a better friend of Mr. Amicus than you say."

"Oh no. That's not it." He blinked hard and squinted. He was having trouble keeping Sylvester in focus.

"Or know more about the barbershop than you're letting on."

"I was just sitting there," Jerome protested. "Like Humpty Dumpty. I didn't know what hit me." His own voice sounded distant, as if it were moving away from him.

Sylvester was talking, and sounded even farther off.

The pressure was coming from both temples, trying to meet in the middle. He sometimes got that feeling from drinking too much Chinese tea, his head tightening fiercely. He was exhausted, and terribly sad. He could look ahead for years, or hours that seemed like years, with everything passing very slowly, a huge wheel turning. The sadness stunned him. He needed time to speak out, to make his point. But who could tell friend from foe at a moment like this? He was too deflated to speak out. His strength was dripping away like thick drops of oil sliding off the slowly turning wheel.

"Hey there, man. You all right?"

"I'm all right," Jerome said, surprised at his own whisper.

"Did I wear you out back there? I'm sorry about that. I didn't mean to wear you out."

"I'm all right," Jerome told him, and suddenly seemed to be, everything bright and sharp. He could see the sparkling silver Jaguar across the street, Olivia Cowan at the wheel, watching. He blinked hard, trying to keep the focus. Her face was like fine porcelain. He knew what it was: she was waiting for him to leave, so she could speak to Sylvester. They had something going, those two. You'd never guess it, a beauty like that, money and class written all over her, and the poor boy scuttling along to make his way. But that was the style these days: mix and mingle. It was okay with him. He was more than ready to clear out of their way, but Sylvester had his arm around him. Sylvester was holding him up.

"I'm all right," Jerome said.

"Sure," Sylvester said. "No problem."

But the edges were washing away. "I can recognize a man . . . of honor . . . when I see one."

"What's that now? You sure you're okay?"

He wanted to clap Sylvester on the shoulder, manfully, as part of the great warm surge he felt. He wanted Sylvester to understand the depth of his feelings. He wanted to share with him, before it was too late, those sweet truths he'd been ready to die for.

"Hey, man," Sylvester said. "No tears now."

He must have directed them, because they got him to his apartment. He slept then. Once he woke when the phone rang and heard the lovely voice from a great distance, making sure he was all right. They were decent, generous people, she and the boy both. He woke again in the dark and slept again and woke and got up because it was day. He sat unmoving as vague shapes slid past his outstretched reach. The sadness still clung to him, but a certain amount of clarity was coming back. It would be a miracle, a thing of awe. Was that to be the pattern now, death and rebirth as recurring miracles until, finally, the string ran out? Better than just old shoes and loosening teeth, gout and gallstones. Draped in miracles: that was the way to go. Gods and goddesses your fit companions, saints and holy men, heroes brave enough to boost you to their shoulders. Every moment a gift now, every hour a sign of true charity, that most marvelous of virtues.

On the radio it sounded like the same announcer with the same composed intonation. Only this time it wasn't his own name he heard to stop his breath; it was Sylvester's.

II.

Sylvester

THE FREE BREAKFAST clinic on McNally Avenue, in what used to be a bar and grill, was going along pretty good serving hot cereal and powdered eggs from the surplus food agency to maybe forty kids every morning. The clothing exchange was also in nice shape, with people trading patched-up jeans their kids had outgrown for faded shirts somebody else's kid had outgrown. The neighborhood ladies were running both setups now, so Sylvester was looking for something new.

"You're insatiable," Olivia Cowan told him. "You have to have something going every minute."

"I'm practicing on capitalism," Sylvester answered. "That's how you do it, you know. You keep on hustling and the loot just rolls in."

She laughed. The lady laughed a lot when they talked. "I don't see any loot."

"I'm just practicing the technique," Sylvester said. "Just honing up."

Dr. Adams was a dentist. Also an Elk or Moose or something, and Sylvester found out, after he saw the ad, that he'd been practicing thirty years in the same front parlor of his old gingerbready house, but was retiring because of high blood pressure and a condition with his heart. He'd already sold his practice to some dentist just starting out, but the equipment was too old to be worth anything. He just wanted it out of the parlor.

Dr. Virgilian, who told Sylvester all about Dr. Adams, said, "No way. I know that cat."

"The ad said no strings."

"You want my advice?" Dr. Virgilian said. "Save your breath to cool your soup."

What the ad said was:

> Dental equipment available free. Complete
> office, all in working order. No strings
> attached, but must take everything.

The choppy old nurse in the reception room looked like she'd been running that room for every one of those thirty years. She looked like she was gripping that place like a chicken neck.

"What sort of business? Do you have an appointment?"

Finally she went in and told the dentist he was there. Sylvester couldn't hear her but Dr. Adams had one of those scrapy fingernail voices that *penetrated*.

"What about? He's not a salesman, is he?"

Quiet.

"Well, what is it then?"

Quiet.

"All right. Let him in. I'll see what he wants."

He sounded angrier at her for announcing him than at Sylvester for being there. Never seeing his nurse again was probably one of the joys Dr. Adams most looked forward to about retiring.

The nurse came to the door and Sylvester sort of edged past her, taking in the scene. Then he let his eyes settle on Adams, who'd planted himself right in the dentist's chair, which he'd swung around to face Sylvester coming through the door. His white jacket looked like twice-a-week, not once-a-day. He leaned back in the chair with his feet on the metal step and his arms on the smooth shiny arms. He wasn't as old as Sylvester expected, but could have heart trouble, and high blood pressure too. A flabby guy, with cheeks as pink as a baby's, and small-boned, hardly seeming strong enough for yanking teeth. The corners of his mouth were turned down into a not at all trusting look. Sylvester was used to that, but got the impression Adams' lack of pleasure wasn't entirely personal, in that he probably disliked puppies and Democrats and small children as much as lopsided Afros that walked in off the street wearing dark shades. But he was scared too. He was trying hard to look both pious and ferocious, and hoping maybe that being in the big chair gave him some special form of status.

"You Dr. Adams?" Sylvester inquired evenly.

"I guess so," Adams said in the pot-metal voice that penetrated doors. "I don't see anyone else around."

Sylvester waited.

"What do you want?" Adams asked when the silence got to him. It was a complaint, like *What are you picking on me for? There's a couple of hundred thousand people running around town, and maybe a couple of dozen other dentists, if that's your particular interest, so why are you coming down on me?* "If it's charity, I'm not interested. I've been fleeced enough for one year."

Sylvester hiked up his dashiki in back and pulled out the clipping. "It mentions here some equipment you're fixing to get rid of."

Adams came near groaning.

Sylvester waited. Then he returned the clipping to his pocket. "Unless of course somebody got here first."

Adams seemed ready to lie his way out, but surprised Sylvester by saying, "It's not going to be any picnic getting it out. You have to know what you're doing. The chair's bolted down pretty tight, for starters. And someone has to know his electricity. There's lots of connections in there, wires all over. Color coding. You have to know color coding. Yank out the wrong wire and you'll burn the whole place down." He had trouble keeping his eyes on Sylvester when he talked.

Sylvester nodded.

"Do you know color coding?"

"I can figure it out," Sylvester said.

"You need an electrician. You have anyone like that?"

"I can do it," Sylvester said.

"I don't know about that."

"I'm real handy," Sylvester said.

"And then what? You gonna tote this chair out on your shoulder?" He looked at Sylvester's shoulder, but didn't say anything. People usually didn't.

"I got help," Sylvester said.

"And then what? You planning to hang out your shingle?"

"The ad said no strings."

Adams' eyes glazed over. His arms were still on the smooth gray arms of the chair, his feet on the corrugated metal step. "For all I know, you'll melt it down for knives and guns."

"We're in no bind for knives and guns right now," Sylvester said.

"I guess not, from what a body reads in the papers."

"What we figured on was dental equipment, like the ad said. And we'll take it if you're still getting rid of it."

"Why should I give it to you? I don't even know your name."

"Sylvester."

"You an orphan?"

"Childs."

"What do you want dental equipment for?"

"The ad said no strings."

"That means no strings for me."

"We're planning to start up a clinic," Sylvester said.

"A *dental* clinic?"

"That's it."

"Godamighty, fella. You need a license for a dental clinic. It's not like a newspaper route. It's not like a shoeshine stand. And you need a dentist. More than anything else in the whole world, you're gonna need a dentist."

"We gave that some thought."

"You keep saying we. Who's we?"

"Dr. Virgilian said he'd help."

Adams' eyes moved. "I figured we'd come to that. What is it, he planning to expand his practice down there?"

"He's pretty busy already."

"But with that special brand of clientele, I understand he doesn't get paid too often."

"He said he'd help. Some people from the school might help too."

"You mean interns? Students?"

"We haven't worked it all out yet."

"Where are you going to locate this clinic?"

"We don't know that yet."

"Who's going to patronize it?"

"We thought it'd be especially good for the kids."

"We've already got a clinic for kids. Over on Washington Street."

"That's pretty far. We thought it'd be nice having an extra one, in another part of town."

Adams studied him, the corners of his mouth pulled down. "The West Side?"

"That was one place we considered."

"What about white kids? Suppose white kids want to come?"

"Some white kids in the West Side," Sylvester said.

"I had the impression it was mostly colored."

"It is," Sylvester said.

"They could go to Washington Street. They could take the bus. They could even walk, if the mood struck them. It's not that far, and most people would rather face a little walk than a toothache. I've been spending Wednesday afternoons there for twenty years, and it seems to me the kids are receiving adequate care." Adams was running out of breath.

"How come you ain't giving *them* the equipment?"

"They don't want it." Adams took a tissue from the dispenser and patted his forehead. "They got equipment."

"We don't," Sylvester said.

With his feet still flat on the metal step Adams looked around at all the stuff, like a little kid in a new dining room. The metal plate on the electric drill said *Ritter.* "I've worked this equipment a long time. I wouldn't want to see it go to waste."

"Won't go to waste," Sylvester said.

"Okay," Adams said, beaten, all his arguments used up. He let out a breath, almost in relief, but the corners of his mouth drooped even more. "You can pick it up the end of the week. Saturday morning. I've got appointments through Friday."

"We'll be here." And then, for the first time, Sylvester gave him a real big smile. "Thanks," he said.

That took the starch out of Adams, "It's all right," he mumbled, looking away. "It comes off my taxes."

Sylvester cut classes to hustle up and down Pendleton and all the side streets, checking out the *To Let* signs and looking for broken and boarded-up windows. He followed up some leads but the prices were steep. The prices were out of sight. He rang bells and talked to people and studied lobby directories. On Wednesday he found a whole three-story building that was empty. It'd been bought to tear down for a new building but the owner hadn't touched it yet and maybe wasn't going to for a while. The first two floors were just one-room offices, but there was a four-room suite on the third floor that would be perfect. The owner was Zero Enterprises.

Which made it trickier, but also more interesting. At least the lines were drawn, and you knew who you were dealing with. You were dealing with Mr. Zero.

"How come he ain't torn it down yet?" Sylvester asked the guy at Zero Enterprises, Mr. Woodstein, who had an office lined with bookcases and a diploma on the wall showing he was a lawyer. They'd met once before, which had been pleasant enough, all things considered, and Sylvester didn't feel any particular grudge against the man. Woodstein, though, not from their one meeting but from other things, was not overjoyed to see Sylvester strolling in with any kind of proposition.

"Certain unforeseen circumstances arose," Woodstein said. He leaned forward with his elbows on the glass top of his desk and made a slanty roof with his hands, his fingertips touching evenly. He had big black frames on his eyeglasses and big bushy eyebrows and was almost bald.

"You mean he didn't have the bread?"

Woodstein smiled. "Hardly. You must understand, he has a good many interests, my client. A good many. Sometimes the appropriate thing to do is to put your money here," he said, placing his left hand firmly on the glass desk top. His hand was square and meaty, with dark hair on the backs of the fingers. "And sometimes it's better to put it here," he said, thumping his right hand down on the other side. "It's not, if you see what I mean, a question of not having the capital, the resources."

"Econ One," Sylvester said, and when Woodstein frowned, he said, "Is he ever gonna tear it down?"

"Why should he leave it standing empty? We pay taxes anyhow. The question in regards to tearing it down is when."

"What's the answer?"

"I don't know the answer. It takes time, you see, to move on something like this, even after you make up your mind."

"We could always vacate when you got around to tearing it down."

Woodstein gave him the evil eye from behind the slanty fingers. "I personally, of course, agree that this is a worthwhile project, even though the rent we would receive would only be a drop in the bucket."

"We could forget the rent then, since it only—"

"No," Woodstein said.

"That way you could really help out, what with it being so worthwhile and all."

"No," Woodstein said.

"But anyhow, you'll check with Mr. Zero? Or can you just give us the okay right now?"

"I'll check," Woodstein said. "There may not be an okay."

"Shame," Sylvester said. "All those poor kids with bad teeth."

"Mr. Zeronski, I'm sure, will recall the difficulties at the Zoning Board."

"That was months ago," Sylvester said. "Besides, it was nothing personal."

"You can come back tomorrow," Woodstein said.

Sylvester considered asking the lady to put in a good word, and maybe Justin Gage too. They both knew Zero, whereas Sylvester himself had never had the honor. He'd never even seen a picture, because Zero didn't like his picture in the paper, so it never was. But the things Zero did, or had people do for him, or one way or another caused to happen, gave you a clear enough picture. And what it told you was: *This is not a forgiving man.* Which would normally mean the clinic was a dead duck, being that Zero would have no great desire to help out Sylvester after what had already transpired between them. But he figured he had something extra going for him, which was that Zero liked to play the big charity man, especially for all the poor downtrodden types in the West Side, so Sylvester didn't say anything to anybody and just went back the next day to Woodstein's book-lined office.

"I'm pleased to report," he said from behind the slant of his fingers, not really sounding all that pleased, "that my client agrees as to the worthiness of the project."

"You gotta be a real Simon Legree," Sylvester said, "to be against fixing kids' teeth."

Woodstein made a face.

They wanted a hundred a month, which was pretty good, especially considering what people were asking for some of the other places he looked at. Sylvester thought Zero might turn the screws a lot harder than that, to get back for being pushed into a corner, and maybe for old times' sake too.

When he left, Sylvester called Olivia Cowan from the nearest phone booth. He didn't want to be taking advantage of her, but she was the only one who could come up with what he needed at the moment.

But over the phone she sounded a little hesitant about it all. "Are you going to need that much every month?"

"I thought maybe you could swing it, at least for now," Sylvester said, leaning against the glass booth with his ankles crossed.

"Okay," she said after a pause. "At least it'll keep you off the streets."

"Only we're gonna need the first month's rent and a month in advance."

"When?"

"Tomorrow. So we can unload Saturday."

"Is that everything or are you keeping the real surprises for later?" But you could tell she was smiling.

"That's everything," Sylvester said. "You know I wouldn't pull any surprises on you."

"All right," she said. "Only why Zero? What'd you have to get involved with him for?"

"It's his building."

"Next time pick another building," she said.

Charles said he had to help his aunt buy a car on Saturday. She was very shaky about motors and needed guidance.

Ruel wanted to know if it was the lady's idea. That was the first thing he asked. It was the only thing he asked.

"It was my idea," Sylvester said.

"She's in there, though, isn't she? She's got her little finger wrapped around it somewhere."

Ruel of course could be a drag. He had his reasons, more than a white boy normally would expect, but you wished once in a while he'd forget his reasons and just relax, just for one minute.

"All right. We'll drop the whole thing," Sylvester told them. "What the hell, why bother? Our teeth don't hurt. Why should we worry about anybody else's?"

So Saturday the three of them headed for Dr. Adams' house, with Charles still carrying on about his old aunt and Ruel just glumping and sulking along in his normal manner. What it was with Ruel, he was really a very remote guy. He'd been alone a lot, through no fault of his own and in a lot of different places, and hadn't had too much good luck with the people he met. Most of them just screwed him one way or another. So given the choice, Ruel would as soon do without people, and just sit in a corner and sulk.

Sylvester drove the two-and-a-half flatbed, which belonged to a guy he knew who did hauling, who lent it to him for the day. It had slatted sides that came off for loading. They also had a dolly and hand truck and a decent set of tools.

They got there at eight and rang the bell. Dr. Adams wasn't wearing his not-so-white jacket but a kind of rumply suit, which made him look even flabbier and less strong.

"It's not that bright in here," Adams said, looking at Sylvester's shades. On the first visit Adams had just ignored them, or at least hadn't said anything. He'd probably been kicking himself for letting Sylvester wheedle the stuff out of him and was looking for a way to make a point. "It's not considered polite," he went on. "It's like wearing your hat indoors."

"I never wear a hat indoors," Sylvester said.

"Or out either, I suspect," Adams said, like this was one more complaint he had. Then he stared at Ruel's red and white wool cap, waiting for Ruel to take it off, which of course Ruel had no mind to do, and didn't. Then he stared at Charles, for no reason he could think of, maybe, except for the fact that Charles was not your normal dusky colored boy but real glossy black, and Adams looked at him as if this was his biggest complaint of all, though of course there was even less Charles could do about his particular failing than Sylvester or Ruel could about theirs.

They worked all morning, Adams staying right with them, zooming in to watch every move. He was like an old lady with a box of kittens she didn't want but was still afraid somebody would steal one of.

"Easy on the walls, okay? There's no law says we have to scratch up each and every one of the walls."

"The way you go on," Sylvester said.

"I'm just asking you to show some care."

"We're showing care," Sylvester said.

At the stroke of noon Adams announced: "Time for lunch."

"We thought of working through," Sylvester said.

"Time for lunch. One hour."

They drove over to the Burger King on Pendleton and ate in the cab of the truck.

"What's wrong with that bitch?" Ruel said, chomping away at a double order of fries. You wouldn't think it from looking at him, because he hadn't any more fat on him than the nearest telephone pole, but Ruel could really stow it away, and did, every chance he got.

"He just appreciates good workmanship," Sylvester said.

"He's a regular pea counter, that mother," Charles said. "When he makes up the Sunday soup, he counts the peas."

"I'd like to lose him down a sewer somewhere," Ruel said.

"Let's get the stuff out first," Sylvester said.

They left the chair for the end. They disconnected the long elbowed arm of the electric drill, and the movable round plate for the dental tools, and the attached sink and the housing, and then unbolted the chair from the floor. The bolts were rusted on so tight they could've been welded. It took both Charles and Ruel,

Charles pulling on the wrench like an oar and Ruel pushing from the other side, to loosen them. Then they tilted the chair and rocked it onto the dolly, sweating like pigs. It must've weighed five hundred pounds. The three of them engineered it out of the parlor, which was no easy job either, Sylvester pulling and steering and the other two pushing with Adams crowding behind, poking his nose right in there. They inched it down the hall and through a couple of doorways with nothing to spare and out onto the wooden porch. They stopped for breath.

"You're gonna have to hand-carry it down those steps," Adams said.

"We know," Sylvester said.

Grunting and sweating, staggering around under the weight and almost losing the chair once, which would have killed Sylvester, who was on the underside at the time, the three of them bumped it, harder than they wanted to, one step at a time, down the porch steps and back onto the dolly. They stopped for breath.

"You're not out of the woods yet," Adams said.

They wheeled the dolly down the cement path to the truck at the curb. The path was downhill from the house and they had to fight back against the chair with all their weight to keep it from picking up speed and smashing right into the truck.

"Whoa!" Charles yelled. "Whoa there, you little fucker!"

The back of the truck was pretty crowded but they'd left room at the edge for the chair.

"Now comes the fun," Adams said, sidling up behind them. He was wheezing away and patting his forehead with a handkerchief, feeling the strain of watching all the heavy work.

"Gonna need more help," Sylvester said.

"Thought you would," Adams said. "Don't look at me."

Sylvester looked up and down the block.

"Won't find many of your friends hanging around here," Adams said.

"White bread and mayonnaise land," Charles said.

"I'll be back," Sylvester said to Ruel and Charles. "You keep an eye on the chair."

"Who's gonna steal it?" Charles wanted to know. "King Kong?"

Sylvester drove the truck back to the West Side and picked up

Ed at the store front and found Billy and George home watching the game on TV.

"Some people got the easy life," Sylvester said to them. "Others are out there trudging along, even on a Saturday."

"Hey look, I got studying," Billy said. "I got a paper due Monday."

"What on, Reggie Jackson?" Sylvester said.

They all drove back.

"Godamighty, there must be a woods full of them back there," Adams said, groaning at the sight of the five guys towering over Sylvester. Except for Ruel, they were all black, which didn't help. "Does everyone grow this big in that part of town, or did you pick out these fellows special?"

"I looked special for size," Sylvester said.

"Sure found it," Adams muttered.

Sylvester and Ruel climbed onto the truck bed. They pulled and lifted from above while Charles and the three others hefted from below, trying to keep the thing from toppling back on them. Adams watched from the path, keeping his distance in case something went wrong. They got it up. Sylvester and Ruel hopped down then and replaced the side. As soon as they did, Billy monkey-climbed over the slats and plopped himself down in the chair for the ride back, spreading out with a big smile, like he'd just been made chief of everything in sight.

Charles climbed right on after him and peered down into Billy's face. "Whatcha got—a pain in your little old decisor tooth there?"

"Oh man, don't touch it. It don't hurt hardly at all."

"Open real wide and we'll look for the misery."

"Oh man. I'm gonna die here. You're gonna kill me right here in this crazy old chair." Billy rolled up his eyes and stretched back, opening his mouth wide enough to catch baseballs.

"Bad," Charles said. "We're gonna have to groom right in there with a brossalosis and acetate the hell out of it." He sighted along his rigid forefinger with one eye, bringing the finger closer and closer as Billy squeezed his eyes shut and knuckled hard on the arms of the chair. "*RHAAANNNGGG!*"

"Owww! You're killing me, man!"

Adams watched grimly, the corners of his mouth turned down. "He the one gonna be your dentist?"

"Just needs more practice is all," Sylvester said.

"God help those little pickaninnies coming in for care," Adams said.

"Let's move," Ruel said. "Let's cut the shit."

"You want a receipt now for these items?" Sylvester asked. "For your taxes?"

"Sign here," Adams said, taking a pen and paper from his suit jacket. He patted his forehead.

Sylvester smoothed the paper on the edge of the truck bed and signed. It was a long typewritten list.

"Aren't you going to read it?"

"Not cheating us any, no matter what," Sylvester said with a smile, handing back the pen and paper. "Cheating Uncle Sam maybe, but not us."

"He's your Uncle Sam too," Adams said. "He pays the welfare, after all."

"We appreciate the equipment," Sylvester said.

"Just don't kill anyone with it," Adams said, looking up to heaven.

They drove into the West Side with Billy riding the dentist chair in back, down Pendleton, past the bars and pizza places, the Taco Palace, the used-car dealers and muffler shops and used-appliance stores. Sylvester backed the truck down the long alley that led to the freight entrance. But the freight elevator wouldn't stir. It was dead. Nothing even clicked. Sylvester drove around to the front entrance then. There was no space at the curb so he double-parked. They made sure the front elevator worked, which it did, and started unloading the stuff from the truck and through the lobby and up the elevator and then into the four-room suite on the top floor of the three-story building.

On one of their last trips down, with just odds and ends left on the truck, they found this big guy in a white jacket—which was at least cleaner than Adams'—standing on the sidewalk with his arms folded and looking at the truck double-parked. He was blocking the space between two parked cars that they'd been going back and forth through. The guy turned to them with his arms still across his chest. A scissors and comb stuck up from his jacket pocket. Sylvester and Charles and Ruel came up to him and stopped. The others were upstairs shoving stuff around. The guy didn't move.

"How ya doing there?" Sylvester said, smiling and cheerful.

The guy came back with a very steely look. "What's going on?" he asked, hardly moving his lips.

"Just bringing in some equipment," Sylvester said.

"Building's condemned," the guy said.

"Not condemned," Sylvester said, still cheerful. "Old maybe, and empty, and maybe on its last legs from the look of things, but not condemned."

"You can't just move in."

"All that's taken care of," Sylvester said. "We been in contact with the owner and everything's all set. Everything's just dandy."

The guy kept his mouth clamped. Real Hollywood Mafia.

"Now if you'll just excuse us," Sylvester said, "we've got lots of work cleaning up, and would like to get finished."

The guy didn't budge. Old Man Mountain Dean. He gave Sylvester a look that told exactly what he thought of him. Worse, he gave the other two the same look, including Ruel, which was a mistake. Ruel was not a person that ever considered he had options when faced with a problem. He always figured his only option was to start blazing away. So when the barber gave him the evil eye, Ruel just took one of those real noisy breaths of his, just this long angry wheeze, and stepped up and grabbed the barber's white jacket in that gigantic strong hand of his, putting his nose about one inch from the guy's face and giving him a look that maybe wasn't as supercilious as the guy himself gave, but had a lot more threat and intention behind it.

"Hey, now," Sylvester said, putting a hand on Ruel's arm. "No need, man."

Ruel shrugged him off without letting go of the barber's jacket.

Sylvester slid his hands real quick up Ruel's sides and rammed a hard thumb up into each armpit, which stung enough to make Ruel let go of the barber. Without shouldering him much, just moving quick enough to catch Ruel off guard, Sylvester eased himself between the two of them and leaned back against Ruel to keep him off balance. Charles had the good sense then to come over and sort of get in Ruel's way too, without actually trying to hold him back, because not even Charles and Sylvester together had any hopes of holding off Ruel if it came to a real wrestling match.

"Okay, everybody—no fights," Sylvester announced. "Just a little misunderstanding, all over now." With that he gave Ruel a real firm look over his shoulder, and before Ruel could say or do anything Sylvester turned to the barber and said: "Maybe it'd be best, all in all, if folks just tried to be friends around here, being that we're next-door neighbors and all."

The barber was still flustered from Ruel coming at him so quick, and so rough, which was just as well, because Sylvester didn't want some mess on his hands before they even finished moving in, and because the barber, even with all the weight he had on Ruel, wouldn't have been any match.

So what the man did was turn on his real best scowl, to show he wasn't being *forced,* and walk back to the barbershop in the next building, with the red and white pole outside, and lean against the window to watch them take up that load, and the rest of the loads. When they were finished and all came down together and drove away in the empty truck, he was still standing there with his arms folded and his mouth clamped shut, watching their every move.

It took almost a month to get the clinic ready. A few others pitched in but Sylvester did most of it, which was easier than trying to round up people every day and having all their excuses laid on you. He'd drop in on a class once in a while to remind the profs he was still alive and spent the rest of the time replacing broken windows, patching walls and ceilings, putting stuff around for the bugs, fixing hinges and leaky pipes and loose floor boards. He got Charles and Ed and Ruel and some of the girls to help paint the walls and finish the floors, with Ed's transistor vibrating away on the window sill. What with the music and horsing around it was more like a party than working. Ed had some grass and fired up and passed it around while they were painting.

"Jesus Christ," Sylvester said. "What the hell you bringing that stuff here for?"

"Wanna toke?" Louise asked, offering it.

"I got better things to do," Sylvester said.

"Ain't he the saint now?" Louise said.

When they finished painting that day, Louise went over to the big sink to wash up and pulled off her sweat shirt. She didn't have anything on underneath. Everybody else just ignored her and she ignored them too but when she was drying up, still with her shirt off, she came over to Sylvester, not saying anything but just smiling away, getting a big kick out of it. Sylvester walked around her with his eyes down to get something from the other room.

"It's just me," she called after him, laughing. "It ain't nothing at all but just little old me."

He scrounged up the furniture at St. Vincent's and the Salvation Army, and got paper and supplies through a guy who worked part-time in the university storeroom. Then he went around the neighborhood knocking on doors, standing in dark halls telling mothers about the clinic through little cracks, the door chains still locked.

He went with Dr. Virgilian to talk to the interns at the Dental School and got a half dozen to sign up. Virgilian said he'd quit the Washington Street clinic and spend one afternoon and one night at their clinic instead, and try to get some white dentists to do the same.

"What's this you got about people's teeth anyway?" Virgilian asked him. "You planning on entering the profession someday?"

"Saw the ad, that's all."

"Were you looking for an ad? Were you holding your breath waiting from some doddery old dentist to die and leave you the equipment in his will?"

"Lots of kids got bad teeth," Sylvester said.

"You telling me something?"

Sylvester shrugged. "I seen kids with teeth so rotten they just fall out."

"I seen a few examples like that too, on a couple of different occasions I can remember."

Virgilian said he'd run the professional end, but Sylvester had to take care of everything else, which he did, with some help from Justin Gage in arranging licenses and permits, and making sure things were cool down at City Hall.

The worst part was getting mothers to bring their kids in.

Then the *Citizen-Times* ran a feature on the clinic. The reporter who came and took pictures of Virgilian smiling at a little girl in the dentist chair really knocked himself out being enthusiastic and helpful. Then Sylvester found out why. Olivia Cowan was a friend of the publisher's. He was an art lover or something, and they just happened to run into each other at this cocktail party, where she just happened to pass along the word to him. The rest was easy enough to imagine. That was okay. That was how it worked. You started at the top if you wanted something, or at some very classy friend of the top, like the lady, who was pretty expert in knowing how to get things done and keeping in touch with the kind of people who could help out if you needed them.

The big spread in the paper got things rolling, and after that they were busy all the time.

Sylvester set up a schedule for the girls who worked as receptionists and the guys who cleaned up at night, but when he couldn't get anyone, or someone didn't show, he'd fill in himself. One way or another he spent most of his time there, and a few profs got uptight. But Sylvester got all his papers done and kept acing the exams so they couldn't lean too hard on him.

Dr. Virgilian and the two white dentists worked afternoons. The interns worked mornings examining kids and giving everyone a good rap about sweets and brushing regular. After a while Virgilian brought in free toothpaste samples for each kid. Sylvester wanted to give out brushes too and was considering a raffle so they could buy some wholesale. Then he thought of Barry, who said toothbrushes would be no problem at all. Barry specialized in stereos and TVs and small appliances, all at very favorable prices, but said he'd produce the brushes for nothing, for a good cause.

Sylvester said okay, and a few days later they had toothbrushes to hand out. Good ones, in plastic cases. Virgilian raised one eyebrow when he saw the cartons piled up in the reception room. He picked up a brush in its plastic case and inspected it, still with one eyebrow up.

"We ran into a benefactor," Sylvester said. "Ain't that a nice surprise now?"

"Don't tell me about it," Virgilian said, putting the toothbrush back.

"I figured you'd be real pleased and smiling."

"Spare me the details," Virgilian said.

The rest of the building stayed empty and Sylvester didn't hear anything from Woodstein. No one else hassled them either, until Olivia Cowan decided one day to come down for a look at the place. She'd never come before, because she'd been waiting for an invitation. Sylvester said he was sorry and wasn't trying to keep her away. After all, she'd been a big help with the rent money and getting the story in the newspaper and all, and they'd be real glad to have her visit anytime she wanted.

What he hadn't counted on was the barber. Sylvester and the lady always got along fine, and after a while each stopped noticing how different the other was, although of course other people didn't. But they made it in very unrelated scenes, as you could see from just one look at her, or her gallery. The Amethyst Gallery. "No, I don't know where it is," he'd told her when she first brought it up. "And I'll tell you something else. I got friends that wouldn't even know how to pro*nounce* it." But that was where she spent her time and did her thing, and she really wanted Sylvester to see it. They had new shows every month or so and she kept inviting him until he finally gave in. It was like walking into a mob scene. He got this faggy little glass of wine he really didn't want, and a cup of coffee with a stick floating in it. "Jesus, what's that?" he asked the gray lady pouring at the draped table. "Cinnamon," she told him in a kind of hushed voice. "Haven't you ever tried cinnamon in your coffee?" The women all looked six feet tall with their boobies half flopping out and their hair falling over one eye and voices like tiny bells. And the smart talk. The kissing. Everybody kept kissing everybody else, coming, going, and in between.

He wasn't going to travel that route again, ever, under any circumstances, for anybody.

But it told you something about the lady, although *she* wasn't so much like that, only her friends. Still, when she showed up at the clinic that day and the first thing she said was "That son of a bitch," he knew right away she'd taken one look at that barber, and he'd taken one look at her, and that'd been it.

How it came about was that the guy was standing outside his shop when she climbed out of the Jaguar, and he stopped her as soon as he saw where she was heading. He said she must be going into the wrong place, because there wasn't anything in that building. She told him she heard there was a dental clinic. He looked at her then, her finery and all, and said he didn't think she'd be interested in that kind of clinic. Now the lady, of course, didn't take to being told what she could or couldn't do, not by anybody, and especially not by someone like that. So she got real icy with the guy, and the barber started laying a long list of complaints on her, that neither Sylvester nor anyone else ever heard before, about kids dumping garbage in front of his place, and coming in for handouts, and how one kid threw a rock that just missed his window, and in general how all those seedy kids and their mothers tromping into the clinic were scaring away his customers and hurting business. He even chased away one kid, he said, who was peeing up against his wall.

Before it was over, the lady gave him a few choice words, and she was still steaming when she got up to the clinic.

"Maybe I'll just drop by and have a chat with the gentleman," Sylvester said.

B. Huddleston, Prop., it said in a corner of the glass window. B. Huddleston, all by his lonesome in his white jacket, was ensconced very comfortably in the chair near the window, reading the paper, with one ankle resting on the other knee. He had really thick, heavy legs. He dropped the paper as soon as he heard the door open and the bell tinkle, straightening right up to flash his customer smile. Then he sort of froze, leaning forward in the chair with the newspaper in his lap and without any kind of smile at all.

"This establishment open for business?" Sylvester inquired.

Huddleston looked at him through real narrow eyes. He was a big barrelly guy and gave the impression of maybe not being too quick mentally, or going in for snappy answers and witticisms, because it took him awhile figuring things through, clump by clump. Finally he said: "What would you want to know for?"

"Haircut time," Sylvester said. "I used to offer my patronage at a different place, but now that we're neighbors, I thought it'd be nice if I came here."

Huddleston listened like his face was set in concrete. But you could tell he was thinking, as hard and fast as he could. "I can't cut that kind of hair," he said.

"I didn't realize it was any special kind," Sylvester said. "Sort of shiny black, is all."

"I'll cut it," Huddleston said. "But it won't look the same when I get finished."

"I'd like to keep it pretty much the same," Sylvester said.

"Maybe you better find some other place then."

Sylvester looked around the shop. It was not what you'd call a high-tone place. It looked like time had sort of passed it by and wasn't about to let it catch up again. "Hair business slow?" he asked.

"I got no complaints," Huddleston said.

"We neither," Sylvester said. "The tooth business, in fact, is actually thriving."

Huddleston said nothing. He was still sitting in the big barber chair, leaning forward with the newspaper on his leg. He easily weighed two times what Sylvester did, maybe more, and was really hovering over him from up in that chair.

"Course, we don't charge for our services," Sylvester said, "so don't have to worry about making big profits all the time."

Huddleston said nothing.

"You see, we en*joy* fixing kids' teeth, just like I guess you get a kick out of cutting hair, without even considering the money."

"I'm not going to put up with vandalism," Huddleston said. "I'm not going to stand by and let a bunch of ruffians run me out of here."

"Ruffians?"

"I could call them worse."

"What's the problem? Offhand, I don't see any damage or anything."

"Because I watch them every minute. If I didn't take time off from my work to watch them every minute, they'd tear the place apart. One kid threw a rock."

"Which kid was that?"

"You tell them apart, if you can. Some little kid."

"White kid?"

Huddleston glared down at him from the chair. "No," he said. "I don't see white kids going in there, if you want the truth."

"I want the truth," Sylvester said.

"I guess white kids, if they got a toothache, just gotta pay their own way, without the benefit of charity. Because I ain't seen any white kids coming around begging for nickels or throwing rocks, or making a pigpen out of the neighborhood by pissing on the wall."

"We don't want nobody bothered," Sylvester said. "By any color kids."

"Maybe you can get them to stop then."

"I'll see what I can do," Sylvester said. "After all, there's room for everybody. I mean, the hair business and the tooth business, they're both kind of noble endeavors in their own way. I wouldn't want my hair falling out, anymore than my teeth."

Huddleston looked at Sylvester's hair and seemed to be trying to come up with a witticism, but never did.

The next afternoon Sylvester went across the street into the old red brick building that was almost soot black over the bricks, two stories high, a small plant with leaded windows where they assembled light switches. He didn't go into the offices or the factory part but climbed the wide metal stairway to the roof. He sat himself down on the little wall at the edge, sidesaddle, with both feet resting on the tar-paper roof, and looked down at the barbershop window and the front entrance to the clinic building. He stayed the whole afternoon, coming down at five to cross the street and knock at the glass door of the barbershop. Huddleston had already locked up and turned out the lights and taken his white jacket off, but was still inside, counting cash at the register. He looked over his shoulder at Sylvester standing in the little one-step entrance outside the glass door. Then he slowly put the money back in the register and slammed the drawer shut and locked it and put the key in his pocket and came over and opened up for Sylvester. He didn't ask him in, though, or let him in. He kept himself planted in the doorway, filling it.

"I watched," Sylvester said.

"I saw you up there," Huddleston said.

"Maybe the kids just didn't feel up to making mischief today. Maybe they were all pooped out or something."

"Maybe."

"Because I didn't see any mischief. I didn't see any customers being hassled."

Huddleston said nothing.

"Matter of fact," Sylvester said, "I hardly saw enough customers to be worth hassling."

Huddleston said nothing.

"I counted four," Sylvester said.

Huddleston stared at him, his mouth clamped.

"Now that we got it cleared up, about kids bothering people, maybe we can just be friends. Work hand in hand, like real neighbors."

"You threatening me?"

"Hell, man, I'm being neighborly."

"You'll see where you get threatening me."

"What's going on, man? What's the problem?"

"Just don't try anything, that's all. Just don't get smart."

Sylvester tilted his head to one side to look past Huddleston, who was still blocking the doorway. He gazed around the shop and motioned upward with his head, to the rest of the building. "Who owns this?" he asked. "Like, who's your landlord here?"

"What's it to you?"

"I was wondering if you were acquainted with a man I'm more or less acquainted with too, indirectly."

"What are you talking about?"

"Mr. Zero," Sylvester said. "Mr. Zeronski."

"What the hell are you talking about?"

Sylvester checked the next day, down at the city clerk's office, and wasn't exactly surprised to find out who the owner was.

He told Olivia Cowan about watching the whole afternoon and talking to the barber, and about Zero turning out to be the landlord. This brought on a little frown, because in her own dealings with Zero she'd gotten to dislike the man and not trust him at all. As far as she was concerned, Zero wasn't only mean and low-down but sneaky too.

"He'd be happy enough to let the clinic stay," she said, "if he could just get you out and take the credit himself."

Sylvester smiled, not wanting her worried, and told her all that nice easy stuff about being the lucky chile, with the big charms on him. "It's true," he said. "Just look at me. Just one look's enough to tell I got the mark."

The lady's frown turned real hard then. She didn't like any talk of that, and never mentioned it herself. That was part of the way she was. Since it didn't bother her the way Sylvester looked, she didn't see why it should bother anybody.

"No, lady," he explained to her. "You got it all wrong. I found that out when I was a kid, and went into the school playground the first time, on the first day, over on Tomaker Street. Every kid in that school was laying in wait for some smaller kid to show up, for his very own, to beat on, and stomp, and kick around a bit. Only no one beat up on me. No one touched me. No one went near me, or talked to me, or smiled or cursed or did anything to me. They all just pulled back and looked. They didn't even try to make believe they were looking somewhere else. Now, I'd never hardly left my block before that, because my mother, she wanted to take real good care of me, and that was it, that first day. That was the sign. That was when I knew about the mark, and the great old charm that was gonna protect me all my born days."

Then he heard—from Dr. Virgilian, who the cops called on—that the barber had gone ahead and actually made a complaint about all the stuff the clinic people were supposed to be hassling him about.

"That creeping guy is gonna get me real mad if he keeps that up," Sylvester said. "He's just gonna edge me right to the end of my patience."

It was all right, Virgilian told him. He talked real nice to the cop, and nothing else was going to come of it. They got crank calls all the time, from old ladies and everything, and had better things to do with their time.

It looked like Virgilian was right because they heard no more about it, and Thursday afternoon he stayed away from the clinic to put in an appearance at some classes and made a little effort toward shaping things up at school. He was coming out of the Econ Building when he saw Olivia Cowan, waiting for him and looking pretty shook up. She said the cops wanted him. She'd tried to get him at home and at the clinic and then cruised around the campus and then started running around on foot, looking for him. They sat in the Jag, under a tree at the edge of the parking lot with students straggling around and kind of eying them on the front seat. The lady was used to getting eyed and paid no attention. Sylvester was used to it too, especially in her company, because then people had three reasons for looking at them, two individual and one collective.

She'd heard the news from a friend with connections downtown.

"What's all this business about a bomb?" Sylvester said. "I don't know about any bomb."

"They don't believe that. They want to talk to you."

"Oh, lady. This is rich."

"I'm sure we can straighten it out. I'm sure it's a mistake."

But she was troubled. And the lady didn't trouble easily.

He kept telling her not to fret about the cops. "I'm not that easy, you know. I'm not that green. We'll just stay nice and loose and take care of things in the right order."

The detective chief was a big surprise. He came on very straight. Ultra cool. So straight and cool you figured something had to be wrong. This wasn't how it went. Simple questions, easy answers. No rough stuff, no wisecracks?

"Where were you that night, Mr. Childs?"

"Home asleep."

"Was anyone there with you?"

"My mother."

"Anyone else?"

"Nope. Just us."

"You had some difficulties, we understand, with Mr. Huddleston."

"We chatted a couple of times. We were neighbors, after all."

"What'd you chat about?"

"Well, Mr. Huddleston got all taken up with some mistaken notions, and I took the opportunity to pass along the accurate information, as a neighborly gesture."

"Did you threaten him?"

"No, sir, I did not. I just didn't want him laboring under the wrong impressions."

"You were angry, though, weren't you?"

"About what?"

"About him threatening to press charges."

"Not angry enough to plant some kind of bomb, if that's what you mean."

The detective chief stayed cool and polite the whole time. Sylvester was sure it was part of the game and that when the man got tired of asking questions he'd just push a button and three uniformed gorillas would tromp in and haul him off like a sack of trash. Only when the detective got tired of asking questions he just nodded and said, "That's it. Thank you for coming," and let Sylvester go.

He was the same with the lady, the lady said. Questions, answers, thank you very much.

"Maybe they're just taking pot shots," Sylvester said, "to see who they bring down."

But later that afternoon the lady came back, after Sylvester finished his stroll with the funky old guy with the white beard, who figured that almost getting his head blown off was enough reason to go tailing after people playing Sherlock Holmes, but who didn't know anything about anything. She came back because she'd been thinking and worrying and wanted to talk to him again, and was waiting for the old guy to leave. He'd seemed pretty game and all, even with that real stiff old man's look, like he was still wearing the hanger in his jacket, but then he just gave way at the end, like somebody'd pulled out the plug.

"Jesus Christ," Sylvester said. "He ain't dead, is he? He ain't dying?"

"I think he'll be all right," the lady said, although she was pretty frantic too. "Get some water or something. Maybe he's just fainted."

He wasn't dead, anyhow, but really spaced out. He'd ramble and mutter and then blink out again, his whole face going slack. They got him into the Jag and drove him to the address in his wallet and helped him through the lobby and up in the elevator and unlocked his apartment with his key and put him into bed. He kept fading in and out and they were on the verge of calling a doctor or maybe even an ambulance. But at the end he came out enough to say he was all right, just tired, and when the lady mentioned a doctor he practically had a fit and said no, no doctors.

"I shouldn't've walked him so much," Sylvester said when they left.

"I'm sure he's all right," she said. She didn't think it was a heart attack because he didn't have any pains in his chest, and she didn't think it was a stroke because her father had had one, and it hadn't been like that.

Still it jolted Sylvester, the guy conking out like that, and he worried about him all alone in the apartment.

"Let me call and make sure he's all right," the lady said, because she was worried too, even though she wasn't too enthusiastic about the man following them and in general making a nuisance of himself. So they stopped and she called and said the guy sounded all right. Then she told Sylvester how she'd been thinking everything over and getting more and more uptight about how it looked. What she decided was that he ought to see Justin Gage, who would be willing to help and know what to do. Sylvester didn't want to bother but could see she was right, as usual, and besides wasn't about to take no for an answer. She drove him to Gage's office and pushed him out of the car and waited to make sure he went through the door.

"I think we've got problems," Gage said, although sounding very cool about it all, which he always did.

"Where's all the faith you're supposed to have in me?" Sylvester said. "I didn't do anything."

"Convince me."

"I was home sacked out that night—whenever the guy who planted the bomb planted it."

"Convince me."

"Ask my mamma. She was home with me."

"That'll do it. A mother proclaiming her only son's innocence."

"What they think is I was sore about the barber for making up stories, and pressing charges. Although I don't know about charges, because that barber wouldn't get involved with a lawyer if his life depended on it. Unless someone else was behind him, pushing him along."

"Zeronski?"

"You know how it is," Sylvester said.

"We won't get very far trying to pin this on Zero."

"I'm not saying he did it. I'm just saying there are other people the cops oughta be suspicious of besides me. That barber, man. I spent a whole afternoon watching that place."

"I know. Huddleston mentioned it to the cops."

"He got four customers that afternoon. Now, four customers don't exactly make a business a gold mine."

"Huddleston wouldn't blow up the place while he was standing right there. What'd he want the insurance for, funeral expenses?"

"Maybe he's smarter than he looks. Or dumber. Maybe it wasn't supposed to go off right then."

"Okay," Gage said.

"Okay what?"

"We'll see what we can do. Assuming you're telling the truth."

"Only I told you, I ain't got the bread."

"If they pick you up, you get one phone call. Call me."

"Just like the last time, eh?"

"That's right," Gage said.

The next morning he was sitting in Comparative Eco-Systems, droozing behind his shades because it was pretty dull going. One of the department secretaries came tiptoeing in and the prof, orating behind the lectern, stopped dead to give her a frosty look. She handed him a note and split, still tiptoeing. The prof curled his lip at the note, then drew a slow bead on Sylvester. "It seems you have an urgent call." Sylvester, scrunched down in his chair, raised his head an inch or so. "Me?" he said finally, and for some reason the class laughed. "You," the prof said.

In the department office the secretary handed him the phone. It was Louise. She was supposed to cover the reception desk at the clinic this morning. "They won't let us in," she said. "They got it all blocked off."

"Who?" Sylvester said. "What're you talking about?"

He hung up thinking, *Christ Jesus but those structures out there get more complicated every day. Those pieces get harder and harder to keep together.* Then he started to dial.

"Students aren't allowed to make personal calls," the secretary said. "There's a booth down—"

"Hello! Hello! I want to speak to Mr. Woodstein. Right away."

"Mr. Woodstein is out of town. Who's calling please?"

With the secretary having kittens at his elbow, Sylvester dialed again.

"They can't do that," Olivia Cowan said.

"They're doing it."

"I'm sure we can stop them," she said.

"We better do it then. We better do it quick."

He ran out to the student parking lot, looking for a black face.

"I can't take you nowhere, man. I just got here. I got a class."

"Fuck the class," Sylvester said.

Three trucks and a really fantastic crane with a dangling iron ball swaying back and forth were parked in front of the building. ZERO WRECKING. Sure. What else would you expect? ZERO WRECKING. Half the street was fenced off by wooden sawhorses, with just the trucks and Mr. Zero's wrecking crane at the curb. About a dozen hardhats stood around, along with a guy in a white shirt and tie with his sleeves rolled up. Two cops flanked the entrance to the building, staring straight ahead and looking bored and separate, just a job, no big deal. The guy in shirt sleeves was talking with some hardhats, pointing to a big unrolled blueprint.

Louise ran out to Sylvester from across the street. A car screeched and everyone looked up but Louise kept running until she reached Sylvester, standing outside the sawhorses in the street.

"What are we gonna do?" she said. "They won't let anybody near."

"We gotta get the stuff out."

"I told them," Louise said.

Sylvester put one hand on the crosspiece and hopped over the sawhorse. The two cops watched him. He moved onto the sidewalk, going right under the swaying iron ball, glancing up. The hardhats pulled back, leaving the guy in shirt sleeves alone to face him. The two cops didn't move but sort of straightened up, playing on their night sticks with the tips of their fingers.

"You the foreman?" Sylvester said.

The guy paused, then carefully rolled up the blueprint and slid it under his arm. He stared at Sylvester's dark glasses. "What can I do for you?"

"What's going on here?"

"What's it look like?"

"You gotta wait," Sylvester said.

"No one told me anything about waiting."

"I'm telling you," Sylvester said.

The guy's mouth pulled back. Then it turned into a kind of smile. "Sorry about that, fella. But the people who sign my check every week, all they told me was to come here and take this building down to the ground."

"We got stuff in there."

"It's supposed to be empty."

"It ain't empty. We got a dental clinic."

"A what?"

"On the third floor. You come with me and I'll show you. But we can get it out. I can get some guys here and take it out in no time."

The guy looked at his wrist watch. It had a leather strap maybe three inches wide and about seven dials, including maybe a couple for the moon and tides. "We're ready to go."

"That equipment's worth a lot of money," Sylvester said. "We gotta get it out."

"Maybe you can sue afterwards."

"Who can make you stop?"

"Nobody who can is going to."

"It'll only take a couple of hours. We can get everything out this afternoon."

"Which means we can't start till tomorrow. Which means all this gear and all these men are gonna sit around for a whole day. You got any idea what these guys get paid, fella? You know what that crane costs for one day?"

"You gotta give us warning. We worked our ass off in there. You can't tear everything down without telling us."

"That ain't my end of it. The building owner takes care of that."

"He ain't done it."

"Talk to him then. Tell him your problems."

Sylvester waited, looking at the guy. Then he looked at the two cops, who were still watching him, touching their night sticks with their fingertips. "What're they here for?"

"To keep people from getting in the way and getting hurt."

Sylvester waited again, staring at the guy, then turned and hurried into the street, under the big iron ball, to the sawhorse where Louise was waiting.

"Listen," Sylvester said.

"They ain't gonna stop," Louise said.

"They're gonna stop," Sylvester said. "Listen. Get in touch with Justin Gage. Get through to him, wherever the hell he is. Tell him to make Zero stop, and if he can't, tell him to try the mayor or the Zoning Board or somebody, he'll know who, and pull off these guys. Tell him all we need is one day, just this afternoon. Then get back and go up to that foreman and don't let him start, no matter what. Take your clothes off, make them arrest you, kick him in the balls, lay down in the doorway. Is anyone else around? Get a crowd and start a fight. Only don't get arrested right away. Stall them off until somebody comes to stop them."

"What if nobody comes?"

"Tell them I'm inside. Wait till the last minute and tell them I'm in there hiding, and they gotta get me out before they wreck anything."

"They won't let you in."

"I'll get in. But make them go looking anyhow. And don't say I'm in the clinic. Tell them you don't know where I am, just hiding in the building somewhere."

"They got cops at the freight entrance too."

"Just go call Gage. Then get back and tie up that guy."

Sylvester stepped over the sawhorse and started walking down the street, easy, not hurrying, staying just outside the barrier. He walked past the boarded-up window of the barbershop in the next building, not turning to look, and not looking back to see if the cops were watching, or coming after him. He turned right at the corner, making sure the cops weren't following him, then circled the block. There was no one at the entrance to the back alley, but there were two cops down inside at the freight door.

The next building had a hardware store at ground level with lofts and offices on the other floors. It was taller than their building and wedged right up against it. Sylvester went into the hardware store and bought a five-foot length of chain and a big combination lock. It cleaned him out. "For your bike?" the guy at the register asked. "Kinda heavy for that."

"Big bike," Sylvester said.

He rode the self-service elevator to the fourth floor and hurried down the hall, past doors with clouded glass panes and embossed names, to an alcove that led to a large window. The window looked out over the roof of their building, a drop of maybe eight or nine feet. Sylvester pushed up the window and tossed the chain and lock onto the roof, then climbed onto the window sill, sitting with his feet dangling outside. He turned around to grab the sill with both hands and lowered himself out the window, his knees and the toes of his shoes scraping down the side of the building, until his arms were stretched full out with his hands on the window sill. After one quick look down over his shoulder he kicked himself away from the wall. His dashiki puffed out and he landed with a hollow thumping sound. The tar paper was soft and giving at first but hard underneath. He rolled over once and waited, lying on his stomach, smelling the tar paper, the bottoms of his feet stinging. He got up, picked up the chain and lock, and headed for the small booth in the middle of the roof. As quietly as he could, he went down the flight of steps to the third floor and listened before peering around the corner of the landing. He unlocked the waiting-room door and slipped inside and locked the door behind him. He moved the big sofa they'd got from St. Vincent's—shoving one end at a time, grunting—against the door. A little card hooked to the bike lock gave the combination. He opened the lock, then tore the card into little pieces and flushed the pieces down the toilet. There seemed to be no rush, as if he'd planned it all out years ago, step by step, and now just had to go ahead in the right order.

In the front room, he locked the door behind him and shoved the white cabinet against it, then climbed into the dentist's chair. He twisted the chain around the steel post of one arm and circled it around his waist, as tight as he could, and slipped the prong of the lock between two links and snapped it shut.

The chain pinched his sides. He tried to get comfortable, crouching to one side.

He waited, hunched over in the big gleaming chair, staring out from behind his shades, sweating. He'd never sat in the chair before. It put you pretty high up. The cushions were soft and cool, the arms hard and cold. His feet were on the metal step. It was like going to the moon, all strapped in and everything. Only it was also like going to the school dentist again, eying the electric drill, the third-degree light, the gleaming sharp tools on the round plate, with this giant looming over you in a white jacket, with a smile like a skull and telling you how he was going to help you out of all your troubles, and you meanwhile praying that with all the other little problems you had to deal with you would at least get a break here, in this regular monster of a chair, that just this once maybe the good-luck charm would really do its job.

III.

Olivia Cowan

SHE DROVE COLDLY, concentrating on street signs, other cars, traffic lights, as if only by such concentration could she keep herself from floating off the earth like a runaway balloon. She didn't even drive fast.

A cop at the intersection was detouring traffic around the block. When he waved for her to stop, she slapped down the accelerator.

The building was barricaded. ZERO WRECKING. She should have known. She had known.

Two wooden barriers had been moved aside to let an ambulance back up to the sidewalk. There were cops around the entrance, more cops across the street, keeping the crowd on the sidewalk. The crowd was all black, maybe a hundred people. They were not straining against the cops. They watched quietly. The whole street was quiet and the air itself seemed altered, as if an eclipse of the sun were coming on. Everyone seemed awestruck, waiting for the unnatural dark.

She was stopped at the building entrance. One of the cops, peering into the vestibule, thrust his arm back. "Watch it. Out of the way."

A man in a white gown walked out, his face lined. The burden flowed behind him, white canvas and white blanket, and then the shock of the face above the open blue collar, the face as white as the canvas, as white as the blanket, the eyes open, stunned, milky, the pupils all but gone, the hair close-cropped, and then the second attendant, his arms sinewy in a short-sleeved gown, his mouth twisting with strain.

She stared, stone, a statue.

The first attendant turned without breaking stride, shifted his hands, and backed into the ambulance. The litter glided in at a slight angle, the second attendant following, as if pulled along in its wake.

A doctor hurried from the building with his small leather case. Dark blotches stained the sleeve of his tan suit. He ducked into the ambulance and the doors slammed shut.

"Can I go inside?" she asked the cop who'd stopped her.

"What? No—what for?"

The engine started, blasting exhaust fumes into their faces. The ambulance eased forward, wailing, flashing.

"Mr. Amicus," she said. "He's a friend. He asked me to come."

"What? What is it, lady?"

"Where's Mr. Amicus? He'll let me in."

"See the sergeant," the cop said.

The sergeant had a walkie-talkie, a black box with a springy aerial. He wrinkled his eyes listening to her. "What name, miss?" He brought the box to his mouth. "Is Mr. Amicus still up there? A lady here wants to come up."

"Cowan. Olivia Cowan."

"Cowan," the sergeant said.

A few minutes later the crackling voice returned: "Okay on that. Affirmative."

The sergeant beckoned another cop. "Take Miss Cowan up to Mr. Amicus. You come down then."

She followed the cop into the dim, tiled lobby, ancient and

empty, scarred, smelling of disuse. "We'll have to take the stairs, ma'am." They climbed to the third floor, and she followed him down the gray hallway. He left her with another cop, who was standing outside the open door with a walkie-talkie.

"You sure you wanna go in there, miss?"

"Yes. Is he still there? The one—who was killed?"

"He's still there. I can ask Mr. Amicus to come out."

"No. I'll go in." She took a breath and stepped into the reception room, ready to pull back, then let out a breath of relief. She remembered the old desk from the other time, the secondhand couches and kitchen chairs, the open cartons of toothbrushes in plastic cases. Only this time there were no people, no kids, no black women with glistening faces and babies squirming on their laps. One sofa lay overturned just inside the door with its stubby legs sticking up, like a grotesque dead bird. The door itself, standing open, was splintered along the edge, the knob broken off, the lock still embedded in a jagged, dangling piece of wood.

Still another cop entered from the opposite door. He stopped when he saw her and called over his shoulder, back through the door: "Mr. Amicus. She's here."

Amicus walked in, in his suit, his hat. He pulled the door shut behind him and touched the brim of his hat, noncommittally. "Hello." His face was like gray parchment, his eyes like gray inserts in that parchment.

"I thought I'd come," she said. She wanted her outrage to show, but wanted it controlled. She wanted it simple and decisive.

He was staring at her oddly, and she realized she was still wearing the bright orange smock over her dress.

"It's all over," he said. "There's nothing to see."

"Is he inside?"

"You don't want to see him."

She paused, struggling for her voice. "What happened?"

Amicus pursed his lips. "He stabbed an officer when they tried to get him out."

"Why did he have to be gotten out? What was he doing?"

"That's a good question," Amicus said. "It seems they were going to tear down the building, and there was all this stuff in it." He gestured, unimpressed, around the room.

"Did they have to kill him?"

"I don't know. I wasn't here. But two officers came up and he stabbed one of them, so I guess—"

"I saw the man being taken out."

"He got cut pretty good."

"Will he be all right?"

"I think so."

"Why couldn't they let Sylvester take the equipment out?"

"I don't know. None of this makes much sense to me right now."

"They didn't have to kill him."

"If your friend was looking for sympathy, he could have left that dentist's tool where he found it."

"You mean he didn't even have a knife?"

"He didn't seem to miss it." Amicus was silent a moment. "With all due respect . . . after looking at him, I'd have to say he couldn't have done anything after he was shot. Which means, I guess, that he cut the officer first, and was shot afterward."

She blinked. "What was he doing when they came in?"

"Sitting, I guess. He'd chained himself into the chair."

"To keep them from tearing the place down."

"Maybe that was it. Unless he figured we were looking for him and wanted a hiding place."

"You *were* looking for him."

"That's right," he said, with no more tone than a robot. "We were looking for him."

"How could he attack anybody if he was chained into a chair?"

"They unchained him. It took some doing, but they finally got him out with a big shears."

"And then he attacked them? With no reason, no provocation?"

"That's right."

"I don't believe that."

Amicus made a little movement with his mouth. "You don't believe he planted the bomb either."

"He didn't. You know that."

Amicus paused. "Don't tell me what I know."

"There's no way in the world he would have done that. Anymore than he would have gone at two cops if they hadn't done something first."

"Okay," he said.

She hesitated, afraid of faltering after having gotten this far. "Can I see him?"

"You don't want to see him."

"Please."

"It's not very pretty."

"I want to see him."

"The photographer's in there."

"What photographer?"

"From the department."

"I won't bother him."

Amicus shrugged and turned toward the door behind him. The cop opened it and stepped aside for Amicus, who stepped aside for her.

She couldn't move at first. The she moved quickly. She saw the dentist's chair first, the high angled arms of the old-fashioned drill, and then the photographer, looking up, surprised, from the big tripod camera. On the floor, drenched in more blood than she ever imagined a bag of skin could hold, the blood spread like paint, the stench incredible, burnt hair and scorched flesh and urine and innards: a flung, small, crumpled doll, with no face, with half a head, oozing clotted red meats.

She reached back, touching Amicus, and screamed.

The sunlight dazzled her. The detective held her arm, steadying her. She seemed to be walking across an infinite distance, an endless landscape of bleached-out angles.

The splash of red caught her eye. They'd stepped beyond the sawhorses and the detective was talking to her. She was looking away, not hearing, when she saw the wool cap across the street, bobbing above heads in the crowd.

She ran through the blaze of sunlight.

The red cap was moving. Ruel emerged from behind the crowd and headed down the block, his white polo shirt hanging loose, his long legs reaching out, his trousers too short.

"Ruel!" she cried.

He spun around to face her, his back against a bakery window, his immense hands spread out on the glass. He seemed transfixed against the background of decorated cakes, pyramids of bread, platters of cookies.

She could smell the warm and yeasty odors.

"What's going on over there?" he demanded.

"He's dead."

Ruel's eyes opened and closed like window shades.

"Sylvester. They shot him."

Ruel drew his head back, his long neck stretching, the muscles pulling.

"They tried to tear it down. They wouldn't let him take anything out."

Ruel seemed to be struggling to pay attention, to sort out his emotions.

"Didn't you know? Didn't you hear?"

"Hear what? I don't know what you're talking about." He blinked in awe. "What in Christ did they shoot him for?"

She could hear the sudden break in his voice, the fear. "Be careful . . ." She reached out to touch his arm but he pulled back. "They killed him," she said. "Just like that."

"That's crazy," he said. "What the hell's going on?"

She glanced back across the street. Amicus was standing on the sidewalk, watching.

"Don't stay here," she said. "Get away."

"They picked up Louise," he said.

"The police?"

"I saw her in the wagon. They were taking her away."

"They'll get you too. Don't stay here."

"I was going," Ruel said. "You stopped me."

She hesitated. "Come with me."

"What?"

"Come with me."

He didn't move. He still seemed unable to absorb what had happened. His eyes had no focus. "That's the sport," he said. "Killing. They did it for the sport. They didn't have to. No one made them."

"Zero made them," she said. "Zero was behind it."

Ruel's eyes flashed. "Hey, now. I don't know about that. There's too much flying around. I can't keep it straight."

"You've got to be careful," she said, "or they'll get you too."

"What?" Ruel said. "What're you dragging me into? What the hell are you talking about?"

"I saw him up there," she said. "I saw what they did to him."

He stared down at her, his lips pulled back.

"I'd kill Zero if I had the chance," she said.

"What?" he said. "You crazy? What're you talking about killing for?"

"Come with me," she said.

"Come where? What are you talking about?"

She looked back. Amicus was gone, but the policemen were still clustered in front of the building, near the wrecking trucks and the giant crane. The crowd across from the entrance was still silent, still motionless.

"Come," she said, knowing he would.

The building was only two blocks away. Not only surrounded by filth but filthy itself, with the same graffiti on the walls as all the other buildings, the same film of soot, the same signs of neglect and decay.

She stopped at the scarred metal door. The whole building was cast-iron, one story high, the sections bolted together. "It's not an easy place to get into," she said, taking the leather case from her bag and dangling the four keys before his eyes. She was very calm. She felt hollow, as if everything had been sucked out of her, but very calm.

Ruel looked at the keys as if they were weapons.

"Don't be frightened," she said.

Methodically, she checked the numbers of the keys and placed one in the circle lock and turned it, then turned the doorknob. She held the knob and inserted a second key in the bolt lock and turned that. She pushed the heavy door open and stepped into the small windowless vestibule. It was like stepping into a closet. Ruel joined her, staring at the second metal door.

"Two more keys," she said, holding up the leather case again. "And you have to know where they go, and the right order. And that's not even the main thing. The main thing is that you have to know something's here worth getting to."

He said nothing.

She reached up on the wall and slid aside the small metal plate to trip the alarm switch and then unlocked the inside door, turning both keys, and pushed it open. She walked in. No light came through the blacked windows and she had, as always, to grope for the switch on the steel post. The two overhead bulbs came on, their metal hoods casting the light down to the cement floor in exact circles.

Silhouetted in the doorway, Ruel did not move for some time. Then he came forward.

"Please close the door," she said.

Ruel hesitated, then closed it. He walked toward her, his heels sounding on the cement and echoing.

"Notice the difference," she said. "No, not the light. The air. That's the humidifier, and the temperature control. Sixty-two degrees, winter and summer. Forty-eight per cent relative humidity."

He motioned toward the two tiers of slotted racks along the opposite wall. "What's that?"

"Paintings," she said.

"Yours?"

"I wish they were."

"What the hell are they doing here?"

"Hiding," she said. "Being hid."

"What'd you bring me here for?"

She fished around in her bag, found the matches, and held them up for him, the way she'd held up the keys.

"Hey, woman. What're you giving me?"

"It's all right," she said.

"You gonna play with matches now? You mean you brought me here to watch you burn those goddamn things?"

"Why not?" she said. "It strikes me as"—her voice broke for the first time—"perfectly appropriate."

"This is crazy, woman. This is driving me right out of my fucking mind."

"You have to understand the . . . appropriateness." It was the only word she could think of.

"There's too much happening today. I'll tell you. It's coming at me from sixteen directions at once."

She started toward the racks but he grabbed her roughly. She tried to pull away. "Let me go."

"I ain't standing here watching no fire. We're getting out of here."

She tried again but he was too strong. She tried to hit him but he caught her hand and held it, his own hand swallowing hers, and then twisted it, twisted her whole arm, and threw her down.

She crouched on the cement floor, gasping, her knee burning. She crouched like an animal and looked up and tried to decide what she saw in Ruel's eyes, beyond the contempt, which had always been there and was still there now.

"Get up," he said. "We're getting out of here."

How did you meet people? The interweavings were always so casual. *Oh*, you would say on looking back. *So that's how it began.*

She met Zero because she attended a benefit for Justin. Later she met Sylvester because she was working on Justin's campaign. At the time Justin himself was little more than a name, serving merely as the means of bringing herself and Zero, and Sylvester, together as faithful workers in his cause.

The benefit was held in one of the smaller ballrooms at the Mayfair, just right for golden anniversary parties and tacky wedding receptions. It could seat a hundred, and when sixty showed up Justin's harried managers were jubilant. "We're off to a great start," one of them kept saying at Olivia's table.

Zero was not even present. He did not, she learned afterward, go to such events. He did not, she learned, go anywhere. But he'd sponsored a whole table, giving the tickets away to friends or employees or deserving waifs, somebody. At the end of the evening, when Olivia was stepping into a taxi, another cab pulled up behind and bumped the one she was entering. The impact was just enough to throw her rather unceremoniously to the ground. A dark face leaned over her, smelling of cloves. He was extraordinarily handsome, a glistening black man with a Caribbean accent and a ramrod posture, wearing his black serge uniform and visored cap with all the severe self-esteem of a general in some grand army. But he was terribly proper and polite. He gallantly helped her to her feet, made certain she was uninjured, offered his enormous white handkerchief. On the little finger of his right hand he wore a huge faceted ruby set in heavy gold. Quite sternly, those cool British syllables as crisp as flint, he dismissed the cab, imperiously waved off the second driver, and announced that he himself would see that she received safe transport home. He drove her back to the gallery in his glossy black limo and helped her out, his cap placed smartly under one arm. She thanked him, and he bowed formally. He was pleased to have been of service. And whose chauffeur was he? Mr. Zeronski's, he replied, explaining about Mr. Zeronski's table, and his guests. He wondered if he could inquire, with all due respect, as to the young lady's name.

It was a break for the gallery, although she didn't need a break there. From the beginning there'd been no necessity to make money, although she'd wanted the gallery to be a success, and it was, and therefore made money. "It's going to be a business, not a hobby," she'd told her mother, who was still alive then, living alone in Philadelphia, with only the vaguest idea of what Olivia was involved in, or why, or exactly what a gallery owner *did*. "And I expect to run it like a business, and not shame the family name."

"Oh, I never feared *that*," her mother said in the soft hush in which she carried on all conversations, her lips forming an O.

She'd expanded the gallery twice in five years and now had Mary Jean to help out, along with a part-time handyman. She'd bought oyster-white carpeting for the showrooms as soon as the income justified it, replaced the old light fixtures with hand-blown glass bulbs. She spent a few hundred dollars on flowering plants, even more on furniture, and had the walls repainted every year.

A few days after her ride home in the limousine she received a call from a Mr. Woodstein, who identified himself as an attorney in the employ of Mr. Zeronski. Would she be kind enough to accept an invitation to visit Mr. Zeronski at home some evening, to discuss mutual business interests?

She'd laughed. "I really don't think any of my business interests coincide with any of his."

"His interests are quite extensive," she was informed. "What evening would you prefer? Mr. Zeronski will be pleased, of course, to send a car."

"Thursday," she said, laughing again.

What did she know about Zero then? It was difficult to distinguish that from what she learned later. She knew he was rich, of course, having worked single-mindedly toward that end. And now, she suspected, he'd suddenly been overtaken by a desire to dignify all that wealth with a few original oils in the living room. She knew that his interests were indeed extensive, including the putting up and tearing down of buildings, the laying out and tearing up of roads. And she knew, of course, that he was supporting Justin Gage.

The handsome black chauffeur arrived at her apartment door precisely on time, cap tucked under arm. Polite, charming, deferential. Scarcely talkative, though. You could hardly blame the man; she sat in back, separated from him by a solid glass partition. The only way to converse was through a tiny speaker embedded in the side of the car. She tried it, pushing the white button. "Does Mr. Zeronski always send you to escort his guests in such style?"

"On occasion he does, ma'am," came the answer, crisp and formal against the background static. It was like talking to someone in a control tower.

Zero lived some miles east of town on a few hundred acres high in the foothills. They swung onto an unmarked private road that angled away from the highway and up through a thick growth of acacia and firs. The house was an enormous one-story structure of semidetached units of glass and softly weathered wood, after the style of Wright's Taliesin West.

After that, and the nice touch of the chauffeur escorting her to the entrance, Zero himself was a letdown. He was dressed in sandals and a camel's hair robe that came down to his knees, exposing his hairy calves. He greeted her with glass in hand: a funny little man, all in all, his eyes large and globy with leathery protruding whites, over which his eyelids seemed to slide very slowly, as if they lacked lubrication. His arms and legs were too short for his body, his head too large, especially in the width of his flat forehead. A brush of toneless brown hair had been trimmed to an exact evenness all around, standing straight up on top and straight out at the sides, stiffly, the same two-inch length everywhere, like a Renaissance ruff.

His age also surprised her. She'd expected him to be older. Zero couldn't have been much past forty, although the dry and burdened eyes and the almost comically fuzzy expression seemed to belie that.

He led her into the living room, where a wall-length window offered a long view of the East Bay city lights. Zero sat in an overstuffed chair with his shoulders hunched, his head settling heavily, his chin resting on his breastbone. He spoke very slowly, with a pronounced accent. He was pleased to see her. It was an honor. Would she join him in some refreshment?

They were served by a pretty black maid, dressed in a tiny skirt and a sheer white blouse over a white bra. She looked, poor thing, like a refugee from one of those gaudy cocktail lounges where the men ogled the waitresses every time they leaned over.

Apparently Zero had three servants, all black, including an unidentified man she'd seen walk by the open door to the room. She couldn't help feeling at least a hint of condescension on Zero's part, and wondered if beneath their silence and impeccable manners all those young and vital-looking retainers indeed felt the kind of gratitude that Zero expected. Marse Zeronski?

She was being unfair. What was Zero supposed to do—refuse to hire blacks?

He took her on a tour of the house, gesturing woodenly with his short arms. The interior decorator must have been the same man who designed the maid's outfit. The furniture was clumsy and ostentatious, the lamps tasteless, the rugs garish. Everything clashed with everything else, and nothing could even claim the virtue of being cheap. The paintings, though, stole the show. The paintings were a revelation. Either, she decided, Zeronski had no use for her at all, or else needed her desperately.

"I own a great many fine paintings," he told her when they returned to the living room. He spoke painstakingly, in pause-ridden hesitations that took some getting used to.

She smiled vaguely and picked up her drink.

"Not here," he said, noticing her reaction. "A safer place. Perhaps you would be interested . . . in seeing them?"

"I would."

"I'm told they are . . . of some value. Although I depend on the testimony . . . of experts."

"What kind of experts?"

"In New York. That is the problem. Distance. I would prefer a more . . . intimate relationship." He gazed at her with his shoulders hunched, his head thrust forward and down, a kind of dulling film over his eyes. He'd been drinking methodically, without gusto or joy, as if merely determined to introduce a certain amount of alcohol into his system within a certain amount of time. Was she the cause of it? Was this funny little man stoking up the fires for his big moment, chasing her from room to room?

"I have some very fine young painters at the gallery," she said.

"You are . . . our leading expert. Your gallery . . . is well known."

"I work hard at it," she said.

But he wasn't interested in her painters. He did not, he assured her, doubt their quality. They simply did not reflect his current interests.

"You can't buy Rembrandt, you know," she said. "You can't buy Rubens. You can't even buy Pollock, or Hopper, or Klee."

He listened stolidly, his eyelids heavy. "That is what I am interested in," he said. "Established figures."

"Like those?"

"The finest," he said, "that are available."

"As an investment?"

"Of a special kind," he responded heavily. "Not for . . . personal gain."

"There are organizations in New York that specialize in art for profit."

"I am not interested . . . in such organizations."

He was interested, he insisted, only in her. He did not want to sign a formal contract. He preferred a simple agreement, a handshake. He would dismiss his agent in New York and Olivia would have full authority to dispose of any paintings that she considered poor investments, and to purchase new works as she saw fit. There would be just one restriction. He would buy only American works. This was his country, and he would support its artists, as he supported its government. Beyond that she would be on her own. He would not require reports. "Whatever is all right with Mr. Woodstein," Zero assured her, "is all right with me."

She was appalled to learn that his paintings had never been catalogued or evaluated. "You mean you've just been piling up all that stuff without even knowing what you've got?"

"Nothing is happening to it. Everything is perfectly safe."

He had no objection to her cataloguing and evaluating. She could do it any way she wished, and pass on her findings to Mr. Woodstein.

"I guess I should be flattered," Olivia said. "Only why should you trust me?"

"Because you are perfectly . . . trustworthy."

She laughed. "Who told you that? Your chauffeur?"

He seemed unsure how to take this. His lids moved down slowly over his eyes.

"He was a real gentleman," Olivia said. "Terribly helpful."

"I was unable . . . myself . . . to attend the function."

"Are you a friend of Mr. Gage's? Or just a supporter?"

"Both, I would hope," Zero said after a moment's thought. It was as if every phrase had to be laboriously formulated on the spot. "He is a fine . . . young man. He has tremendous . . . potential."

"Will he win? You must know about these things. You must have contacts."

"He can win," Zero said slowly. "From the beginning . . . before the beginning . . . I have told him that."

"Were you in on it from the beginning?"

"Before." He stared at her somberly, as if trying to summon up his dignity. It was difficult. He wasn't built or dressed for dignity. "If people like myself didn't . . . work for good men . . . people worse than myself . . . would give us bad men." He paused to let his words sink in and then blinked once, more rapidly than usual, and invited her to the pool.

"The pool?"

"I neglected to point it out . . . on our tour."

He led her slowly, portentously, to an all-glass wing that she hadn't even noticed before. The pool was very large, surrounded by a tiled walkway. The massive wall panels were steamed over from the rising mist. It was like walking into a hothouse.

"The roof . . . can be withdrawn."

"A little air might help," she said.

He pushed a button on the wall and raised his protruding, leathery eyes to watch the midsection of the glass roof slide noiselessly to one side. "We hardly need . . . all this light." He rotated the dimmer knob on the wall until the lights spaced around the pool served only as glowing markers. "Every night," he announced, "I swim."

"How nice."

"Perhaps you will join me. The water is . . . luxurious."

"I'm afraid I didn't bring my suit."

"No suits," he said.

"I'll just skip it then."

"You would find it . . . enjoyable."

"Some other time. When I remember my suit."

"No suits," Zero said.

The maid brought in a tray with two glasses.

Zero nodded heavily toward a lounge chair next to a small table. Olivia sat down. The girl handed them the glasses and left.

"Are you sure . . . you won't join me?"

"Quite."

"Very well." He waddled toward the diving board at the end of the pool, perhaps thirty feet from where she sat. "Your . . . last chance," he called back when he reached the diving board ladder.

"No thanks." Her eyes had become accustomed to the dimness, and she could follow his movements although his face blurred at that distance.

Methodically, certain that she was watching—what was she supposed to do? cover her eyes in mortification?—he untied his belt and spread apart the robe, pausing apostlelike, his dark and indistinct nakedness framed by the open robe, then let the robe drop noiselessly to the tile walkway. He climbed the ladder and proceeded, woodenly, preoccupied with the placement of each foot, to the edge of the board.

He'll kill himself, she thought. He'll conk his head on the edge and sink like a rock.

But his dive was perfect, and Olivia pulled back, startled, when he burst chest-high out of the water in front of her. He'd traveled half the pool underwater. "That was not . . . one of my best." He swam toward the other end, reversed himself skillfully off the wall, and swam the length again, his short arms chunking steadily through the dark water.

Olivia watched from the lounge chair, sipping her drink and counting. He made ten laps without faltering, then headed toward her again. Maybe that was the nightly regimen, ten laps and ten drinks.

He swam up to her and placed his hands on the edge to boost himself out, dripping, his neat ruff undisturbed. He was enormously hairy all over his body, as if to disguise the pudginess. He picked up a towel and faced her, drying one shoulder, his nakedness distinct now. He drained his glass; the maid must have been watching through the glass door, or listening, knowing that as soon as the splashing stopped he'd be ready for a refill, because she reappeared then with her tray, her tight little fanny wagging under that wispy skirt. Olivia hadn't finished her drink but the maid removed it and gave her a fresh one. Wordlessly, she took Zero's empty glass and handed him a full one, then left, a very pretty girl with a light cocoa complexion, and nice legs.

"To our newly formed . . . relationship," Zero said, raising his glass. "May it prosper, and be fruitful."

"I've never been toasted in the nude before."

Zero resumed drying himself, taking his time. She wasn't sure just where she was supposed to look—the protocol of the situation eluded her—and so, smiling, almost laughing, she watched his wrinkled little dickie nodding back and forth, keeping time as he rubbed away with the towel. The swim seemed to have revived him somewhat, and he finished by vigorously massaging his head. The ruff emerged as stiff and neat as before. He stared down at the towel then, as if debating the various uses to which a piece of damp terry cloth might be put, and ended up by draping it carefully around his waist, tucking the ends in.

"Modesty above all," she said but he didn't respond. Maybe it was all part of the ritual: covering himself now so that at the right moment he would be able to unveil his manly pride to full dramatic effect. *Voilà!*

He stood over her, short and flabby in his white loincloth, and offered her his hands. She hesitated. Touching them only lightly, she stood up without his help. He took her hands and held them. Now, she thought. Here it comes. She hadn't expected it quite so soon but was sure it would at least be direct and straightforward. Subtlety hardly seemed Zero's style, let alone the disguised approach, the symbolic overture. But she assumed he'd at least say something. Instead he rose up openmouthed for a kiss while at the same time going for her breast with all the delicacy of someone grabbing a grapefruit.

He seemed surprised when she pushed him back. He seemed genuinely puzzled. "What's wrong?"

"I don't need work that bad," she said.

He frowned. "Are you talking about our . . . agreement?"

"Is this supposed to be part of it?"

"This has nothing to do . . . with our agreement."

"Are we sure of that?"

"Of course. This is entirely . . . separate."

"Good," she said. "We'll shake on that."

In the foyer the maid brought Olivia's jacket. "Thank you," Olivia said. Zero brooded a few feet away, chin down, having again donned his robe for the occasion of Olivia's departure. The maid stepped back after helping Olivia. Her eyes, wide and white against that smooth cocoa face, flashed at Zero, not angrily or accusingly, not even fearfully. Checking out the weather, that's all, hoping to stay out of reach of the grope she assumed was coming. She was ready to jump, maybe even with a smile, a playful wag of the finger. But Olivia could see the contempt in her eyes, the cool and unyielding resentment.

Zero, heavy-laden, glass in hand, did not notice the girl's look: he was staring dully at the white bra beneath her frilly blouse.

Riding down the dark road in the back seat of the limousine, with the silent chauffeur on the other side of the glass partition, Olivia wanted to laugh, shaking her head over it, but instead felt terribly sorry for the poor girl back there. She could envision her at that very moment scooting breathlessly through the halls and doorways with Zero huffing and lurching in pursuit, his wrinkled little dickie jiggling away as he grabbed for her like someone swatting flies. Would she eventually be caught, to be pounded flat beneath that pulsing flabbiness? Oh, God. Ravished by a clown balloon. Fucked by a teddy bear.

But anyone who'd started as far down as Zero—with nothing; an immigrant kid who couldn't even speak English—and still managed to acquire that much money and power must have had some kind of special energy. Surely he could have done more with it. She'd seen that in so many people, even in her own family, men who would have been so easy to admire if they'd only given you the chance. At one time someone must have believed in Zero; he must even have believed in himself. Why did he have to end up not only repulsive but pathetic, a joke, a jerk, a buffoon, grabbing at titty as if it were pure gold?

And why, if he were such a joke, couldn't she just laugh him off? It was as if he'd rubbed rough and hard against her, leaving a raw spot.

She pushed the white button, startling the chauffeur, and asked: "Am I the only one to escape alive? Or have some of the others returned to tell the tale?"

"Excuse me, ma'am?" came the formal, crackling reply.

"Nothing," she said. "Forget it."

The next day she talked on the phone to Woodstein, who offered to show her the collection. "Mr. Zeronski, of course, has many demands on his time. His associates, therefore, are granted a great deal of independence." That sounded fine to her, and when she saw the collection that afternoon, with Woodstein leading her through the pair of locked metal doors and standing by, bored, as she slid out paintings at random from the two racks, she decided to take the job. Just the idea of going through those paintings to catalogue them was exciting. She wondered if Zero had any idea how good they were, or even, more in his line, how much they were worth.

No, Woodstein said, he didn't think Zero had seen most of them.

"You mean not even looked at them?"

"Not that I know of," Woodstein said. "He has—"

"I know. Other things on his mind."

"That's correct," Woodstein said.

She was never sure whether she'd have started the gallery if Bob hadn't died.

After law school, Bob had taken over his father's import business. He could have been a terrific lawyer. He'd edited the *Review* at Georgetown, graduated right at the top of his class; he was the kind of person who seemed to glow with potential. But his father's business was there for the taking, and he took it, devoting all that capability and energy to the task of importing fabrics at fat profits from impoverished countries. He traveled all the time (they lived on the Peninsula then, in Atherton, so he'd be near the airport), flying to Hong Kong, to Singapore and Rangoon and New Delhi, to Beirut and Johannesburg and London. For their first anniversary she presented him with a magnificent Swiss watch with twelve dials encircling the main dial, giving the time in different capitals of the world.

He'd called from Hong Kong to tell her about the amethyst. It was a beauty, he said, the find of the trip. Jewels from the Orient.

The next day he accompanied a wealthy Hong Kong merchant, a Britisher, to a local airport where the man maintained a glider. It was a first for Bob, soaring through the air in that sleek plywood craft. His whole life had seemed tentative up to then; she was still waiting for the moment when he would discover his possibilities.

They plummeted down in what she always imagined as a horrifying shriek of wind rushing past. The plane was not recovered from the bay, and she wanted to believe he'd had the amethyst with him, because it wasn't found at the hotel and she didn't want to think of it being heisted by some houseboy as soon as it was learned he was dead.

Hardly then, a good-luck piece, and not easy to explain as the name of her gallery. Her mother, when told of her choice, simply noted in her hushed voice that the amethyst was not a precious stone. Bob had been twenty-eight, and was gone, and she would never escape the feeling that the bottom could again drop out of her life, without warning or reason, announced by nothing more ceremonial than a garbled cablegram. She moved across the Bay and opened the Amethyst Gallery, with as much ceremony as she could devise, three months after the glider, the wind screeching past, hit the water.

Sylvester was already part of the campaign when Olivia joined up. About a half dozen people were working in the second-floor office, with Sylvester at a small table off by himself, flailing away at a vintage Underwood that must have been borrowed from a museum. He seemed so small that she thought they'd lucked onto the star of the high school Bus. Ed. course to do all their typing. What he was doing though, at what sounded like a hundred words a minute, was writing copy for their handbills, their press releases, their mailings and throwaways.

When she was introduced, Sylvester looked up to nod, his eyes shadowed behind his dark glasses. He didn't smile, and returned immediately to his work. It wasn't until he took a walk to the communal bathroom down the hall that she realized he truly was as small and frail as he looked in the chair, and that his twisted sideways hunch over the typewriter remained when he stood up, and when he walked.

It wasn't until Olivia's third or fourth evening that she had anything resembling a conversation with Sylvester. He was hunched over an enormous chart, plotting schedules for the volunteer canvassers. Olivia had nothing to do at the moment—political campaigns were hardly models of efficiency—and was pouring herself a cup of coffee. The urn was on the table next to Sylvester, and she paused to watch him work. Sylvester finally stopped scribbling. He held the pencil motionless for a moment, then turned slowly to look up at her, his dark glasses shadowing his eyes.

"I haven't a thing to do," she said. "Maybe I can lend you a hand."

He considered this cautiously. "I'm almost finished."

"You'll finish even sooner with help. Then we'll both have nothing to do."

"I got some other things after this."

"I can help on them too. I'm really quite useful. I can type, although not quite like you, read names in a clear voice, do simple sums in my head, print with a neat hand. It seems a shame to let that kind of talent go to waste."

He hesitated, then finally smiled. "You a regular gold mine, lady."

It was an indication of how shy he was, and maybe of how reluctant he was to let down his guard with thirty-year-old liberal females, in that it took a few more evenings for him to loosen up enough to say anything to her first, to initiate a conversation on even the most trivial subject. By then Olivia had been put in charge of organizing door-to-door and telephone canvassing for the entire city, except for the West Side. Sylvester handled the black wards, and helped out on everything else.

"What I can't see," she said to him one night, "is why somebody like Zero is backing us. Why should he want Gage on the Council?"

"You know Mr. Zero?"

"I've met him," she said. It was late and they were the only ones left in the room, sitting at the big table drinking cold coffee from Styrofoam cups, surrounded by stacks of literature and precinct lists. "You know that those people always end up running things," she said, "but you hate being reminded of it. Especially with Zero. He's a buffoon."

"He manages," Sylvester said.

"He's got those darky servants to scurry after him."

"Those cats, you know, they got about the best paying deal, counting eats and all, of anybody in the whole West Side. Hell, lady, they're our success stories. They're our *gentry*, those people working out there on the mountaintop."

"Have you met Zero?"

"What would a man like that bother meeting me for?"

"What about Gage?"

"That's different," Sylvester said. "Sure. I know Mr. Gage."

"I don't."

"You seen him around."

"But we've never really met."

"You oughta get to know Mr. Gage. Being such a faithful worker and all."

"I haven't had the opportunity," Olivia said.

From the beginning the West Side seemed solid for Justin, but the blacks were mostly straight-line Democrats, and not terribly interested in anyone running as an independent. Sylvester worked hard in the hope of getting them to the polls and having them take the trouble, once they got there, to find Gage's name on the ballot. All in all Sylvester showed more energy and intelligence than anyone else in sight.

"We downtrod masses got a real stake in being quick and flashy and full of inborn wit," he explained with a little shrug. They usually worked later than the others, and when they were finished would sit around the big table talking. "That gives us the element of surprise, see, because no one expects us to do much more than count on our toes. I mean, that's why white people are so pious about old G. W. Carver. He lasted near a hundred years, which was what they allowed one bright colored boy every century, so Mr. Carver and his peanut butter jar filled the quota all by himself, and kept the field from cluttering up."

"You know what?" she said. "You're not really a radical. I'm more of one than you are. You're not caught up enough. It's too easy for you to step back and look at things."

"Radical's your vocabulary, lady, not mine."

"You know what I mean."

"What? Yelling and screaming and marching up and down? Guns and riots and beating up on people? Guns and beating up, I would go so far as to say, are exactly the things I appreciate least about this country, and would most like to see changed. So maybe you're right, and I ain't no proper kind of radical a-tall, but just a poor hard-working fellow trying to make his way out there in the raggedy world, and will just have to live with that fact."

She laughed. "If you put your mind to it, you'd end up rich. You'd be a millionaire."

"Lady, I have considered it. I have considered more things, lady, than you ever dreamed of in your philosophies."

"Only don't become *like* them. Don't let them turn you into their flunky."

"I'm just trying real hard not to be a child of my era, if you know that feeling."

Sylvester probably had more scholarships than anyone on campus, and took some pleasure in confounding the various professors and deans who were so anxious to shower their charities upon him.

"You know what it is, I'm a regular *advertisement* for those people, showing how cheerfully they're providing us types with educational opportunities."

"Take advantage of it," she said. "Get it while you can."

Sylvester had straight A's but wouldn't let himself be caught working at it. He enjoyed being in control, not playing anyone's game but his own. His confidence seemed so pure that she warned him about it. But back then she did it almost as a joke, a genial parody of the realist lecturing the blissful dreamer: "Don't let your pride get you either. Don't put all your stock in the magic touch. Things can turn, you know. The luck can run out."

He laughed. "Hey, now, lady. *You're* the one who just told me to grab while the grabbing was good. All I'm doing is riding the tide, and following my lucky star."

They worked awfully hard on the campaign, especially at the end, and on election night Olivia stood next to Sylvester in the crowded Mayfair ballroom, exhausted, her feet aching and her eyes burning, shouting in exuberant relief when the final votes were tallied at 3 A.M. and they realized they'd won. People in the crowd cried from joy. Justin thanked them for what they'd done and for the dedication they'd shown. He had a magnificent voice and they cheered and shouted *Yes! Yes!* when he said they'd only begun, that now the real work would start.

It'd been very close. There were five seats on the Council and Justin had barely come in fifth. The man he edged out wasn't even one of the party hacks they'd hoped to unseat, but the closest thing to a liberal in the whole city government.

Justin had played football at the university, and something else, baseball or basketball, one of those guys who'd always been taller and stronger than anyone else and therefore became cautious about asserting himself for fear of being taken as a bully. The few times they'd met during the campaign Justin treated her politely, discreetly, almost with deference. He was like that around women, with his shy soft resonant voice and his habit of lowering his eyes when he spoke. You realized what a surprisingly gentle man he was and wondered how he could make it as a lawyer, let alone survive the gutter battles of politics. But the strength was there, and you could see it transformed on the platform or before a TV camera into the kind of excitement that had finally given him the election, and that made him the only politician in the city who had a chance of going anywhere.

It was at a cocktail party that she finally spoke to him alone, without his wife on his arm, without the half dozen or so people who'd always flocked around him during the campaign. This was months after the election. She'd said something innocuous and he'd lowered his eyes, tinkling the ice in his glass: "I guess that's true, Miss Cowan."

She'd stared at him, smiling, until he raised his eyes. Then she laughed. "Really, Justin, why don't you just start by calling me Olivia and we'll see where it goes from there."

It went further than she expected. Or maybe just faster, in directions and with nuances she hadn't been prepared for.

She'd invited Justin to an opening at the gallery and he'd come, without his wife. Sylvester came too, but in no condition to enjoy himself; the poor guy just couldn't stop perspiring, couldn't find a place to stand. He kept backing toward walls and corners, as flustered as a kid at a high school dance. She felt terribly sorry for him, but the more she tried to help the worse he looked. Finally he bolted. She saw him scuttling through the crowd for the door but fought off the impulse to call after him.

"Poor Sylvester," she said to Justin. "I really hoped he'd enjoy himself. I thought he'd be interested in meeting some new people."

"I guess he wasn't," Justin said, avoiding her eyes.

He stayed until the end, as she hoped he would. A small group was going out for dinner with the artist, and she invited Justin to join them. He sat next to her at the restaurant. He was woefully self-conscious, and not very good at hiding it. He still seemed undecided, still clinging to the possibility of turning back at some almost-final step. But he didn't. She was the one who suggested a drink together afterward. He was the one who suggested the suite at the Mayfair. All along he remained very polite, almost formal. It wasn't that he was unsure of himself; he was perfectly sure, but simply not yet convinced that she would be interested.

"Of course I am," she told him, laughing. "Do you think I would have come here otherwise?"

"Maybe you were counting on being able to fight me off."

"I don't want to fight you off."

The suite was very nice, with a lovely bedroom and a big fine bed. He was gentle and unhurried, and not in the least bit vain about that marvelous athlete's body.

It was the next night that they first mentioned his wife.

"We really have to get the whole guilt business straightened out," she said. "I'm not stealing you from anybody. I don't want to steal you, or anybody else. If that's how you see it, we should stop now before we go any further. We can't have that hanging over us every minute."

It wasn't like that, he said. It wasn't a question of guilt at all. (Although of course it was for him. Both of them simply wanted to ignore that fact, at least for a while.)

"I want to be good for you," Justin told her that night, lying with his arm around her on the bed.

"We'll be good for each other," she said. "That's the point of something like this, isn't it?"

They met every afternoon in the suite at the Mayfair. Some of his supporters had provided it as a place for small meetings and political receptions, not because a councilman needed it but because a potential candidate for mayor did, and his wife refused to have her living room overrun by politicians. He rarely mentioned his wife, but they obviously weren't getting along; she resented Justin's ambitions and seemed to feel personally affronted by his success.

Justin was a terribly decent person, and there was nothing like five years as an unattached widow to make you appreciate decency. She'd had her introduction, and more, to the battering-ram mentality: "Let me stick it to you!" one had wetly breathed into her ear. He was on top of her, grunting and rasping and shoving his beloved member against her, playing hit and miss in the hopes, it seemed, of eventually muscling into the right opening, and that was his final outburst of passion, his *cri de coeur*: "Let me stick it to you! I want to stick it to you!" He'd been the worst, and she'd never seen him again. They'd met at a party in Beverly Hills; she was down there visiting an old friend from Smith who did P.R. work at one of the studios. The guy was a musical director of some sort and had worked on a whole list of films she'd never heard of. He'd seemed all right at first, and she went to his place in the hills, where they ended up balling on his chaise longue, an absurd king-sized affair on his second-story patio, overlooking the lights of Hollywood and the valley. "Really, that couch out there is almost too much," she told him afterward. "It's so strategically placed with the view and everything, and for God's sake, orange blossoms. Did some set designer fix it up for you?"

"The girls seem to like it," the fellow said, almost primly.

They weren't all like that, but they weren't always that much better. You wearied of the cringing self-defeated ones, and got tired too of the strutting peacocks, the loudmouth little Caesars.

She would meet Justin at the suite in the late afternoons, as soon as he could get away from the office or the courts or the Council meetings. They both had keys and each would enter without knocking, to walk in upon the one already there, as a kind of intimacy. They would have a drink together, she would smoke cigarettes, they would talk, they would make love, and then he would return home to his wife.

"I was going to be an artist," she told him, the first person in years she'd admitted this to. "My parents insisted I do the Smith thing first, and then I studied at the Art Students League in New York. I was waiting for a sign, a revelation. I guess I expected a big booming voice to shake the room: *You are an Artist!* I was terribly young then. What happened was that I got a part-time job in a gallery and loved it; it was exciting and exhausting and exactly what I wanted. That was the revelation and it came from a small, quiet, but very firm voice."

He'd assumed she was divorced, and listened in silence when she told him about Hong Kong, and the amethyst, and the glider plummeting down toward the glassy sun-drenched bay with the wind shrieking off the wing tips.

"We had a lot of money," she told him when he asked about her family. "Not just my father. My mother's side was deep into carriage parts around the turn of the century and managed to make the transition to automobile bodies, or body parts, I'm not sure which. Except for one uncle on my mother's side, who made his pile buying up rights of way in Ohio until he died falling off a train, although there was a school of thought that believed he was pushed. He was not known, my mother would say, as an ethical man, and it was presumed he had powerful enemies. Deaths in the family have always tended toward the bizarre. One of my father's brothers choked to death while eating. He was only in his fifties, in the prime of his life, and head of some gigantic rubber processing company. My father, of course, committed suicide, but it wasn't as bad as it sounds. He was already in pretty bad shape from a stroke when he got cancer too: he'd always been a regular dynamo and the prospect of gradually wasting away simply didn't fit in with his flair for the dramatic. He was a financial wizard of sorts, and had been an ambassador. My mother was the only one who died quietly and normally. The women were mostly spectators, lovely but lacking in spark. And very genteel. *Your monthly flowers* was how you were supposed to refer to your period. And she was a real push-over for babies, although she never had any great number herself. I can still remember her cooing over someone's baby. The kid smiled at her and someone, one of the men, said it was probably gas. *Oh no,* my mother said. *He sees the angels. That's what it is, isn't it, baby? You see the angels.*" Olivia paused, enjoying the recollection. "But the men were pretty dynamic. The men in that family were the passionate ones, the buccaneers."

In the years since Bob died she liked to think she'd learned to accept tentativeness as the normal state of things, to be suspicious of good luck and prepared at any moment to have the bottom drop out of her life again. But it was very good with Justin and she couldn't help feeling that it was solid and assured and would be protected.

The only person she wanted to tell was Sylvester, even though he was terribly moral and she wasn't at all sure how he'd take it. But she didn't want him learning about it as a piece of dirty gossip.

She thought she'd found the right moment. They were sitting together in the university cafeteria after one of his classes, just the two of them at a corner table, and Sylvester was in an awfully good mood, telling her of his experiences with the draft board a couple of years back.

85

"What do you mean, they gave you a hard time?"

"I mean they practically formed a line, to see who could give me the hardest time."

"Are you sure you didn't go there to give *them* a hard time?"

"Lady, I went there because they told me. I went because they sent me this super-simple notice saying I sure as hell better go there if I knew what was good for me."

"Who gave you the trouble, the army people?"

"The doctors," Sylvester said.

"What on earth for? Did they think you were faking?"

"Maybe they figured I stopped off at the local hoo-doo woman on the way over for a hex."

"Didn't they even examine you?"

"Afterward. First they asked questions. You born that way, boy? You ever see a real doctor about that? You ever try to get it fixed up? You ever do any exercises, or imbibe any pills, potions, or pharmaceutical preparations for that peculiar condition you got there?"

She laughed. Even Sylvester was laughing. "But that's terrible," she said. "That's indefensible."

"Then they started talking about limited service. Maybe, one of the doctors said, I would be interested in helping my country by offering whatever form of limited service I was capable of performing. Man, I allowed, that is *it!* All my life I have been thinking about how what I owe my country is very definitely limited service."

"They must have appreciated that."

"They mulled it over some. But they could tell I wasn't mad at them. I even told them I wasn't. You are just little old ineffectual cogs in this great big machine, I said, doing your duty as you see fit."

"You told them that?"

"I think they were real moved to hear me tell them that."

"What'd you do then? Snap to attention and give them a crisp salute when you left?"

"Aw, c'mon, lady. Who told you?"

Then she mentioned Justin.

"I'm in love with him," she said. "It's as simple as that. We're both in love."

Sylvester's face had already changed. "I didn't think you were that dumb," he said. It was the first time he'd ever gotten angry with her. "I didn't think *he* was that dumb."

"What are you talking about? We're not planning on renting billboards. I'm not trying to hurt him. I want to be good for him. I want to help him."

"Only what's wrong with him? One woman ain't enough? One wife ain't enough? What kind of ambitions he got in that line anyway?"

"I thought you'd want to know. I thought it'd mean something to you."

"It don't mean nothing to me—okay? Not coming, going, or sideways. You're the ones having fun, so don't think it means anything to anybody else, except maybe a few voters and an occasional wife here and there. But not me, okay? It don't mean the littlest tiddliest thing in the world to me."

"Sylvester . . . please . . ."

Right after that, everything changed between her and Justin. At first she feared Sylvester had said something to him. But he hadn't.

It was almost as if she went to the suite that afternoon expecting something to be wrong. When he arrived Justin seemed tired. He'd been working hard, trying to keep too many things going at once. They couldn't seem to find much to talk about, and after a drink Justin came over and took her hands, almost as if in apology for the awkward silences. They went inside and made love then.

"Sometimes it's like that," she said afterward.

"I guess I'm worn down," he said. "It's been a busy stretch."

They each showered and got dressed, hoping it would rejuvenate them.

"I'm going to have to leave early," he said. "I got into a thing over some new fire ordinances, and we're going to have to meet on it."

"Can you stay awhile?"

"Awhile," he said.

It would have been better if they'd just written the evening off. She asked about the meeting, the fire ordinances, and learned of the incredible series of fussy little accommodations that not only Justin but the whole Council was going through.

"But it's all so petty," she said finally. "You'd think five grown men could settle a problem like that in five minutes."

It annoyed him, and should have, because he was trying very hard to do the right thing. What she really wanted to say was that politics like that had never worked, and never would, that you couldn't be cool and accommodating and practical in that situation without eventually being swallowed up into that colorless paste that politics in this country had always been. Justin deserved better. And the people who believed in him deserved better too. But no matter how she tried to say this it sounded wrong.

"It's not that I'm expecting miracles," she told him. "I know what you have to put up with. But if you start playing the game their way, they're going to wear you out over nickels and dimes while at the same time they're making off with the crown jewels."

It turned out that Zero had some interest in the new fire code.

"Is that why you're spending so much time on it?"

"Everyone who owns property in the city is interested," Justin said.

"And Zero owns most of the West Side."

"A good part of it," Justin said.

"I've never really understood what he does down there."

"He does a few things. He builds, he tears down, he owns, he controls."

"And makes money."

"He's also set up a pretty nice scholarship fund for black students. He gave the space for a neighborhood center, supports a lot of charities."

"It's good business, dropping a few crumbs here and there."

"Look, I've never been the P.R. man for Zero. I don't have any delusions about him."

"Doesn't it make you uneasy then, having him as your big supporter?"

"You can't let every grabber in sight scare you. I can handle Zero. I can handle most of those people."

"I'm not saying you're a push-over. But don't you get—angry, infuriated, outraged? Don't you get the urge to rattle the brains out of some of those people?"

"What good would that do?"

"What good does it do to treat them like philanthropists? That's exactly what Zero wants, to be the goddamn white savior for all those poor unfortunate people down there. You've seen him with his servants; it's the same thing. That's why he's so unhappy with Sylvester. It rankles the hell out of him to see some kid running even a ragtag shoestring clinic in *his* territory. It's not simply greed. He wants medals too, for his great benevolence."

Justin was silent a moment. "If you feel that way, why do you work for him?"

"Because he's paying me well for something I like, and that I couldn't do on my own, and because it's all straightforward and aboveboard and without any question of fringe benefits for him."

"He's not getting any fringe benefits from me," Justin said.

"I didn't say he was."

They stopped then. They both realized they were saying things that offended the other.

It was better the next night, and then for three days they didn't see each other. She flew to New York for Zero, to attend a sale at Sotheby Parke Bernet. It was the first time she'd ever bid at a large auction. She purchased three works, all for Zero, including a small very fine Mary Cassatt, and flushed with excitement when the auctioneer gaveled the bidding to a close at her final nod. Everyone in the crowded room turned to look, wondering who she could possibly be.

When she got back, still high from her success, she called to ask Justin to come to the suite early that afternoon. He said he would try.

She called Zero then. The Mary Cassatt was the best piece in his collection, and maybe the most valuable: an exquisite softly rendered portrait of a young woman in a red velvet chair. She was sure Zero would at least want to look at it. She hadn't spoken to him since the night of his pool-side grope and grab.

The operator, though, gave her Woodstein instead. Mr. Zeronski was busy at the moment, but would of course be pleased with her acquisitions.

"I'm sure he'll want to see these," Olivia said.

"I'll inquire, but I don't think so," Woodstein said. "Meanwhile, you can add them to the rest, in the usual manner."

She struggled to maintain her elation. At the suite, hours before she had any hope of Justin arriving, she poured herself a drink. It hit her immediately. She was exhausted and could hardly keep her eyes open. Pulling off her shoes, she stretched out on the bed. She couldn't fall asleep and got up and took off her clothes and lay down again. She wanted Justin to discover her lying there waiting for him, and fell asleep imagining herself being awakened by his touch, his fierce breathing.

It didn't work out quite that way. But he did arrive and they did make love, and afterward she told him about New York. He seemed pleased for her, but hardly excited. She'd hoped he'd share her enthusiasm, but realized that she hadn't really expected him to. Justin was polite, gentle, terribly restrained; and she could have predicted that.

The following day Justin said he'd been retained by Zero to do some legal work in connection with the paintings, but that Zero hadn't explained what the work would be.

The news annoyed Olivia. "It would have been nice," she said, "if Zero had at least told me about this."

"He asked me to tell you."

She shrugged, unsatisfied. "Did you play innocent, and ask for my phone number?"

Justin frowned. "This has nothing to do with us."

"Why does he have to be so mysterious about what he wants?"

"He's like that. He never says anything unless he has to."

"Why do you have to see the paintings if you don't even know what you're supposed to do?"

"I don't have to. He just suggested maybe I should. I thought we could go tomorrow morning, and then have lunch together."

She narrowed her eyes at this. He was trying hard to sound casual.

"It'll be the first time we've ever gone anywhere together," she pointed out.

He was still self-conscious. "It'll be perfectly proper," he said, hoping to turn it into a joke. "Strictly business. If we want, we can even have Zero pay the tab."

"I don't want Zero paying the tab," she said.

"I didn't mean anything by that."

"If we're going out, I'd like us to do it on our own, without his help."

Justin had never been good at dissembling, and she could see this disturbed him.

"What is it?" she said. "What's wrong?"

"We don't have to go anywhere afterward," he said. "We could just . . ." He shrugged and didn't go on.

"Come back here?"

"Whatever you'd like."

She looked around the living room of the suite. It was one of those simple revelations that left you perfectly calm, because you realized you should have known it all along. "You never told me," she said quietly.

She could tell from his expression that he hadn't tried to hide it from her. He simply never imagined she would find the idea offensive.

"That's it, isn't it?" she said. "Zero's our benefactor, providing us with this nice little hideaway."

"It's not him alone. In fact, it's not his money at all. He just has an interest in the hotel and gave us the suite at cost."

"Oh," she said.

He picked her up precisely at eleven the next morning. They were both silent on the drive into the West Side. Justin parked in front of the building and she unlocked the outside metal door and disconnected the alarm high on the vestibule wall and unlocked the inside door, after a little trouble getting the keys in. Her hand wasn't shaking but seemed clumsy. She stepped quickly inside and Justin followed her. He looked at the two racks of paintings, only the edges of the frames showing. He shrugged then, as if to say that was fine; he'd seen everything he wanted to. She brought out the Cassatt anyway.

"It's very nice," he said.

Carefully she returned the painting to its slot in the lower rack. She hesitated, wondering if she should show him any of the others. She was standing, facing the rack, with her back to him. She heard him walking toward her and waited, stiffening. From behind he gently placed his hands on her arms. He didn't say anything. She didn't either. She remained rigid in the awesome silence. She could hear neither the humidifier nor the air conditioner. That meant the readings were right; everything was perfect.

"We could go," he said. "I really don't have to see any more of these."

"To lunch?" she asked, without turning around. Her voice seemed to waver. She tried to keep a column of air under her words. "Maybe there's really no need—for a business lunch."

"Can we go?" he said, very quietly.

She slipped her arms free, lightly, and turned to look up at him. The light was behind him, and his face was shadowed. "Do you really want to sit somewhere and talk about everything?" she asked.

He was a moment answering. "We ought to talk," he said.

"Maybe if you understand and I understand we can just leave it at that, and not muddy things up."

He was silent again, looking down at her. He put his hands on her waist, drawing her closer, until her thighs pressed against his. But she kept her head back, looking up into his shadowed face.

"We'll start out by trying to be nice and considerate," she said, "and just end up by hurting each other."

"There's no reason to hurt each other."

"I know there isn't," she said. "That's what will make it so frustrating."

He was silent again, holding her, then bent down and kissed her. He was terribly strong and held her tight against him.

Finally she pulled her head back slowly. "We could make love here," she said.

"Here? It's like a tomb."

"I don't want to go anywhere else. We could do it now, and not have to say anything."

"The floor's cement."

"There are some tarps over there." She laughed then, softly, trying to make it easier for both of them. "Really," she said, "there's no law that says we can only do it in the afternoon. The doors are all locked; this is probably the safest spot in the whole city. We've even got a thing monitoring the environment. A hygrometer-thermometer. Have you ever made love before in a monitored environment?"

He tried to smile.

She took one step back, paused, then started unbuttoning her jacket. He watched, not moving. "My hands are freezing," she said, and just then a button ticked lightly on the cement floor and rolled away.

"Let me," he said quietly.

She dropped her jacket and turned around and waited for him to unbutton her blouse. He didn't move. The silence was like the after-ringing of a bell. "Well?" she said.

Methodically he unbuttoned the back of her blouse.

"You know how you like to slip it off," she said, only partly turning her head, not able to see him behind her. "You push it forward off my shoulders and then slide your hands over my breasts and hold them as the blouse falls the rest of the way off, quite delicately, almost airily."

He didn't move.

Again she waited. Finally, turning to face him, she hunched her shoulders forward and removed the blouse herself, from the cuffs, one sleeve at a time, and dropped it delicately, airily, to the floor.

"Olivia . . ."

"We're not going to talk, remember?" She took his hand and led him to the pile of quilted tarpaulins in the dark corner of the room, near enough to the wall to smell the cold metallic odor. She felt suddenly careless and lighthearted. She took a corner of the tarp on top of the pile and started pulling it off.

"I'll give you a hand," he said.

Together they spread it on the cement floor. He flapped it twice to straighten out the folds. She smoothed down the corners. She laughed. "It's like setting up for a picnic. All we need is a wicker basket and a nice bottle of wine."

He didn't seem to know how she meant this. She wasn't sure herself.

They took off the rest of their clothes and hesitated, facing each other. Again she smiled; she didn't know why she felt so lighthearted; it was as if for the first time she could be perfectly relaxed with him. He was very small. He looked like a little boy who'd been out playing in the cold. She sat on the tarp and patted the space next to her. He sat and put his arm around her; she shrugged free and stretched out on the tarp. It was like rough leather, and cold. She pulled him down alongside her. Justin lay on his side, facing her, his hand like a weight on her breast, making it hard for her chest to rise and fall. She reached down along his stomach and touched his penis, startling him. She took her hand back. "Hardly coming on like gangbusters, are we?"

"It'll be fine," he said. "Once we get started."

"I though we were started."

He kissed her, very softly, on the lips. Then, resting on one elbow with his head over her, he toyed delicately, using one finger of his other hand, with her nipple. "It's different here," he said. "I guess I just wasn't prepared."

"Maybe that was a problem," she said. "Always doing it in the same place, at the same time of day. All that orderliness. Maybe we were too serious, and never really let ourselves go."

He was silent a moment. "Wasn't it good the way it was?"

"See," she said. "As soon as we start talking about it, everything comes out wrong. Anyhow, it was very good, you know that. It was great. I'm really glad about it. Only let's not talk about it. Let's not be serious and rational and responsible. Let's just have ourselves a nice happy fuck, all right? No holding back, all right?"

"I'm not holding back," he said.

She laughed. "You're not letting go either. You're not doing anything."

"All right," he said. He eased her—gently—onto her back and moved one leg over her. He moved his hand over her and kissed her nipples. He became hard and wanted to enter her, but she put her hands on his shoulders and pushed him down, and pushed again, down, arching her back, holding him down and not letting him up until he was thrashing at her, grabbing and scratching, his breath as harsh as trumpeting between her legs.

She kept him from discussing it at the restaurant. She was sorry she'd given in and come with him. "Everything's fine," she insisted. "Let's just leave it like that."

The poor guy didn't feel right giving up, and struggled pathetically for the one phrase that would let him begin. He wanted so much to do the decent thing.

"I have a suggestion," she said. "The gallery's practically around the corner. When we leave, why don't you just give the nice man outside the ticket for your car and then while you're waiting for it I'll just stroll on back to work. I have all sorts of things to do there."

"I'd like to drive you."

"I'd really prefer to walk."

"I'll walk you then."

"I'd rather you got your car."

"All right," he said after a moment. "If you'd rather." But he still didn't feel off the hook. He glanced, frowning, around the restaurant.

"That's right," she said. "It's not the place for long good-bys."

"We shouldn't have come here," he said.

"It was nice and it's over," she said. "Let's leave it at that."

He looked so unhappy she wanted to reach across and pat his hand. Either that or announce, as a little joke to go out on, how tender she was from all that heaving and bumping on the tarpaulin. *Man, have I got a sore ass!* But the tone would have to be right—a little gleefully shared mischief—and she was afraid she'd botch it and make him feel bad. She really didn't want to make him feel bad. "Why don't you just ask for the check?" she said.

"We could go to the suite. I don't have to rush back to the office."

"Oh no," she said quickly.

Outside he handed his ticket to the attendant and turned to her, but she put out her hand before he could speak. He took it but she didn't give him a chance then either. Coolly, briskly, she slipped her hand from his and started walking away, suddenly realizing that she was fingering the buttonhole for the missing button on her jacket. She hoped she hadn't been doing that all through lunch.

There was enough catching up to do; Mary Jean had been struggling vainly to stay on top of things. It amused Olivia that people considered running a gallery something you did wearing white gloves. Olivia took pleasure in the heaviest and dirtiest work, and prided herself on her skill in building crates, pounding away enthusiastically with claw hammer and tenpenny nails. She'd never yet had a piece damaged in transit.

With twelve artists on her list, she spent a lot of time getting everything accessioned and priced and catalogued, and a lot more trying to keep all twelve happy. She flattered them, scolded them, lent them money, promoted their reputations, listened sympathetically to even their zaniest dreams, extricated them from their profound depressions, and patiently tugged them back to earth when they began elevating from too much alcohol, or dope, or undisciplined euphoria. She also sweated over tax records, mailing lists, accounting procedures, government forms. Beyond this she had to behave pleasantly in the company of, and do the dance of the dollars with, those few rarefied and necessary individuals known as collectors.

She'd joke—usually with her painters when they got overbearing—that she was well aware of not being privy to the Muse's luxurious secrets. But someone, after all, had to make sure the pictures hung straight, and fill out the REA manifests, and as long as she had the job she was damn well going to see that it got done right.

She kept up with the art journals and every couple of weeks would drive over the bridge to see what was going on at Hansen-Fuller and the other San Francisco galleries. Occasionally she'd take the morning shuttle flight to L.A. to check out the County Museum and the La Cienega galleries, and twice a year she'd fly to New York for a four- or five-day binge of walking and viewing.

She lived over the gallery, and did not mind spending time there alone. When she stayed home at night, either in the apartment or working by herself in the gallery, it was by choice. There were always invitations, places to go, people to see. After the breakup she went out a few times with old friends but put most of her energies into the gallery. She'd missed that commitment during the weeks with Justin.

She liked Justin very much, and felt no desire to belittle him. Justin would succeed; she didn't doubt that. He'd almost surely make it as mayor next time. He'd have a good shot at Congress then, and would probably settle there; liberal, competent, responsible. It wasn't that she expected him to aim for the White House. She just wished he wouldn't always find it so easy to discover perfectly good reasons not to become excited, not to get angry, not to strain or test or commit himself to anything. She just wanted him, no matter where he ended up, to take that final scary step of believing in himself.

Maybe that was asking too much, of anyone.

She was pleased, after a few weeks, to meet Justin at a party for some friends leaving for Europe. She wanted to set the tone for the future.

Before she talked to him she asked the host to introduce her to Justin's wife, Beatrice. The woman was pleasant but guarded. You got the impression she knew or at least suspected that Justin had been involved with someone, but was not sure who. She therefore approached every woman with a certain reserve, just in case.

"We're still friends, I hope," Olivia said when she managed to speak to Justin alone. "We'll meet on occasion, say hello, pass a few cheerful words. That'll be better, won't it, than putting paper sacks over our heads?"

"Of course," he said, jiggling the ice in his glass, his eyes down, as shy and deferential as the first time they'd met.

She enjoyed seeing Sylvester and they got together occasionally for a cup of coffee, usually at the Student Union. He took a lot of pressure from his friends about her: the smart-aleck stares, the sly jokes, the barely disguised obscenities. He hardly took notice, although she always felt uncomfortable on campus, even with the kids who were friendly. Some were barely out of their teens and made her feel like a maiden aunt. But he never wanted to meet anywhere else. "You think we get looks here?" he said. "What're you expecting other places?"

He was working hard on the clinic, running the whole operation and filling in at the last minute for people who didn't show up. The clinic was terribly important to him and there were stretches when he didn't set foot on campus for days. "They'll flunk you out," she warned, but Sylvester refused to worry about it. He was easy in the confidence that he could glide along forever, cheerful and untouched.

She didn't have to tell Sylvester she'd stopped seeing Justin. Nor did Sylvester mention it, except indirectly, right afterward, when she was still feeling the disappointment.

"You gotta smile once in a while, lady. I mean, it's good every now and again to peek out from under all that gloomy."

"You're not smiling."

He smiled. "Although I don't have the need as much as some others," he said, going into his dialect. "I'se a head nigger, lady. Most niggers, now, they soul types."

"Am I a head white woman?"

"Surely you is not. You is all heart, lady, from top to toe, fretting all the time about all the good things you could do for people and such. That's why you gotta smile. You need a little felicity to play off against all the conscience weighing you down."

She laughed. "You should have been a big fat mammy, Sylvester—passing along wisdom and folklore to all the spoiled kids from the mansion."

"Oh no. Mammies *all* soul. And I live up here, behind the eyes. That's where it all happens for me."

"Have you ever had a girl, Sylvester?"

"No, ma'am, I ain't never touched any of that stuff. And I ain't fixing on doing so either, if that's okay with people."

"Aren't you even interested?"

"No, I ain't even interested. It just don't make anything happen up here where I live, so why mess around, I say. I mean, you dig that? Or you want me to draw you pictures?"

"You don't have to draw me pictures."

Eventually Justin's name came up, in connection with some vote that the Council had to contend with. Sylvester thought a lot of Justin, and was always quick to defend him.

"But don't you ever have doubts?" she asked. "Don't you worry about him turning out like all the others in the end?"

"Hey, lady—you down on the man now? You beginning to feel distrustful about your old friend?"

"I was just asking about how you felt."

98

"Tell me how you feel. You're the one with the changed feelings."

"Oh no," she insisted. "They haven't changed at all."

After she completed the cataloguing for Zero she drew up a three-page prospectus, evaluating the collection, very conservatively, at $700,000.

She wanted to give the prospectus to Zero personally, standing over him to make sure he looked at it. She was tired of clearing everything through Woodstein and wanted Zero out in the open, where she could deal with him.

She talked to Justin over the phone and learned that he still hadn't done anything about the paintings, still didn't know what he was supposed to do. That was how Zero operated, Justin again assured her. Even his closest people, even Woodstein himself, hardly knew what he was up to half the time.

"Is he paying you?"

"Not so far," Justin said.

"Well—he's paying me."

"Maybe you can get an answer then."

"I expect to," she said.

"How are you doing?" he asked when she was about to hang up. "How's everything going?"

"Fine," she said. "I'm working hard and having fun at it."

She wondered if Zero was avoiding her because he was embarrassed over what happened at the pool. At any rate, she'd had enough of the house on the hilltop. She intended to see him at his office, without the cocoa-brown maid around to charge up his libido and ply him with tumbler-sized shots.

"One moment, please," the switchboard girl said and then, after a long dead space, Woodstein answered.

"The girl must have made a mistake. I asked for Mr. Zeronski."

"Mr. Zeronski, unfortunately, is tied up right now. Perhaps, if you could tell me the problem . . . ?"

"There's no problem. I'd just like to see him."

Woodstein was silent a moment. And then, in his most avuncular manner: "If it's nothing pressing, perhaps—"

"Actually, it's quite pressing. Would you pass that along to Mr. Zeronski? Say I called about an extremely pressing matter and expect him, as soon as he's free, to find a space for me in his incredibly busy schedule. I'll be waiting to hear from him."

She hung up.

The rest of the morning she worked around the gallery. She stayed on through lunch, asking Mary Jean to bring her back a sandwich, in case the call came then. Shortly before two, Alfred Lester showed up with four new canvases, backing his pickup truck to the curb and unloading them from the tail gate. He'd been working on the series for some time, each canvas nine feet high, each posing a single larger-than-life nude against a realistic landscape.

"These are major works," Alfred announced after he'd leaned the paintings in a row against one wall of the main showroom. He and Olivia had stepped back to view them from the opposite wall. "They are not to go cheap."

She agreed. Alfred was the best, and best known, artist on her list, and she like the canvases very much.

"If you can't manage real money," he said, "don't sell the fucking things. I'll store them in the attic."

"I can sell them," she said. "Don't worry."

The outside door led into the smaller front room, and Olivia had not heard anyone enter. She first realized someone else was present when Alfred stopped in midsentence to stare past her. She turned to find the handsome black chauffeur standing in the archway with the visored black cap under his arm, the huge ruby ring flashing on his finger.

"Pardon me, ma'am," he said with a slight bow. "I didn't mean to disturb you."

She couldn't help but smile at his formality. "I was only expecting a phone call. What is it? Has he sent a hand-lettered scroll?"

"No, ma'am," he answered gravely. (Had he come from a whole line of chauffeurs, his grandfather sitting out in the rain to snap a thin hard whip over the horses while the ladies gossiped inside the elegant carriage? She was tempted to say something terribly outrageous, to see if he'd flinch.) "Mr. Zeronski asked me to inquire if you were free."

"You mean he's here?"

"Outside, ma'am. If you're free."

"I'd be delighted to see him." She felt a real achievement in having flushed him out.

The chauffeur turned and strode out through the small room, not quite reaching the door before Alfred, who'd been watching with puzzled interest, demanded: "What the fuck is this? Is he some goddamn buyer?"

"Not really," she said. "Well, yes, actually. In a way."

"I was just going," Alfred announced and headed for the door, almost catching up to the chauffeur.

Olivia stepped into the smaller room and watched through the glass window. Alfred leaped into the cab of his red pickup just as the chauffeur leaned forward to open the limousine door. A puff of smoke exploded from the exhaust and Alfred roared out from the curb. The chauffeur, leaning into the limo, stepped back and Zero's face appeared, the stiff ruff of hair, and then, slowly, his whole body. He wore a dark suit and dark tie. He let go of the chauffeur's arm and walked past him. The chauffeur slammed the car door and hurried ahead to open the gallery door. Zero stepped inside, his head down, his chin forward, his eyes also down, although not with the deadened alcoholic rigidity he'd shown at his house. The effect was odd. Even sober, even in his business suit, Zero was still that funny little man with comically bulging eyes. Yet something suggested a sadness and resignation so burdensome that it was all he could do, it seemed, to drag himself drearily about.

The chauffeur came in after him. Maybe he tagged along everywhere, not only driver but bodyguard too, with a small pearl-handled pistol strapped somewhere beneath his trim jacket. He would, of course, be a cool and expert marksman.

Zero nodded somberly to Olivia.

"What a pleasant surprise," Olivia said. She walked across the white rug to offer her hand.

He took it with a nod, his expression unchanged. "I have heard so much about your place."

"All good, I hope."

"Everyone speaks in complimentary terms." The long pauses were gone and his accent seemed less prominent, although he still spoke as if each word were crucial, to be chosen with the most intense care.

The chauffeur, a good head taller, remained just inside the door behind Zero.

"I have been hoping, for some time, to visit your establishment," Zero said. He looked at the prints and lithographs hung in that room, turning slowly in one spot as his gaze shifted from one to another, around the three walls.

"There are more inside," she said, and led him into the large showroom. Zero stopped as soon as he entered, staring up at the four huge canvases leaning against the wall. He studied each painting for some time, then moved forward to examine each one close up, as if looking for flaws. He backed to the opposite wall and stared some more, his short legs spread firmly, his short arms at his sides.

Olivia waited; she would love to call Alfred with a sale a half hour after he dropped the paintings off.

Zero had apparently singled out for special attention a painting of a young nude woman—Alfred's wife, who modeled for him—against a very Cole-like landscape of river and fields and soft green hills. The only break from pure realism was in the exaggeration of the figure, with the woman's breasts and hips and thighs swelling out to glorious proportions.

"The moral qualities," Zero began, breaking the long silence, "are all that matter."

Olivia couldn't tell if it was a compliment or a complaint. "I'm sure the artist would agree," she said.

"But the body is distorted. It drags down all the beauty around it."

"I don't think so at all," Olivia protested.

Zero moved close again, his nose practically touching the canvas, to focus on one enormous breast, one huge erect nipple. He straightened up and looked at Olivia. "Is there somewhere we could talk?"

"We can sit in back," she said.

The chauffeur followed them into her office, remaining more or less at attention just inside the door. Zero seated himself upon the small couch, Olivia behind her desk. There was no other furniture besides a file cabinet and a smaller slide cabinet.

"I've finished the cataloguing," Olivia said, taking the

prospectus from her desk. "It's an impressive collection. Whoever put it together for you did a good job."

"I always rely on experts."

"Times change though. Most of the pieces are solid, but there are some we might want to reconsider. From an investment standpoint. After you go through the list, maybe we could sell off those items—de-accessioning is the genteel term—that don't look so good for the long run." She leaned forward to hand the list to Zero.

He held it a moment, looking at the top sheet. She noticed that the backs of his hands were speckled with brown liver spots. He placed the list beside him on the couch. "Whatever you recommend. You are my expert."

"I want to be sure you know what I'm doing."

"You have just told me what you will be doing."

"I want to be sure you approve."

"I approve."

"That's not good enough," she said.

He didn't seem to understand. "If you are reluctant to take the responsibility, Mr. Woodstein will be—"

"Will you look at the list?"

He glanced at the papers on the couch. "Why are you so . . . hesitant to act?"

"It's like working in a vacuum. I feel sometimes I could just put a match to everything and you'd only shrug, for all you care about those paintings."

"I care."

"Why don't we sell the whole batch and convert to government bonds? That'd eliminate the storage problem right off the bat."

"You are not serious. You are joking with me."

"I'm supposed to be in charge, is that it?"

"I made that clear at the beginning," Zero said.

"Then why don't you tell me when you bring somebody else in?"

Zero blinked, puzzled. "Mr. Gage?"

"That's right."

"He has not interfered, has he?"

"He hasn't done anything, as far as I know. But what's he supposed to do? And why didn't you tell me when you brought him in?"

"It was no secret. I asked him to tell you. I saw no conflict, no change in your work. You are in complete charge."

"What do you need him for then?"

"That is a separate matter. It has nothing to do with you."

Olivia took a breath. "This is really exasperating."

"Why? You have full authority. You should simply do what you think best." He paused, looking at her. "I do not understand. If you enjoy your work, why should anything else bother you?"

"Okay," she said. "Forget the whole thing."

"You will continue then?"

"I guess so," she said. She laughed, shaking her head. "I just feel as if I'm dealing in smuggled goods or something."

"There is no reason," Zero said. He waited to see if she was finished, then picked up the prospectus, apparently ready to go. He paused. "Your friend."

She thought he meant Justin, and it struck her that Zero might have been staying away because he knew about Justin, and had come out of hiding now on the assumption that she was once again available. "Which friend?"

"You have many, of course."

She smiled. "More than one, I hope."

Zero did not smile. "The young boy."

"Sylvester?"

"He was arrested not long ago. For promoting a riot, at a hearing."

"That was before I knew him."

Zero seemed to be searching for the exact words he wanted. "He has . . . inflammatory opinions. About many things, I understand, but particularly about me." He watched her face closely.

"I really can't speak for him," Olivia said.

"I mean no one harm," Zero said. "I have worked all my life to help people."

"I guess Sylvester just sees certain conflicts between your interests and his."

Zero seemed to be grappling with this possibility, as if it

hadn't occurred to him before. "Perhaps he does not understand the true source of my interests."

"I guess he thinks he does."

Heavy-lidded, his head like a weight, Zero spoke slowly. "People do not understand what they do not choose to understand. The boy has not had an easy life. I am aware of that. But I am not responsible for—"

"I'd rather not discuss my friends."

"I am not asking you to speak against him. But it is always possible for our ideals, our principles, to turn into self-glorification."

"What are you talking about?"

"He knows only how to use people. To abuse them. To take advantage of them. If his motives were truly pure, why would that be necessary?"

"Are we talking about his clinic?"

"*His* clinic. See. You understand."

"I don't understand."

"I will not be intimidated by ruffians. I will not be made a fool of by urchins in the street."

Olivia bit back her anger. "I really don't want to talk about him," she said.

His lids slowly slid down over the bulging whites. "Very well." He stood up.

The chauffeur stepped briskly to his side, offering an arm, the ruby ring flashing. Zero raised a hand to keep him at his distance and slowly, ponderously, walked out of the room. Going through the large showroom he paused to look again at Alfred's paintings.

"I am pleased, in spite of my own reservations, that Mr. Lester is doing well."

She hesitated, not sure what he meant. "He's doing extremely well," she said. "They're fine paintings."

For the first time, Zero smiled. "I was referring to his growing reputation."

"Oh—?"

"He might be, on that basis, a good addition for us."

Olivia stared at him.

Zero was still smiling.

"Mary Cassatt," she said. It was all she could think of, and she blurted it out like an accusation.

"Miss Cassatt," he said, "was an outstanding American artist. One of the finest we own."

Olivia narrowed her eyes in astonishment, then laughed. "What's this been—a game? I thought you didn't know anything about painting. I thought you were too busy to bother."

"I have always been interested in art."

"You could have told me. You didn't have to pretend ignorance."

"I never," Zero said ponderously, "pretended ignorance." He was still holding the list in his hand. He nodded to the chauffeur, who hurried ahead through the front room to open the door for him.

She didn't like the idea of Zero trying to trick her. Was that his standard procedure, hiring "experts" to work on their own, all the while waiting to pounce gleefully on their first false move?

What he'd said about Sylvester also disturbed her.

"You know how it is," Sylvester said. "He saw big money in this pet project of his. Redevelopment. That was the nice name for it. We weren't too keen, though, on that particular project, no matter what they named it, and managed to get it stopped. Only what with one thing and another it turned into a lot of noise and yelling down at the Zoning Board."

"I saw something in the paper, I think. I saw your name."

"Zero especially didn't like that. He was gonna be the big hero, you see, coming in there and helping out by getting rid of all those slummy run-down houses people were living in."

"How'd you stop him?"

"Mainly by getting the word out. Because the people already living there were just gonna be left on the street, since they sure as hell couldn't afford the kind of apartments Zero was fixing to build. Where it was gonna be, you see, was right on the edge of the West Side, because what he had in mind wasn't apartments for the raunchy coloreds, but just carving out a nice chunk of the West Side and sort of separating it from the rest, to make the kind of high-tone place white people would like, and pay for. So it wasn't dumb, what he was doing. No matter what you might say about it, you couldn't call it dumb."

"He lost a lot then, when you stopped him?"

"I wasn't the only one. Mr. Gage was a real help all the way through."

"But you were the one that got the publicity."

"Part of that, I guess, was being arrested. Although of course when they had to let me go that turned out all right too, and just got Zero that much more riled up."

"Why'd they arrest you?"

"There was this little hassle when we got all the tenants to turn out for the meeting, and one of the city guards got roughed up, it seems, and the police thought maybe I was responsible."

"Were you?"

"No, which was why I got off."

"Zero's still angry over that," she said. "And I think he's even angrier about the clinic."

"He doesn't want anybody else having any say down there, except him."

"You should never have used his building."

"It's not only that. It's just that he owns so much of the West Side already he likes to think he owns it all, one way or another, and doesn't want any back talk about it."

She was sure Sylvester didn't like her working for Zero, but he never mentioned it, and didn't then. She was beginning to wonder, though, if she really wanted to continue serving as Zero's hired hand. She hadn't ever liked the man, and liked him even less now, with his tricks and grubby little secrets.

She wondered if Alfred Lester might feel the same way. Alfred had been getting two or three thousand for a painting, with one going as high as five. Zero, she decided, would pay ten, and in a couple of years would be pleased he had.

Only she felt obliged to explain the situation to Alfred. She wan't sure how eager he'd be, no matter what price he got, to let one of his paintings be sealed up in a room where no one could possibly see it, bought and stashed away by someone with no more feeling for it than he'd have for a stack of bank notes.

"Fuck it," Alfred said. "Take the money."

Much as Sylvester talked about the clinic, it never occurred to him to invite her to see it. Hinting to Sylvester was a waste of breath. He was one of those people you couldn't fool in a thousand years, whose antennae were infallible, yet who could miss the most obvious feelings of people around him. Finally she simply came out and asked.

"Hey, lady, you should've said. When you want to come? You just come on up and say hello anytime you want, and I'll be right there to greet you, and show you all around, and everything."

Her mistake was in stopping for the barber.

"Miss," he said, moving along the sidewalk toward her like some bulky thick-skinned animal. "I don't think you wanna go in there."

She glared at his hand on her arm until he removed it, and then glared at him: a large, dull, unpleasant man in a white jacket, with steel-rimmed glasses. His expression seemed pained, as if he were trying to figure out something that both puzzled and annoyed him. *The eternal redneck.*

"I'm looking for the dental clinic," she told him.

He gave her the eye then, up and down, with an arrogance that infuriated her. "You don't wanna go in there," he said. "Not with those people."

She told Sylvester when she got upstairs. "That son of a bitch," she said. She was so angry she hardly noticed what the clinic was like, never asked to be shown around. Ruel was there, and some women waiting with their children. She could hear the high insistent whine of the drill from another room but never met the dentist.

"Maybe I'll just drop by and have a chat with the gentleman," Sylvester said. "We don't want none of our neighbors having complaints like that."

"I wouldn't waste my breath," she said. "I wouldn't lower myself to talk to him."

Sylvester saw the barber that afternoon, and the next day hid away somewhere and watched for hours to make sure the kids weren't bothering him. Then, and this surprised her, he went down to City Hall to see who owned the barber's building.

"Why did you think he was behind it?" she asked. It still

seemed farfetched that Zero would actually *do* anything about the clinic.

Sylvester shrugged. "Just a hunch, that's all. Of course, the man there, he owns enough buildings around here that one more or less don't really prove anything. It's just interesting, that's all, that he by chance happens to be the barber's landlord."

"Maybe if you're really worried," she said, "you ought to check into things more."

"I ain't worried," Sylvester said, and he really didn't seem to be. He was still gliding along, easy in his confidence. "He's not getting me out. And he's not hurting me either. You know how it is, lady. I'm the lucky chile, born under the good star, with all the big charms laid on me."

She should have argued against that, and almost did. She should have warned him. But she wanted to believe in Sylvester's innocence, and share in that unruffled assurance.

Whose pride was it, then, that brought him down?

"Oh my God," she said when she heard about the bomb.

He wasn't home, wasn't at the clinic or the store front. He was supposed to be in an economics class, but it still had forty minutes to run and she couldn't burst in, frantic and wild-eyed, to drag him out amid the hoots and catcalls. Besides, he hardly ever went to class. She scoured the Student Union looking for him, then in desperation returned forty minutes later to find him strolling casually out of the class with all the other students.

He took it calmly, still hostage to that belief in the special providence of his fortune. "I'm not that easy, you know. I'm not that green."

By then she realized how vulnerable he was and tried to warn him. She knew he wouldn't stand for anything and was afraid everyone else saw only that light and casual boy, willing to trade jokes even with people he found contemptible. But he'd been pushed too much already, had too long a list of humiliations bottled up inside him, to take a threat or an affront as a joke anymore.

"Only what's all this business about a bomb?" he said. "I don't know about any bomb."

"They don't believe that. They want to talk to you."

"Ain't nothing I can tell them, except I didn't do it."

She hesitated. "You didn't, did you?"

"Hey, now, lady—what is it? You gonna get on me too?"

"Maybe the barber said something to you. Maybe you got angry, lost your head. Maybe the guy threatened you."

"Aw, c'mon, lady. You're making up stories now. You're dreaming things."

"Tell me you didn't do it."

"I already told you. I didn't do it."

"Good," she said. "But don't let them trick you. Don't let them push you into a corner."

The police called him down for questioning, then let him go. She was sure that wouldn't be the end of it. The police knew about Sylvester's run-in with the barber and were probably already convinced he'd done it. As far as they were concerned he was the campus radical, the black rabble-rouser who'd no doubt already planted a few bombs here and there, just for kicks.

She didn't really want to believe Zero was behind it but didn't know what else to believe. She'd known people like Zero and had learned never to underestimate their capacity for barbarism. There'd been enough of them in her own family, the grabbers, the knife-edged entrepreneurs, the buccaneers. It wasn't a delicate concern for the rights and feelings of others that rewarded you with bowing servants and racks of original oils and a direct claim on half the city's paving and construction contracts. If someone got in your way, you had him moved aside. If you wanted to make your next million on a housing project and somebody—especially some wise-ass half-crippled kid—threw a monkey wrench into your plans, you did whatever seemed necessary to make sure he wouldn't be able to do it again.

The next morning the police phoned her. The man was very businesslike, and asked if she would mind talking to him.

"I'm worried," she told Sylvester. "I don't like this at all."

"Well, good Lord Jesus," Sylvester said, "don't *look* worried when you get there, all right?"

She tried not to. "What did you want to see me about?" she asked the detective after he guided her to a seat alongside his desk and a secretary brought in a mug of coffee. The room, the whole building was incredibly bleak. How could anyone spend his entire life in a place like that?

He introduced himself: Mr. Amicus. He was cold as ice but took pains to be polite. He wore a business suit instead of a uniform and offered her a cigarette, stood up to light it, apologized for the inconvenience, assured her that she was not in any difficulty or under the slightest suspicion. "I'd have been glad to go to your home if you—"

"I wanted to come," she said. "I've never been to a place like this."

"It's hardly a tourist attraction," he said with a little smile. A half smile, crooking up one corner of the straight gray line of his mouth, his eyes remaining flat and lusterless. His face could have been made of gray cardboard but you knew he would remember every word you said, was already passing judgment on your every look and gesture and intonation.

"I hope you understand, Miss Cowan, that we're not prying into your personal life. But sometimes we—"

"You needn't be so circumspect. What would you like to ask?"

"We understand you're acquainted with a young man by the name of Sylvester Childs. You do know him, don't you?"

"Yes."

"And I guess you're aware that he's a leader of various black groups at the university."

"I'd hesitate to swear to that, since I'm not a member of any of those groups. Besides, they're not all black. Some of his best friends, I understand, are white."

He was silent. He picked up the pen from his desk set—the kind you could buy in Woolworth's—and started turning it over and over in one hand. "Perhaps I should explain. We're not trying to get anyone in trouble. The information you give might even be a real help to Mr. Childs."

"I understand. I really do."

"Why was Mr. Childs angry enough at Mr. Huddleston to threaten him?"

"Who said he threatened him?"

"Mr. Huddleston."

"Well, Mr. Childs said he didn't. So I guess it depends on who you believe. I believe Mr. Childs."

"But he was angry at Mr. Huddleston, wasn't he? Why?"

"For the same reason I was maybe."

"And what was that?"

"I guess we could start with Mr. Huddleston's rudeness, along with the lies he was spreading. And the fact that he seemed to consider a free dental clinic part of the Red Menace."

"Did Mr. Childs ever mention the possibility of taking some sort of action against Mr. Huddleston?"

"I can't imagine what in the world you might be referring to." She laughed, annoying him. "Why don't you just ask me if I know anything about Sylvester blowing up the place?"

"Do you?"

"No."

"Do you know of anyone else who might want to do it?"

"No."

There was a soft knock at the door. It eased open and a face peered around, the eyes hesitating for a moment on Olivia before darting to Amicus.

"Yes?"

"I didn't know you were busy."

"Come on in."

The man carefully closed the door behind him. Unlike Amicus, who worked so hard to impress you with his cool, this man, pudgy and bland, bulging a bit against his rumpled suit, seemed to have all he could do to keep from appearing hopelessly befuddled. Maybe he was the ace of the force, with a razor-sharp mind, the hesitation and uncertainty part of a brilliant disguise. But looking at him, you had trouble suppressing a smile.

"It's about that lab report . . . ," the man began.

"This is Mrs. Cowan."

"Oh," the man said.

"This is Mr. Cunningham."

"Hello," Olivia said.

"It can wait till later," Cunningham said.

"Was there anything else?"

"Oh no. I'll check back later, when you're free."

"Here," Amicus said, picking up a folder from his desk. "Take a look at this, okay, and leave it with Ida."

Cunningham took the folder and turned for the door. But he was holding it at the bottom, along the crease, and when he turned some papers slid out from the top and fluttered to the floor in front of Olivia, who was sitting with her legs crossed.

Cunningham hesitated, then bent quickly to retrieve them,

flushing a bit at having to thrust his face so close to Olivia's legs. He kept his eyes rigidly averted as he swept the papers together with his hand. He stuffed them back into the folder and hurried out.

There was a brief silence. Olivia was smiling. "Is he working with you on the barbershop business?"

"Actually, he's pretty much running it."

"And one of your best men, I'm sure. With a razor-sharp mind."

Amicus allowed himself the smallest of smiles. "That's true. I don't know what I'd do without him."

Every court needed its jester. Every prince liked to keep a few bumbling retainers around to spotlight his own wit and urbanity.

"About that argument," Amicus said. "We really don't care who started it. But we would like to find out if it could've gotten Mr. Childs angry enough to bomb Mr. Huddleston's barbershop. After all, it was hardly a prank. Someone did get killed."

"I understand," she told him. "It's just that I happen to know Mr. Childs very well. And it's utterly inconceivable that he would, under any circumstances, plant a bomb anywhere."

He raised one eyebrow, dubiously. Then he noticed her staring, amused, at the pen slowly twirling in his hand. He put it down. "I guess I don't have any more questions," he said.

Sylvester listened without expression when she told him what the cop had asked. He was driving and noticed the old man following them. "Hey—maybe that's who their spy is."

"Don't be silly."

"What's he got, eyes for you? Is that what he's doing, chasing the skirts?"

"The hell with him. What difference does it make?"

"What did he want on the sidewalk back there?"

"I don't know. Nothing. He was in the barbershop when the bomb went off, that's all."

"Maybe he knows something."

"Does Justin realize they're after you? Maybe you should tell him. Maybe he can help."

Sylvester had his eyes on the mirror. "He's still there."

The old man rumbled on through the campus and followed them right into the West Side.

"What does he think he's doing?" Olivia said.

"Solving the big mystery, I guess. Maybe I'll chat with him. Maybe he knows something."

The man named Jerome Tinney was cheerful enough about it all but exasperating. She left them standing on the sidewalk, Sylvester giving Tinney the cool, unruffled gaze that he used on white people, new white people. The old fellow waved her goodby with a frozen smile, determined to play the gallant to the bitter end.

She drove to the gallery and tried to work but couldn't. She drove back, trying to suppress the flutter in her chest. Tinney's car was still at the curb but neither he nor Sylvester was in the store front. Ruel was there, along with Louise. Not exactly her two favorite people. Louise didn't like her because she was white, and Ruel didn't like her because, as far as she could tell, Ruel didn't like anyone.

"They're out traipsing around somewhere, I guess," Louise said.

"Where did they go?"

"I wouldn't know," Louise said.

"When are they coming back?"

"I wouldn't know," Louise said.

Ruel was sucking on a Pepsi and lounging back on a wooden folding chair in a contemptuous spread-legged slouch. "I'm here," he announced. "You can talk to me."

She could never understand why Sylvester put up with Ruel.

She waited in the Jaguar until they came back, and waited then for Tinney to stop jabbering away. Then, suddenly, he crumpled, and Sylvester had to grab him to keep him from toppling over. Her first thought was *Someone's shooting at Sylvester!*

They couldn't imagine what had happened. It didn't seem like a heart attack. And it wasn't a stroke; her father's stroke had left half his body paralyzed. Tinney wasn't even unconscious; he kept fading in and out but insisted he was all right. He wouldn't hear of a doctor, but as soon as they left him at his apartment she regretted not having taken him right to the hospital. Maybe he'd been injured somehow by the bomb. Finally they stopped and called. The man insisted he was fine.

"Maybe you're just in a worrying frame right now," Sylvester said.

"They can't just go around arresting anybody they want."

"Lady, they can. They can and they do and maybe they will, in which case I guess we'll just have to see how it goes."

"Maybe you shouldn't wait. Maybe you ought to go away."

"Where to, you think? Palm Beach? Hawaii for the surfboarding maybe? How about Vegas?—a few fun-filled nights, like they say, around the gaming tables."

She insisted he talk to Justin. She drove him to the office, waiting to make sure he went in, and left then feeling that Justin at least would be calm, and reasonable, and would know what to do to keep everything from falling apart.

Early the next afternoon she was working in the back room when the call came. Mary Jean was in the office, straightening out the slide cabinet. Olivia, wearing her bright orange smock over her dress, was packing a small unframed print to be returned to its owner, who'd lent it for a show. The phone rang and Olivia heard Mary Jean pick it up at the desk. Olivia unrolled a strip of wrapping tape from the big spool and wet it with a sponge. She placed it carefully along the center to seal the flaps of the mailing carton. She was so absorbed in that long piece of brown tape that Mary Jean startled her.

"It's Mr. Childs. . . ."

She raced inside to the phone.

"Calm down," Sylvester told her. He sounded calm himself, but very tight. "Listen to me."

She listened. "They can't do that," she said. "You've got all that stuff in there."

"They're doing it."

"Zero's doing it. That shit. That limp dick."

"You got ideas?"

"We can stop him," she said.

"We better move then."

She called Justin. His secretary said he was out. She called his home and his wife answered. "Mr. Gage isn't at home," she said, as formal as a duchess. "I'm sure you can leave a message at his office."

She did, and then called Zero.

The girl on the switchboard said Zero was gone for the day. She asked for Woodstein.

"I'm sorry but he's with Mr. Zeronski."

"This is Olivia Cowan. It's very important. I've got to get in touch with him."

"I'm afraid that's impossible."

"You must know where they are."

"They're out inspecting property."

"Where? You must have a number."

"Actually, they're up in a plane."

"What?"

"They're in a plane, flying over the land. There's really no way to—"

She slammed the phone. It could crash. That would at least be something. They could both get killed.

"I'm not sure I'm following, Miss Cowan," the detective said. "Exactly what do you want me to do?"

"You've got to stop them. This is utterly indefensible and you know it. This is the worst kind of persecution."

"Really, Miss Cowan. What am I supposed to have to do with all this?"

"You're out to get him. You have been from the beginning."

"As a matter of fact, we *are* looking for him."

"What? What did you say?"

"I said we were looking for him."

"Oh," she said. "Oh."

She called Justin again. He'd just got back, the secretary said, but was on another line. It was urgent, Olivia told her. It was an emergency.

Justin finally came on and she told him what was happening. "I just talked to the detective down there. He came right out and admitted it."

"Wait a minute. What have the police to do with the clinic?"

"They're out to get him. They're trying to arrest him right this minute."

"We sort of expected that," Justin said.

"But what are they tearing the clinic down for?"

"I don't know," Justin said, sounding not at all worried or excited but merely curious. As if she'd presented him with some kind of intellectual puzzle.

"Zero's doing it," she said.

"Zero?"

"Maybe you could check. Maybe you could find out what the hell is going on."

He was silent a moment. "All right," he said, annoyed but very restrained, very controlled. "I'll get in touch with the police and call you back. Stay where you are so I can reach you."

She stayed, waiting for Justin to call. It was almost a half hour before the phone rang, and it wasn't Justin. It was Amicus.

"No," she said. "No."

She drove coldly, concentrating on the steering wheel, the other cars, the traffic lights. She felt as if she could float, weightless, right off the earth.

The building was barricaded. Then she saw the trucks, the enormous crane. ZERO WRECKING. She should have known. She had known. God damn him. That slob. That limp dick.

She gagged at the stench. She reached back, touching Amicus, and screamed.

IV.

Jerome

A COUPLE OF HOURS after he heard the news on the radio Jerome
Tinney found himself seated on a high wooden stool, his heels
hooked on the bottom rung, a faded green bath towel draped
over his shoulders and pinned at the back of his neck. The For-
mica table with aluminum legs had been pushed aside, leaving
four black indentations in the flowered linoleum. He sat in the
middle of the low-ceilinged kitchen facing the black burners of
the stove. It was a little after five o'clock and he could smell pork
cooking in the oven.

"Really," he protested. He sat with his hands folded under the
enormous towel, like the class dunce. "You don't have to bother."

"Just take a minute," Budd said.

It wasn't what Jerome had come for. The news had hit him
hard. What kind of world was it, with kids being shot down
dead, snuffed out like insects? He'd tried to get a handle on it

but couldn't. It must have been the bump on the head he'd got tumbling out of the barber chair that made him drift off, and that left him, even after a day's dark sleep, still feeling ragged. You looked for a solid purchase, and found the ground shifting everywhere.

He had bathed and changed the gauze bandage over the cut. It was healing well enough, the redness all but gone.

He'd asked nothing from anyone. He'd survived good times and bad, a whole life of hard scrabbling. No one ever suggested it could be different. As a kid he'd scrounged around Fenway Park after the game picking up the score cards the fans tossed away. The same teams would play the next day; he'd hitch a ride on back of a trolley, clinging with one hand and holding the rescued score cards in the other, and sell them for a penny each to that day's crowd. He was maybe ten or twelve then. He made a couple of bucks. That hadn't been the worst, scrabbling from the word go. The worst was now, trying to make things add up in a world that no longer showed signs of believing in anything.

You didn't get blasted out of a chair, another man dying at your feet, without some lingering sense of awe and dread. No wonder his legs had given way. He recalled Sylvester and Olivia Cowan, that mismatched pair, driving him home the previous afternoon. Good people, the woman even calling afterward to make sure he was all right: considerate to strangers, both of them, and now the boy dead. The thought burned hard within him. Except for the woman, he might have been one of the last to see Sylvester alive.

He had left the apartment then, to walk back to the West Side for his car, which was still, as far as he knew, parked near the store front. He felt stronger as he went along, but couldn't shake off a disquieting sense of obligation. The boy's death left him that much more determined to work things through, at least to his own satisfaction. He was involved, after all, whether he appreciated it or not, and it was too late now to put on his hat and stroll away, whistling like a bird on the breeze.

On the way he had to pass the barbershop, and paused to view it again. No cop this time, watching for suspicious characters. The door and the plate-glass window had been boarded up, the barber pole an odd slash of red and white against the light pine boards.

Who arranged for the boards? Budd? The police? The insurance company?

Budd: He'd hardly given him a thought. The poor man had spent his whole life in that shop and now it was rubble. It'd provide little comfort to point out that you always had to be prepared for the worst, and that the worst had a habit of coming suddenly, explosions, eruptions, batterings of one sort or another that left you too stunned to pick up the pieces. Budd could hardly be asked to take the philosophical view. Where could he turn now, deprived of his livelihood? What reasons could he invent in the morning for dragging himself out of bed?

Jerome looked up Budd's address in a phone booth: it was only a few blocks, hardly out of the way. He walked there, the street no better than the street the shop was on; not yet as bad as the West Side but a despairing place nonetheless, caught in a downslide.

Budd was flustered to see him. He didn't know how to react to a customer at his apartment door.

Jerome said he'd been thinking of him, of his troubles and his loss, and had come to offer sympathy.

He still couldn't believe it, Budd said. He'd been sitting there hour after hour, staring at the four walls.

He wore old slippers, baggy gray trousers, a plaid shirt. He looked like a man scraping bottom and seemed heavier and flabbier than he ever had in his white apron, with nothing to firm up the bone and muscle beneath all the spiritless bulk. Standing on his feet for twenty or thirty years, maybe more, wielding clippers and comb and scissors, gulping down a sandwich between customers and taking pills for indigestion; the world had hardly been Budd Huddleston's oyster.

At first they sat in the living room, a dim place with dark wood baseboards, a fringed carpet, lacquered TV tables. Conversation did not come easily. And then Budd said: "It needs finishing up. It don't look right half done."

Despite Jerome's protest, Budd shooed his wife—a pale, worn woman, uneasy in the presence of a guest—out of the kitchen, where she'd been preparing dinner, the pork or whatever already in the oven, a colander of string beans left in the sink. Budd shoved the table out of the way and fetched the high stool and bath towel and his leather barber's bag, like a doctor's.

That changed everything. Clicking away in his own rhythm, stepping back to study the results, squinting through his steel-rimmed glasses, shifting his weight from one foot to the other, holding up the hand mirror for Jerome, Budd became himself again. With scissors and comb in hand, he could talk freely to the man perched on the stool, duncelike, beneath the tented towel.

"What I wanna know is, is it supposed to be my fault? Even the cops. What am I supposed to tell 'em? It's their job, not mine. Who ya think done it? they ask you for two days running, and I tell them I don't *know* who done it. *You* tell me who done it. *You're* the cops."

"You'll fix the place up, won't you?" Jerome said. "You were covered."

"Covered? I mean, I'm the guy that got it in the ass. I'm the one that lost his shirt. Only I'll tell you something. They treat you like a goddamn criminal. They treat you like you're the one that caused all the trouble and they're doing you a favor just even talking to you." Wheezing, he snipped angrily, with quick darting jabs.

"What's the problem? Are the insurance people giving you a hard time?"

"They're worse'n the goddamn cops. Everybody thinks I'm making money out of this. I'd like to see some of that money I'm making. I really would. My place is turned into a junk pile, my wife's so nervous now she can't sleep, my business, my whole life goes up with a bang, just like that, and everybody tells me how much money I'm making. Suppose I fix up the place? Who'd be crazy enough to set foot in it?"

"I'd come," Jerome said, although he really hadn't thought about it. What would it be like climbing again into that throne-like chair?

"Sure—you'd come. You're a friend. But I get a lot of mothers bringing their kids. What mother's gonna bring her kid in there again? What, to get his head blown off, or beat up by a bunch of hoodlums hanging around throwing rocks? Only you tell that to the insurance company and they just give you a look and hand you ten more forms to fill out."

"Hoodlums?"

"Troublemakers. I mean, what the hell is ruining that neighborhood anyhow? I ain't just making it all up, you know. You try to chase those goddamn kids away to keep them from wrecking the place and what do they do? They give you the finger, that's what they do. They tell you to go fuck yourself."

"I didn't realize you were having that kind of trouble."

"Well, now you know," Budd said, clipping away, breathing harshly into Jerome's ear. "Only I heard that got taken care of. I heard they got the guy, although a hell of a lot of good that's gonna do me."

"I heard that too," Jerome said.

"Well, it wasn't me that told them to go out and shoot anybody."

"I'm sure not," Jerome said.

"Although if you wanna listen to the way his loier talks, you'd think maybe I did."

"His lawyer?"

"That politician guy. What's his name. I mean, I couldn't even afford a guy like that. But naturally for all the criminals and troublemakers and stuff, it's nothing but the best."

"The boy wasn't a troublemaker for you, was he?"

Budd grunted deep in his throat. "I'll tell you something. I think maybe if they wanna dress like savages, and act like savages, maybe they ought to load themselves right back on the cattle boat and go back and *be* savages, running around bare-ass in the jungle, where they'd be more at home and not have to go blowing up places just to make themselves feel better. Maybe it'd get rid of a lot of problems and general hard feelings around here if they did that."

"Well now," Jerome said. "I don't know if that'd be the answer."

"Only the guy that got killed, you know, the schoolteacher, he was an old customer of mine. I known him for years. What the hell did he ever do to anybody? He never hurt a fly."

"That was a terrible thing," Jerome said. "But it doesn't mean the young boy did it."

"I ain't the one that said he did. The cops are the ones that said he did."

"I met him," Jerome said. "I don't think he'd have done a thing like that."

Budd stepped back to look at Jerome. "What's that supposed to mean?"

"Nothing. Except that someone else might have done it."

Budd's breath wheezed. "You got names? I mean, is that it? You gonna set the cops straight on this whole thing?"

"That wasn't what I said."

Budd paused, looking hard at Jerome. He shrugged then, giving Jerome the benefit of the doubt, and stepped close again, bulkily, to work the scissors. "Maybe you're another one that thinks I'm cleaning up," he said, gesturing angrily at the kitchen, the whole apartment. "Tell me something then. Do I look like a guy that's cleaning up? Is this supposed to be some kind of millionaire's mansion?"

"I guess not."

"I guess not either," Budd said, going back to Jerome's hair. "Sure, there's all kinds of crazy talk around. Only I don't even wanna hear it. I'm sick and tired of the whole thing, you wanna know the truth. I'd be happy if I never heard another word about it as long as I live."

"Suppose the police are wrong? Wouldn't that bother you, not knowing who did it? You could've been killed, after all."

Budd stepped back slowly. "Are you gonna start now? Are you gonna be just like all the others?"

"What others?"

"I ain't gonna stand around and be accused by nobody," Budd said, his face reddening. "I put up with too much already, and I ain't gonna take any more."

Jerome turned his head: a young woman stood in the open doorway. It had to be Budd's daughter, with the same dull eyes, the same look of grinding discontent. In her early twenties maybe, more buxom than need be, with a kind of street-corner coarseness. She wore a long robe and fluffy slippers, both pink. Her hair was still wet, wound like fat sausages around spiky pink curlers.

"What's going on?"

Despite the towel around his shoulders, Jerome felt he ought to stand up, but realized how foolish he'd look.

Her eyes were as bleak as an alley cat's. "Is that what you're up to now? Giving haircuts in the kitchen?"

"He's a friend," Budd said.

"What were you arguing about then?"

"Who said we were arguing?"

"Hasn't he had enough?" she said to Jerome. "What more do you want from him?"

"I don't want anything," Jerome said.

"What were you yelling about?" she demanded of her father. Every time she moved her head the curlers jiggled.

"Nobody was yelling," Budd said. "I'm just getting sick and tired of everybody talking like I'm the guy that did something."

"Who said you did anything? Is that what this guy said?"

"No," Jerome said.

"Maybe I'm the only guy that didn't do anything," Budd said. "Every goddamn one of them, the cops included."

"Shut up," the girl said. "Who is this guy anyhow?"

"I could tell people about the cops," Budd said. "They're no better than anybody else. Merry Christmas and grease my palm. Only it's all right if the niggers throw rocks and piss on your window. Nobody lifts a finger until somebody blows your place up with a bomb and kills somebody."

"Shut up," the girl said.

"You shut up. Everybody keeps telling me to shut up. What are they doing, doing me a favor? You shut up, okay? I don't want to shut up."

His wife appeared then, like a gray wraith. She looked at her daughter, her husband: a sorrowful woman in a bleached-out dress, her eyes set in hollows, a woman resigned to suffering, cleaving misery to her narrow bosom. "What's wrong?" she asked in a voice as woeful as her expression.

"Nothing," Budd snapped. "What do you want?"

Slowly the wife's gloomy eyes found Jerome's face. The daughter was also staring at him, and Budd too, his arms hanging at his sides, had taken a backward step to fix Jerome in his gaze. No one moved, no one spoke. Jerome sat rigidly upon the kitchen stool with the towel draped about him, only his head showing. Wisps of hair dotted the towel, wisps lay scattered on the worn linoleum. Were there still others, he wondered, a maiden aunt maybe, a bratty brother, waiting inside to join the family in staring the intruder down? You put one foot forward and you're hip-deep in the muck. Extend a single hand to help somebody and suddenly you're everybody's patsy.

Finally the daughter broke the silence. "The show's over, mister." She gave her father a hard look, waiting for him to agree.

Budd stirred, looking down at the scissors in his hand, and then at the pinned towel, Jerome's hair. He took a deep breath and placed the scissors and comb in the black bag on the table and snapped it shut. "I guess that's it," he said hoarsely. "You're all set now." He held the hand mirror in front of Jerome's face while mother and daughter watched stonily.

"That's just fine," Jerome assured him. "All set."

But the barber in Budd died hard. "Unless you want the beard trimmed?"

"No. That's fine. Leave the beard."

Budd placed the mirror face down on the table. He moved dreamily, a burdened man. He unpinned and removed the towel, arms outspread, and shook it without interest, the tufts drifting to the linoleum.

Jerome stood up. "Sorry to mess your floor."

"No mess," Budd said. "Can't go around with half a haircut."

Jerome hesitated, caught at an awkward moment, then reached for his wallet.

"Oh no," Budd said. "No charge. Not for a friend."

"Good Christ," his daughter muttered, and Jerome fled, like a man leaping off a merry-go-round, the floor spinning beneath his feet.

An unsettling piece of business; hardly a high point in the moral education of Jerome Tinney. Only what difference would it make to anyone? What could he possibly do for Sylvester now that wouldn't be a day late and a dollar short? *See, I'm innocent; I didn't do it.* That'd been the message Sylvester had worked so hard to get across, and a first-rate performance too, spiced up with tales of kids dropping pennies and exhibitions of escape artistry. Down the side of a building in seconds, from roof to street in the blinking of an eye. You had to keep your eyes open with someone as shrewd as that, as polished, as cheerful. You had to watch for the sharp edges he might be trying to hide, the sleight of hand. You had to watch too for your own sentimentality and vanity, and keep reminding yourself of how even the best intentions produced their share of confusion and heartache. Yet Jerome wanted to believe the boy, and did.

He wasn't so sure he believed Budd.

Jerome was no babe in the woods, after all. He'd never touched it himself but knew bets could be placed in some barbershops, with hoodlums controlling the whole sleazy network. He could see Budd trying to make a dollar on the side and then getting greedy, skimming off a few bucks here and there, not reporting bets, destroying slips, whatever, but too slow-witted to get away with it. And the local boss, no more than a petty crook himself but smarter and tougher than Budd, deciding to teach him a lesson by making a shambles of his shop.

And what about Budd himself? He wouldn't be the first sinking shopkeeper to pull a fast one on the insurance company. Debts and troubles piling up on all sides, the business dying on its feet, Budd trying to sell but without a buyer in sight. For months now dreaming of the kind of windfall that could solve all his problems in a minute.

Was that so farfetched? We strolled, unblinking, past more fantastical scenes every day. If you went after the answers to anything more complicated than the daily crossword, you had to be ready for a few surprises, and a reasonable amount of disillusionment.

His car was right where he'd left it, but he didn't get in. Instead he walked to the door of the whitewashed store front. It was padlocked. By the police maybe, after herding up Sylvester's friends. Or by the friends themselves, to keep the police out. It wasn't easy making head or tails of any of it.

He turned from the door and saw the other one—Ruel—across the street in his red and white wool cap, watching him, and only then realized how deserted the street was. No black faces this time, no sullen young men lounging on steps, leaning on the tops of cars to give strangers the eye. It might have been a quarantine sign, that padlock on the door, warning everyone away. Only Ruel within sight, a single white face. Was this home for Ruel, friendly territory? Was he spared the insolent looks and accepted as one of them?

As Jerome approached, crossing the street, Ruel watched with one shoulder against the window of the dingy café, his arms folded. He wore a white T-shirt hanging loose, and the sinews of his long arms looked as hard as stretched hemp.

"We met," Jerome said. "Remember?" He offered his hand but Ruel ignored it.

"What're you doing over there?"

"Coming for my car, mostly. Seeing if anybody was around."

"Nobody's around."

"You're around," Jerome said.

"You're really a funny man."

"It was an awful thing that happened to your friend," Jerome said. "I heard it on the radio."

"I heard it too," Ruel said. He inhaled harshly, his nostrils flaring. You could see the fierce tenseness, yet he stood loose-limbed in that lazy stance of athletes, careless with their fine bodies and liking the cockiness of the display.

"I understand your feelings," Jerome said. "I've lost close friends. I've seen fine young men die."

"You don't know what the hell you're talking about."

"Oh?" Jerome said.

Ruel said nothing.

"Don't accuse me of ill feeling," Jerome said, but gently, without scolding. "I'm no happier over this than you are."

Again Ruel was silent. He seemed to be testing Jerome, waiting to see if he could be trusted. It was understandable. Your buddy shot down like that; it didn't make for kindness toward strangers.

"Are the police looking for you too?" Jerome asked. "Is that the problem?"

"What?"

"I heard on the radio they'd been looking for Sylvester."

"That doesn't say they're looking for me."

"I was just wondering."

"Wonder about something else, will you? Don't be giving anybody ideas."

Jerome looked at the café window behind Ruel, squinted to look through it. He made a face. There wasn't much choice though, since it was the only place in sight. "How about a cup of coffee?" he offered. "On me."

Ruel pursed his lips. His long face seemed remarkably flexible, the expressions shifting quickly, although none came out very friendly. He glanced over at the padlocked store front, then up and down the street, maybe looking for an excuse to say no. Or making sure no one would witness him saying yes.

He avoided saying either by simply heading for the door, leaving Jerome to follow.

Jerome paused inside the café. He sniffed. The place was practically empty, one man alone at the counter, one behind it, both Negroes. The signs over the counter were glazed with yellowing grease, and you could practically watch the germs executing squads-right in the mustard pot. The man behind the counter nodded to Ruel, who more or less nodded back and headed for a booth.

They sat across from each other, the table between them covered with tacked-down oilcloth. Jerome decided to stick with black coffee; Ruel ordered a bottle of Orange Crush and two doughnuts. He looked like one of those lean hard types who eat endlessly but never relax enough to put on a pound, burning it all up in nervous energy. He tossed his head back to gulp the soda and clamped into the sugar doughnuts, the powder whitening his lips. He licked at them and noticed Jerome watching.

"You don't like that," he said.

"Like what?"

"The way I eat. You think it's dumb. You think it's really funny." Ruel pulled up the bottom of his T-shirt and wiped his mouth, keeping his eyes on Jerome, waiting for him to say something. Then he slouched back, still watching Jerome.

"Your friend got killed today," Jerome said. "And you're worried about the way you eat."

Ruel drank from the soda bottle. "You know something about that?"

"The radio said he attacked a policeman."

"Sure," Ruel said.

"Do you believe that?"

"That's the way it goes, right? That's the sport, the big gamble. You play the game and take your chances."

"What kind of game was Sylvester playing?"

Ruel toyed with the soda bottle. "The wrong one, I guess. With the wrong guys, the ones with the uniforms."

"You weren't there when it happened, were you?"

Ruel raised his eyes. "What're you always dragging me into this for?" He picked up the second doughnut, looked at it top and bottom, then bit into it.

"Why did they have to kill him?"

"Maybe they didn't have to," Ruel said, chewing. "Maybe they did it for the sport."

"He was your friend," Jerome said.

"And not the first to get taken, either. Some guys pick up the chips, the rest get their balls fed to the cat." He drank from the soda bottle.

"Your friend didn't talk like that."

"Sure. Sylvester was a real talker. Look where it got him."

"It's easy to play the wiseacre," Jerome told him.

"C'mon, man." Ruel had finished the doughnuts, finished the orange drink. He was trying to sound bored and cynical, but trying too hard. His eyes gave him away, even his voice. You could see he was unnerved by the vision of his friend sprawled dead, and that he was scared too. "That's the sport, killing. That's the heavy stuff."

"I believed Sylvester," Jerome said. "I still do. I think he was innocent."

"I don't even know what you're talking about. I don't know what that means."

"Yes, you do."

"I'm the dumb one, you know. Not like Sylvester. When people start dumping words like that on me, I get feeling very pressed."

"Are you afraid?" Jerome asked.

The question seemed to catch Ruel off balance. "What are you supposed to be, on my side or something? You my big buddy now?"

"I'd like to feel Sylvester was a friend," Jerome said. "We met only once, but I felt a bond."

"Only what about me? You met me twice now."

"We could be friends. We've nothing against each other."

"Everybody you meet on the street, you're suddenly their big buddy?" He'd been balling up a paper napkin. His fingers were long and hugely jointed, the knuckles like knobs. He began tossing the napkin straight up and catching it, his mouth half open and his eyes following the wadded ball up and down. It could have been insolence, an insult to Jerome's seriousness, but looked like a simple inability to sit still. There was too much confusion and fear working over him, too much to burn off.

"If they hadn't blamed him for the bomb," Jerome said, "they wouldn't have been after him, and wouldn't have killed him."

Ruel caught the napkin, his hand closing like a trap, and shifted his gaze to Jerome. "What are you messing around with all this for?"

"A man was killed right before my eyes. I could've been killed myself."

"Only you weren't, so you were lucky. So maybe you just oughta forget it." He tossed the napkin onto the table, weary of that game, and looked around for something else. He picked up a spoon and started tapping it, insistently, into the palm of one cupped hand.

"You were Sylvester's friend. Why are you pretending you don't care?"

Ruel bristled at this, then shrugged. "I guess I just don't have all the connections figured out as good as you."

"I had decent feelings for Sylvester."

Ruel looked at Jerome, at his beard, his clothes. "You and Sylvester don't somehow seem exactly the type, to be friends and all."

Of course Ruel hardly seemed Sylvester's type either. Beyond the difference in their temperaments, Sylvester had showed some real drive, determined as he was to make his mark in the world. It was hard to envision Ruel doing much besides feeling sorry for himself on street corners, or at best, at his most energetic and least harmful, running up and down a basketball court.

"I didn't grow up in any mansion," Jerome said. "Maybe I've even had as many hard knocks as you."

"That's right. I forgot. You're my big buddy now."

"Do you know whether Sylvester planted that bomb?"

"I told you. I don't know anything about it. I don't know what the hell happened." He picked up the salt cellar and turned it upside down over his hand, to see if it worked. It did. He put it down and brushed the salt off his hand, getting the last few grains by slapping his hands together.

"Do you know the barber?" Jerome asked.

"I see him around sometimes, that's all."

"Do you think he could have done it for the insurance?"

Ruel pulled his mouth to one side, thinking it over. "Like I said, I don't know the guy."

"I hardly do either. But I've gone there for years for my haircuts."

Ruel raised his eyes to Jerome's hair.

"I don't like to think he'd do anything like that," Jerome said. "I don't like to think anybody would."

"I'll tell you something. It don't matter. Because the bomb didn't have anything to do with what happened to Sylvester."

"But that's why they were after him."

"The cops've been after him a long time, for a lot of things. For general principles. Because that's the sport, that's how it goes. The bomb's just gonna be their excuse now, to fool a lot of people. What happened is they wanted him out of the way, so they got him out of the way. They fed his balls to the cat."

Jerome was silent a moment. "That's not something a man takes pleasure in believing."

"You wanted the truth."

"Then who planted the bomb?"

"I told you, I don't know. And I don't even care, because it don't have anything to do with me."

"And the other does? The killing?"

"Now you're catching on."

"If the cops are after you, should you be sitting around here like this?"

"I gotta sit somewhere." Ruel started picking at one of the tacks holding the oilcloth, forcing his thumbnail under it. He got it up, looked at it, and then carefully replaced the point in the same hole and pushed it back in. "When they want me, they'll get me, no matter what. I ain't running the show, you know. They're running it. They're wearing the uniforms."

"Maybe you're exaggerating things a bit."

Ruel laughed. "You just watch tonight. See how much I'm exaggerating."

"Tonight?"

"Sylvester got friends around here, and they ain't gonna like what happened to him, with the cops. They're gonna make some trouble tonight. They're gonna tear things up a bit."

"That won't do any good."

"It won't do me any good, but they ain't worried about me. I mean, let's face it. Nobody's worried about me."

That was the cry catching in Ruel's throat: *Now that Sylvester's dead and gone, can't somebody pay a little attention to me for a change?*

"Is there something I can do?" Jerome asked. "Maybe I can help?"

"What—like you helped Sylvester? Thanks, man, but I already had enough of that kind of help."

"All this hatred and killing," Jerome said. "It's not a thing to be proud of. It's not the heritage a man wants to leave behind."

Ruel had been trying to scratch a cross into the oilcloth with his thumbnail. He stopped and looked up, the corners of his eyes wrinkling in his long harsh face. "What are you doing? Shitting me?"

Jerome drove through the West Side. His heart went out to Ruel, even to Budd. It was a distressing thing to see the human soul eaten away by bitterness. They all knew what the short end of the stick looked like, Budd and Ruel as much as Sylvester. They'd all asked for bread and got a stone. What consolation could you offer those unfortunates, either that boy struck down or those other two, their lives stunted by spitefulness and distrust?

Still, a person had a responsibility, even in the worst of times, to do what he could to keep things from falling apart. You were always being told that morality was nothing but the first remembered voice—your mother's—saying *No!* Maybe so. But Jerome could also remember a *Yes* from that vague past. Ages ago in front of their tenement building: his mother's younger sister hesitantly climbing those ancient brown steps, bearing in her arms a boy infant, already called *bastard* by certain relatives and neighbors. "It's not his fault," his mother said, reaching forth. "Here—let me hold him."

He drove steadily through the West Side, blinking to clear his eyes, his mouth set. Was there no one but himself who still believed deserts could be made to bloom?

V.

Zero

THE NIGHT ALMOST sleepless, shredded by nightmare. He would not go to bed until it was that or collapse, that or paralysis. Randolph would help him to the bedroom, help him undress, leave. He would get into bed without washing his face, for fear of being revived and having to go through it all again. He would bring the last full glass of the evening into the bedroom and place it, always in the same spot, on the night table. He would lock the door, turn off the lights. He could find the glass in the dark if need be, knowing exactly where it was, although on some nights it was too much effort to reach over and he would fall asleep without it. It was thick and wide-bottomed and not easily tipped. He had cut himself once on a broken glass. Every morning the glass, full or empty, would be the first thing he saw upon opening his eyes. He slept best just before dawn; on the worst nights that was the only time he slept. If the glass was full when he woke, he would empty it in the bathroom and leave it for Ben to remove when he straightened up.

This morning he left the office with Woodstein at ten-thirty. They drove for almost two hours, Randolph driving, out of the city, beyond the suburbs and the foothills, over the ridges and into the central valley. The pilot joined them in the tiny café attached to the main building, the only building, of the airport. Woodstein spread out the map on the table. The property was outlined in red, with the creek, the hills, the marsh, and the high dirt road starred in blue. These in particular, Woodstein told the pilot. But first around the perimeter, as low and as slowly as safety permitted. No stunts. Then back to the southeast corner to begin traversing the interior in parallel lines. How close together —a quarter mile? Woodstein looked at Zero. A quarter mile, Woodstein said.

A twin-engined plane, four seats. Zero lacked faith in engineers, mechanics, aviators, the weather, and would not fly with one engine. Woodstein sat on the pilot's right, comparing the features starred on the map with the landscape below. Methodically. Woodstein was a methodical man. Details were important to him. Zero sat behind the pilot, not looking at the map, gazing steadily out the window. They flew at five hundred feet, the cockpit noisy and rattling, the whole plane vibrating. With his feet flat on the floor, he could put his hand on his knee and feel the kneecap vibrating. At the creek bed, the marsh, the rolling hills, Zero nodded when Woodstein glanced back and Woodstein instructed the pilot to circle each area for a second look. As the plane banked, Zero clutched the arms of his seat.

The right wheel struck the runway first, like a blow. The plane lurched, causing the left wheel to strike. The plane bounced from side to side, the wing tips shuddering like sprung steel. When they came to a stop in front of the little building, Woodstein spoke to the pilot, then looked back at Zero. Woodstein spoke again to the pilot, who protested until Woodstein cut him off.

On the drive back Zero listened to Woodstein and his details. Woodstein unfolded the map and pointed with a blunt forefinger. The creek was low for this time of year; still, the marsh seemed to offer sufficient drainage. The road had perhaps

136

been cut too narrowly into the hills and there were signs of erosion. They could blast out a wider road. That would cost, but would be worth it. Woodstein folded up the map and slid it into his briefcase. Overpriced, that was his feeling. They should underbid by at least 20 per cent, and might even want to wait for the geologist's report. But, on balance, a sound move, from an investment standpoint.

There is no need to wait, Zero said.

Are we ready to move right now?

Zero nodded, and Woodstein made a notation.

They got back to the office, and promptly at three o'clock Miriam brought in the tray with the bottle and glass and the small hand-carved ice bucket. The schedule had so long been observed that it now seemed as natural as a path worn through a woods, the easiest way around trees, boulders, obstacles.

Woodstein came in a few minutes later; the agent did not like the bid, but would relay it, and wanted two days to contact the owners; the several sons and daughters living far apart, the widow in poor health.

Not two days. Today.

He might turn that down.

See.

Some minutes later Woodstein returned. Could we give the agent until tomorrow morning?

Yes. For a sick widow and her scattered children.

I think they're going to take it, Woodstein said.

I know, Zero said, and Woodstein left.

It was a good piece of property, although no more or less tempting than a dozen, a hundred other possibilities, projects, undertakings. There was no shortage of such opportunities; the siren song could be heard throughout the land.

Justin entered, followed by Miriam. Justin declined the glass and waited for Miriam to leave.

Sit down.

I haven't time to sit down.

Very well. Stand.

The boy's dead.

What boy?

Childs. The late Sylvester Childs. Justin was like an Old Testament prophet, full of wrath and righteousness, as he recounted the story.

I cannot understand, Zero said. It is awful. How could it happen?

That's what I'd like to know.

It couldn't have been a surprise. Licenses have to be procured. Permissions. You know that. Agencies have to be notified. Even the police have to know. Demolition is very public. You cannot tear down a building in secret.

Maybe everybody else knew, but the kids didn't.

I don't see how it could have happened.

It's your building.

No. The building was sold. It is not mine.

You sold it?

Yes. It is out of my hands. I have no interest whatsoever.

What are you talking about? When did this happen?

A month ago, two months. I can check with Woodstein. But it was no secret. All the papers were filed.

But Justin was not to be mollified. You still knew about the demolition, he insisted.

You mean Zero Wrecking?

What do you think I mean?

Zero Wrecking hardly pays overhead. What do you think, that I drive the truck, that I write the job orders, shovel up the debris? I didn't know they were involved. What was it, a two-day job, three days? I don't even see the summaries anymore. Woodstein takes care of it. Let me get him.

Why didn't you tell them you sold it? Why didn't you tell the new owners to give them notice?

You can't believe I had anything to do with this. A boy shot dead by the police. Justin. How long have you known me? Of all people, would I have anything to do with the taking of a human life?

What was it then? An oversight?

I don't know what it was. Why did the police have to shoot him? He was only a boy. He was half-crippled.

I was supposed to represent him. I was going to keep him out of trouble.

You represented him before. Have I ever told you not to? Have I ever tried to influence you against him?

The police are saying he planted the bomb.

They talked to me about it. The boy seemed to think I was connected with the barbershop, somehow behind all their troubles.

What'd you say to the police?

That I had nothing to do with that barbershop. With any barbershop.

Did you suggest he might be involved with the bomb?

They didn't need suggestions from me. They were already investigating him.

I'd just like to know, for my own benefit, what happened.

Justin. I am not a maker of stories. I do not tell tales. I have worked for you as honestly as you have worked for me. Have I ever lied to you? Have I ever been even remotely involved in anything like this?

As soon as Justin left, Zero called in Woodstein. Woodstein was confused.

I want to know what happened, Zero told him.

I don't know what happened.

You can find out.

He saw no one else until five, when Miriam brought in the message from the mayor's office.

Tell him yes. Tell him I will be there. Tell him I will have news for him, an announcement.

Miriam glanced at the tray. Is there enough left? I'll be leaving now unless you need me.

That will be fine.

Miriam left. Everyone left except Woodstein, who at five-twenty knocked and entered. He had been on the phone continuously, had talked to everyone, the owners, Zero Wrecking, the foreman, the police. He had even talked to the dead boy's friend.

Zero raised his head abruptly. What friend?

The ex-convict. The one we put on scholarship that time. Ruel. Don't you remember?

Why did you call him?

You wanted to find out what happened. I thought maybe he would know.

I expected discretion.

I was discreet. I only mentioned the scholarship so he would remember me.

Did you say I asked you to call?

No.

Did you mention my name?

He knows I work for you.

We promised him privacy. We promised it to all of them. It will look like we are presuming upon him. That we expect favors for the money.

I don't think so. At any rate, he knows nothing. So, at least, he claims.

You don't believe him?

He doesn't go out of his way to sound believable. Let alone likable.

What did he say?

Hardly anything. It was his manner. Did you meet him back then, the tall one?

No. You handled it. I never saw him.

Anyhow, he was no help. It occurred to me, though, with the other one dead—do you think this one will take his place?

He's white. The group is not white.

He and Childs were very close. If he does take over, he will be even more trouble.

More than Childs? No. Less. Much less.

His bitterness is deeper.

Childs was bitter enough.

Anyhow, I learned something from the others.

What?

No one told Childs. No one even mentioned it.

Why not? Are they deaf, dumb, and blind, those people?

It got lost in the shuffle. That's why they were in a rush to buy, because they were in a rush to tear down. There was considerable cash involved, a quick turnover. They were grabbing their chance, and didn't pay attention to anything else.

Imbeciles.

No one seemed to feel the responsibility.

Those people wouldn't last ten minutes here.

At any rate, the equipment was worthless. It was junk.

Is that what you spent two hours finding out? That it was junk?

I told you what I found out.

And that's what I'm supposed to explain to people, when they ask me what happened? That it was all an oversight?

The police might have handled it better. Although Childs did attack them first, with a dental tool. There seems no dispute about that.

You just told me Childs was not bitter. That he was a genial and charming boy.

I didn't say that. I just said the other one might be even worse.

I am not interested in the other one. The other one did not blow up a barbershop in one of my buildings. The other one did not attack a policeman. The other one was not killed.

I found out everything I could. I don't know why Childs attacked the policeman.

Perhaps it was part of his charm. Perhaps it was another aspect of his geniality.

After Woodstein left, Zero walked through the empty outer office to the storeroom. He had to open a new case, tearing off the lid. He removed a bottle and brought it to his own office. He rotated the glass on his thigh, leaning back in the chair, his eyes open and unmoving. He could feel the slide of his lids, a single brief closure, like a pulse. Blinks, pulse beats, breaths, minutes; the count, once begun, could not be stopped until there was nothing left to count.

In spite of everything, he had tried to help the boy, only to be spurned, as if Childs were possessed of a purity so elevated that everyone else, by comparison, stank with corruption.

Why? Zero had asked Woodstein.

He said he didn't need it.

I thought he was poor. I thought he lived from hand to mouth, had no father. A cripple. But he has money? He lives high.

He's very bright. And deformed perhaps, but not crippled. He has other scholarships.

Did you make it clear that no one would know, that nothing would be expected of him in exchange?

Of course.

What do you think of him? What is he like?

Very sure of himself. Very quick. Rather pleasant, if anything, on the surface.

Proud? Too proud to take money?

He takes money from other sources.

It's the source, then, that bothers him? He ridicules the source?

He didn't indicate that.

What kind of group has he set up?

It's designed, I would guess, to make noise, to get attention, to cause trouble.

Only for me?

I don't think so.

Only in the West Side then?

All the members are from there. Almost all the members are black.

He doesn't believe I have ever done things for those people?

I don't know what he believes.

Zero knew. It was not difficult to draw conclusions about a person who claimed heroism by arousing ignorant people against their own best interests, by convincing them that it was somehow noble to live with vermin and rats and filth, by turning them against the very person trying to free them from vermin and rats and filth. It was flamboyance and vanity, not dedication, not virtue, that propelled a person to seize the platform at such moments, and with such messages. What Childs wanted was his name in the papers, his motives praised, his exploits hailed. He would ruin one hundred worthwhile ventures before he would share an ounce of glory with anyone else.

Zero had seen him on television: this cheap boy in his flashy clothes, with his wild hair and dark glasses, his white teeth flashing, full of street talk and tasteless jokes, being interviewed on a news show like a visiting dignitary, an elder statesman. And for what did he receive this honor? For disrupting a public body, for starting a near riot, for attacking a uniformed guard, for subverting in a single flamboyant action the careful planning and work of years, for making a mockery of an investment of time and energy and hope and wealth beyond anything that grinning boy could even comprehend.

And not stopping there.

What do you mean, clinic? Zero had demanded. What kind of clinic?

Woodstein had explained.

He didn't cause enough trouble before? He didn't cost us enough money and aggravation? What is he planning now? To picket and ruin all the dentists in town?

He wants to start a welfare clinic, and needs space.

He cannot have it.

We are not using the space, and can always say it was for a good cause. He's even willing to pay rent.

A thousand a month then. That is our rent. Two thousand.

That would be a refusal.

We will refuse then.

Perhaps we should let him try. I don't envision a great success.

He thinks this is a joke. A humiliation. He thinks he can laugh at me, and then use my generosity to promote himself. To show what a humanitarian he is. With my space. My property.

The point is, it would not hurt us when we return to the Zoning Board. It would illustrate our continuing interest, despite our setback, in the well-being of the area.

We've done enough to illustrate our interest ten times over. He has not a nickel in his pocket. He is a step removed from a ragpicker.

Even if he does succeed, it would be only through your generosity.

I feel no generosity toward him.

Although failure seems much more likely. Suggesting that some inexperienced boy who cannot even run a hand-me-down operation in an abandoned building, the whole thing hardly worth the cost of printing up a lease, lacks the qualifications to serve as spokesman for his people, or to discuss the virtues of an undertaking worth over a million dollars.

I don't want to bother with him. He doesn't deserve such attention.

It will be no bother. We will just give him what he wants, and sit back and watch him make a fool of himself.

He is trying to make a fool of me.

Believe me, he will not do that.

He used Justin the same way, shamelessly, for his own glorification. That is not going to happen with me.

But it did. He let himself be convinced, and should not have. It only made the boy more reckless, convincing him that even shabbier frauds could be perpetrated, that even easier victories lay ahead.

Sell it, he told Woodstein after he read the story.

We've tried before.

Try again. Let the new owners worry about the clinic. It won't be my concern. It won't be my space he is using.

Perhaps the newspaper exaggerated his success.

Sell it.

I doubt if we can sell without a condemnation.

Then have it condemned. Make arrangements.

The policeman in the hospital; the other one, the school-teacher, dead, blown to smithereens. Another Jew taken out of his misery, and nothing to waste tears over. Had that been the extent of Childs' remorse? What about the barber, Zero's tenant for years, his business, his livelihood ruined? And all the while the others played into the trap, encouraging the worst in him, the spoiled child showing off for guests. His picture in the paper like a conquering hero, not only for his ruckus at the Zoning Board but also for the clinic, as if that were some marvelous achievement, a cause for celebration.

With Zero meanwhile cast as the villain, the culprit.

He had never made one dollar, not one, that did not give full value to others.

And your wrecking business? they would say, smiling at their own archness.

He had learned to expect such comments. There was an elemental appeal to demolition. One moment a structure is there. Then, before your eyes, it disappears, gone forever. But replaced, of course, by something more useful, more beautiful. No one credited that—what rises from the ashes. People were drawn to rubble and wreckage like maggots. For every person who stopped to admire a structure rising from bits and pieces, a hundred would press forth to cheer the raucous spectacle of even the ugliest tenement being rendered back to bits and pieces. He had seen their faces, heard their little cries, their gasps. An iron ball crashes through a brick wall, and they cheer. Men, strangers, had begged his foremen, offered money, to be allowed just once to control the swing of that iron ball.

What gratitude did the people in the West Side show for everything he had done? What acknowledgment did Olivia Cowan make for his recognition of her talents, for his unwavering trust in her judgment?

(Had she ever let the boy see her, touch her? The haughty aristocrat aroused by pity, by exotic disabilities, by the suggestion of depravity beneath the grinning surface? Maybe to tempt him she would wear a clinging blouse with nothing underneath, brushing against him like a whore. Uttering the words shamelessly.)

He had tried to reason with her, but like everyone else she saw only innocence and sweetness there, never arrogance, never selfishness, as if he were some pathetic waif to be pressed to her bosom. They'd all been like that, but she was the worst, letting her sentimentality wash over everything.

Zero had suffered as much as any victim in the West Side, had prevailed over the same cruelties and degradations. He not only understood their needs, but admired, without benefit of illusion, their vitality. They were strong in an age gone bland; they alone could still make you believe in beauty and hope, in radiance, in energy, in ambition and dedication. They alone still possessed the thrilling possibilities that Zero himself had once known.

He blinked, his lids clicking. A quarter of six. He refilled and emptied his glass, then rang the garage. He locked up, dropping the keys and stooping cautiously, one hand clutching the doorknob, to pick them up. Randolph drove up and got out to help him in.

He did not go to the conference room but to the mayor's office. The mayor was still there, preparing for the meeting. Zero spoke to him. The mayor was pleased. Such a gesture, more than a gesture, a sign of real concern, would be a great help. It would reassure people, and for that reason he wished to make the announcement immediately.

But anonymously, Zero insisted. Anonymously, he repeated stickily, trying to keep the syllables distinct.

He left the mayor and joined the others in the conference

room, his eyes fixed. Justin was there, of course. After a few minutes, the mayor entered and spoke. Phillip Ryder was a leaner, without strength, and had become mayor simply by leaning on the right people. This night he intended to lean on both the police chief and Justin Gage. The chief would threaten war, Justin would preach peace. Only Justin's anger had not yet subsided; he clashed with the chief, and the mayor had strained to pacify him. Zero's eyes remained fixed. The mayor announced the donation of the new clinic: everyone turned. Zero nodded. The faces were set, the eyes blank. The mayor was not the only one in that assemblage who lacked imagination.

On the drive home he recalled the hard unyielding thump of the wheel against the runway, the plane rocking violently from one side to the other, the wing tips shuddering. He had faith, though, in Randolph, and dozed briefly in the back seat.

He was changing in his room when Pamela knocked. She placed the tray on the bureau and left. The phone then: the mayor, to thank him once more for his generosity. Everyone appreciated it, even Justin. The mayor had spoken with Justin, who already regretted his outburst. Justin had not intended to make light of Zero's offer, but was merely upset over the boy's death.

It is nothing. I am not a man to hold grudges.

The new clinic will be a fine thing.

It will only be a beginning, Zero told him. There is more coming.

Pamela tiptoed in, replacing the empty glass. He reached out but not quickly enough, barely grazing her skirt.

Will you be staying home tonight? the mayor asked.

Yes.

I just hope those people show a little sense. It'd be nice if nobody went out of his way to make trouble.

I am not worried, Zero said.

I'm not either. We can handle it.

In his robe and slippers he sat down in the dining room. Ben served, poured. He had prepared carbonnade and fresh asparagus. Zero watched the early edition of the news, the announcer's face orange against the green background. The boy's death was reported; the warrant outstanding for his arrest. The policeman was not in danger. The meeting was not mentioned. But the mayor, on camera, his face red against a blue background, announced the offer of a new clinic. *A-non-y-mous-ly.* No suggestion of trouble, of preparations by the police.

I was delayed, he told Ben. It's your pool time. You may go ahead with the others.

When he finished dessert—Ben had prepared chocolate mousse—Zero went to the phone, taking his glass with him. Methodically, concentrating, he dialed Ruel's number. He was not in his room, the landlady said. Would she take a message? She was not required to take messages. It is a matter of grave importance, Zero told her. Have him return my call, as soon as possible. It is urgent.

Ruel had been a mistake. Zero regretted now that he had been swayed by Justin's sentimental hopes, and by his own natural sympathies. He should have foreseen the extent of the boy's confusions, and the inevitability of his falling prey to someone like Sylvester Childs.

He went to the pool. The tray was set for him on the glass-topped table. He sat on a lounge chair and waited for them, twirling the glass slowly on his thigh. Steam rose from the water. The smell of chemicals. Randolph and Ben arrived together, dropping their robes and diving in from the ledge. Pamela came then. She checked the tray, took the glass inside, and came back with another.

Will that last you now till we're finished?

Yes, he said. Go ahead.

She dropped her robe and dived, her legs pressed together to form a dark dividing line from the small of her back to her toes. She was not a swimmer. She made it two or three times across the pool, the short way, then talked the others into throwing the ball back and forth. She boosted herself out on the other side of the pool. The others followed. They sat together across the pool joking with each other, taking advantage of the full half hour.

I do believe you're getting fat, Ben.

You're the one that'll turn to lard, girl. Long before me.

Randolph smiled but did not join in. He was more reserved than Ben, more conscious of his dignity. He wore his opulent blood-red ring even in the pool, as token of that dignity. Tall and proud as a chieftain, a descendant of island kings.

All three bodies sleek and wet, shiny as oilcloth. Pamela's nipples black, the area around them almost black, her breasts still lighter, wet and glistening in the overhead light.

Randolph bigger than Ben; longer and heavier; it swung when he walked.

Maybe he would surprise them at it one day, Pamela and Randolph. Pamela flung back like a victim, crying out. Randolph enraged beyond any suggestion of reserve, two furious shadows on a white sheet. Even now she would glance, dewy-eyed, at that purplish rope lying carelessly across his black thigh.

I don't know about that, Mr. Zeronski. I mean, I didn't think swimming was part of the job.

It's not, he had explained. It is simply available, if you feel inclined.

I hardly know them fellas.

It is up to you. No one will force you.

I guess I'll have to think about it.

There will be a robe for you to use, walking back and forth.

I'll have to think about it.

Tell me when you make up your mind.

She made up her mind, he assumed, after talking with Randolph and Ben.

Okay, I think maybe I'll try it. Once anyhow.

I will be present on occasion. I will swim then, when you are finished.

That's okay. They explained all that.

I have a robe here for you.

It's real pretty. What is it, silk?

You can put it on now.

Randolph said you would leave me alone. He promised.

Of course.

He said you never bothered any of the other girls.

Go ahead. Put on the robe.

It was not the first time she had taken off her clothes for someone. She didn't mind him looking, didn't cover anything with her hands or turn away. The blackness of her nipples surprised him that first time. Blacker than any of the others. She took her time putting on the robe, didn't hurry to belt it closed. Perhaps she was testing him, to see if he would try anything. Perhaps she wanted him to, or simply liked showing herself. Most of them did. He wanted to touch her then, but waited, so that she would understand. A few days later when he touched her the first time she said, Hey, now, we're being a naughty little boy, aren't we? But she paused, smiling, before moving his hand away.

Not down there, she said the first time he tried that.

Down where?

You know. There.

Where? Tell me.

Pussy.

No.

Snatch. Muff. Jelly roll. Poontang.

No.

Cunt.

That's it. Don't be afraid to say it.

It had worked out with Pamela. It had worked out with all of them. He never had to explain. They would come to understand. Only once had there been any confusion. No, he had to tell Helen. Don't do that. Don't touch me.

—Or was it Eunice? No. Helen had come first, then Eunice. Eunice was taller. Her thighs were heavier. Her hips were smooth and plump. She would let him, almost from the beginning, touch her anywhere. She would wait longer than the others before moving his hand away.

Pamela liked talking about it more than any of the others. She would giggle, making it a joke, but that was all right.

You know girls ain't supposed to go talking to men 'bout things like that, she would say, but she never stopped him. The language you use, she would say. The things you do ask questions about.

He wanted to touch Olivia Cowan again. He wanted to see her. Olivia's nipples would be large, and dusty pink, and stippled with tiny bumps under the pinkish circles. They would be soft until he touched them. They would thicken then. Her breasts would be larger than Pamela's. The darkness between her legs would seem darker than Pamela's, cradled by the whiteness of her thighs. He would have her sit with her legs together, and only after a long time have her slowly spread them apart. He could hear her voice, speaking the words. That aristocratic voice.

He could not believe she had done it with the boy. Justin was her style, tall and handsome, a big hard athlete's body, smooth-faced, the darling of the crowd. So Justin gave it to her and ran. Zero would have done the same. Making her cry out. Pounding her until she screamed. And then good-by. Her naked body, not so delicate now, bruised and raw, all its secrets shamefully revealed.

They stood up across the pool and put on their robes to leave, their half hour over. Zero stood up too, steadying himself on the arm of the chair. He let go and got his robe off and waved to them. They waved back, Pamela giggling. He stepped carefully across the wet tiles and plunged.

The warm water was like a flush of intimacy. The pool an enormous electrical field, the veins and arteries of your body a circuit, magnifying the impulses.

He counted. The laps passed between one number and the next. Like blinks, breaths, minutes, pulse beats.

He dried himself, rubbing hard. Twenty laps. He could have done thirty. If need be, if his life depended on it, he could have done fifty. There was no way to foresee what threats you might one day face, what tortures you might have to endure. You could be trussed and gagged, abandoned like a sack in the desert. You could be smashed onto an empty beach. You could be thrown into a cell with garbage for food, no windows, no light, no air. You could be forced, for reasons you would never be told, to stand for hours with your arms overhead, your hands flat on a cold wall. You could be tattooed with a number, your head shaved, and hounded like an animal through a forest, a ruined landscape, under railroad bridges. Your nails could be plucked, one by one, your fingertips dripping like rose petals.

Had it not already happened often enough, to himself and others, to convince the skeptical?

No. To them it was something distant and abstract, and too long ago. The victims were all dead. Their torturers were dead. Even Justin saw it only as some vague historical event, which all right-thinking persons naturally condemned, on political grounds.

My father . . . an alien in his homeland . . . hated . . . in the town of his birth. The Fascists . . . killed him. My mother died also . . en route to freedom.

A terrible thing, Justin admitted, anxious to get on to something else.

I saw my father . . . seized by bullies . . . in the middle of the night. My mother died of pneumonia. Do you know . . . what that is like? Your lungs fill with fluid . . . and you drown. That is how my mother died. Beneath a railroad bridge . . . hunted like an animal . . . despised . . . not even a bed, a pillow. I watched her die, struggling for breath. I remember every horrible . . . detail.

Justin politely sympathized.

It was not that Justin lacked feeling. Justin was full of honest feeling. He merely could not distinguish, in the end, between injustice and tragedy, between truth and the meaning of that truth. Justin was quite sincerely opposed to suffering and oppression but had never known either, and saw them only as varied forms of injustice. And, as with everyone else, the very nature of Justin's limitation prevented him from understanding that limitation. Justin slept nights. For Justin there were no agonizing nightmares but only occasional bad dreams, shrugged off in the morning. Horror did not cling to him, like some gamy animal smell that would not wash.

Pamela, dressed now, handed him a glass at the edge of the pool.

Tell Randolph I want to talk to him.

A few minutes later Randolph walked into the study. Zero, in his bathrobe and slippers, sat behind his desk. He pushed forward the slip of paper. I want you to call this number now, and every half hour. City Hall, a special number. Say you are calling for me, for the news. Tell me if anything is happening.

Is something wrong?

There may be some trouble. I want to keep in touch.

Here?

Not here. The West Side.

Randolph accepted the news stolidly.

Do you go down there? Zero asked. He'd never asked before. He did not wish to intrude upon their outside lives.

No, Randolph said.

You have no friends there? No hangouts?

No, Randolph said. What kind of trouble?

There was a fight, an exchange. A young man attacked a policeman, and was shot.

Dead?

Dead.

There's often trouble among those people, Randolph said.

Randolph was a Jamaican, a proud man. He had come to America with ambitions, as Zero had.

Here is another number, Zero said. If I do not get a call from a Mr. Frank Hopkins within a half hour, call this number and ask for a young man named Ruel. It is urgent that I speak to him.

Very well.

Listen to the radio too. Get the news. The rest of the time use the police band.

Perhaps Ben could listen. I could stay with you, as a precaution.

You listen. There will be no trouble here.

I'll tell Ben to keep an eye open.

There is no need to worry. Nothing will happen here.

I'll tell Ben anyhow, as a precaution.

From the living-room window he stared at the lights of the city. Would every bulb blaze tonight, making even the dimmest alley so bright that no one would dare move? Or would it be so dark, with shades drawn everywhere, that the city would become as ominous as the dead side of the moon?

Sitting on the chair nearest the window, he turned the glass slowly on his thigh. He would survive, no matter what. The horrors that were visited upon you night after night, as you lay terrified upon your bed, encompassed both by what you had already known and what you might yet have to face. That way you were prepared, and would survive, not in spite of those nightmares, but because of them. That assurance, and the kinship of all those innocent dead, finally set you apart, once and for all, from the others, and provided you with the burden and the glory of your dedication, your commitment.

Pamela brought in the phone. He had not heard it. She handed it to him but it dropped, clattering. Pamela handed it to

him again. He turned it around, methodically, using both hands.
Miss Cowan, Pamela said.

Miss Cowan? he said into the phone. Olivia?

She sounded very calm, very precise.

Yes, he said. Of course you are welcome. I would be honored.
I have been thinking of you. If there is anything I can do . . .

She had already hung up.

Pamela, waiting, took the phone.

Tell them Miss Cowan is coming. Tell them to let her in.

Pamela turned to go and hopped out of reach as he made a
swipe at her. He yelled but she was moving away, still giggling,
trailing the extension cord behind her. His arm hung over the
side of the chair, his fingertips grazing the carpet.

VI.

Ruel

HE WAS AT THE store front when the cops showed. They were okay at first, because Louise and some others were there. Not Sylvester though, who was out diddling somewhere with his lady friend. The cops already talked to Sylvester and were looking for Ruel to talk to, and came in with a big smile and very friendly because of the others being there. The cops wouldn't pull anything when people were around. Also they like being nice at first, to set you up for when they got you alone. That was standard. They even helped him into the squad car, with the wire screen between the front and back seat. But one cop sat in back with him and as soon as they drove off he started in, just enough to let you know there was more coming, meanwhile keeping you hoping maybe this was the worst. He put his hand on Ruel's knee, almost friendly, and then tightened his grip, and then patted the knee, like warming up, itching to get at you.

But all they did was horse around getting him out of the car at the station, more for the sport than anything else, and to remind him what an old friend he was, with the sheet they already had on him. The one cop reached into the back and yanked him out, not letting him get set, so that he whacked his head on the doorway coming through. It sorta took his breath away but Ruel just sucked in his lip and said nothing.

Cops were experts at things like that. Guards too. They knew just how much shoulder to give you after sticking out their foot, and how to grab at you when you were going down, like they were trying to save you, to make sure you were off balance when you hit the floor.

At Woodward, the guy there, the foreman, said, Well, you look like a big tall strong boy now. I'll bet a guy like you could work these other bastards right into the ground if you half put your mind to it. That was always part of it, being taller, which gave everybody a reason to want to cut you down. The guy put him out in the sun and said, You see this pile of dirt here now? And you see that hole there? Good. You got till noon. Only there was no way one guy with one shovel was gonna move all that dirt in that amount of time. Still, he tried, working all morning in the sun without even a break for water and biscuits, which the others got but which the foreman said, seeing Ruel still had more to go, he might be better off skipping. The dirt was dry and he could taste it in his mouth the whole time. When noon came he still wasn't finished. The other guys broke for lunch under some trees, eating from pails brought out by the kitchen hands, but it was so important to get all the dirt into the hole, the foreman said, that maybe it'd be a good idea if Ruel just skipped lunch. The foreman waited for Ruel to say something, but he didn't. So he digged through lunch and finished around two o'clock. The foreman came over then and said, Hey, you know what? We made a mistake.

When he finally finished, it was after dark, and all he got was leftover mashed potatoes, because he missed the regular dinner. But there was plenty of potatoes, cold now and gray and sour, and he must've ate five pounds, tasting like dirt.

Of course that's the way it was, and no big news. That's what those places were for, to teach you who was boss, and to shut up mainly, and stay in line. He wouldn't have been surprised if the potatoes had been specially allowed to go bad just for his benefit. The point was, somebody had to run the show. A work farm or anything else. Somebody called the shots, and somebody else ate shit. When you finally got that straight in your head it was really pretty simple and logical, and you might just as well go along, because otherwise you'd end up rotting there for the rest of your life, and no one would even notice. All because some little broad puts her hand inside your pants and you give her exactly what she should've expected, starting in like that. And frankly, it wasn't that big a deal, knocking off a piece, and sure as hell not worth the goddamn mess he got into because of it.

Especially that one, who had her hand in on him, pulling away and all before he even knew what was going on, or had a chance to warm up or anything. But he figured, what the hell, I might as well get cracking, since she seems to be in such a hurry about it, so he stuck his hand up under her dress, sort of skipping the preliminaries. That's the way I like it, she said, what you're doing. You mean *just* like that? Ruel said. Yes, she said, sort of in a big whisper in his ear, because you could tell she was really getting hot, which naturally by that time Ruel was too. So he said, I don't just like it that way. I mean, I like it all the way. No, she said. Just this way. Whatd'ya mean, just this way? Ruel said. I wanna get *in*. I don't want just diddling around. I'll make you come, she said. I wanna get *in*, Ruel said. You don't have to worry about me coming then. I'll make you come this way, she said. You're practically doing it already, Ruel said, if you don't stop. I don't want no babies, she said. What the hell'd you start playing around for, Ruel said, if you don't wanna do anything? I'm doing something, she said. It ain't enough, Ruel said. I'll do some other things, she said. I'm getting in, Ruel said. I don't want no just playing around. Because what the hell, she shouldn't have started it if she didn't wanna finish it. So he made her, that's all, which of course, in the long run, maybe he shouldn't of, for all the goddamn trouble it caused, and for how much good it was.

By the time they brought him in to the detective, after about fifteen minutes waiting in another room, he had his breath back but still could feel that whack on his forehead. The detective was wearing a suit and tie behind this desk in his nice office, and very friendly. Like, Won't you have a chair and make yourself comfortable? It was really something. Because when you're their man, you know it. You don't see any fancy office then, or hear any of that Won't-you-have-a-chair? business. What you get then is a wooden bench if you're lucky, or a stool, but more likely a nice hard cement floor to stand on while they ram it to you. One two three, that's it. But this time Ruel wasn't their man, Sylvester was, so he got a very different treatment.

No, he told the detective, he didn't really know the barber there. Like maybe he saw him around a couple of times, but no, he never actually *knew* him.

I thought there was some sort of argument between you fellows and Mr. Huddleston.

Well, not that I ever knew anything about. Now whether maybe somebody else had some kind of argument, I couldn't tell you, because if they did, I wasn't around when it happened.

And no, he never heard Sylvester or anybody else talk about getting back at the barber, with bombs or anything else. Sure, he was a friend of Sylvester, but that didn't mean he was covering for him. He'd been in enough trouble before this and wasn't looking for any more, either by lying or any other way. That was right, he was going to school now, the university, on a special program. Well, he was doing all right. He was hitting the books regular and keeping his nose clean, and trying to stay out of the way of any stray cops that happened to be wandering around. That last thing maybe sounded funnier than he wanted, and the detective naturally picked it right up. Cops can hear one wise sound in your voice ten blocks away. So he gave Ruel a look and asked, very cool, just how he was managing to stay out of the way of all these cops wandering around, to see if any more wise stuff was coming, because if there was, he wanted Ruel to know he could handle it, which of course Ruel knew. So he just said he was doing it mainly by putting all his time and energy right into the books, where it belonged, and staying away from any kind of trouble, which was a lesson he learned a long time ago.

Not so long ago, the detective said, opening up a folder on his desk and pulling out a sheet, like he was handling something real special that he didn't want to get any kind of smudge on.

Eight months, Ruel said. But that's only since I got out. I was in five and a half months that time, and you can check the record at Cheney, I was clean that whole time. So that makes it really over a year, altogether.

I hear tell, the cop said, that you're having some difficulties over there at the university.

Well, you know, Ruel said, it ain't the easiest thing in the world, hitting those books every night.

He wondered if the detective ever went to college. Christ, you got it one way or the other. If they didn't ram you because you were this regular jerk of an ex-con, they rammed you because you were supposed to be a real Joe College, thinking you were something special and everything. What was the point of going to the goddamn college, he'd like to know, if it just gave people one more reason to put it to you?

Which means you've finally decided to stay out of trouble?

That's right, Ruel said.

And what made you decide that?

I smartened up, Ruel told him. That's the God's honest truth. I wisened up.

The cops in the other room gave him the eye when he left, but let it go at that. Outside he stood on the sidewalk, looking up and down. The cops were great that way. When they had you nailed to the wall, they provided transportation. When they couldn't pin anything on you, you walked. He hadn't been too worried about how it would go, but you were always glad when it was at least over. The thing was, they already had their sights on Sylvester, so Ruel could just stay cool and not let it get too complicated.

That always got him about Sylvester. Sylvester *liked* making things complicated, so nobody but himself could figure out what was going on.

Ruel felt good leaving the station, even if he had to walk. He'd let the cop think he was getting what he wanted, which maybe he was. Only Ruel was getting what *he* wanted too, and so was really the one calling the shots, because he'd taken the trouble to think everything out ahead of time and not just let himself be a sitting duck, with everything suddenly coming at you from a hundred directions at once and leaving you so dizzy you couldn't tell which end was up.

The hardest part, he knew, would be getting in, and then getting out, so he worked hardest figuring that part out before-hand. He got in then by staying in, hiding under the stairs on the top floor late in the afternoon, with the shopping bag on the floor alongside him. He picked the top floor because nobody would be going up that stairway, which only led to the roof. There was a paper box company on that floor, with these great big rolls of paper stacked in the hall that must've weighed a ton each, right in front of the space under the stairs. It was dark and musty under there behind the big rolls, and he waited a long time, until he heard the people from the paper company go home, coming out their door and walking down the hall and then getting into the elevator, talking and joking until what they were saying was cut off by the elevator doors closing. After a few minutes he peeked around the paper rolls, and saw lights still on behind the cloudy glass door. He heard sounds too, so had to scrunch back under the stairs. That wasn't what he had planned on, people staying late, but it didn't make too much difference, except for more waiting. The time really dragged, sitting in the dark with nothing to do but wonder what kind of bugs were crawling over you. But actually, he felt pretty good. He was exactly where he wanted to be, with no one else in the whole world knowing what was going on except him.

Finally the people in the office came out, two guys talking until the elevator doors cut them off. It hit him then that maybe there was money in the office, and since he already went to all the trouble of getting in and hiding, maybe he ought to give it a try. He decided not to. It wasn't what he'd come for, and he didn't want any sudden changes screwing things up, especially for a few lousy dollars, which didn't really excite him, and never did, to tell the truth.

After he made sure the office was dark he took the shopping bag and strolled down the hall and pushed the elevator button. It was part of the whole plan he worked out ahead of time. If he walked down the stairs he might meet a janitor, or somebody from one of the other companies. This way, by riding the eleva-tor, the chances were he wouldn't meet anyone, and even if he did, they'd just think he came from working late on a different floor. At least that's the way he figured it. Maybe it wasn't per-fect, but he spent a lot of time on that part, and it was the best he could come up with.

He got the elevator and pushed the 1 button and the doors slid closed with a little whispery sound. He practically held his breath the whole way down, listening to the cables scraping and flapping and hoping the hell there wasn't some kind of jerk around pushing a button on one of the other floors. When the elevator stopped at the first floor he pushed the B button, for the basement, as soon as the doors started opening. Then he stuck his head out. That way, if he saw somebody, or something looked funny, he'd pull back and let the doors bounce closed and ride down to the basement and get out through the exit down there before anyone could figure out what was going on. If the first floor was clear, he'd just hop out before the doors closed again.

It was clear, so he hopped out.

From there on it was like just gliding along. The door to the little hall behind the barbershop was locked but he had his pocket knife, which was thin enough to slip into the crack. It worked and he got in and locked the door behind him.

He flicked on the little flashlight and put on the garden gloves he brought with him. The hall was narrow, with no windows, and served all three of the stores on the street, because it had this little john they all used. There was a basket under the sink in the john, practically overflowing with paper towels. He took it out into the hall where there was room to work, because the john itself was about the size of a postage stamp. He put the flashlight down and took the pipe out of the shopping bag. He handled it carefully, but not really that carefully. It didn't make him uptight or anything. It was just something you didn't fool around with, that's all. Then he scooped out most of the paper from the trash can, some of it still wet and cruddy, and put the pipe in on top of the paper that was left. Then he took out the little cheapo clock he bought for $2.98 at Wiley's Discount, which he already had wired to the battery. He had it set for eight o'clock, because he figured he'd be all finished and out of the building by six-thirty and decided ahead of time he was going to give himself an hour and a half leeway. He didn't know what the hell for. You could be halfway to Nevada in an hour and a half. Still, that's what he decided, to give himself an hour and a half, and with the guys in the paper company working late it was now seven-thirty, so he set it for a little after nine. Then he checked the connections to the battery, to make sure he hadn't jiggled them loose carrying it around. He wrapped one end of the wire, which he'd stripped ahead of time, around one end of the pipe. Then he took the other end of the wire and just looked at it, and looked at the other end of the pipe, which it was supposed to be wrapped around. Breathing very steadily, he twisted the wire around that end of the pipe, being more careful now, not wanting to bump anything. Then, very carefully, he scooped back in all the paper towels he'd taken out, covering everything without pushing down too hard, and set the wastebasket carefully against the back door of the barbershop. He played the flashlight on the wastebasket then and stood there looking at it, feeling both really good at how smooth it went and kind of let down and wishing there was more. It was like getting all warmed up and loose for a game and then hardly even playing.

But he wasn't that dumb, to hang around any more than he had to. So he climbed out the little bathroom window that led to the alley and beat it.

It was a quarter to eight, and dark. He didn't have far to go, just out to the street and down to the next building. It took him right past the front of the barbershop. That was a funny feeling, strolling by real innocent and being the one guy in the world that knew what was ticking away inside.

He climbed the three flights of stairs to the clinic. A couple of big fat mammies were there with their kids, because this was a night they were open, and Ruel was supposed to help out, which he said he would. He was late, of course, but it didn't make any difference. They already had Louise and another girl at the desk and there wasn't even enough for them to do, let alone him too. It was always like that, which was one reason he hardly ever came. That got him about Sylvester, always hassling your ass off to come when he didn't need you anymore than the man in the moon, except to show people what a big deal the clinic was, with all these terrific volunteers helping out. Besides Ruel didn't like working there. The whole idea was dumb, and more bother and screwing around than it was worth. People were supposed to be trained for things like that, and he couldn't see why you couldn't just let those people do it, that were supposed to be the experts. Because the truth was he couldn't stand it there. Just the smell practically made him puke, all the medicines and stuff that the dentists used, and the soap they washed their hands with every three minutes, which one whiff of could just about do you in. But the worst was the drill. You could hear it in the outside office, and all those kids in there screaming bloody murder. It was more than he could take.

But this night he said he'd come, because that way he'd just be working up in the clinic with the others when the thing went off, and all of them, he figured, would go down together to see what the hell the commotion was.

Virgilian was the dentist that night. They had a couple of white dentists too, but this was Virgilian's turn, which meant that including the dentist and Louise and her friend at the desk and all the Aunt Jemimas and their kids, in other words, everybody in sight, Ruel was the one and only white man.

Sylvester liked to ride him about that, the same way he made fun of everything. That's all right, he would say to Ruel. You are the one person in this whole crowd here eligible to join the Country Club.

Fancy seeing you here, Virgilian said when he came out to tell Louise what to write down on this little kid's card. I thought you'd given up on us. I come a lot when you ain't around, Ruel told him, which the smart-ass girls thought was real funny, which Ruel was on the verge of giving them the finger for.

At first, when he grew up over on Ainsley Street, the place was all white. But then they started coming in, and one of the first things he remembered as a kid, when he was still with one of the foster families, was the family saying how every time you turned around there'd be another busload of jazzbos moving in looking like they owned the place. He really noticed it when he first came back from the Home and could hardly find a white face. Sure, he could go somewhere else, but what were you supposed to do, live in some kind of penthouse? Besides, it was his neighborhood, not theirs, where he grew up and everything. So he found this old house cut up into rooms that was cheap and where at least the old lady only rented to whites.

Of course, when you got sent away then you *really* got the chance to live with them. Places like Cheney were full of them, like they were buying tickets for the circus. Actually he got along better with them inside than out. At least then you had the feeling you were all in the same boat, getting shafted from the same people.

Outside it was different. Sylvester was the only one he ever had much to do with outside, and he never felt in any same boat with Sylvester. They met at school, where Ruel was in this special small group, of which he was naturally the only white guy, of guys who served time but had their high school behind them, one way or another. Ruel got his certificate at Cheney, where they at least gave you a break, because they were very hot on showing how many guys they were turning out in the great education program they had. This dean at the college was supposed to be in charge of the special group, but he was never even around and what it turned out to be was just another deal for Sylvester, who had the touch for finding deals.

The thing about Sylvester was that he could just toss rings around anybody he wanted to. Like at school. The first thing he did, which wasn't exactly what Ruel was figuring on, was drag him right into the dean's office, jiggerbooing up to the secretary there and saying, My name's Sylvester Childs, and I'm one of the dean's regular right-hand men in that great special education program of his, and I have here a brand-new member of that program that I'm sure Dean Whatsisname is just dying to meet. Ruel was ready to turn and run right then and forget the whole thing, before the secretary tossed them out on their ass. Only Sylvester just grabbed his sleeve and hung on, and the secretary went inside and must've told the dean what Sylvester said, because before Ruel even knew what was happening Sylvester was easing him into this real classy gigantic office and introducing him to the dean, who was smiling away like a yokel and leaning across this mile-wide desk to pump Ruel's hand off and say how great and terrific it was to have a guy like him show up on campus. You take a real good look at this fellow now, Sylvester told the dean, because not only is he going to bring down the whole gymnasium when he puts on a show for the folks with the big round ball in his hand, he is also going to raise eyebrows among the professor crowd with the kind of brains and intelligence he is going to exhibit.

And the dean, this kind of pudgy guy who kept blinking and

smiling at the same time, didn't seem to know whether Sylvester was just joking or not. Ruel, for Christ sake, didn't know if he was joking or not. What the hell you trying to do anyhow? Ruel asked him afterward, when they were leaving the building. Get everybody figuring I'm some kind of nut or something? Just introducing you around is all, Sylvester said, skipping along like a regular hustler except for sort of dragging that one foot with every step. Just seeing that your merits are all properly appreciated in their rightful mode. Because you don't wanna just ride your jock. You break a leg then and where are you? You wanna ride your head in this place. Only what happens, Ruel asked him, if I break my head?

The thing was, Sylvester was an expert at parading himself around as this kind of special underprivileged type that deserved all kinds of special attention. Having the right kind of dark skin didn't hurt, of course, and Sylvester got good money to handle the class, signing up their courses and tutoring and everything, and seeing that they got their share of the loose money floating around from Mr. Zeronski's pockets, which eventually even Ruel got a part of, even though Zeronski, like everybody else, figured that white was the wrong color now, if you wanted any kind of break.

Actually, Sylvester just figured Ruel was a convenient guy to have around, for odd jobs and shit work, and to show how the store front wasn't just a bunch of raggedy niggers. Besides, when Ruel got involved Sylvester said there'd be action, only his idea of action was something like the clinic. That wasn't Ruel's idea of action. Because Ruel was giving stuff a lot of thought, and had some real changes in mind. Like the school, for Christ sake. The goddamn university. It was the worst-run place he'd ever seen, with everybody jumping around like a chicken without a head. What Ruel wanted was to get people together, the students and all that were always being kicked around, and plan out some kind of logical organization. And then, once it was set up, that would be it. People would do what the hell they were supposed to, and if they didn't, screw them. Because somebody would at least be in charge then, to keep things in order.

Only Sylvester wasn't interested in anybody else's ideas. He had his own. Ruel was ready to just forget about Sylvester and his whole frizzy crowd, and would have, if it wasn't for the money.

It was still only a quarter to nine, so he had fifteen more minutes. And that was when, suddenly, he started feeling jumpy, and funny in the stomach. The minutes dragged on like dead horses, and he wished the hell he had something to do.

Whatcha doing that for? Louise wanted to know, who had a wise way of saying everything.

What?

Jiggling your foot. You gotta harness that, man. You could churn butter or something that way and earn yourself a good dollar.

I'm doing it because I like doing it, he told her, although he didn't know he was doing it, and stopped.

Anyhow, that ended that conversation, so he just sat there, on one of those crummy chairs that the Jemimas and their kids sat on waiting for the dentist to work them over. And that's what it felt like, waiting for the goddamn dentist. He wondered how loud it would be, whether they'd just barely hear it up there, like it was real far away, or whether it'd really rattle their brains, with everybody jumping a foot. He sat there, ready to jump a foot.

Only it never came. Nothing the hell happened. The last kid came out from the dentist office and left with his mother and Virgilian said, Okay, that was it for tonight, because it was nine-thirty and closing time. It took about fifteen minutes to get everything closed up, and still nothing happened. They walked down the stairs together, Ruel and Virgilian and the two girls, and when they got out on the sidewalk Ruel looked over and there was the goddamn barbershop just sitting there like a big-assed bird, like nothing in the world would *ever* happen to it, and Ruel began to think maybe he lost his marbles and just dreamed the whole thing.

Virgilian offered them all a ride home and Ruel figured maybe he'd better take it. At least then he could say he was with them when it happened, in case the clock was just a little slow and would go off any minute. Although he wasn't exactly sure what difference it'd make if he was riding in a Buick with some jazz dentist and a couple of high-tone broads, or just walking along the street by himself. He just felt it'd be better.

Back at his room, he had time to think. Only there wasn't anything to think *about,* because nothing had happened. All right, maybe the clock was screwed up, and ran the wrong time or something. What did that mean, that it'd go off at some other crazy time, or not at all? How were you supposed to figure that one out? For all he knew, the goddamn clock could be running backwards.

What he finally came up with was that he could do one of two things. He could just leave it there and see what the hell happened, or he could go back and try to figure out what the hell was wrong, and just hope it didn't go off in his face.

He decided to wait, and see what happened. He killed time watching TV until the eleven o'clock news. No one mentioned any bomb, so he figured he'd have to wait till morning to see what happened, and meanwhile might as well hit the sack. Which he did, after first scrounging up a bowl of cold cereal because he was practically starved and couldn't sleep on an empty stomach.

Sometimes at the Home you didn't think you'd make it to morning you'd be so starved. Of course he was only a kid then, without any real clue. He was hardly old enough back then to know what he was even doing there. For a long time he actually figured he must've done something real bad, like poisoning a cat or something, when he was practically a baby, so long ago that he couldn't remember what it was anymore, and that was why he'd been sent away.

And then, Jesus Christ, somebody died. That wasn't what he wanted. That was crazy. Only what the hell could you do about it?

Actually, why it went off at nine o'clock in the goddamn morning instead of nine o'clock at night was beyond him. He set it for nine o'clock at night. It wasn't his idea for the clock to get the time wrong. He didn't make the fucking clock.

Still, it was a hassle, someone dying. Right then he decided the important thing was to keep your head, no matter what. You could really get iced because of just one little thing going wrong like that.

Although there were times he could've been killed himself, if it just worked out that way, bam, the end, and no big deal as far as anybody cared or would even know. That's how it was, and you had to take your chances. Like, actually, when he was hiding away under the stairs up there, without even room to turn around, someone could've just come along and pinned him under there, with no way out, and kicked the shit out of him. In his whole life he was never so freaked out of his head as that once when this guy trapped him in a toilet booth, jumping up over the top of the door at him. Ruel had to scrunch down as far as he could in front of the bowl, that smelled enough to make you sick, because it was the john for this cruddy bar, and the guy's boots kept kicking against the metal stall. It sounded like an army coming at you, the kicks banging and echoing all around you like shots, like goddamn gongs, your heart jumping every time and the guy yelling and screaming and drunk out of his mind, jumping up on the stall with his fat red face sweating and twisted over you and spit dripping from the corners of his mouth, until finally some guys came and dragged him off.

And if you wanted to talk about dying, well, he'd seen dying. He'd even seen a kid die at the Home, because he had some kind of disease that this old nurse that came in once a week gave him some pills for, but he died anyhow, maybe because they were the wrong pills or because he was already so far gone that even the right pills wouldn't have done any good. Nobody knew. But you couldn't expect a Home like that to have doctors and specialists all over the place to take care of every little kid that might come down with some kind of oddball disease. He seen others too. Once at Cheney there was practically a regular war between the guys in this one cell block and the guards, who naturally started dinging a few heads to show who was in charge and bring the place back to order. Two guys died then, that he knew of for sure, although he heard there was even more. Nobody would bet on it, one way or the other. But there was this one dead con he could see from his window down in the yard, that was supposed to be running for the wall to escape, which was a joke, or trying to attack a guard with his bare hands, which was an even bigger joke, and got cut down from the towers. The dead body just laid there for hours, with all these officials diddling around looking at it and taking pictures and writing stuff down. Things got brought under control and back to normal, the only difference being that some guys got in a few licks along the way, and some got killed. None of which anybody thought was any big deal. The guards had to run the place, after all, one way or another.

He'd never seen an explosion. He'd never even heard one, now that he thought about it. The TV didn't say much and he wondered what it was like. Did it actually blow you up, like your stomach busting open, or tear off an arm or leg or something, maybe even your head, and send it bouncing off a wall? He wondered. Maybe it was just the noise and everything, the pressure, like, that did it, sort of crushing your brain from all that sudden pressure. Did you bleed then, or end up all black and blue, or not have a mark at all, with all the damage being sort of inside? Maybe you couldn't breathe, maybe that was it. The explosion maybe just blew all the air out of the room, so you suffocated. He didn't think so. Mostly he thought it'd be like being hit with something all over your body at the same time, but without blood or anything. And very sudden, very quick. One two three.

The point was, he had to decide whether he ought to do something, or just lay low. The answer of course was lay low, which he figured he would do all that day and night, and not even go out of the room. So he did, that whole day and night. Only it was a drag, sitting around with nothing to do, and the more he thought about it, the more he thought it'd look suspicious, suddenly dropping out of sight like that. That really got him. He could drop dead on the spot and nobody would even notice, but if he was trying to *hide* from people, everybody and his brother would probably start wondering where he was. He figured the smart thing would be just to do normal things, but nothing that looked funny. So he decided the next day to just mosey over to the store front, very normal, which would at least give him something to do and at the same time let him see what the hell was going on, and what anybody knew.

What they knew, it seemed, was the cops already had their eye on Sylvester. He didn't learn it from Sylvester, who wasn't around, but from the others, and it really threw him. He never figured on Sylvester being fingered like that, so quick and everything. What it was, was the cops were just dying to pin something on Sylvester, and figured this was their chance. Ruel thought they'd at least look around first for clues and everything, and check out a lot of guys that could've done it, even the barber, instead of just jumping on Sylvester. As far as Ruel was concerned, he figured he was doing a *favor* for Sylvester, screwing the barber like that. He even figured on telling Sylvester eventually, once things settled down, so he'd at least know Ruel done him a favor.

When Sylvester finally sauntered in, though, there wasn't any chance to tell him anything, because he had this goofy old guy with him. That was just like Sylvester. You never saw him alone, but always with some patsy tagging along. The old guy was supposed to be the one actually sitting there when the bomb went off, which was supposed to be worth some kind of special medal. And the lady'd been with them, too, but was gone by then, which was okay with Ruel. Sylvester and the guy went off then, and after a while the lady popped back, all bothered about the cops being after Sylvester, and wanting to know where he was.

Which really got Ruel, the way the lady was always worrying about something happening to Sylvester, like he was this real delicate guy that could hardly take care of himself. So Ruel said, I'm here, you can talk to me, just to make the point, which naturally went right over her head.

Anyhow, that changed things, knowing the cops were out for Sylvester. It let him get prepared. So the next morning when the cops showed up at the store front to take him down for questioning he was able to play it very cool. Because he knew what the detective was after, which was Sylvester's ass and not his, and could stay on top of things without actually saying anything against Sylvester, but also without getting himself into any kind of trouble.

So he left the station feeling pretty good at how it went, even though he had to walk. He didn't actually mind though. Because all along the TV news and even the paper that morning didn't really say that much, and didn't have pictures of the place or anything, and he naturally wanted a better idea of what happened, and how it looked now, because after all he was the one that planned it out from the beginning to end, and it felt funny not knowing exactly how it worked out. To walk home he practically had to go right by the barbershop, so it was the perfect time to just sort of casually check it out as he strolled past.

Only for Christ sake, there was a regular freaking mob scene there, with cops, and ambulances, and barricades, and trucks and everything, and this big gang of pretty-mean-looking jazzbos across the street watching. Only they weren't watching the barbershop. What everybody was watching, and what all the cops and everything were crowded around, was the goddamn clinic building.

The first thing he thought of was the goony barber must've flipped his lid and decided to get back at them by blowing up the clinic. But then this squad car pulls away, practically under his nose, and who the hell's behind the screen in the back but Louise, with this cop on the seat beside her, watching her like a hawk. He just had no idea in the world what was going on, but whatever it was it didn't have anything to do with him, and he was already on his way, getting out of there fast, when he saw her coming across the street at him, Sylvester's goddamn lady, yelling *Ruel* loud enough for every cop on the street to hear, and wearing this bright orange thing you could've spotted a mile off, and right away, with everything flying around in his head in sixteen directions at once, he knew it was trouble.

That was something else that got him about Sylvester, who was supposed to be so smart and everything. If Ruel could get her number with one look, what was taking Sylvester so long? He wasn't making it with her, that was for sure. All she wanted from Sylvester was a toy to play around with, like a little dog on a string to tag after her. She had ideas about putting Ruel on that same string but he wasn't that dumb. How Sylvester could be that dumb was beyond him.

Who's dead? he said. She had him pinned against the window, practically shoving him right through the glass. What're you talking about?

She wasn't even making sense. She was wearing that orange thing over her dress that made her look like some lady that worked in Woolworth's or something, and she wasn't even making sense. "You've got to be careful," she kept saying, all of a sudden his big buddy now, "or they'll get you too." She was throwing so much at him he didn't know if he was coming or going.

Come with me, she said. What? he said. Come with me, she said. He just looked at her. He didn't know what the hell she thought she was pulling, but she looked really weird and spaced out, which was not, no matter what else you could say about her, her usual way of looking.

Zero wanted to get rid of Sylvester, she said.

Jesus K. Christ, he thought, what the hell's going on here? I don't know, he said, trying to keep cool and get some kind of handle on things, because she was beginning to make him very jumpy. But she kept plowing right on, and he just hoped the hell she wasn't really as spaced out as she looked. I'd kill Zero if I had the chance, she said. Hey, now. What do you mean, killing? What are you talking about killing for? Come with me, she said, really spaced out, really dopey and faraway-looking. And for some goddamn reason he didn't say anything, but just went.

He didn't know why. Because even if she was crazy enough to talk about killing Mr. Zeronski, it wasn't his problem. He wasn't getting anything to protect Mr. Zeronski from crazy women. Besides, it wouldn't surprise him if Mr. Zeronski did have something to do with it, because Sylvester practically made a profession out of giving him the finger, even though Mr. Zeronski was nobody to mess around with, and Sylvester should've been smart enough to see that. Only Ruel didn't want any part of it. He didn't even want to hear about it. He could practically feel things falling apart all around him as it was, with the lady right in the middle of it, yelling and screaming and shooting her mouth off at everyone in sight.

But, like a jerk, he went, and she took him to this old building with rusty iron walls and the windows all painted black and covered with iron bars and more locks than some First National Bank. It was pitch-black inside until she found some kind of hidden-away switch. Christ, he'd been in prisons that weren't that tight. And what it was, was paintings. That was it. A whole bunch of paintings stacked in bins along this one metal wall, and what she wanted to do was burn them all up. There's too much happening today, he told her. I'll tell you. It's coming at me from sixteen directions at once. But she actually took out matches and headed for the paintings, so he had to put her down. He just grabbed her arm and when she tried to haul off at him he put her down, right there on the floor. She must've felt it too, but that look on her face said no, she wasn't feeling anything. She stayed down on her knee and looked up at him, with her dress at regular half-mast up one leg, and with this really wild look on her face.

Get up, he said. We're getting out of here.

Because he really had to get away from her. She was giving him the creeps and he needed time to think and pull things together.

Because in spite of things you could say about Sylvester, they were friends, and it made him feel funny, him getting killed like that. Sylvester even helped him some ways, although maybe not as much as Sylvester liked to think, because they really weren't that *close* friends, when you came right down to it. The truth, of course, was that Mr. Justin Gage was really the one that got the ball rolling. If it wasn't for him, Ruel would've never met Sylvester, or got any scholarship money or anything, or even met Mr. Zeronski. So if you were giving credit, it ought to go to Mr. Justin Gage, for bringing everybody together in the first place. Although of course he could be a drag too, and just as bad as the lady in the way he was always buttering up to Sylvester, who you could tell was really his big pet.

Only that didn't mean Ruel wanted Sylvester to get killed, for Christ sake. Only it was too late to worry about Sylvester anymore, and feeling sorry for some other guy's troubles wasn't going to help your own any.

He decided to call Mr. Zeronski. He didn't have to. It wasn't part of any deal, warning him about the lady. And he knew all about her and Mr. Zeronski. Maybe she went around with her nose in the air but she wasn't fooling him. She was hooking into some of that loose money too, out for all she could get like everybody else, maybe by serving up a little hot nookie on the side. But it had something to do with those paintings too, which must've somehow belonged to Mr. Zeronski, which was why she wanted to burn them. So actually he really did Mr. Zeronski a favor, stopping her, which he wasn't even being paid to do, and maybe ought to be.

He wouldn't say anything about burning paintings, or how he stopped her. Maybe some other time, when things calmed down a bit. He'd just say how she was all shook up about Sylvester dying. Which was something else, because Mr. Zeronski probably didn't even know about that yet, and would want to.

So he called and asked for this one secretary he was supposed to only ask for, Miriam, and said, This is Mr. Frank Hopkins calling, to speak privately with Mr. Zeronski. Only he was out flying around somewhere in a goddamn airplane, and couldn't be talked to. No, he told the secretary, no message. And no, she didn't have to say he called or anything. Just skip the whole thing.

Because as soon as the secretary came on he suddenly felt very jumpy about the whole thing. It was dumb. Why should he tell Mr. Zeronski or anybody else about the lady? That would just make all these things look somehow connected, and make Ruel look like he was in on all those connections. First of all there weren't any connections, and second he didn't even have a clue about what happened to Sylvester, or why, or what Mr. Zeronski or his goddamn paintings had to do with it, or even what the lady knew about anything, or thought she knew, because he could never get a straight answer from her. So he decided then, definite, he wasn't calling anybody. He wasn't talking to anybody, about anything. He had nothing to say.

Play dumb, he figured. Go home and watch the goddamn TV and mind your own business.

It was just as good he got that straight in his head then, because later, at home, the lawyer called and said he was calling for Mr. Zeronski. That threw Ruel at first, because the lawyer wasn't supposed to know about Mr. Frank Hopkins or anything except the straight scholarship money. No one was. That's what Mr. Zeronski promised. Not even the secretary, who was supposed to only figure Mr. Frank Hopkins was some kind of guy he had private dealings with. But the lawyer just said he heard of Mr. Childs unfortunately being wiped out by the police, and was feeling bad about it, and Mr. Zeronski too, and they knew Ruel was his friend and thought maybe he knew what happened.

I don't know what happened, Ruel told him. I ain't got the foggiest notion what happened. I just heard it on the radio like everybody else, and feel very bad about it too.

The lawyer didn't push it, which Ruel figured was a good sign. But then he started thinking maybe he shouldn't just sit around watching TV but maybe try to find out what did happen, for his own good. Just in case somebody tried to tie him into it. Because it was getting complicated, and it wasn't going to be that easy staying on top of all these things at once. Christ, who knew what the hell Mr. Zeronski or his lawyer might pull, or what the lady might be shook up enough to say to somebody. Or even what Louise might say if the cops really started leaning on her. Maybe without Sylvester around anymore, the cops might be looking for someone else to blame the bomb on, and just decide to finger the next guy in line, especially if they already figured him for a sitting duck. Because when the cops wanted to cut somebody down, they didn't need reasons. They had reasons.

He headed back to the store front, only nobody was there, not even on the streets, except for the goofy old guy with the white beard, that Sylvester brought around the day before. That was all he needed.

He was just looking for his car, the guy said, and seeing if anybody was around. No one's around, Ruel told him. But the guy really had an itch, and kept going on about how terrible it was for Sylvester, who was such a good personal friend and everything, and just wondering offhand if maybe the cops weren't looking for Ruel too. Wonder about something else, will you? Ruel told him.

The guy was so full of shit he was overflowing. What are you supposed to be, on my side or something? You my big buddy now? Everybody you meet on the street, all of a sudden you're their big buddy? The guy had it in his noggin about Sylvester being so innocent and everything and kept carrying on about how it was really his duty to prove it. Christ, Ruel thought. What the hell is going on around here anyhow?

So he tried to get the guy to forget about the goddamn bomb, but could've saved his breath. Anyhow, he had better things to worry about than some goofy old man, and left.

He wondered about the lady. What would he do if he really

had the chance, not like at the building, where she was all freaked out of her mind, but under what you could call normal circumstances. Suppose for instance she just one day came up to him and invited him for a ride, say, in that big silver boat of hers, that Jaguar. Out in the country somewhere, or the woods, and he suddenly realized he could score. Sure, she was older and everything, but not that old. She was stacked, after all, and not ready for the junk heap yet. So they park somewhere and he starts in nice and slow, and she goes right along. Nothing heavy, but just sort of really smooching around. Maybe with his hand just sort of sliding onto one of those nice big soft boobs, and her just leaving it there. And then she says, Hey, let's not do it out here, in the car or anything. Let's go back to my apartment, because I have this real nice apartment that would be just perfect for what we have in mind. And he thinks maybe it's just a stall. But no, they get back to the apartment, and it really is this fantastic place, with everything spotless and spiffy and all kinds of fancy furniture and stuff. So she fixes them drinks from this very high-class little bar that swings out from the wall or something, and takes his hand and brings him in and shows him this bedroom there which is enough to knock your eye out, with a gigantic bed and all kinds of fancy covers and everything, and then she just makes one little tug on her zipper because along the way she's already changed into this real clingy outfit, a robe or special kind of pajamas or something, and with just one little pull on the zipper there she is, without a stitch and just looking up at him with these great big moony eyes, waiting for him to make the big move, practically saying with her eyes, We can do whatever you want, Ruel. You're the boss. Any way you want it.

Only what would he do? It was a good question, because he wasn't so sure. He really wasn't. It'd be one thing if she was just some piece he picked up somewhere, because in that case it'd be just one two three and forget the whole thing by the time you got your pants buttoned. In and out and down the spout. After all, what the hell was she always shoving her nozzles in everybody's face for if she didn't expect you to do something about it. Only suppose that wasn't the real story. Suppose she hadn't boffed maybe sixteen million guys over the years. Suppose there'd only been a couple of guys say, or a very few, and now she really had eyes for him, as something really special. Of course that was an awful lot to suppose. But it could be. What then? He just didn't know. The problem was it meant she'd have to be different, somebody entirely else, for it to work, and if she was somebody else then it wouldn't be her, and what the hell then, he might just as well ram it right to her and forget all about it. Because he could really get turned on thinking about her standing there, or laying there, without even a stitch on. But even just thinking about it, he never really seemed to get far enough along to where he actually got *in*, because all these other things, a whole bunch of other crap, would start bothering him. He just couldn't get comfortable with it. Because he didn't just want a quick bang out of her. He could get that from anybody, and no big deal as far as he was concerned, because nine tenths of the girls were as bad as the guys, the way they talked and everything, and what was so special about some dumb slob that could melt a goddamn lamppost the way she talked, and sat around with her friends all the time talking about crotch rot and the size of some guy's whang?

Only she'd never, not once, ever done anything but treat him like shit. How were you supposed to feel good about somebody like that? She never even looked at him unless she had to, and never once said a decent word, except to ask, Where's Sylvester? That was it, the only time she even noticed he was alive, to ask, Where's Sylvester?

He'd see them together sometimes, and it really got him. You'd think she was being treated to royalty or something, the way she'd knock herself out laughing at every goddamn thing he said, and fluttering those goo-goo eyes like it was all she could do to keep from fainting dead away from all the excitement. And Sylvester, naturally, figured that made him pretty hot stuff, with this classy broad falling all over him, and he'd go mincing and swaggering around and sort of just give her a break once in a while by maybe smiling in her direction, or letting her treat him to lunch, or have the privilege of driving him around wherever he wanted to go in that little old silver boat of hers.

It was getting late and there wasn't anything to do except twiddle his thumbs. It was funny, having nothing to do. Like at Cheney you didn't mind because that was the way it was, you sat around. You didn't get any choices. But outside you didn't *have* to sit around, because there were a million things you could do, so sitting around was really a drag, and just made you jumpy.

The gym was open in the afternoon for pickup games. He changed in the locker room and went out on the court. Some guys were screwing around and he got into it. He'd seen most of them before and they weren't exactly what you'd call sensational, but it was a game at least, and better than sitting around. One of the guys had tried out for the team the same time Ruel did, the difference being the guy didn't even make the first cut, because he stunk. Still he always wanted to buddy up to Ruel, like they were two of a kind, teammates and everything, and not like the others. So Ruel kept taking him one on one, just to remind him that *he* made the team, and hadn't been cut, driving for the basket and then stuffing as hard as he could, just daring the guy to put a hand up.

He was starved and ate early, at the Student Union, where he could use the punch card. That really pissed off the lawyer guy, when Ruel tried to get a card for regular restaurants too, instead of having to eat the cafeteria crap all the time. Like, you know, I already *been* places where I got lousy food free three times a day, so that ain't such a big deal. But he couldn't swing it. The lawyer said the punch card was only good at the school, and if Ruel was so fussy about his menu maybe some different arrangement could be made, with him taking care of his own food, along with his own books and tuition and expense money too. Nah, Ruel told him, this'll be all right. Of course that was at the beginning when the lawyer, who was never too friendly anyhow, was the only contact Ruel had for bringing in the goodies.

He really wouldn't mind turning the tables, just once, on that lawyer. Actually, he'd really like to do it on Mr. Zeronski. That would be something. But of course you didn't play games with people like Mr. Zeronski. Without their uniform, you could wrap most guys up in a ball and bounce them across the room. But the ones you really had to watch out for didn't need uniforms. The funny thing was those guys were usually nice and polite. Guards never were, and the cops of course would ream you out as soon as look at you. But a man like Mr. Zeronski, who could get rid of you just by nodding his head, was always very polite. Although you could see he stayed on the juice pretty steady, and wasn't exactly as logical all the way through as you'd expect a man like that would be. You really had to try to follow, and Ruel did, because he was sure the guy was pulling something. Only he'd given him money before that, for nothing at all, for just going to school. Still, this was different. It was actually the first time in his life anyone ever came up and *offered* him money for doing something. Absolutely the first time. Of course all the other guys that got the scholarship money, that Mr. Zeronski could've picked, were all regular weirdo jazzbos, which was maybe why he turned to Ruel, being the only white guy. Still, it made him edgy, thinking it had to be some kind of trick, to get him in trouble. Only why would a man like Mr. Zeronski waste his time inviting Ruel to his house just to get him in trouble? So what the hell was it then? Ruel just felt like saying, It's been guys like you that've been screwing me all my life. Now suddenly you're knocking yourself out being nice. What's going on? Where's the catch? He didn't say it though. He just said, Sure, he'd do his best. And he meant it, even though what Zeronski was paying him was just peanuts. After all, it was a chance to show what he could do. Only at the same time it pissed him off. Don't do anything I don't tell you to do, the guy must've said three times. Do only exactly what I tell you. Do you understand that? Yeah, Ruel kept saying. I understand already.

Suppose what happened was Mr. Zeronski figured he'd had enough of Sylvester, so snapped his fingers and had the cops take care of him, once and for all. What was going to stop him from maybe snapping his fingers just one more time and taking care of Ruel too, because he didn't have any more use for him now that Sylvester was out of the way? It could happen. It could be exactly what Mr. Zeronski was thinking. Which meant, of course, that Ruel had to be on his toes, and do a lot of thinking and planning out, just in case, because he didn't want to give Mr. Zeronski any kind of clean shot at him. He didn't want to even go *near* the man, or any of his strong-arm bodyguard types either. That'd be just putting his head right in the noose.

At the cafeteria you got your food on a tray, and when you finished you were supposed to carry the tray back to the hole in the wall for the dishwashers. Just like Cheney. Only Ruel never did. He just left it on the table and walked out.

He felt better after eating. He always did. Because you could always say, after getting through a meal, Well, at least I got *that* under my belt, which nobody then could take away from you. So all right, the food was lousy. You got used to that. It was funny, because at Cheney everybody always bitched all the time about the food. Then at Thanksgiving they'd put on this big fancy meal, with real turkey and stuffing and sweet potatoes and actual pumpkin pie covered with whip cream for dessert, and what happened was that night half the guys were puking all over the place.

There were two notes. He opened the door and just stood there with the key in his hand, looking down at them on the floor. Two notes. He never got two notes under his door in his whole life put together. He didn't even want to pick them up. He didn't want to touch them. He took a giant step over them into the room and leaned back over them to shut the door. He tossed the keys on the dresser and went into the bathroom to take a leak and came back out without even looking at them and pulled out the TV button and waited for the picture. Then he adjusted the picture and turned up the sound. It was an old movie, with everybody in old-fashioned clothes in this classy room, talking. He looked down at it with his head to one side, trying to figure out what they were talking about. They were talking about some big party they were going to have, and who they should invite. The lady, with her legs crossed on the couch, didn't want to invite this uncle they had. He shrugged and turned around and went over and picked up both the notes, and jiggled them up and down in his hand, sort of weighing them. The first one the landlady must've wrote, although it wasn't signed by anybody. She wrote like a goddamn chicken. Please call back Mr. Zorowski, it said. Shit, he said. Then he opened the other one, which you could tell the landlady wrote too. Please call back Mr. Gage, it said. Shit, he said. He crumpled up one of them and faked left and then right and tossed a nice soft lob toward the basket, but missed. He made a face. On the other one he put on a real move with his head and hooked it, and that one went in. Shit on all of them, he said, and took what was left of the peanut butter cookies, which was mostly crumbs now, from the dresser and stretched out on the bed to watch. They were already having the party, with people all dancing around under this great big chandelier hanging from the ceiling that he figured, if somebody just shimmied up there and snipped the cord, could've splattered half the people in the room to smithereens.

What was it, everybody had nothing to do but sit around writing him notes? Fun and games for all the gang, giving Ruel the old stick. Zeronski especially. Only there were things Ruel had on Mr. Zeronski, too, which maybe ought to be worth something if he handled it right. What the hell, Mr. Zeronski wouldn't want people knowing about paying Ruel, even if it was peanuts, to keep track of Sylvester. That would look very funny and suspicious now, with Sylvester suddenly being wiped out by the cops. Of course it *was* very funny, which was one reason why he'd have to play it careful, and not put himself in any kind of position where Mr. Zeronski could just wipe him out too, or have the cops do it for him. What he wanted was to plan it out so Zeronski would feel that it'd be worth his while to give Ruel a break maybe, and help him out a bit.

Although, Christ, not by *threatening* him. Ruel wasn't about to play that kind of game. As far as he was concerned, no matter what happened, it wouldn't be as bad as what would happen if he was crazy enough to ever open his mouth about Mr. Zeronski.

The point was, if you wanted to really think things through, you needed a place to *start*. After that it was really easy, and you could take your time and work it all out logically, with organization and everything. That was the difference. The other guys, no matter how complicated things got, were always very well organized.

At Cheney, it was funny, the guards really had things under control. Like one time Ruel and this other guy got in sort of a fight because the other guy started giving him a hard time. Well, Ruel put it to him pretty good, and the next morning the guy had to show up on line with this face that everybody wondered what happened to. Only the guards never said a word. What it was, was the guards were very careful never to notice anything like that, unless there was blood, which they always had to report. But by morning when they rang them to breakfast the guy had the blood all washed away and dried off, so as far as the guards were concerned there wasn't any blood, so nothing had to be reported.

There were lots of things like that, little things, that showed how, no matter what happened, the guards would know just how to handle it, to keep things in good order.

On the TV they were still dancing, around and around in circles. Ruel crumpled up the cookie bag and tossed it on a quick turn-around, swish, right into the can, then switched off the set. The hell, he wasn't about to call Justin Gage, and he wasn't about to call Mr. Zeronski either. He had a better idea, that suddenly seemed all perfect and planned out in his head. He'd call the goddamn lady, and see if she was really so anxious to be his buddy now or not.

VII.

Jerome

AMICUS SEEMED IN a better mood than the other time. Not exactly bubbling over, of course. Hardly bubbling over. But not quite so grim and sallow-faced. "And what brings *you* here, Mr. Finney?"

"Tinney."

"Tinney."

"I've been seeing some people," Jerome explained.

Amicus gave this a little thought. "It's good keeping active."

"Do you have a moment? I'm not taking you away from your work?"

"Oh no. I appreciate your interest." Amicus was as smug as the cat that swallowed the yellow bird whole.

"It's not just the bomb," Jerome said. "The death of that boy too. It disturbs me, his being blamed for the barbershop and then being shot down like that."

Amicus made a face. "Do you know how that happened?"

"Not the whole story, I suspect."

"That's what we're after," Amicus said. "The whole story."

"Is there a connection between those two things?"

"You're assuming we did blame him for the bomb."

"The radio said you were looking for him."

"That doesn't mean he was guilty."

"Are you telling me now he didn't do it?"

"We try to maintain a strict presumption of innocence, until the courts decide one way or the other."

"I'm sure you do. But when you kill someone, it doesn't much matter to that person anymore what the courts decide."

"It's too bad there weren't any witnesses. I'd give anything for a few good witnesses, or about sixty seconds of instant replay. Ten seconds."

"Is that how quick it went?"

"I suspect so."

"Now that he's dead, I guess the case is closed as far as you're concerned."

"I never said that."

"Then it's still open?"

"Just because one of the suspects is dead doesn't mean our work is done."

"Are you close?"

"Closer than we were."

"And it looks like Sylvester?"

"I wouldn't want to name names."

"But he was the one you were picking up."

"I wouldn't deny he was a suspect. He had a little run-in, after all, with the barber."

"I heard about that."

"Which gave him what you might call a motive."

"To blow the place up?"

"You never know."

"I'd still like to believe he's innocent," Jerome said.

"Why is that?"

"A feeling I have. I met him only that once. Bright young fellow, though, pleasant and energetic despite his handicap. He had something wrong with his back, you know, and a bum leg."

"I know."

"Still, he was going to college, getting an education instead of sitting around feeling sorry for himself."

"Sometimes, you know, I wish those college kids would just stay over there on their nice green campus, playing with their Frisbees. Or even studying if they felt like it, or going to class. None of those things, it seems to me, cause half the problems bombs do."

Jerome frowned. "You're making light of this because you've already made up your mind. You've got your man and everything else is just for show."

Amicus pursed his lips. He shrugged then and reached for the phone. "Ida—Cunningham around? Ask him to come in, would you?" He replaced the phone and waited.

Cunningham entered after a polite knock. He was older and bulkier than Amicus, more florid in complexion, with a kind of uneasiness about the eyes. His dun-colored suit was in the same league as the one Amicus had on.

"You wanted me?"

"We'd like the latest update on the Big Case," Amicus said.

Cunningham hesitated. "Huh?"

"You know. The Big Case. The Bomb in the Barbershop. The thing we've been working on day and night."

"Oh yeah . . . ," Cunningham said. "That."

"This is Mr. Tinney. You remember, the gentleman who was sitting right there when it all happened. We have his statement."

"Sure," Cunningham said and gave Jerome a brief smile.

"Mr. Tinney's of course very interested in our progress."

Cunningham waited.

"So I thought it'd be nice to fill him in on things. He's wondering, for instance, if the case is still open."

"Well, sure. We're still . . ." His voice faded off. He shrugged.

"Still looking into things," Amicus said. "Still checking out every shred of evidence."

"That's right," Cunningham said.

"Mr. Tinney knows about our prime suspect, of course. But I've been pointing out that he's not the only suspect."

This seemed to leave Cunningham completely at sea, and Jerome, glancing between the two, thought he saw a flicker of uncertainty cloud Amicus' expression, as if he suddenly feared he'd put too fine a line on things.

"You mean the ex-con?" Cunningham began dubiously.

Amicus' frown darkened. "I didn't mean any one person. I just wanted to reassure Mr. Tinney that we're still keeping everything wide open, trying to find the right man."

"Oh sure," Cunningham said quickly. "It's still open."

"Thanks," Amicus said.

"Sure," Cunningham said with an uneasy glance at Jerome.

"Actually," Amicus said, "we've got several real possibilities. Like the man says, everything's still wide open."

"I thank you for your time," Jerome said, picking up his hat.

Naturally you were treated as a bother, barging in on people with no more excuse than a kind of itch that wouldn't let you be. Once you pass a certain age, every move you make begins to look funny to the rest of the world. Maybe the Chinese honored their graybeards, and the Cherokee and the Sioux, but hardly the American city dwellers. Jerome could remember those Civil War vets of his youth, heroes of the GAR turned out for Decoration Day, or marching in their brass buttons and campaign hats on the Fourth. The Boys in Blue, still stepping right along, bringing a lump to everyone's throat. Just yesterday, and in a twinkling they were all gone. You expected that. What hurt was the way those once marvelous boys became, at the end, no more than a mild embarrassment to all concerned, pitiful doddery geezers good only for a wink and a laugh.

Jerome didn't believe Amicus, of course. The police had their minds set on Sylvester. It was easy enough to see why: some kid from the wrong side of the tracks, with a black face and pretensions to a college education, with a ball of black frizzled hair that he wore like a declaration. Who then turned out to have even one more strike against him, some run-in with the authorities at a demonstration maybe, or getting picked out of a crowd at a protest against that insane war, making him an ex-con too, and all the more tempting as the fall guy.

"May I ask about what?" the girl inquired from behind her little desk. Budd's convictions to the contrary, you didn't feel you'd stumbled upon the richest lawyer in town, too fancy for the likes of barbers. The reception room was hardly opulent, with only one girl and one desk and one couch, not even a ragged magazine around to help pass the time.

"It's sort of complicated," Jerome said.

The girl smiled, with all the worldly wisdom of someone two years out of high school, with maybe a six-week shorthand course thrown in, and said, "I'll see if he's free."

Apparently he was, for the girl returned to usher Jerome inside.

Gage's own office was no classier than the reception room, except for the lawbooks on the shelves. The fellow himself, though, was impressive, large and manly, with a sensible air. A man who, you'd guess, knew where he'd been and where he was heading and thus, for whatever it was worth, someone you could feel comfortable voting for. But a bit haggard at the moment, irritable and worn down.

"We've never met," Jerome said, "but I know you from the election."

"You were the one in the barbershop, weren't you? What is it? Are you thinking of suing?"

"Oh no," Jerome assured him. It'd never even occurred to him. "I just thought you might have some idea what happened. Without violating professional confidences, of course." Jerome waited for some reaction.

Gage sat hunched forward in his chair, those powerful shoulders drooping a bit, one arm resting on the desk. "It hardly makes much difference anymore."

"Do you know who did it?"

Gage was silent a moment. "The police seem convinced it was Sylvester."

"You're his lawyer. I want to know if you're convinced."

"Maybe I'm going to have to be."

Jerome stared hard at him. "What does that mean?"

"It means maybe if I were Sylvester, and grew up where he did, and how he did, and took all the guff he did, I might feel I had some pretty good reasons to blow up a few places too. Maybe I'd even feel justified in going after a cop with a dental tool, if he was going to tear down the clinic I'd spent all that time and sweat building up."

Jerome felt a terrible draining sadness, almost a nausea. He tried hard to keep his eyes steady. "He did it then. That's the open and shut of it."

"Maybe there were reasons. Maybe it's not all that simple."

"I never thought it was simple," Jerome said. Did it always have to work out like that? You followed your instincts, your feeling for people; you staked your best on the bright and lively ones you believed in and got slapped in the face for it; wrong from the start, pigheaded and sentimental, not half the savvy guy you thought you were. And each time it left you with the same ache, sharp enough to make you wince. Nobody's fool but your own.

"I'm afraid I have to leave for a meeting," Gage said.

"Why did he make it go off in the morning?" Jerome asked. "Was he *trying* to kill someone?"

"I'd like to think he wasn't too experienced setting bombs, and miscalculated."

"A man was killed because of that miscalculation," Jerome said.

"Sylvester was killed too. Does that make you feel better?"

"I'm not concerned about my feelings," Jerome said.

"I really have to go."

"Don't let me keep you," Jerome said.

And where did that leave you?

One of Jerome's grandchildren, now a grown woman with children of her own, had years ago run off from her parents. Only twelve or thirteen then, something like that, she'd been brought back against her will, a pathetic creature in ragtag runaway clothes. There was a boy involved, some kind of fierce puppy love. Jerome tried his best to help smooth things over, to make head or tail of the whole mess, which seemed with every question and answer to grow that much more entangled. And all the time he couldn't help but remember the girl's father as a baby, snuggled up to his mother's bosom, nibbling away at her little pink butterflies, as warm and peaceful a scene as you could imagine, producing for Jerome the awe that miracles always stirred up in him. And there they were, but a third of a century later—and a third of a century ago!—a blink of the universal eyelid, consoling that squalling babe's offspring, a shy petite girl overwhelmed by the world's stormy complexities, with her boy friend vowing to carry her off forever, her mother on the verge of operatic collapse, and her father—that squirming, suckling infant—raging and stomping like an Aztec king.

(All that frenzy and hubbub, all that passion, over a girl still with braces on her teeth . . .)

It was difficult enough, it seemed, just finding an answer—to be able to say, *This is the way it was; this is what happened*—without also expecting that answer to be congenial and reassuring.

Maybe the lawyer was right. Maybe Sylvester had his reasons. Still, it was hard to shrug off the thought of that lighthearted boy fastening wires to an old clock, packing in explosives, leaving an innocent man dead.

The temptation was to forget the whole thing and head home for the soft side of a big chair. But he was struck with the thought of the other person who, like himself, had pledged so much to her belief in the boy. Beneath all her exquisite poise you knew how deeply Olivia Cowan could be touched, although perhaps not everybody saw that. No one enjoyed playing Miss Goody Two Shoes, passing out bits of fortitude like so many damp bouquets, but was there anyone left to sympathize with her now, to take her hand amid all this pain and disappointment?

He found her in the phone book, as he'd found Budd Huddleston earlier. The Amethyst Gallery. He jotted down the address and climbed back into his car.

VIII.

Justin Gage

You HAD TO BE careful what you asked of people. Once, late in the fourth quarter, and only a few points behind, the coach looked down the bench and threw a straight finger at a third-string offensive tackle, a big sweet guy who hadn't played five minutes all year but loved the team with all his heart. "Get in there and roll around on the ground like you broke your leg. We need a time out." So the kid hustled in for one play and rolled around and broke his leg and spent three months in a cast.

"I'm not looking for a life history," Justin explained to Trow. "I just want to make sure my client didn't do it."

"Sure," Trow said. He looked like a tailor, squat and rumpled, squinting, nearsighted through bottle-thick glasses, and was the only dependable private investigator in the city. The lawyers used him, the businesses, the credit agencies, maybe even the police when they got desperate. He groped a bit, Trow did, and legend had him bumping into telephone poles on foggy days, but he managed to come up with what you wanted. Because Trow was, above all, a foursquare realist, a man who had no argument with the world as it was, and therefore never frittered away precious energies wishing it were different, or trying to shape it to his own desires. He entered your office diffidently, waited until you offered him a chair, took no notes, made no witticisms, wasted no time. He would, though, allow himself a pinched, squinting glance around the office, storing up impressions for the day when someone might want a run-down on you. That was all right. If you were going to be tailed, it might as well be done by a pro.

"I don't particularly care who did it," Justin told him, "except to clear my client."

Trow raised a magnified eyebrow behind his chunky lenses.

"Although if you find out," Justin added, "I guess you can tell me."

"That's two things then," Trow pointed out. "Who didn't do it, and who did."

"I'm only interested in making sure my client didn't."

"The best approach would be to identify the responsible individual. Then either it's this Childs fellow, or it isn't."

"Okay."

"Only that'll be two things."

"For the price of one?"

"I never haggle over rates."

"Let me know what you find. Keep in touch."

Don't break your leg, Justin wanted to warn him. *Don't do any more than I'm asking.*

So they'd have a riot. That seemed the general consensus, and Justin wasn't up to arguing. Maybe it'd even serve some purpose. Get the kids out for a few wind sprints with the beet-red cops in hot pursuit—and Justin himself, as the delegate of Reason and Neatness, surveying it like a parade, from a reviewing stand maybe, through binoculars.

"Okay," Justin finally agreed. "I'll go. I'll keep an eye on things. But I'm not risking my neck to save anybody's store window. As long as we understand that."

He would have gone anyway, without being asked, and the

mayor knew that. Councilmen were elected at large but each was expected to watch over a single district as his very own. Justin's baby, by common consent, was the West Side. He knew more about it, had more contacts, cared more, got more votes there than any of the other members. "Essentially," he'd explained to Olivia, "I'm the nearest thing they've got to a token nigger."

"In that bunch, I'd take it as a compliment."

"Christ, I do," Justin said.

They started at six, not a Council session but an informal meeting of councilmen and other interested parties. The mayor could have opened with a stirring pronouncement that it was but a scant hour to nightfall, at which time all manner of perils would threaten the dark and ordinary streets of their city. But high drama was not the mayor's forte. Phil Ryder did not have a forte. Phil Ryder had been into office equipment for twenty years and was now into local government, and there it was, the whole story. Not that he was any worse than the others around the table. No worse than Zero certainly, or the chief of police, no worse than the president of the university, the other four councilmen, the mayor's special assistant, the civil defense chief, the commander of the state guard.

At least the mayor occasionally demonstrated a certain amount of genial self-deprecation. "You like this office, don't you, Justin?" he'd said one time, gesturing expansively around the room. "You approve of the furnishings, I take it—the decor, the official air. You could feel at home here."

"You're not worried, are you?" Justin said.

"Not in the least. By the time the revolution comes and you're ready to move in, I'll be off sipping a slow martini and watching my azaleas grow."

"Don't underestimate the forces of truth and righteousness."

"I always estimate them, Justin, at precisely their true strength —which has enabled me to beat them bloody every time."

They'd both laughed back then. This day, Justin would have loved simply to erase Phil Ryder, and everyone else around the table, like chalk figures on a blackboard, up and down in straight lines, pure fourth grade, afterward slapping the hard-backed felt eraser vigorously against a curbstone.

They weren't even notably vicious, these men. What impressed you was their staying power, their turtle-back toughness. You could picture them arising, perfectly composed, from the still-smoking rubble of some universal upheaval to gather once more around a table like this, in a room like this, settling into their smooth leather chairs with all the rectitude of certified virgins.

Zeronski was the lone surprise. Zero rarely appeared at any sort of meeting, preferring to work his magic *in absentia*. He looked flushed and heavy-lidded. He had been keeping to his schedule. He always kept to his schedule. Three o'clock was the dividing line, the glorious moment, and when three o'clock came, nothing, neither flood nor famine nor impending riot, could deter Zero from his appointment with the long bottle and the round glass. Today, however, it hadn't done much to allay his fears. Everyone else in the room looked concerned enough, but only Zero looked downright scared. Maybe he had a better imagination than the others.

The police chief briefed the men around the table. His forces would be ready at any sign of trouble, although he naturally hoped cool heads would prevail. He discussed with pontifical gravity the location of field headquarters, the positioning of police units, the availability of crowd control equipment, the contingencies that might require the mayor to declare a curfew or, if it went that far, a state of emergency. He was a veteran of the troubles of the sixties, and had confronted enough marchers and demonstrators and rioters to have become quite businesslike about it. Everyone was fascinated by his crisp references to *exploratory contact, variable response, retributory force, preventative presence*.

After a while the mayor turned to Justin. Justin said what he had come to say, and what everyone expected from him and had therefore already discounted.

"No one's arguing with that," the mayor said. "No one wanted the clinic destroyed. No one wanted anyone killed."

Sourly, Justin gazed around the oval table. "Of course not. We're the good guys."

"I made a point of not inviting the bad."

"You're meeting them later, I take it?"

The mayor laughed. "Maybe I should."

Justin didn't laugh.

"We understand how you feel," the mayor said, sobering quickly. "But we've been working hard to ameliorate the—"

"I don't want to hear about amelioration. I'd just like us to make a little effort to understand what made that kid go at the first person who tried to get him out, even if it happened to be a cop with a gun in his hand."

"The injured officer," the chief said, "did not have his weapon drawn when—"

"I don't give a damn. Is that what we're doing here? Seeing what we could pin on the kid if he were still fortunate enough to be alive? And what about the girl? Are you going to make her an accessory to the assault on an officer?"

"She wasn't any accessory," the chief said. "She was downstairs, assaulting an officer on her own."

"She was trying to keep them from going in after Sylvester, because she knew what would happen if they did."

"Maybe if she'd just explained things," the chief said, "instead of calling them every name in the book. . . ."

"What are you going to charge her with?"

The chief hesitated. "Disturbing the peace."

Justin looked at the mayor.

"I don't think there'll be any problem with the girl, Justin. Let's not get sidetracked over that."

"Okay," Justin said, sitting back.

Eventually the mayor sprang his big surprise. "I think you'll all be glad to hear that a private donor, who'd like to remain anonymous beyond this room, has already pledged to provide a new and larger location for the clinic, along with whatever equipment is needed to run it. What we'll end up with, actually, is a much better and more professionally oriented facility than we had in the first place."

Everyone turned to Zeronski with the same look: *So that's why he's here*.

Zero lowered his head.

"That's very fine," Justin said. "That's commendable. And meanwhile the old clinic, I understand, is still standing."

"The demolition has been postponed," the mayor said, "until things settle down."

"Which means we can still get that stuff out. Which was all the kid wanted in the first place."

"There's really not much need for it—now that we've got a new facility in the works."

Justin paused. "I don't suppose there's any chance of our new, improved clinic being named in honor of the boy who died for it, is there?"

The mayor looked pained.

"I didn't think so," Justin said.

The meeting ended with the sun already set, although the dark night had not yet fully descended. Justin tried to make it to the door but the mayor caught his arm and led him aside. "We didn't do too bad, did we?"

Instead of answering, Justin turned to watch Zero, the last to gain his feet, methodically making the long circle around the table, each step tentative, his bulging eyes like whitened cowhide. Justin got out before Zero reached them.

Justin first met Zeronski a few years back, when he consulted for him on a building project for the West Side. The whole thing was pretty vague. "We are merely exploring possibilities," Zero explained. "The exact nature of the project remains undecided." Justin developed area studies and spent a few days in Washington picking his way through the maze of guidelines for federal funding. He made some trips to Sacramento and appeared before the Zoning Board with Zero's application for Prime Developer Status. He heard no more about the project and assumed Zero had abandoned it.

Back then Justin got his first chance to observe Zero in his hilltop house, hunched over in his bathrobe, settling heavily into the downy cushions of his chair. You sat there maintaining your untenanted smile as his lachrymose fantasies achieved their full flower, Zero emerging as unabashed moralist and self-appointed savior, as mushmelon, as the *genius loci* who thrived on acquisition and alcohol, who sustained his ambitions through a combination of sweet dreams and nightmares.

Zero would insist on accompanying you to your car. It got complicated. First the maid had to be summoned to refill his glass. Then the elegant chauffeur would appear to help Zero out of his chair, digging in his heels to draw Zero—the now full glass in his hand making the operation even trickier—up and out as if from the suction of some oozing swamp. The good man would then steer Zero through halls and doorways and out to the parking area. The last image of the long evening would be that of Zero turning to jelly on the uniformed shoulder, his eyes almost closed, his head drooping, one hand still clutching the glass as he lifted the other in a bleary farewell.

Later, much later, Zero invited Justin to dinner. To meet a few friends. "People you'll like. And who would like to meet you." It was stag, with eight at table, Justin and seven millionaires. Heavyweight silver and vintage wine, rare Chateaubriand, foot-long H. Uppmanns to smoke over coffee. And of course the stealthy black servants, as genial as lap dogs in the service of their beneficent master. *Here it is,* Zero seemed to be saying. *All this can be yours, just for the asking.* And the talk. It straightened you up, that talk. Money. That was the blood, the marrow bone, the soul of it all. *Élan vital* indeed. The greenback symphony. *Mon/ey, mon/ey, mon/ey. Boom, boom, boom.* It reminded you again how easy wealth was in this country, as common as clay, every city and hamlet nurturing its own marauding band of getters and spenders, its cool wielders of power. Those princely entrepreneurs of plumbing supplies and auto accessories, of electrical fixtures, of corrugated boxes and insurance policies. It was pure and surreal, that evening, straight from *Alice in Wonderland.* With Zeronski plop in the middle, fuzzy-eyed and frumpy, the Mad Hatter presiding over the festivities, whistling along in sheer exuberance to the beat of his favorite tune.

"How did you like them?" Zero inquired the next day.

"They were marvelous."

"Good men. They can help you. They know what they're doing."

"I know what they're doing too," Justin said with a smile.

"You mustn't be too picky," Zero advised. "You mustn't be pious and moralistic."

Cut and Fill: that was Zero's fundamental instinct, his *modus operandi,* his philosophy, his religion. He knew a few other hard-nosed ways of piling one dollar on top of another, but what really excited him was digging into and rearranging the land itself, almost as a mild rebuke to God for not putting things in the right place to begin with. Cut the hills, Fill the valleys. The great leveling influence of democracy, and no more complicated than pressing out wrinkles. In one instance, having purchased a huge hill, Zero proceeded to top off its peak and transport it, clod by clod, down the road to fill in someone else's valley. He then decorated the flattened hill with a tract of one-family homes. The beauty of it all was that no one else (except maybe a few openhanded members of the Zoning Board) made a buck out of the whole deal. Zero's earth movers did the digging, his trucks carried the dirt, his construction company built the houses, his real estate office sold them. "Who makes your business cards?" Justin asked, and Zero, after a moment's thought, said, "A little firm downtown. Why?"

There were variations, such as tearing down old buildings to get flat land for new buildings. All the world's contours, natural and man-made, were thus subject to the principles of Cut and Fill. All matter, ultimately, could be shaped to your desires.

It was a philosophy more American than most. *The country, see, the land, was full of wrinkles when we arrived. So we proceeded to iron them out and, presto, became rich.*

Still, Zero gave full value on the dollar. When he built a house, it stood foursquare. When he tore down a building or developed a property or repaved a road, he did it with a craftsman's pride.

Putting aside—as he was sure Zero managed to do—all the inside deals he'd bought and paid for, all the guys he'd demolished for being foolish enough to get between him and his next dollar, you had to grant Zero his points. Zero truly believed that without energy all you got was a lot of dull afternoons. That without ambition nothing flourished. That without greed and lust to get us going we'd all be shivering naked in a ragged tent instead of living the sweet life in one of Zero's sturdily constructed Colonials. (Justin's house, in Baywood Hills, had been built by Zero.) Only that argument gave you all those friendly millionaires with their rare wine and their easy arrogance, not one of whom, least of all Zero himself, would hesitate to parcel off his grandmother for the right offer.

Justin had always been careful not to ask favors of Zero, and broke that self-imposed stricture only once, not for himself but for Ruel. People considered Ruel his protégé, although Ruel himself probably didn't quite see it in those terms.

"I don't much like that boy," Beatrice said after they'd had him for dinner.

Justin hadn't expected Ruel to entertain them with upbeat anecdotes of life behind bars. He could understand how ostentatious even Beatrice's plain white tablecloth and everyday silver must have seemed after six months of slop on tin trays. But one smile would have been appreciated, one pleasant word.

"I think it's very nice helping these people," Beatrice said. "But why pick one like that?"

Ruel hadn't done much to encourage Justin during their first meeting at Cheney. Justin's being a lawyer didn't help, nor his connection with the parole board, nor anything else. Robbery; assault; statutory rape reduced to contributing to the delinquency. There were extenuating circumstances, of course. There always were. But Ruel was guilty enough, even though the robbery didn't net him a cent, the assault turned out to be a fight in a garage, and the statutory rape emerged from a couple of sweaty encounters with a fifteen-year-old sexpot. But it seemed just as stupid dumping a guilty kid into prison as an innocent one, for all the good it did anyone. What caught Justin's eye, beyond Ruel's pretty fair test scores, was the fact that people had started locking him up long before he had the chance to be guilty of anything. He'd been bandied around between foster parents until finally, at the ripe age of eleven, he was sent off for five years at the Juvenile Home. That impressed Justin. He'd seen the Juvenile Home.

The first time at Cheney, a guard delivered Ruel into the room where Justin waited. It was a small plasterboard room, tucked away in the corner of a Quonset hut with only a picnic table for furniture. Justin could see right away how shrewd and tough and whip-hard Ruel was. He could also see that somewhere along the line he'd been turned inside out by that whole sequence of guards and directors and cops and judges.

"Sit down," the guard ordered.

Ruel eyed him maliciously, then sat across from Justin.

"Okay?" the guard inquired.

"Okay," Justin said, and the guard left.

Ruel waited with his eyes down.

Justin explained that he used to work with the parole board, that he was now legal adviser to an organization of ex-cons. Ruel did not respond. Justin explained some more, coming on as easy as he could, hoping to find, somewhere, a crack in that wall of distrust.

"What're you giving me?" Ruel said finally. "What're you trying to set up here?"

Ruel's only show of interest occurred when Justin mentioned basketball, the single item Ruel had listed on his form under *Interests*. "I used to play a little too," Justin said.

Ruel looked him up and down, gauging his height, his weight, his toughness.

"What do you play?" Justin asked.

"Forward," Ruel said, still studying him. "What'd you play?"

"Forward," Justin said. "That was fifteen years ago. You could play up front then at six-three, especially if you weighed two-ten."

"I'm six-five," Ruel said.

"But you don't weigh two-ten."

"Hundred and eighty," Ruel admitted after a moment, reluctantly.

"I played a little football too," Justin said.

"I never played football," Ruel said.

At the end, Ruel more or less consented to see Justin again. "I'm just not making promises," he said. "I'm not getting dragged into anything."

"You're already in something. You're in here."

Justin visited him a few more times, and Ruel would sometimes let a smile show through, just long enough to suggest some possibilities beyond unrelenting suspicion. He wanted to know exactly what Justin was doing for ex-cons, because this was what he couldn't understand. "I mean, you're a lawyer. What do you care?"

"Some lawyers care."

"I don't know, from what I seen of lawyers."

"We're not defending what goes on here, or even in the courts. We know that system."

"I guess I do too. Because if there's one thing I know, it's the goddamn system."

"Maybe we could try to change it."

"I could give you some ideas, I'll tell you that much."

That was the high point. All of Ruel's defensiveness seemed for a moment to have melted away, and that long harsh face revealed some signs of the boyishness that had so long ago been obliterated.

But on the day of his release, when Justin picked him up at the gate, Ruel leaned rigidly against the car door during the ride into town, as far from Justin as possible, looking out in dismal silence with his ratty suitcase on his lap. Justin could understand: you weren't just being let *out* of prison; you were being sent back *into* a world that had given you nothing but trouble. Ruel seemed to be contemplating those familiar affronts as he stared out the window, and didn't say a word until Justin stopped for a light at Pendleton and Forrest.

"This is okay," Ruel said and shoved open the door.

Justin watched him cross the street in front of the car, hurrying, his suitcase dangling, that long harsh face showing as much fear as contempt, his eyes stunned in puzzlement. But he wore his toughness like a badge. He looked ready to deal with anything, except maybe good will.

"I guess obnoxiousness is the price we have to pay," he told Beatrice after they'd had him for dinner, which had been a mistake, and from which Justin was trying to salvage some encouragement. "Maybe after what we've done to someone like that, it's too late to expect politeness."

Ruel was so used to being offended that he discovered offense everywhere. Justin soon realized how long it would take, how much had to be done and undone. Either you gave Ruel every break and every benefit of the doubt or you wrote him off, and quite impartially stood aside to watch him charge the buzz saw head-on.

The biggest disappointment was in basketball. Not that Ruel wasn't good. He showed real class on the court, and Justin hoped that a few hot games, a few big cheers from the crowd, might start him toward becoming the easy self-assured kid he had every right to be. (And would have been, maybe, if he'd gotten half the breaks Justin himself had gotten.) Justin practically guaranteed the university a conference title if they'd come up with a grant-in-aid, and when Ruel told off the coach one afternoon and stomped out of the gym, Justin talked him into returning, talked the athletic director into reinstating the scholarship, talked the coach into taking him back on the squad. Justin slipped into the gym and sat alone high in the portable bleachers to watch the final preseason practice. Ruel looked fine in the drills and even better in the scrimmage. He had the moves, the speed, the hands, the whip-hard strength. He played a hard and cocky game, conceding nothing. But the fellow covering him, after getting burned a few times, started muscling up. He wasn't as tall as Ruel but heavier and stronger, the bullnecked forward every team needed to pound it out under the boards. Ruel swore at the guy, loud enough for the whole team to hear, and started coming back at him during the play, with his elbows, his knees, his hip.

No, Justin wanted to shout. *Play it smart, just this once.* As they scrambled for a loose ball, Ruel slashed the other fellow from behind and flailed away at him. The coach tried to whistle them off but Ruel was already throwing punches. Several players pulled them apart, two of them struggling to hold back Ruel. The other fellow already had a welt under his eye and a bloody mouth, and was hustled off to the locker room. The coach reamed out Ruel and sent him to the bench when the scrimmage resumed. He seemed perfectly content there, sitting with his sharp knees up and a white towel around his neck, taking the whole thing as a matter of course. But a few days later, just before the first game, he quit the team for good. He was fed up, he said, with taking a lot of shit.

That was when Justin, after some agonizing, asked Zero for a favor. He explained that Ruel had not made the team, and would be forced to drop out unless he got some money.

"The fund was designed for Negroes," Zero said.

"You could make an exception. It's your money. You can give it to whoever you want."

"The program was not designed for ex-prisoners."

"You've got some."

"Because they are Negroes."

"This guy might as well have been, for all the breaks he's gotten."

Zero pondered this for a moment. "I take it you feel he is particularly deserving."

"He's had a rough time," Justin said.

"So have we all. But I have faith, as you know, in your judgment."

Ruel thereby became the only white student deemed worthy of Zero's charity.

There were still glimmers that kept Justin hoping, times when Ruel would open up enough to reveal the struggle he faced trying to make sense of things. It was a starting point, Justin would tell himself. But then Ruel would elevate dizzyingly from that starting point and leave Justin shaking his head in disbelief.

"What the hell," Ruel said. "I can pass history. I can pass any course they wanna throw at me."

"No one threw it at you. You picked it."

"I hadda pick something."

"What kind of course are you looking for? Suppose you could just make up your own?"

For a moment Ruel seemed tempted. But it sounded like a trick, and he wasn't about to be taken in.

"There are all kinds of independent study deals," Justin said when he saw Ruel hesitating.

"What are you trying—to get me into something?"

"Cut the crap," Justin said. "Talk sense."

Ruel glowered for a moment, then shrugged. "I ain't trying to take you down."

"You can't take me down."

"Okay," Ruel said, not bullied but willing to go ahead on that understanding. "First of all, you could set up a regular procedure. You could get everybody together to make up their own minds."

"About what?"

"The kind of stuff you have to take. I mean, this ain't Cheney. If everyone just got together you could plan it all out ahead of time."

"Plan what all out?"

"Like, you have to have some real organization first off. You need publicity, so people know what's going on. And if you really wanna go all the way, well then you gotta feed everybody, naturally. You could use the regular halls though. You could decide on the rooms, work it all out ahead of time, who'd be in charge and everything. You could get somebody that just specialized in that, and hire him."

"In what?"

"Organizing. Because it could get complicated. But once you set it up, you'd at least know what was going on, as long as somebody saw that everything was kept in order."

"This is supposed to be a course?" Justin paused. "Maybe we could start with something simpler."

"It'd just be to show them we could do it."

"Show who?"

"Everyone. That's why they get away with things. They ain't just sitting around. They're out grabbing the big chance."

"Just passing would show them something. Christ, it'd show me something."

"Don't lay that on me, all right? Just don't."

"I'm trying to keep you from getting thrown out on your ass," Justin said, exasperated.

"You're always saying, change things. Well, if you wanna do something, you gotta *do* it."

"Maybe that's not the place to start."

"What place to start? Everything's already started. No matter where you wanna start, it ain't the start anymore."

"What about starting where you are, and moving on from there?"

"Only where the hell's that? You got sixteen things coming at you at once. You could just rot, sitting there, before anybody even noticed."

Justin took a breath. "What about the course?"

"What course?"

"The one you're flunking."

Ruel shrugged. "I don't know. What about it?"

Justin could have arranged the meeting with Sylvester's group himself, but wanted to give Ruel a chance to help set up something simple and practical.

Even before Ruel's release from Cheney, Justin had been working on the dean of students about a program for ex-cons. There were only a few on campus, but the number was growing, mostly through Justin's efforts. By the time the proposal dragged its way past a few dozen quibbling deans and committees, Ruel had gotten out, and Justin talked him into joining the program, even though it offered only counseling and tutoring, not money. Most of the ex-cons were black, and the dean wanted a dark-skinned assistant. He picked Sylvester, who went out of his way to help Ruel, maybe because he *wasn't* black, and therefore seemed odd man out, a role Sylvester could sympathize with. Whatever the reason, Justin was delighted. With a trio as mixed as Sylvester, Zero, and himself rooting for him, Ruel had to have *something* on the ball.

Before long, Ruel drifted into the group that hung around the store front, again as pretty much a white minority of one. The surprising thing wasn't that Ruel had joined a black group, but a political one. Ruel had no truck with politics, and considered Justin's interest in running for office about as strange, and meaningless, as a trip to another planet.

Eventually, though, with a little prodding, Ruel arranged the meeting. Four fellows and two girls faced Justin across the long table in the store front. Justin knew he'd need the West Side, and that if he couldn't even get the college kids from down there behind him he might as well chuck the whole idea. He sweated it out for over an hour, talked as straight and openly as he could, without getting one nod or smile the whole time, not even from Ruel. Least of all from Ruel, who sat through it all like a statue with a bellyache. The guy who saved it for him was Sylvester, who up to that point seemed to be dozing behind his gigantic sunglasses.

"I appreciate your kind words," Justin said afterward, towering over Sylvester like a sideshow giant and feeling a need to be very gentle—a ludicrous notion, he soon learned, given Sylvester's knack for making the world perform tricks for him. "I hope we can get together on this."

"How about a little stroll?" Sylvester suggested. "You game?"

It was late afternoon, and Sylvester led him through the worst streets of the West Side, enumerating all the obvious horrors with a kind of proprietary interest. "Let you see how the other half lives," he said.

"I've seen it before. I've been here before."

"So I hear. Another look won't hurt though, will it?"

He took him through the streets, into buildings and stores, through alleys and across vacant lots.

"Only what's a man like you getting messed up with politics for? Successful lawyer, big good-looking guy, fancy talker. You could make the dough, man."

"I haven't so far."

"You ain't eating regular?"

"We're eating regular."

"Maybe you just wanna line your pockets good on the Council, and then move right up to mayor and really hit pay dirt."

"Maybe the sky'll fall tomorrow. Maybe we'll wake up in the morning and hear everybody singing hosannas."

They passed some pretty-cool-looking dudes and Sylvester casually raised a hand, his eyes shrouded behind those enormous shades.

"They at the university too?" Justin asked.

"Nope."

"How do they feel about you being there?"

"People like to see a brother making his way. After all, big day coming. Wide open now, from what I hear, for a hard-working colored boy. One of these days we'll all be driving off for the weekend in a nice shiny aluminum camper. Wearing a baseball cap, right? And towing the big power boat behind."

"You forgot the American flag decal," Justin said.

"And the gun rack," Sylvester said.

Back at the store front, Sylvester stopped in front of the whitewashed window. "We could do worse than you," he said. "You got friends here, you know. People say you help out."

"Good."

"Only you gonna keep helping?"

"I'd like to."

"Maybe I'll take you up on that in a couple of days," Sylvester said, opening the store-front door and bowing Justin inside.

Ruel was there, and most of the kids from the meeting, along with a few new ones. All of them, except Ruel, were black.

"I brung him back for you," Sylvester said to Ruel. "All safe in one piece."

Ruel was sitting behind one of the long tables, drinking orange soda from a bottle, his chair tipped back, his long legs spread. "Where you been? I been waiting."

"I didn't realize you were in a hurry," Justin said. He'd picked up Ruel on the way over, and had promised him a ride back.

"We would've asked you to come," Sylvester said.

"Sure," Ruel said.

"I didn't mean to keep you waiting," Justin said.

Ruel shrugged.

"It was good bringing your friend around," Sylvester said. "We had some nice conversation."

Ruel seemed on the verge of saying, *Friend? He ain't no friend of mine.* Instead he just said, "If you two are all finished walking, we can go maybe."

The worst of it was that Ruel as a protégé left you a bit short on accomplishment, and long on uneasy moments. Sylvester would have been a pleasure; you could just stand to one side and watch him make his way. All you'd have to worry about would be overconfidence.

A few days later Sylvester showed up at the office. By then Justin knew what he was coming for. That morning Zero announced a redevelopment proposal for the West Side. It was the same project Justin worked on two years before, and had since considered abandoned.

"The people don't hardly know what's going on," Sylvester said. "Somebody's gonna have to do some yelling about this. Somebody's gonna have to make some noise for the man to hear."

"Do you know Zero?" Justin asked.

"We never had the opportunity. You know how it is, though. We sorta both have some interest in the West Side, only those interests are not exactly convergent."

"Let me talk to him before you do anything," Justin said.

"Talk to him real good," Sylvester said.

Justin dropped by Zero's office—in the brisk, sober light of morning—to explain what Zero understood better than anyone in the city: the Zoning Board would have to approve the details of the proposal.

"The details are very good," Zero said.

Then the Council itself would have to consider the long-range impact.

"The impact will be favorable," Zero said.

"It's not a bad plan," Justin said.

"It is a good plan," Zero said. "If you were already on the Council, I think you would support it."

"Not as it stands."

"Why not? We have worked hard on it. We have had advice from experts. The federal authorities have approved funding. The state authorities have approved. The mayor is enthusiastic."

"There are too many units," Justin said. "And there aren't any provisions for resettlement. None of those people being evicted can afford the new apartments."

"I have no wish to leave people homeless. But I am producing a thousand units. I can't produce another thousand for the people displaced, and still another for the people *they* displace. It would go on forever, a merry-go-round. The city has the responsibility. My project is a separate matter. If the city approves, I will go ahead. My conscience will be clear."

"I'm going to work against it," Justin said.

"You must always feel free," Zero said, "to act as you see fit."

Zero could afford to be magnanimous. The mayor and the Council were solidly behind him.

"There's no way we're going to stop it," Justin told Sylvester. "But we've got a chance on relocation and maybe can cut down the density. Zero's pushing for as many units as he can get."

"We gotta get the word around," Sylvester said.

"I'm going to make a statement on it. The papers will run it, and maybe the TV will pick it up. I've got some friends there."

"That ain't gonna do it."

"We have to stop it at the Zoning Board. We don't want it to even reach the Council."

"The Zoning Board's bought off."

"They'll bend though. Everybody on the Council's got his flunky on the Board. If they think there's going to be trouble, they'd rather it took place down there. They want all the hassling over with before they touch anything."

"We can give it a try," Sylvester said.

Sylvester had still been in high school back during the war protests, but was sufficiently involved to learn a few things. As the movement faded, he more or less took over the remnants, and was smart enough to realize that the days were gone when you could pull ten thousand students onto the Plaza for their daily outing and demonstration. He worked quietly the next couple of years, not producing any miracles but getting more accomplished than anyone had a right to expect. He worked on the student-faculty committee for minority education, organized the picketing of businesses that refused to serve or hire local blacks, fought for rent control enforcement, for a beefing up of the Pendleton Street welfare office, for some movement from the city on recruiting an occasional black on the police, fire, or garbage collection forces. He never had more than a handful of people behind him but was very good at using the right approach on the right person, applying the pressure where it'd do the most good.

He did just that at the Zoning Board hearing on Zero's project. He spread the word through the tenements and got over a hundred people—most of whom never heard of the Zoning Board before—to turn out for the occasion, firing them up just enough to scare a few people but not so much as to give the Board fits. When he got his turn to speak, resplendent in his flashiest dashiki, Sylvester not only showed the Board how well he understood the intricacies of Zero's plan but also how effectively he could convey that understanding to the sullen crowd packed into the room and overflowing into the hall.

Justin also spoke, and the board agreed to table the proposal until the relocation and density questions were resolved. Happily, the vote was taken some minutes before Ruel decided to lay into a security guard.

Ruel hadn't made it into the hearing room, and so spent the whole time grumbling around with the overflow in the hall, feeling deprived and itching for something to do. "The guy was shoving me around," he said later. "He was stomping away like a goddamn bull out there."

Justin was still inside the board room when the scuffle started. Sylvester, however, had just emerged to tell the people in the hall about the vote, and he rushed over to pull Ruel off and keep the thing from turning into a free-for-all. By that time two cops were shouldering their way toward the trouble. Their instincts proved less than unerring. They brushed past Ruel and pounced triumphantly upon Sylvester.

"I didn't mean to knock him over," Sylvester said. "We just kinda bumped, by accident."

Ruel never realized Sylvester took the rap voluntarily. He assumed the cops grabbed Sylvester simply because he was the ringleader.

Justin tried to have the charges dropped. Sylvester got a break from the guard, who insisted he'd been slugged in the neck from behind by a guy he never even saw but who must have been a big guy, not this little half-crippled kid the cops had in tow. He was positive it was a downward blow, with real muscle behind it.

"There's really no reason," Justin pointed out to Amicus, "for pinning it on Childs just because you can't find anyone else. A phony conviction like this would make a hell of a mess for the kid."

"That's the way it goes," Amicus grumbled. "A shipwreck at sea can ruin your whole day."

"He only admitted to a little bump. How was he supposed to know the guy'd been slugged?"

"Even you don't believe that. What's he doing—covering for somebody?"

"All I know is he didn't do it. Christ, he can't hardly reach that high."

"I guess not," Amicus said.

"Will you release him then?"

"I guess so," Amicus said, making a face.

Sylvester therefore got off unscathed. Ruel also got off clean, not even suspected. Beyond that, their efforts had achieved something of a historical first by stopping Zero in his tracks, and the *Citizen-Times* and the TV newscasts covered it in some detail, rightly giving most of the credit to Sylvester.

"I worked on it too," Justin pointed out to Zero, who was naturally somewhat vexed. "Don't just blame Sylvester."

"The situations are different," Zero said. He had listened patiently, his face set, to Justin's explanations. "Your motives were legitimate. I respect your motives."

"The boy's motives were just as pure."

"No. He is a self-glorifier. He impresses people at first, but lacks substance. He is all flash. He cares only about himself."

Zero would listen to no more. He wasn't interested, he said, in Sylvester. But he was eager for news of Ruel, curious about the fortunes of the one white boy he had agreed to help.

"He's doing well enough, all things considered," Justin said. "He's got a lot of ground to cover, after all."

"I was just wondering."

"Have you ever met him?" Justin asked.

"Woodstein handles the details. But I take an interest in the students. I wish them all well."

He also, he insisted, still wished Justin well. He did not favor large campaign donations but would be honored if Justin saw fit to accept a modest contribution of two hundred dollars. Zero of course was too shrewd to overplay his hand. Besides, he could afford to go easy, and be patient. Even setbacks like the one he'd just received, despite his anger at Sylvester, did not seem to disturb him for long. He remained confident that sooner or later he would get what he wanted.

Of course that wasn't the whole of it. Zero genuinely seemed to like Justin, beyond any question of personal gain. And once you got past his single-minded devotion to the gathering up of riches you discovered, almost as a letdown, that Zero was pretty much a liberal. Justin liked to think it was their agreement on political issues that made it impossible for him to do wrong in Zero's eyes. Justin's defections were forgiven as easily as his little jokes; he had become son and protégé, and nothing he said or did seemed capable of destroying Zero's misty-eyed faith in him.

It took as much time and energy, Justin decided, to run for councilman as it would for President. It had to, because it took all the time and energy he had. Still, he found it exhilarating, at least on his better days.

There were five seats, and since the office was supposed to be nonpartisan the party leaders got together every two years and divvied up the pie to produce a Good Government slate of five names. Until Justin came along the only independents who ever appeared on the ballot—"Bus drivers and English teachers," as Zero characterized them—provided little more than laughs.

"That is why," Zero said, "you must run as if it were the most important thing in the world. You must set yourself apart from the others."

The main problem was to fire up the West Side sufficiently to give him the support he needed in the black wards without letting that support turn the whites against him. And then to win over the middle-ground whites without letting them scare off the blacks, or the liberals, or the radicals. Beyond that, the main problem was money, and exposure, and luck. Beyond that it was getting someone to man the phones and write letters and hang posters and keep track of the petty cash and butter up the media for coverage and finally, on election day, to drive people to the polls, especially that whole subculture of the sick and infirm and shut-in, who never saw the light of day except on such noteworthy occasions as weddings and funerals and, it was to be hoped, that great November celebration of Democracy, when they came out in droves not because of any particular political commitment but because it was the only time anyone paid attention to them. They got a kick, God bless them, out of being chauffeured around like visiting royalty, which in a way maybe they were on that day.

Justin himself spent most of his time, as Beatrice liked to put it, with his mouth open. One time, at an open house that some dreadfully-well-meaning couple sponsored for him in their awesomely neat living room, he spent a couple of excruciating hours talking to three people, the benumbed couple and their one hesitant friend, all the time praying for the door chime to ring and averting his eyes from the women's club coffee urn surrounded by a couple of dozen untouched cups and saucers and maybe twenty pounds of cakes and cookies and a great glass bowl of sour cream dip that remained throughout as virginal as new snow. That was the worst. The best was when Sylvester turned out two hundred surprisingly attentive students for a campus rally. The rest fell somewhere between, although hovering generally around the bottom of the scale. He got pretty good at sniffing out a group and deciding whether he ought to quote Kennedy or King, or FDR, or Ralph Nader, or anybody, whether he ought to sound solid and knowledgeable or bright and exciting, whether he ought to go through his paces on jobs, or schools, or taxes, or prisons, or housing, or the generally crummy state of mankind. He was also prepared to present a closely reasoned analysis of the way the present system of city government managed to keep people from exerting even the smallest influence on the decisions that affected their daily lives. It was, he felt, his big winner, but he gave the talk only once, to a group of Concerned Parents who that evening must have been Concerned about something else. The only woman to raise her hand during the question period wanted to know how he stood on the high school's dress and grooming code.

During this time Justin saw less of Ruel and more of Sylvester, simply because Sylvester was involved in the campaign. By the end, Sylvester was running all West Side projects and helping out on just about everything else, all the while claiming to have no faith and little interest in the political process. For a guy who seemed almost Calvinistically dedicated to Good Works, he spent an awful lot of time denying any suggestion of idealism.

"Then what are you wasting your time for?" Justin asked.

"Practice, that's all. Learning the ropes. Maybe figuring out a few changes."

"How are you going to make them? No one's out marching anymore. Somebody's taken down the posters. You can go for weeks without seeing a single banner."

"Everyone knows that," Sylvester said. "The parade's over, man. Everyone's standing around, pitching pennies against a crack."

"I'm not."

Sylvester shrugged. "We manned a few barricades back then. Back when they were dropping tear gas from the governor's helicopters. We maybe even said a few things worth saying. But it seems like everybody's gone now, out selling shoes maybe, or blowing weed in Colorado, or dead, or crazy. Only I was *born* here. I had to hustle these streets long before those people showed up, and I'm still hustling them, long after they're gone, trying to pick up a few of the pieces they left behind. For some of those guys, you know, the big parade wasn't much more than a cakewalk."

"Some people just like the idea of marching up and down."

"Funny thing," Sylvester said. "I been in crowds where no-body'd think twice about charging a whole line of police all decked out in riot gear, knowing they'd get their heads banged in. That wouldn't bother them. But one drop of rain and they'd go home. You couldn't get a crowd together in the rain if your life depended on it."

"People get tired too," Justin said. "They get bored. Their feet begin to hurt, and that's the end right there of all their nice help-ful notions."

"Who was that dude now, that wrote about helping? About how when somebody wakes up in the morning with this gleam in his eye to do you good, your only chance is to run and hide."

"Thoreau," Justin said.

"That's the dude," Sylvester said.

Sylvester became something of a celebrity within the cam-paign. (The only other person whose political instincts were as shrewd and useful was Zero.) And even during the busiest weeks right before the election Sylvester still found time to do what Justin no longer could: to serve as guide and mentor for Ruel.

Sylvester even tried to entice Ruel into the campaign, and one time brought him along to the second-floor headquarters. It was one of his rare mistakes.

Justin wasn't there, and afterward had to piece together the accounts. A couple of high school toughs picked that evening to wander into the room, asking to look around. They begged to be allowed to pitch in, with the show of moony-eyed sweetness that teen-agers thought of as polished satire.

They were of a good size, one wearing a football jersey, and had probably downed a couple of beers or a swig of Zapple be-forehand. Three or four women were working that night, along with an elderly accountant who helped out with the books, and Sylvester and Ruel. The accountant grew testy and told the kids he had no time for foolishness. They started bullying him and one of the women, an older schoolteacher, stepped forward to see if her standard classroom scolding would work. It didn't. The bigger kid, the one in the football jersey, cursed her out and turned threateningly to the accountant.

Sylvester moved so quickly no one saw him coming. He executed a sweeping soccer-style kick that caught the kid at the ankles and quite crisply knocked him off his feet. Kneeling, glaring up at Sylvester, the kid pulled a knife. His buddy backed off, leaving the two of them to go it alone.

"If you come at me with that," Sylvester informed him evenly, "I'll kill you."

The schoolteacher, who'd taken a shine to Sylvester, insisted afterward that he was bluffing. The others disagreed. "He meant it," the accountant swore. "He would have—somehow—killed that kid."

Justin believed the man. For all his glib patter, Sylvester was no easy mark. He wouldn't panic if he got backed against a wall. He would simply do whatever he had to do, coolly and without remorse.

But with everyone's attention on Sylvester and the kid with the knife, Ruel took off like a shot, not so much running at the still-kneeling kid as flying at him, head-on, knocking him over so violently that the knife flew halfway across the room. Ruel yanked the kid up by his jersey and threw a punch that could have felled a tree. But the kid wrenched back frantically and took it on the shoulder, or maybe the neck. It was still enough to put him down again.

"Okay!" Sylvester commanded. "Enough!"

Ruel leaped for the knife and turned back to the kid, who had groped up to a sitting position, looking pretty dazed. Ruel started toward him, maybe intending to stop, maybe not, depending on whose version you believed. Sylvester sprang at Ruel, throwing him off balance and spinning him around. Caught by surprise, Ruel dropped the knife and Sylvester picked it up. The second kid, the spectator, ran for the door, and the one on the floor, seeing his chance, scrambled after him. The people in the room listened to them flying breakneck down the stairs and out the front door.

Which left Sylvester with the knife and Ruel facing him, apparently humiliated by the ease with which Sylvester had disarmed him. He seemed angrier at Sylvester, everyone agreed, than he'd been at the kid.

"Catch," Sylvester said, and tossed over the knife, lightly, in a soft arc. Stupidly, Ruel tried to catch it, and cut himself. He

dropped the knife and looked at his hand. The gash was somewhere around his thumb, hardly serious but deep enough for the
blood to start dripping off his hand as he stared.

"Knives can hurt," Sylvester said. "You don't want to mess
around with knives."

The words seemed to startle Ruel. He looked up abruptly,
glaring at Sylvester. Then, after a long pause during which neither moved, Ruel bent slowly at the knees, keeping his back
straight and his eyes on Sylvester, and picked up the knife. The
two of them were standing, by general consensus, something like
fifteen feet apart. It mattered, because when Ruel threw the
knife at Sylvester, as hard as he could, he missed. Maybe he
wouldn't have if he'd been closer. The knife flew past Sylvester's
ear and slammed into the wall behind him. It ricocheted to one
side and clattered along the floor. Sylvester, according to the reports, had not flinched. He probably didn't have time. But he
remained motionless—and seemingly composed—as the knife
whistled past his ear.

The apparent composure might have been enough to intimi-
date Ruel, or at least calm him. He jerked his head, impatiently,
and said, "I'm going." He stormed past Sylvester and pounded
down the stairs, not as frantically as the kids had, but stomping
away pretty good.

"I better go talk with him," Sylvester said to the others, and
left.

"What'd you say?" Justin asked the next day.

"Nothing too much," Sylvester said. "We just had a little rap, is
all."

"What'd *he* say?"

"There wasn't much saying either way."

"How's his hand?"

"Fine. Little Band-Aid was all it needed."

"Why'd you toss him the knife in the first place?"

"I thought he wanted it."

"To throw at you?"

"I figured that was his choice."

"Did he at least apologize?"

"I wasn't looking for apologies. We're friends."

"Still?"

"He's all right underneath. Just a little jumpy sometimes."

"At least he didn't start it. At least he wasn't the one that pulled the knife."

"He could've," Sylvester pointed out cheerfully. "He carries his own."

Justin did not see Ruel again until after the election. He made a point of having him invited to the Mayfair on election night, as part of what he hoped would be a large and enthusiastic crowd of well-wishers. The turnout was fine but Ruel didn't come. Sylvester did, and so did Olivia Cowan.

Olivia had drifted into the campaign casually, just showing up one evening and offering to help.

"Jesus Christ," one of his aides said a few days later. "Have we got a munchie. If I were you, Justin, I'd drop by later to chat with my loyal staff. I'd mosey in, old man, and press a little flesh."

"Which one should I be looking for?"

"You'll know when you see her," the fellow assured him.

Olivia turned into a gold mine, and she and Sylvester worked closely together. When Justin saw her in the election crowd, standing next to Sylvester, he told himself that they formed the sort of couple you'd notice even in a packed ballroom. But he'd been looking for her. He'd spent a lot of good time and effort working toward that night, and had enticed a lot of other people into working toward it with him. He was still hanging on, precariously, to the fifth spot, barely ahead of his one friend on the Council, the last guy he wanted to beat but the only one, it seemed, that he had any chance of beating. He'd begun by believing he could win if he'd just work hard and shrewdly enough to put all the pieces together. By election night he realized the only time anyone won anything was when the pieces—through luck, fate, faith, coincidence, or clean living—somehow fell into their appointed places all by themselves. He was more excited than he'd expected: the chalk boards, the votes coming in, cameras, shouts, even balloons, the sudden and excruciating need to pee, the headiness of being surrounded by all those friends and strangers who by some odd political chemistry had adopted your cause as their own—and in the middle of all that, with Beatrice at his side on the platform, he'd been searching the crowd for a woman he hardly knew, and when he saw her, standing next to Sylvester, it was like a nerve flashing.

After that, for months, it seemed as if the sight of her that evening would remain, slowly dimming, as one of those curious images that have to be recalled with effort, wistfully, years later. Then they met a few times socially; they reminisced about the campaign; one more stylish woman at a cocktail party. But afterward he could remember exactly how she looked, every word she'd said. He would discover himself recalling the precise intonations of her voice. One night he lay uneasily in bed after having made love to Beatrice, envisioning Olivia, naked and luminous.

The most dignified moment, he decided after a while, had been the swearing in. That showed some class, with the Council chambers handsomely decorated for the occasion, the wives and relatives all dressed in their Sunday best. After that, the job lost a bit of its grandeur. But if you were looking for unabashed, bone-gristle practicality, you'd come to the right place. Whatever the Council lacked as a deliberative body, however it fell short of lofty sentiment, by God it was practical.

"And how many tons of waste products," Justin would ask, leaning forward from his seat at the far left of the great curved table, "do you estimate such a facility would produce?"

"Solid or liquid?" the witness would inquire.

"Let's take the solid first," Justin would say, in all dignity.

The invitation came addressed to both of them, and Justin argued, with more insistence than seemed called for, that Beatrice ought to come with him. She wasn't interested; she rarely accompanied him to any of the functions he felt obliged to attend. She had not wanted him to run, had not been pleased to see him elected. She never asked what he did and hardly glanced at the news coverage of the Council. They'd married in his third year of law school, and she'd expected him to be content writing wills and contracts, with maybe an occasional trial thrown in for variety. Politics bored and annoyed her.

"You might like this," he said. "It's not a political thing. It's an art opening."

"Would you really mind going alone?" she said. "I'd as soon skip it, if that'd be all right."

Half the women glittered, with bare arms and backs and acres of powdered bosoms: the patronesses, lavish and slightly condescending. The rest of the women were younger, dressed in jeans and work shirts. The young men were bearded. The older men, clean-shaven and forlorn in their business suits, stood around clutching stemmed wineglasses in bear paws.

The gallery was unmistakably Olivia's: the white carpeting, the polished wood benches with black leather cushions, the curved chairs placed in exactly the right spot, the freshly painted walls, the flourishing plants with their polished leaves. Even the paintings seemed elegant.

Seeing Sylvester then was a shock.

The poor kid had backed himself into a corner behind a large ceramic vase, pressing one shoulder against the wall as if trying to worm through the plaster to freedom. He wore, as always, his oversized sunglasses. The dashiki partially disguised the sideways twist of his body, and his legs were encased in the narrowest black trousers imaginable. His pointed black shoes gleamed.

"I didn't know you were an art fancier," Justin said.

"Jesus," Sylvester said. He was sweating.

"Is something wrong?"

Sylvester grimaced, baring his teeth briefly. "This is crazy, man. It really is."

"Is it your first visit?"

"Yeah. Really. My first visit."

Justin laughed. "You could run rings around this bunch."

"I'm running rings, man."

"Do you want to meet some people? We could drift around a bit."

"You drift around, man. I'm all right. I'm doing wonders."

Again Justin laughed. "Why'd you come?"

"Go ahead. Go meet the people. I'll watch."

The next time Justin looked, Sylvester was gone.

"What'd you drag the poor guy here for?" he said when he got to speak to Olivia.

She seemed genuinely dismayed. "Was it that bad? I was hoping he'd have a good time."

She kept busy greeting new arrivals and then, at the end, saying good-by. The crowd had thinned out by the time she got back to Justin. A few people were getting together for dinner. "Would you be interested, or do you have something on?"

"I'm not sure," he said. "I'll have to check first."

She smiled, taking his hand. "We'd like to have you." And then, frowning: "Poor Sylvester. I really thought he'd enjoy himself."

Later, in the bedroom of the Mayfair suite, his clothes on a chair, hers on another, she again took his hand, took both his hands to form a circle with their arms.

"Shall we dance?" she said.

"After."

"I've been wanting you to make love to me."

"I've wanted to."

"There's nothing to stop you now," she said.

Beatrice had grown used to his coming home late for dinner, or after dinner, or late at night. It was to his secretary that he had to keep giving excuses for the blank spaces on his calendar every afternoon.

Sometimes they would make love as soon as he arrived, sometimes in the evening, right before he left.

Olivia was fascinated by his work on the Council. Having been active in the campaign seemed to make her feel, in a very flattering way, a special involvement in everything he did. She loved to hear him talk about the meetings, the votes, the debates, loved his stories of the Byzantine intricacies of city politics, loved even the backstage gossip. He would find himself during the day deciding which stories she'd most enjoy, savoring the prospect of telling them to her. He delighted in her mere presence; it was a new world, full of discoveries, and he wanted to bring to her something as good in return.

She'd talk about the gallery, her shows, her sales. Business was good, and you couldn't miss the sheer joy she found in working with her painters. She glowed over their successes, bristled if she felt any were being neglected or unfairly criticized. Her belief in them amounted almost to a sense of mission.

She sometimes spoke of the husband long dead; it had been a good marriage. But the shock of his death had transformed itself into a farewell gesture to the conventions of home and church and marriage; she'd paid her dues and received nothing but pain and loss in return; she would not be bound by those rules again.

For years she'd done volunteer work in the West Side, mostly at the school for the retarded, playing games and digging in the sand pile right along with the kids, reading them stories, changing diapers not for babies but for five- and six- and eight-year-olds. She still kept in touch with the children and mentioned once, casually, shopping for a gift; she made note of birthdays, and brought a present to every child she'd worked with at the school. "Some of them don't even understand it's their birthday. One just grabbed the box and ran. He thought I'd made a mistake and would want it back."

She wanted to be tough-minded and realistic, but the world's brutality shocked her. Maybe growing up rich did it. Her early years had been very gentle.

"It must have been something my parents drilled into me when I was still in the cradle," she said. They were having a drink in the suite, Olivia sitting on the green chair with her long legs crossed. "But I had so many advantages that I decided there simply had to be a reason behind it. It couldn't just be luck, it couldn't be aimless. It had to serve some purpose, or else the waste would be terrible, throwing away all that money and education and intelligence—I was a very bright kid—on some scatterbrained little goose. So it was either some kind of really sick joke, or else for God's sake I'd better decide what to *do* with all those breaks I'd gotten."

"And that was the tough part?"

"It has to be better than handing out toys. That whole place, the whole West Side, is like a running sore. I'd like to just go down there very calmly one afternoon and wipe it out, so we could start all over. I wouldn't leave a single brick standing."

"Zero's already doing that, only more gradually."

"Don't say it's like Zero." She stood up abruptly, holding her empty glass, then took Justin's, as if this were the reason she'd jumped up. "Zero doesn't want to change anything and start over. He's doing too well the way things are."

"He tries to help, in his own way. I think he really feels a kind of identification with those—"

"Jesus Christ, Justin. You try to help too, don't you? In your own way. At least compare me to you." She poured drinks and handed Justin his glass.

"You're not doing anything down there anymore, are you?"

She paused, still standing. "I got tired of the looks I got, and deserved, and the names I got called, and deserved." She sat down and sipped at her drink. "There's nothing we can do down there anymore. We might as well put on desert helmets and hire native bearers for our luggage. They're going to have to do it themselves. People like Sylvester. That's what we've been waiting for: someone to come along and make us obsolete. Everything's turned sour and flat for us. The only excitement we can feel anymore is through someone like that, who at least has energy and enthusiasm and can really believe the day's coming when things will be better. We don't believe that anymore, not for ourselves. We've already got everything we ever thought we wanted. Our day came and went before we even knew it arrived."

"There are things I want," Justin said. "There are things I'd like to see changed."

"But it's not something burning in your gut. It's not something ripping you apart. After all, isn't that the great historical irony? The conquerors turn bland and sophisticated while their victims, because they have no choice, become tougher and shrewder and more energetic. Even from the beginning, with the first settlers, they worried about the white men who suddenly chucked it all and joined up with the savages. Cotton Mather gave some pretty hairy sermons about that, the danger of good Christians becoming, as they called it, Indianized. What the hell caused that? There must have been something pulling them. And it never went the other way; the Indians didn't move into the settlements. What happens is the people we think we're subjugating are really sucking the vital juices out of us. When we want some kicks what do we do? We go hear the grandchildren of slaves sing and play the saxophone, or hit a home run for that matter, or run up and down a field carrying a ball."

"I never could sing much," Justin said, "but I used to be pretty good running up and down with a ball."

"That's not the point."

"I'm not borrowing my energy from anyone. I don't think anyone's sucked the vital juices out of me."

She paused and then said, as if the connection were obvious: "You know what they did with Sylvester his first day in school? They put him in the retarded group. They took one look and decided he was defective. Isn't that marvelous? Those sweet people were going to help this poor unfortunate boy by putting him on to finger painting."

He learned then that Olivia was providing the rent money for Sylvester's dental clinic: coming maybe from the fees Zero paid her, passed on to Sylvester, and then completing that not wholly surprising circle by finding its way back into Zero's pockets.

She enjoyed wheeling and dealing for Zero, but hated the thought of being beholden for favors to anyone she so thoroughly detested, who wouldn't even give her the satisfaction of paying attention and didn't know a Rembrandt from a blank wall. At the same time Zero was precisely the kind of man—a throwback to those fondly remembered buccaneer uncles and grandfathers—who awed and excited her. That, Justin finally decided, was why she was so hard on Zero. God knows the man was no saint, but Olivia had gotten herself into such a state over him that she wouldn't allow him mere human shortcomings; his faults had to be monumental.

With all this, she saw no problems for herself. It was only Justin's purity that she worried about.

"We've got enough virgins around," he told her. "I don't want some plaster saint decorating the mayor's offices while everybody else robs us blind. I don't want less politics. I want more. I want to be right in the middle of things, and not be too fastidious to do a little arm wrestling with Zero for a good cause."

"I couldn't manage that," she said.

"Sylvester manages. He's a better politician than I'll ever be."

She seemed genuinely surprised. "Really. He's not like that at all."

She longed for some single grand gesture that would allow peace and loveliness to reign forever, and seemed to have convinced herself that Justin was destined to ride at the head of that great crusade.

"I've only been elected to the City Council," he reminded her. "No one's appointed me the Avenging Angel. We deal in sewer extensions and property easements. We haggle over the sales tax. No one's asked our opinion on the larger discontents of the age. No one's called for our vote on the eternal verities."

Olivia went to New York for three days on some kind of buying spree for Zero. On two of those evenings, Justin had meetings that kept him out late, and he strained to convince Beatrice that they were real, feeling compelled to make the truth sound more convincing than the lies. On the third evening he came home for dinner and sat around with Beatrice afterward. She seemed a bit distant but not angry.

"You don't have to make excuses," she said. "I know how it is. You're busy. I don't expect you to stay home every night keeping me entertained."

"It's nice staying home," he said. And then added: "It's been a hectic stretch—these past few weeks."

"I know," she said, and he realized she did know.

She went no further, but the message was clear: she would be willing to give him time to get it out of his system, to bring his little affair to a civilized conclusion, and even, if that was the problem, to make up his mind which way he intended to go. There would be no need for recriminations, but she'd appreciate his being good enough to decide what the hell he thought was going on.

Fair enough, God knows. More than fair.

He made love to Beatrice that night, and she took it as a sign. Afterward, she pressed close until she fell asleep, leaving him listening open-eyed to her soft breaths and thinking, for the first time, of the foolishness of hoping to change your life without changing your life.

Olivia called the next afternoon, back from New York. Could he make it to the suite early? She had grand news.

He let himself in with his key at a little after five, the earliest he could get away from the office, and was startled to find her asleep on the bed, her face in solemn repose. He did not move. Her clothes lay on the chair; her hair was spread against the pillow as if blown and then allowed to set. Her legs were stretched straight down, but as he watched she slowly raised one knee until that leg formed a graceful triangle behind the other, the hair at her groin ruffling delicately against the moving thigh.

He would have liked, tenderly, to make love without disturbing her, bringing her a contentment not limited by her consciousness of it. It seemed now as if all along she'd been waiting for some kind of assurance from him, some revelation. She'd tried very hard to be good for him, to help him; now her nakedness seemed to indicate how fragile and complicated that concern was. Not consciously, and certainly not selfishly, she'd really been crying out for him, somehow, to save her. *See; this is how it's done,* was what she'd been saying by her generosity, what maybe everybody said through even their most decent gestures. *Now, please, do the same for me.*

He sat on the bed and put his hand over hers; she moaned softly and moved her head. Her eyes snapped open. She smiled dreamily. "You're here."

"Have you been waiting long?"

"I was tired. I thought I'd nap." Without moving her head she glanced down at her body, and looked up to smile again. "Stripped for action. In case you couldn't restrain yourself after three whole days."

"How are you? You sounded great over the phone."

"I feel great." She swung her legs around and sat up and kissed him, then laughed, wide awake now. "I was so excited the whole time back there I hardly slept a wink. It was fantastic, Justin. I had an absolute ball." She placed one hand under his chin and tilted his head back to look into his face.

He rested his hand, softly, on the inside swell of her thigh.

"It's been days and days," she said.

They made love as a kind of celebration of her return, her triumph in faraway lands. It was a good moment; for once she didn't seem to be straining for an exuberance that simply would not materialize. *Easy,* he would sometimes whisper to her. *Don't try so hard.* But this time she glowed with assurance.

Afterward she told him about New York, and he tried to share her elation.

"All those people are regulars," she explained. "They all know each other, and it was really marvelous making them sit up and take notice. Suddenly, here was somebody they had to contend with, this woman from nowhere, with some sort of mysterious commission behind her. Here was somebody who was going to have to be watched in the future."

"I'm sure they were watching from the minute you showed up."

"I wore my most smashing outfit to make sure. I got a kick out of turning them around, making them look at me another way."

He waited for the right moment, not wanting to ruin through some final clumsiness what had been so good those few weeks.

She spoke the next evening of Sylvester; she mentioned him often, unaware, it seemed, of how little Justin said in response.

"What I can't understand," he said, "is why you're so quick to boost Sylvester but absolutely refuse to give Ruel the least benefit of the doubt."

She stiffened. "I really don't see the comparison. You can't lump those two together." And then, more softly: "Ruel makes it awfully hard to like him. I really admire you for sticking with him, but I just can't warm up to that guy—not with the looks he gives me, not with the things he says."

"You can't write people off. I'm just not sure enough of my own virtue to want to put a rope around someone else's neck."

"For God's sake, Justin—I'm not suggesting you *execute* him!"

"You're suggesting I ignore him, because he lacks the social graces, and all that cheer and easy wit you like so much in Sylvester."

"C'mon now. Sylvester's got as much right to bitch about his deal as Ruel does. The difference is Sylvester's come out with some ambition and understanding. It hasn't just turned him mean and spiteful."

"Maybe Ruel would like to be different."

"He could try harder then."

"To be like Sylvester?"

"Admit it: it'd be an improvement."

226

That evening he drove out to Zero's; they had important matters to discuss, Zero had told him. The argument with Olivia had left him out of sorts, and the prospect of a few hours with Zero didn't do much to cheer him up.

As sodden as ever, Zero spoke of some new and exciting project he had in mind, involving what he called the "ultimate disposition" of the art work that Olivia was overseeing for him. "You know Miss Cowan . . . do you not?" Zero inquired without, so far as Justin could tell, any irony. It was close to ten o'clock and Zero spoke heavily and slowly, with that excruciating deadness of tone, his voice thickening through some deep congestion.

"Yes," Justin said. "She worked on the campaign."

"Of course," Zero said. He went on then to talk of the help he wanted from Justin in his new venture, but always with the coyness that he enjoyed so much whenever he discussed his plans, staring into his smoky bourbon as if searching for even more ingenious and mystifying phrases.

"Exactly what am I supposed to do with those paintings?"

"Nothing. Not yet. I am just . . . preparing."

"Isn't Miss Cowan taking care of them?"

"Your responsibility will be different. I need you both. You are . . . an expert too."

"In art?"

"You will have other . . . obligations."

"Sweeping out?" Justin said. "Screwing in picture hooks?"

"You are always joking," Zero said. "But you should view them . . . at your leisure. You should become familiar . . . with the items."

He rambled on then in great self-serving effusiveness, but coyly, coyly, in circles and figure eights, loops and curlicues, drunk enough to wax poetic but not so drunk (never so drunk) as to reveal one more detail than he wished. "It is not yet time. But the time is near. And when it comes . . . I will need your help. When it comes . . . we will clasp hands. We will aim . . . for the stars."

Zero got himself pretty fired up and almost fell out of his chair swiping at the little maid, who pranced out of reach, balancing her upraised tray with impressive dexterity. Zero settled back then, catching his breath, and regaled Justin once more with the old sad song, Zeronski's long and mournful saga, proving again that reality lost something in the translation, that a thin line indeed separated the pure poetry of tragedy from unadulterated bullshit. "I'm a man who's known prejudice . . . hatred. I'm a man who's known . . . homelessness and despair. . . ."

Those glorious rolling phrases, drowning in bourbon and self-pity: Justin was hardly listening, and looked up abruptly when he realized Zero had stopped.

Zero was eying him with glazed sadness. "Justin. It is not for me . . . to intrude."

Justin stared at him uncertainly.

"Miss Cowan . . ."

"What?"

"The future . . . I want only . . . to help . . ."

"What are you talking about?"

"For your own good," Zero said. "For everyone's . . . good."

Justin was on his feet, blazing. "Who asked you for advice? What the hell business is it of yours?"

He left in a fury, and seethed, clenching his teeth, on the drive back. He was enraged at himself for not having settled everything with Olivia before Zero had the chance to come blundering in.

By the time he got back to town the irresolution that had dogged him for days was gone. He wouldn't move a moment sooner because of what Zero had said, but wouldn't hesitate an extra moment either. He'd agonized over it long enough, and had no reason, or right, to postpone it any longer.

It was clear to him that he could never truly satisfy her. He was not a saint, and could not be; he had never been to the mountaintop, possessed no dreams that could not be put into words, had no inhuman enemies dedicated to his destruction, had no visions awesome enough to enrapture her. He dealt, as she still refused to acknowledge, only in the lower, steadier orders of virtue.

Was everybody expecting miracles from him? Maybe you asked for it, sticking yourself up on a platform and milking the crowd for cheers.

Only Sylvester seemed willing to accept him as he was. Ruel wanted goodies by the bushelful. Zero wanted support and enthusiasm, and a kind of blessing for every scheme he came up with. Beatrice was better, of course; Beatrice asked less of him than anyone.

Olivia demanded the most of all, not for herself but for him. She didn't seem this way with other people. She could deal with Zero and Ruel, both of whom she heartily disliked, and with Sylvester, whom she admired with a special warmth, because all of them confirmed her exacting vision of them. Justin alone kept disappointing her in a way that distressed both of them; he could never become marvelous enough to satisfy her without first being weak enough to give in to her.

"It's very nice," he said, looking at the painting she'd brought back from New York, the sign of her triumph. The painting *was* nice, soft and delicate and finely done, but it was the place itself that stole the show. The place was incredible. Who else but Zero would buy a metal building to protect his treasures and then, just to make sure, put bars across the blackened windows and install four locks and a safety alarm?

"We could go," he said to Olivia after she wrapped the tarp around the painting and placed it back in the rack. He was anxious to leave, to talk to her.

She seemed equally determined to stay, knowing by then what was coming. "Maybe if you understand and I understand we ought to just leave it at that, and not muddy things up." She was smiling, almost lighthearted, trying hard to mock his seriousness. "We could make love here," she said.

Eventually they did, in a dark corner of the metal room, practically under the racks of paintings, Zero's treasure trove. He made love to her without restraint. He had always been gentle because he felt that was what she most wanted, and found hardest to accept. *Easy,* he would tell her. *Take it easy.* But this time, the last time, he clawed frantically at her, forced the breath from her, his own breath harsh and loud, because it seemed the only way he could make love to her in that place and at that moment, and because, this last time, she seemed to want it that way.

And then, eventually, they got to the restaurant, and then, without having discussed anything, all his painful rehearsals useless, they said good-by to each other under the sidewalk canopy, he waiting for the attendant to bring his car, she walking away alone in that tall and graceful and determined manner that made her seem always committed to some sure destination, even when she was not walking away from, or toward, anything.

He'd seen her a few times after that, although never alone. He would look up at a party, startled, and see her face. Beatrice would be with him, because she made a point of going places with him now. Things were better between them. Things were as good as they'd ever been, as real and substantial and inevitable as anything in his life would ever be.

Olivia always seemed more relaxed than he. She could even chat pleasantly with Beatrice, who didn't know but maybe suspected. For him, it was always a shock seeing her. He would stand in the middle of someone's living room, clinging to a glass, and envision the woman beneath those shimmering clothes, beneath that incredible self-assurance. It was an odd sensation, looking at her as a stranger would. At one party she wore a pale blue cocktail dress that made her seem even more cool and certain than ever, and he wanted to cry out *No! I know that woman! She's not like that at all!*

She called once, at the office. She was still troubled about working for Zero, and wanted to know if Justin had done anything yet about the art collection.

"No," he told her. "I still don't even know what I'm supposed to do."

He didn't learn until some weeks later, during another dreary visit to Zero's house on the hilltop, and another narration of bourbon-soaked woe that finally came to its point:

"It is up to those of us . . . who have suffered . . . who have known hatred and bigotry . . . to help others . . . rise above . . . their deprivations . . ."

Zero wanted to transfer all the paintings to an irrevocable trust. The Zeronski Foundation. Eventually, when market conditions were most favorable, they would be sold to provide not only scholarship aid, but education and training at all levels for blacks and other minorities. He wanted Justin to handle the details, to make sure everything was done properly.

"That's quite a move," Justin said.

"It is what . . . I have always aimed for . . . my lifelong ambition. . . ."

It was no doubt true. The problem in dealing with Zero wasn't his vulgarity and greed. The problem was his refusal to be *exclusively* vulgar and greedy. He had to keep messing up things in your mind with fitful bursts of unabashed generosity.

Maybe that was the answer, the way to keep everything manageable and reassuring: people ought to find a place to stand, and stand there, instead of squirming away every time you thought you finally had them pinned down.

Sylvester and Ruel remained close. They were almost always together, the incident with the knife apparently forgotten. For a while, earlier, Ruel had begun to have second thoughts about the store-front group. They weren't, he'd complain, interested in *doing* anything. But he stayed with them and became one of Sylvester's big helpers on the dental clinic, and Justin felt encouraged.

No one, though, could match Sylvester's dedication. The clinic was his baby, and he worked on it in a kind of sustained euphoria.

"But what the hell is it," Justin taunted, "if it isn't politics?"

"It ain't politics," Sylvester said.

"Sure it is. It's managing the best you can with the means at hand. It's forgetting, for the moment, the vaster philosophical questions in order to get a few aching cavities filled."

"You're stretching."

"No," Justin said. "Planning and running something like that—those are political acts. Even the goals are political."

"It's only," Sylvester said, "that when the big day comes, we're gonna need good strong teeth to help us prevail."

"Are you hoping to smile your way into the halls of power?"

"The temples of sin, man."

"Beating off the moneylenders with toothbrushes?"

"Now you got it," Sylvester said.

The bomb came as a shock. Justin had in no way been prepared for that. He heard it over the radio, then read about it in the paper, struggling to come to grips with it, going back over things in his mind and working his way forward again, trying to reach different conclusions from the first one that had come to him.

"Only I ain't got the bread," Sylvester said when he appeared at the office, looking not at all worried. Nor did he seem to notice how worried Justin looked. "So if you're willing to take me on, I guess it's gonna have to be gratis. Again."

"You're turning into a steady customer."

"That ain't hardly my fault. I don't start these things, just to give you business."

"Convince me," Justin said when Sylvester, with a shrug, declared his innocence.

"Ask my mamma. She was home with me."

"Sure," Justin said. "That'll do it. A mother proclaiming her only son's innocence."

Sylvester had two suggestions. The first was Zero. The other was the barber himself, whose business had been going to pot for years, with the whites moving away and the blacks going elsewhere to get their Afros shaped.

"Those are a couple of great choices. A guy blowing up his own shop, or a guy blowing up a piece of his own building. You know, if I were a cop, I'd lean toward another explanation."

"Me."

"That's right."

"Only you ain't a cop, and I didn't do it."

"You're sure now? I mean, you didn't one day just decide to take care of all that business, the barber hassling you and everything, once and for all, and meanwhile knock a little chunk out of one of Zero's buildings, just for good measure?"

"No," Sylvester said. "I told you that."

"Okay," Justin said finally. "We'll see what we can do. Assuming you're telling me the truth."

"I'm telling the truth. But look, it wasn't my idea. The lady practically pushed me through the door."

Justin raised his eyes. "I thought you just wandered by."

"Actually, she drove me over."

"If they pick you up, you get one call. Call me. Meanwhile, I'll check around a bit, if that's okay."

"Feel real free," Sylvester said, getting up with a smile. His sunglasses had slid down his nose, and he guided them back up with an extended index finger.

Budd Huddleston didn't even want to let him in, but finally relented, looking as if he feared Justin would yank open a closet and discover the neatly pressed white sheet and eyehole hood draped over a hanger. Nor was he delighted to learn who Justin was representing.

"You mean the goddamn kid's got a loier now?"

"He may need one. The police seem pretty interested in him."

"Well, good for them. I'm glad they're interested in something. I'm glad they're at least awake for a change."

"I thought you might have some information that could help us."

"Help who? That kid, that comes around acting like he owns the place? Look, I'll tell you something about that kid, only it ain't gonna help you any. That kid oughta learn to shut up and mind his own business, and not go around threatening people about what he's gonna do to them if he just happens to feel like it."

"I understand you two had a bit of an argument."

"It wasn't no argument. It was threats, if you wanna know what it was."

"And you mentioned this to the police?"

"You're damn right I mentioned it to the police, because it's what happened."

The more obnoxious Huddleston sounded the more Justin had to admit that if anyone could freak out Sylvester sufficiently to make him do something as dumb as blowing up a barbershop, it would be someone like Budd Huddleston.

"Look, enough, all right? I'm sick of talking about it. I said everything I got to say. I said it to the cops and I said it to the goddamn insurance guy. I said it enough times over already that I don't feel like saying it anymore. I just wish the cops, if you want the truth, would get off their butts and do their job for a change."

"Thanks for your time," Justin said.

"After all, he's your boy," Justin said. "He's your only boy."

"That's right," she said.

"If he got in trouble, you'd rush to his aid. If he hurt himself, you'd tend to him. You'd do whatever you were called upon to help him."

"I surely would," she said. "He was a sickly baby. There were times we thought the Lord had marked him just to die."

"I'm not his mamma," Justin said. "But I'm his friend and his lawyer and I'd like very much to help him."

"I believe that. He tells me your name. He tells me everything he does. It makes me feel I know his friends."

"His father's dead, isn't that so?"

"Killed in the war, back when Sylvester was a baby."

"Which war?"

"The Korea war. He was a sergeant. It's the Negroes, you know, who get killed in the wars."

"I'd like to help as much as I can."

"I believe that."

"But you've got to tell me the truth. You don't have to tell anyone else the truth, like the police, or a jury, or anyone like that. You might want to clam up with those people and say nothing, to protect Sylvester. But you can't clam up with me. You've got to tell me the truth."

"I told you the truth."

"He was here every minute that night? You swear to that before God?"

"I swear it before God."

"If I believe you, and it's not the truth, it's going to cause a lot of heartache for people, and most of all for Sylvester."

"It's the truth. I swear it before God."

"I'll do the best I can for him," Justin said.

"We thank you for that. We're all grateful for your help."

He got in touch with Trow. It was nice enough to discover that his doting mother, at least, still retained an unshakable faith in Sylvester's innocence, but Justin couldn't quite bring himself to share it, and figured he might as well learn the worst, and sooner rather than later. "Let me know what you find," he told Trow. "Keep in touch."

But then Sylvester had to illustrate his social conscience by

234

slicing up a cop who afterward, or right before, or at precisely the same instant, demonstrated his enthusiasm for crisp law enforcement by blowing Sylvester's brains out.

That afternoon then became the perfect time for an even better than average variety of scolds and malcontents to wander in with their complaints. Some woman who didn't like the way they taught algebra in the high school; some man who wanted two or three hours of free advice on filing dissolution papers, so he could get rid of his wife without having to pay some shyster lawyer for the privilege; and finally, right before he had to leave for the mayor's meeting, even the old guy, stiff-jointed in his dandy's suit, smirking and wincing behind his white beard, who'd managed to luck through the bomb and now felt solemnly anointed as guardian of the late Sylvester Childs' good name and reputation.

The guy wasn't even that bad. His heart was no doubt in the right place. Justin had simply had it, and his patience was gone.

"It means maybe if I were Sylvester, and grew up where he did, and how he did, and took all the guff he did, I might feel I had some pretty good reasons to blow up a few places too. Maybe I'd even feel justified in going after a cop with a dental tool, if he was going to tear down the clinic I'd spent all that time and sweat building up."

It didn't make the man feel any better, and didn't do much to cheer up Justin either, but that was all he had now, and he'd have to make the best of it. He just wished the hell Sylvester could have managed to stay away from the barber, and from Zero, and from whoever or whatever had introduced him to the intricacies of bomb making, and finally and most of all, from those two cops who came into the room after him with their hands slapped to their holsters.

After the meeting with the mayor and Zero and all their friends at City Hall, Justin walked one block down the street and around the corner to police headquarters, on the chance that Amicus might be working late. He was.

Amicus drained the last of his coffee and, after studying the residue briefly, tossed the plastic cup into his wastebasket. "What are you coming to me for? I thought the chief was supposed to fill you all in at the big meeting."

Justin made a face. Amicus knew what Justin thought of the chief, and Justin knew what Amicus thought. It was one of the tenuous confidences they shared.

"What the hell happened at the clinic this afternoon?"

"That's a good question," Amicus said.

"I mean, it's one thing to sign out a warrant. Killing him is something else."

Amicus leaned forward for his pen and twirled it slowly, the fingers of his right hand flicking. He was very good at it. "You want to know what I think? I think maybe two grown cops should've been able to get that kid out in one piece, and without anybody having his belly cut open. That's what I think."

"Good," Justin said.

"Only I went over there, you know. I checked things out. The kid was shot once, and believe me, that one shot did it. He was dead the minute the trigger clicked. So the only way he could have cut up that cop was before the shot was fired. Before any shot was fired."

"You know what? Even with a dental tool handy, most people wouldn't attack a couple of armed policemen without at least a little provocation."

"Maybe you're wrong about that."

"I think I'm right," Justin said.

Amicus shrugged. "That's why I'm not a politician. I lack that fine sense of my own infallibility."

"When you issued that warrant, did you make a point about how dangerous he was? Did you get those cops all hopped up expecting trouble from him?"

"I didn't expect trouble. He struck me as a guy who wouldn't go at a fly. Of course, I was wrong. Still, I wish the hell they hadn't popped him. I'd a lot rather still have him running the local crazies than some of the others we've had. Now we'll probably end up with a certified Mau Mau, who'll start issuing blowguns to all the street freaks."

"Did you have proof on the bomb?"

"Bombs are hard to prove. Bombs, in general, if you want my

honest feeling, are a nuisance. They kill people and wreck the furniture and leave a mess for the cleanup crew."

"What was it? Were you just ready to throw him to the lions?"

"The lions gotta eat too. Only look, don't jump on me because we were picking him up. I had my doubts from the beginning."

"About what?"

"About him being our man."

Justin stared. "What'd you want him for then?"

"C'mon. We had enough stuff, Christ knows. He'd been hassling the barber and the barber was filing complaints all over the place. They hated each other's guts. Besides, what the hell was he doing up on a roof for a whole afternoon? Taking a traffic survey? Or maybe studying cloud formations. Cumulus, nimbus, and—I can never remember that other one. Anyhow, you know how it is. Everybody else around here just figured he was the guy, and I didn't have much to make an argument with."

"Do you now?"

Amicus shrugged. "I'm still looking into a few things."

"Jesus Christ. You mean you don't think Sylvester did it?"

"I never did."

"This is a hell of a time to say so."

"If he hadn't been so quick to go at that cop, it wouldn't be such a bad time."

"Jesus Christ," Justin said.

Amicus said nothing.

"What was it? Did you just decide you liked his looks? Did you take a fancy to his style or something?"

"If I started liking people it might interfere with my professional judgment, and screw up the orderly process of justice."

"Cut the shit. What did you really think of him?"

"I thought he ought to remove those glasses when he came in out of the sun."

He went home for dinner and found Trow patiently waiting for him in the living room.

"God damn it," he yelled when Trow removed a little plastic Baggie from his pocket, containing a few bits of colored insulation and some shreds of copper wire. "Anybody could have planted this stuff in his room."

237

Trow squinted at him from behind his bottle-thick lenses. "I thought that's what you wanted. I thought you were interested in clearing your client."

"God damn it," Justin said.

"What's the problem?" Trow asked. "Were you interested in clearing his friend too?"

That wasn't even the worst of it. Trow saved the worst for last.

"Someone else had been there," he said.

"Who?"

"No way to tell. But not amateurs."

"Are you positive?"

"They were good enough at it to leave something behind for me. They didn't want to clean things up too much or it'd look suspicious."

"Maybe it was Ruel himself."

"I don't think so," Trow said. "It was professionals."

The landlady answered the phone and said Ruel wasn't in.

"Are you sure? Could you check?"

"I'm sure," she said. "He ain't in."

"Do you know where he is?"

"No."

"Do you know when he'll be back?"

"I didn't even see him go. I can't keep track of everybody."

"Would you leave him a note? Tell him it's urgent. Say it's very important."

He couldn't think of anywhere else to call. Where did Ruel spend his time anyhow? What did he do with himself all day?

He told Beatrice, who'd been holding dinner, that he'd better skip it. She was put out and he explained.

"I can't say I'm surprised," she said. "That guy gave me the creeps from the beginning."

They haven't all been like this, he wanted to tell her. They haven't all taken me for a jerk. Some of them were real successes. Some of them were great.

He drove onto the campus and parked alongside the gym and went inside to check the basketball court. Some students were playing pickup, and one said he thought Ruel had been around earlier. He wasn't sure. He didn't know where he might have gone.

Justin drove into the West Side and pulled to the curb in front of the house: Ruel's third-floor windows were dark. He drove to the store front: it was padlocked. He couldn't think of any other possibilities.

The streets were practically deserted, except for the cops, some in cruisers, some moving along warily on foot. Waiting for the riot to begin.

Maybe that'd be the logical place to look for Ruel, hip-deep in chaos and disorder. Besides, Justin had promised the mayor: he was supposed to walk around, keep an eye on things, stay calm, try to spread that calm around like oily salve, try to keep the natives from burning down buildings and the cops from turning the occasion into open hunting season. All those rational and responsible things expected of him as a rational and responsible man, an elected official, a believer, a man who distrusted fanatics and disapproved of frenzy as a public stance and had, more or less of his own free will, joined the forces of domestic tranquillity.

Just as, with equally free will, he'd decided to represent a guy who'd got his head shot off, and play big brother to another—who only needed a few kind words and a couple of decent breaks to blossom forth like a rose—who for one reason or another then decided to turn a barbershop into a shambles.

But you weren't supposed to lose hope. That's what your parents, your teachers, everybody, taught you when you were dewy-eyed and impressionable: that doughty Franklinesque belief in piety, good sense, and charity, and all the sweet profit that accumulated upon those who tried and tried again, and never for an instant doubted the evenhanded nature of God's beneficence.

In truth he wouldn't mind a little noise. He wouldn't mind seeing something broken, hearing an occasional shout, a few obscenities, watching a couple of bricks whistle through the air. Riots, after all, were standard fare from way back and no speciality of any country or age. They were the gritty raisins in the cake. Or better, the odd piece of nutshell that every so often you had to expect to crack a tooth on. You couldn't fault those

239

scroungy kids in the West Side for wanting to smash everything in sight. And Sylvester's death wasn't the reason. It was the excuse. If riots were caused by reasons, there'd be one every day.

He stopped at a corner phone booth to see if Ruel had called in yet to the answering service. He hadn't.

Four cops were stationed outside the grocery store that had been designated, God knows why, as field headquarters. A couple of large police vans were parked at the curb, containing, he assumed, stacks of visored helmets and riot batons. The chief was nowhere to be seen, but a half dozen captains and lieutenants were lounging about near the detergent shelf. A coffee urn stood on the counter next to the cash register; a tube of nestled Styrofoam cups, white plastic spoons, a box of neat sugar cubes, a jar of CoffeeMate. The atmosphere hardly seemed charged. Phil Ryder, the city's highest elected official, was leaning against the ice-cream freezer joking with a reporter from the *Citizen-Times*.

Phil Ryder saw Justin and came over. The reporter remained behind, busying himself checking the flavors through the plastic top.

"How's it look out there?"

"It looks fine," Justin said. "It's a lovely night."

"The quietest of the year, if you ask me. We haven't even had an arrest. We haven't even had a lost dog. Coffee?"

Justin poured himself a cup from the urn.

"There's doughnuts somewhere too. What the hell, are they all gone already? These friggin' cops eat like there's no tomorrow."

The cops laughed.

"We'll have to swipe another box off the shelves," the mayor said and the cops laughed again. Then he looked over at the reporter and said to Justin, with a motion of his head, "Let me show you something in back."

Justin followed him past the cold cuts and the loaves of bread into the back room. It was stacked with cartons.

"You were kind of rough on Zero at the meeting, Justin. You didn't give him a break at all."

"I wasn't in much mood to congratulate him on his virtue."

"It wasn't his fault. He doesn't even own the building anymore."

"It wasn't anybody's fault. The kid obviously died from natural causes."

Phil Ryder glanced at the open door leading to the store, then around the back room. That was always a sign—searching for eavesdroppers—that the mayor was about to impart a confidence. "Between you and me, Justin, I'd be a lot happier if the cops could've handled it differently. Only what the hell, the kid started it."

"You don't know who started it. I don't know who started it. The cops don't even know anymore because by this time they've convinced themselves that it happened just the way they said it happened."

"Where the hell does that leave us?"

"It leaves us not knowing who started it."

"They didn't shoot him in the back, you know."

"They shot him in the face."

"I'm trying to level with you, Justin. I know how you feel. I just wish the hell—"

"Okay."

"He's been on the force three months. Sure, he should have played it cooler. But it's a lot easier for us—"

"Okay."

"I went to see him—in the hospital. That's one of the prerogatives of my high office, visiting wounded policemen. Anyhow, the guy's taking it a lot better than I would. You'd like him, Justin. He's very pleasant, and remarkably sane. One of the few sane men I've run into in the course of my official duties."

"Sylvester was also remarkably pleasant and sane."

"Why the hell were they trying to kill each other then?" The mayor shook his head, musing over the wonderment of it all. "Anyhow—this Zero business."

"What about it?"

"You ought to say a decent word. Look, I've been dealing with Zero for a long time. I've got no illusions in his regard. But the first thing he did when he heard what happened was come in and offer us a new clinic. He can afford it of course, but that's not the point. The point is no one else made any offers. No one else even thought about making any."

"Maybe no one else felt pressed."

"What are you talking about?"

"Nothing."

"He likes you, Justin. He's your big booster."

"Part of my vast army of supporters."

"Don't knock that army, Justin. It's done all right by you, and so has Zero. What the hell are you jumping on him for anyway?"

Justin shrugged irritably.

"Okay," the mayor said. "Are you going to wander around now, or just hang on here?"

"I thought I'd go off for a look," Justin said.

"We've got a couple of cops to go with you. We don't want any of your friends mistaking you for just another street-roaming honky."

One cop was white, the other black.

Justin checked in again with the answering service and then began walking the streets in their company. They were young and healthy and as unobtrusive as possible for two armed men in crackling blue uniforms and four-inch-wide cartridge belts.

"We're looking for the goddamn riot," Justin muttered after a while. "Where the hell's the goddamn riot?"

"It's pretty quiet now, sir," the white patrolman responded.

"So it is," Justin said.

And so it was. There were other cops around, and now and again he'd spot a civilian getting in or out of a parked car, or peeking cautiously from behind a door. The police were stopping everybody, explaining the situation, advising them to return home. Most people, obviously, already were at home, behind a couple of locks and watching TV or listening to the radio for the bulletins that would tell them what, if anything, was really happening. To them. The West Side was holed up waiting for news of the West Side.

It was all paralysis, nerveless and static, as if a whole population of vigorous high-spirited people had been drugged to numbness by some odd sweet scent in the night air.

It left him in a foul and unforgiving mood. He felt a million miles from everything, as if that godawful day had finally come when no one read anymore the books you used to curl up with for a whole afternoon, or knew the names of the ballplayers and movie stars you assumed would be famous forever. The Empire State Building wasn't even the tallest in the world anymore, and what the hell could you make of that? The tabs in the soda fountain jukeboxes bore the names of Martians, and your heroes had so long ago been shot dead that they weren't people anymore but junior high schools and football stadiums. He'd met John Kennedy once, during the 1960 campaign, when Justin was one of the whiz kids on the state committee. A few of them were taken up to Kennedy's hotel suite but there was a delay; the senator was taking a bath. He appeared in a robe, barefoot, his face ruddier than Justin had imagined, and chatted easily with them. After that it had to do something to your perceptions when you could pull from your pocket a shiny fifty-cent coin of the realm engraved with his unreal likeness. But we hadn't even started, you wanted to protest. Where did everybody go? How did the world suddenly get taken over by Rotarians?

They decided they deserved a break, Justin and his two escorts, and sat on the stone steps of an old brownstone for a smoke. Why'd they ever become cops? Justin inquired. What was the lure for a couple of clean-cut young guys like themselves? (As pleasant, surely, and probably as sane, as their compatriot in the hospital.)

The black cop said he'd been on the force two years, and it'd been a revelation. Sitting on the dark steps, dragging on his cigarette, he went through the list in a low steady voice. The battered children. The derelicts in alleys. Husbands going at wives, or vice versa, with knives, clubs, hunting rifles, weed whips. Eleven-year-old girls raped. Women flying through windshields to end up splattered on the pavement. A guy shot seven times and stuffed into the trunk of his car. A baby wrapped in the Sunday paper and suffocating to death in a garbage can. "But nobody thinks about that part of it. Nobody smiles at a cop. Especially around here. Especially if he happens to be one of the brothers."

"That's not true," the white one said. "They're glad to see you often enough. And I'll tell you something. They're even glad to see me sometimes."

"We ain't out to bust heads," the black one said.

"Where'd they be without cops?" the white one said. "I'd like to see a vote on that, on everybody doing their own dirty work. And if they voted no cops, that'd be okay with me. I'd give them a week then, to see how fast they came crawling back."

"Who did this?" Justin said.

The sergeant shrugged.

Justin stepped inside, avoiding the shards of glass on the floor. The sergeant came behind him, followed by Justin's two escorts. The sergeant played his flashlight beam slowly around the big room, the shadows lurching as the glare slid across overturned tables and broken chairs, a smashed mimeograph machine, toppled cases of empty pop bottles, scattered papers and pamphlets.

"How'd they get in? Through the window?"

"Looks like it," the sergeant said.

"I'm surprised they didn't just burn it down."

"I think maybe they were planning to. But some officers discovered them and—"

"Did they arrest anyone?"

"No, sir. They escaped before they could be apprehended."

"This is the only damage I've seen tonight."

"I haven't seen anything else either," the sergeant said. He moved the beam again, scanning the walls, then abruptly brought it back to the large sepia poster, so that Justin could study the gigantic enlargement of his own face smiling down with enthusiasm and hope and sure-fire vote-getting confidence:

The Time Is Now!
JUSTIN GAGE!

"Okay," Justin said. "Let's go."

He was more than willing to write it off as coincidence, a gang of kids happening upon a dark store front and thinking, *This would be a good place*. Otherwise, it had to be the cops themselves, fixing those smart-ass niggers once and for all. Or else, this the least happy possibility, some real straight Toms from down the block, who didn't want Sylvester and his gang of gonchos giving the neighborhood a bad name.

That covered just about everything: random chance for the wandering kids, revenge for the cops, and something you could call self-destructive fastidiousness for the Toms. Only what about avarice? What about stupidity and ambition and pure innate viciousness? What about all the various forms and shades of irrationality? The world offered a cornucopia of possibilities, with no end to the list of villainies—to say nothing of the virtues, all those good and noble reasons that could have provided a starting point way back somewhere, and were as likely of leaving a mess behind as any of the standard corruptions.

Maybe they'd voted for him, whoever they were, having their own reasons for that as surely as they did for smashing up the store front. Maybe, Christ knows, they were the same reasons.

He used a corner phone booth to check in with his answering service. Ruel still had not called back, but there was a message from Olivia.

"She wanted me to tell you it was very important," the girl said.

"If she calls again, tell her I'll get back to her as soon as I can."

He hung up and dialed the landlady again.

"Oh yes," she said. "He's here now."

"Did he get the message? Why didn't he call?"

"I don't know. Do you want me to get him now?"

"No," Justin said. "I'll drop by. You don't have to say anything."

He told his escorts he was going home. They seemed reluctant to let him out of their clutches. "Nothing's going to happen," he said. "You people have everything nicely under control."

Ruel lived on Seventh, not in one of the larger brick buildings, layered with generations of grime, but in an equally dismal shingle and clapboard frame house that had, ages ago, been converted to rentals. Ruel's third-floor room was part of what used to be the attic. It was always, Ruel complained, either too hot or too cold.

The second-floor hallway had a small light; the third floor was dark. Justin knocked, and Ruel, after asking who it was, and asking again, and taking his time even then, finally opened the door.

Ruel wore tire-tread sandals and a red tennis-net sport shirt. Lean as a whippet, his stomach flat and hard; he still looked as if he'd just got his growth, springing up overnight and not yet used to his height; his eyes blinking in confusion, surprise, resentment; trusting no one in his awkwardness.

"Hey," Ruel said quietly, his eyes steadying. He still had one hand on the doorknob, enveloping it.

"I called before," Justin said. "I left a message."

"Oh yeah," Ruel said. "Yeah."

"Can I come in?"

"Sure," Ruel said without emphasis. "Come on in." He closed the door behind Justin.

The room was large and square, the walls a claustrophobic green. An open door led to a small bathroom, a closed door to a closet. The bed was made, the covers stretched tight. The blaring TV faced the bed, away from Justin. Ruel had one worn armchair, a dresser, a wooden chair; the furniture came with the apartment. The room was very neat, with no dirty clothes lying around, no newspapers or soiled paper plates; just one well-scuffed basketball on the floor next to the bed. Maybe that was the argument for getting them young; it taught them neatness, all those cell checks at all those institutions. Although he hadn't cleaned up that good. If he'd really done the job, vacuumed the floor and emptied the trash can, Trow wouldn't have found anything, and neither would the cops.

"What's up?" Ruel asked. He talked loud over the TV.

Justin shrugged.

"Hey, you been out there? What's happening? I keep waiting for the big noise."

"It's pretty quiet," Justin said.

"Well—sit down. I mean, you staying?"

Justin walked to the TV, coming up from behind it, and reached over the top to snap it off, looking down as the distorted picture shrank to a glowing dot. He straightened up and looked at Ruel, who was standing in front of the dresser. He had to raise his eyes just slightly to meet Ruel's.

"Sure," Ruel said. "I wasn't even watching."

Justin sat in the armchair.

Ruel remained standing. "You mean nothing at all's going on out there? I figured there'd be at least something." He shrugged. "That was a real shit deal."

"What?"

"Sylvester. They oughta get it for that. Somebody should've really ripped some things up."

"Why don't you sit down?"

"I'm all right," Ruel said.

"Sit down," Justin said.

Ruel hesitated, then went to the bed. It ran the long way against the wall, between windows. Ruel sat in the middle, leaning against the wall. He hooked his heels over the frame with his toes up, showing the chunky tire treads of his sandals. His knees were pointed high, his arms angled down to the mattress with his hands outstretched flat against it. "What's the big occasion?"

"Why'd you do it?" Justin said.

Ruel's eyes moved; he glanced around the room, as if reassuring himself that it was the same place, that nothing had changed. "What're you talking about?" He blinked. He couldn't seem to decide what expression he wanted.

"I'm interested," Justin said. "Tell me."

"Hey, man. C'mon." Ruel's eyes flitted to the open bathroom door, then to the wooden chair.

"Don't come at me," Justin said. "Don't take anything in your hand and try to come at me."

Ruel took a breath. "I been fucked over by a lot of people. You gonna try now? You gonna take your turn?"

"You haven't answered my question."

Ruel wet his lips. "You wanna know something? You're flying around up in the clouds. You're not even making sense."

"Give me an answer."

Ruel's eyes changed. He laughed abruptly. "Hey, you know what, man? You wanna hear something? I'll tell you, I went out before. Just to see what the hell was going on, where all the noise was. And I saw this goddamn cop getting out of the goon car. He got out and the other one, not the driver, stayed inside writing something in his book. What it was, the guy hadda take a leak, only he didn't see me. So he spread out, you know, nice and comfy, and whips out the old joint, up against this house there, right on the next block. *Go piss on your own house!* I yelled. That really blew his mind. I just took off then and the guy, you know, he didn't even bother coming after me, what with it flapping in the breeze like that."

Justin said nothing.

Ruel's face sobered. "Hey, man." He spoke softly: a friend, a confidant. "What's going on here? What's the deal? I mean, you never came at me before."

"I want to know why you put that bomb there," Justin said.

Ruel was quiet a moment. "What is it—you playing games with me?" He studied Justin heavily, then pressed his lips forward into a pout. His features changed with startling quickness. He became very businesslike. "Okay. I ain't gonna shit you. Only look, you can figure that out. The guy was asking for it. He was giving us a bad time."

"The barber?"

"The barber. I mean, what we had there was a clinic. We were fixing kids' teeth, for Christ sake. What the hell was he giving us a bad time for?"

"I don't know."

"Well, he was asking for it." Ruel's eyes moved. "So all right, maybe I shouldn't of. Only I never figured they'd jump on Sylvester like that. You know what it was, don't you? They were out for him. That's what I didn't even know. How bad the cops were out for him."

"Did you give any thought to what'd happen if they caught you? Or were you looking forward to a reunion with your old buddies at Cheney?"

"Don't tell me about Cheney, okay? I know all about Cheney."

"You must have thought about it then."

"What am I supposed to do? Have a goddamn sign on the wall that says *Think* all the time? I think about things, all right? I think about as many goddamn things as you do."

"Did you ask the others to help out?"

"There was nobody to ask. Nobody was ready to go that route. Like Sylvester, you know, he didn't have the first clue. You know how he is. He just wanted to talk about it for six months. He didn't wanna *do* anything."

"What about the money?"

"What money?"

"Zero's money."

Ruel frowned. Then he smiled, he laughed. "C'mon. Is that what you're worried about? Shit, man, you're the one that set it up. Don't you even remember? You're the one that *got* me the money in the first place."

"Not that money. The other money."

"What other money? There wasn't any other money."

"Sure there was."

Ruel didn't react. Then he looked around again, at the dresser, the open door to the bathroom.

"Don't try anything," Justin said.

Ruel seemed surprised. He might even have been mildly offended. Then he laughed, stretching his legs out and shifting around to sit on the edge of the bed. He bent forward, long and supple, not an inch of fat rolling up beneath the tennis-net spaces of his shirt. "You know what's the trouble? I see the trouble now. You got a piece of the story, and then somebody piled a lot of shit on top of that one little piece. We gotta straighten this out, man. We gotta get together on this and get back on the track."

"Okay," Justin said.

"I'm glad you came now. I can see where the trouble is now."

"Did Zero pay you extra for the bomb, or was it just part of the regular job?"

Ruel stared at him. He sighed. "That's the bullshit part, I'm telling you. That's the part you wanna forget about. You ain't listening."

"I'm listening."

"Who's been piling this on you? The lady?"

"What's she got to do with it?"

"That's what I'd like to know."

"I had a private detective look into it."

"You what?"

"He told me some things I didn't know."

"He told you a lot of shit. That's what he told you."

"He paid you a little visit here, only you weren't home at the time."

Ruel pulled his head back slowly, his long sinewy neck tightening. He looked around the room, trying to figure out if anything was missing, anything disturbed.

"What difference does it make?" Justin said. "You already said you did it. We already agreed on that. Next time just clean up better. Especially those little shreds of copper wire, and the plastic insulation with all the pretty colors. Of course maybe you were just fixing a lamp or something. But the real problem isn't that my man found the stuff. Someone else got here even before him. Maybe you can think of someone besides the cops who'd want to come looking around in here, but I can't."

Ruel jumped up, his arms loose. He glared down at Justin but made no move. Justin stood up slowly, giving Ruel plenty of time to make a move, all the time in the world, and then reached forth slowly and placed one hand on Ruel's chest, feeling the narrow bones. Ruel still did not move. Justin pushed hard, as hard as he could, getting his shoulder behind it and sending Ruel toppling back on the bed, hard, his head cracking against the wall.

"Hey!" Ruel yelled, grabbing the back of his head.

"Come on," Justin said. He wanted to say it calmly but was hardly moving his lips. He tried to control the catch in his voice. "Come at me. Give me an excuse."

Ruel still had his hand cupped over the back of his head. "What the hell's going on?" He removed his hand and stared at it, looking for blood. "What you hauling off at me for?" He lowered his hand slowly. He didn't seem angry, just surprised. In a way he seemed subdued, ready to continue where they left off.

Justin let out a breath. He was still standing, looking down at Ruel on the bed. "There are other people who'd like to take you on too, if they knew some of the things I know."

"What people?"

"Sylvester's friends, for one. Zero, for another. And finally, of course, the cops."

Ruel worked his tongue at one corner of his mouth. He winced and touched again, gingerly, the back of his head. "Christ. You got everything coming at me from sixteen directions at once."

Justin slid the toe of his shoe under the basketball on the floor next to the bed and goosed it straight up in the air and caught it. He hadn't done that in ten years. He twirled the ball casually between his hands and then, not moving his arms but getting all the power from his fingers, shot it as hard as he could at Ruel on the bed. Surprised, Ruel still reacted fast enough to catch it. He held it a moment, then dropped it to the floor and let it roll across the room.

Justin sat down. "Zero's not going to want people knowing about your little arrangements. Money changed hands, after all. Zero's not going to want you running around loose, dragging his name into all this."

Ruel said nothing. He looked down and traced a long straight finger along the bedspread.

"Did Zero pay you extra for the bomb, or was it just part of your regular chores?"

"He paid me," Ruel said after a moment, not looking up. "Extra?"

Ruel raised his eyes. "Extra."

"So it was Zero's idea, not yours?"

"That's right. I did it for him. It was his idea."

"And he paid extra, over and above what you got for school, and over and above what you got for keeping tabs on Sylvester?"

"That's right."

"Christ, you had arrangements all over the place, didn't you? You should have incorporated yourself for the tax breaks, what with all the deals you had going."

Ruel said nothing.

"Did he pay you before or after you blew up the place?"

Ruel's face was rigid. He was concentrating as hard as he could. "Before."

"Did he take care of getting the bomb, or leave that up to you?"

Ruel hesitated. "He left it up to me. It was part of what he was paying for."

Justin shook his head. "No."

"He wanted Sylvester's ass. Everybody knew that. So when he heard about the trouble with the barber he figured he could use it to get Sylvester."

"No," Justin said.

"Whatd'ya mean, no? I'm telling you yes."

"And you went along? For the money?"

"I needed the money."

"Only some guy got killed."

"It went off at the wrong time. It wasn't my fault." He ran his tongue, exploringly, over his lower lip.

"Sylvester was your friend. You were buddies."

"It wasn't exactly buddies."

"So you sold him out."

"If you mean him getting killed, you can forget it. That's just too much shit. I didn't have anything to do with that."

"I'm talking about the bomb."

"I did it for the money. How many times am I supposed to tell you? That's what people do things for. Money. That's how it goes."

"Even if it got Sylvester sent away?"

"I told you. I never figured on that. That's the part you don't understand." He waited, watching Justin. "What I was *really* doing, if you wanna know the truth, was screwing *Zero*, not Sylvester. What the hell would I wanna screw Sylvester for? Besides, I knew how he operated, and never figured the cops would get him. How could they? I mean, he didn't do it. What I figured, to tell the truth, was that you'd make a case out of it right away, like at the Zoning Board, and get him off. I mean, that's how it works. You'd fix it up. You're a lawyer and all. You got connections. So what would happen, I figured, was he'd get off, no matter what, and meanwhile I'd have Zero's money. So the guy getting the shaft was Zero, not Sylvester."

"No," Justin said.

"Fuck this *no* business."

"Zero didn't pay you for any bomb. He paid you for going to school, and then for keeping an eye on Sylvester. But that was it. That was all. Zero wouldn't trust you with a bomb. If Zero wanted a bomb, he'd hire an expert."

Ruel shrugged angrily and twisted around. He bent one leg up and started toying with the strap of his sandal, bending it back and forth, then looked up. "Shit, man. There ain't just up and down, you know. Things are going around too. Things are flying all over the place."

"Where'd you learn to make a bomb anyway? Did you take a course in it? Is that one of the things you learned at Cheney?"

Ruel answered soberly. "I can do things, you know. I can figure things out."

"You're lucky you didn't kill yourself. You couldn't even get it to go off at the right time."

"The clock was *broke,* for Christ's sake."

"What gets me is Zero really thinks Sylvester did it. Since he was paying you to tell him things, I guess he figured he ought to believe you, just to get his money's worth. Except Sylvester got caught in the middle, and ended up dead."

Ruel was silent for a moment, flicking at the sandal strap. "If you really wanna know, I'll tell you what happened. No bullshit." He took a breath and swallowed. His hand was still now. "What it was is, I was playing it very cool, as part of an over-all thing, that was a lot more complicated than you think. That's where you're going wrong. Because I was screwing Zero from the beginning, by not giving him anything for the money he was paying me to watch Sylvester. He never learned a goddamn thing from me. I had him actually going in circles, if you want the truth. I was taking him for a ride."

"So he *didn't* pay you for the bomb?"

"What the hell would he pay me for, when it was just a way of screwing him?"

"You just *said* he paid you for it."

"Only now I'm giving it to you straight. I was out to screw Zero."

"You screwed Sylvester."

"Look. Sylvester's crazy sometimes. I could've told him, you don't go at a cop like that. Only Sylvester figured he was special, and no one was gonna touch him, no matter what he did. So how was that my fault? Because I was involved in something else entirely, and playing it very cool. That's what you gotta understand. Zero thought he was getting all kinds of inside stuff from me, only he wasn't getting a goddamn thing, because I was running him around in circles."

"How?"

"I told you, it's complicated. It ain't always like it looks. But the main thing is I was just taking Zero for a ride."

"What'd the bomb have to do with taking Zero for a ride?"

"Jesus, man, you gotta understand. The bomb didn't have *any*-thing to do with it. The bomb, you see, was part of a different thing entirely because, for one, the goddamn barber was asking for it, and because it was just something to get things *moving*, instead of everybody sitting around on their ass talking about things. So the bomb really was actually a *favor* for Sylvester."

"It was a favor for Zero."

"It wasn't, I'm telling you. It was one of the ways I was *screwing* Zero. I mean, if you wanna know what it had to do with Zero, *that's* what it had to do with Zero. Can't you see that? Because he didn't want me to do a bomb. He didn't want me to do anything. The guy had a fit, for Christ's sake, telling me *not* to do anything. Because what was gonna happen was Zero was gonna get screwed, and not anybody else." Ruel took a loud breath, his nostrils flaring angrily. His forehead glistened. "Man, you're stringing me out," he said hoarsely, dropping his voice. "I don't even know what to say to you anymore."

"My big mistake," Justin said, "was letting you get within ten miles of Zero. He took you so beautifully he didn't even know he was doing it."

"No one took me. I did the taking."

"Zero just sat back and laughed while you nailed your friend to the wall for him."

"Don't talk to me about friends."

"Didn't Sylvester do enough for you? What does a guy have to do to be your friend?"

"He was no prize, you know. He could be a drag too when he wanted."

"He kept you from being sent back. Where do you think you'd be right now for slugging that guard?"

"What guard?"

"At the Zoning Board. How many guards have you slugged?"

"It wasn't my fault they jumped Sylvester for that."

"But he covered for you. So you paid him back, first chance you got. When are you going to learn something? Have you signed a contract promising to be stupid all your life?"

"Hey, man."

"Why were you out to get Sylvester?"

"I was getting the barber."

"Christ, are we back to that now? That's where we started."

"You wanted the answers. I'm trying to give you the goddamn answers."

"Were you just having so much fun playing around with the idea of a bomb that you never even gave Sylvester a thought?"

Ruel's brow furrowed.

"I like that reason," Justin said. "Can't you at least tell me it's the right one?"

"You're blowing my mind, man."

"Or maybe Olivia. She really got you, didn't she? Her and Sylvester?"

"You're losing me. You got things going in sixteen thousand directions at once."

"Maybe it was Zero throwing all those dollar bills at you. I've seen people go crazy lots of ways in this country, and maybe that's just one more. You spend your whole life getting kicked around, then suddenly this character starts stuffing money into your pockets. That's got to get your head going in funny directions."

"It got my head thinking how I could take him, that's what it did."

"Only he took you. He wiped the streets with you."

"Hey, now."

"Did you just figure you owed him something for all that money? After all, he was helping you out, so you ought to help him too, by getting rid of Sylvester."

"What am I supposed to be, the only one? What about all those other people? What are they, saints or something?"

"What other people?"

"All of them. How come no matter what the hell goes wrong, *I'm* the guy that gets it in the ass?" He was breathing harshly. Then, as abruptly as it came, his anger subsided. He spoke dully, without confidence. "Sylvester never took any rap for me."

"He sure did."

"I told you, I never said a single word about Sylvester. I was trying to *help* Sylvester. And I'll tell you, the first thing I thought when I heard about him getting killed was how glad I was being clear of that, in case that son of a bitch tried to drag me into it."

"Zero?"

"You don't think it was an accident some cop shot Sylvester, do you? I mean, if Mr. Zeronski wants to get a message to the cops, the message goes through, if you know what I mean. And I wasn't gonna let him make me any fall guy, for taking that rap."

"For Sylvester getting killed?"

"I'll tell you, the whole thing is a lot more complicated than you think. What you gotta remember is, I was *protecting* Sylvester. It was Zero I was trying to *get*."

"How, for Christ's sake?"

"How the hell am I supposed to explain if you won't even listen? You got everything so goddamn mixed up I don't even know if I'm coming or going anymore."

"It's not mixed up. It's very simple. Sylvester's dead, and you're in more trouble than you can count, and Zero's sitting around having a good laugh."

"He ain't laughing."

"He's laughing."

"Fuck him then. I ain't gonna worry about him." Ruel frowned, thinking, then said: "That guy better not try anything."

"Sure. Okay. Only one more thing now."

"What?"

"Why'd you do it?"

"Jesus Christ, man—I've been *telling* you why I did it!"

Justin let out a breath. He could feel himself sagging. "I'm a lawyer, you know. A public official. An officer of the court. It's my duty, if I have knowledge of a crime, to report it to the authorities."

Ruel stiffened, focusing hard. "Hey, man. Are you pulling something now? What is it, you working for Zero too? Did he send you here to get me?"

"It would also be my responsibility," Justin went on, "to make any reasonable effort to bring a suspected felon into custody." He paused. "Except of course if he were my client, in which case we would have a privileged relationship. So if you'd like me to be your lawyer, there's nothing I have to do then, and we could just hang around to see whether the cops get to you first, or Sylvester's friends, or maybe even Zero."

"I ain't hanging around," Ruel said. "I ain't waiting for anybody to lay into me first."

"I guess that means maybe you're thinking of getting pretty far away from here." Justin paused. "Or are you so crazy you can't even understand what I'm saying?"

Ruel ran his tongue over his lip. "What do you know about

crazy? Everything's all nice and simple for you. You got nothing to worry about."

"Jesus," Justin said, and couldn't help laughing.

Ruel stared, his mouth partly open, his long face darkening. Then he bolted.

Justin sat in the chair, listening to him flying down the stairs.

He waited only long enough to give Ruel time to get comfortably hidden away somewhere. He didn't want to wait too long and keep him from coming back for a couple of shirts and some extra socks before taking off, his red and white wool cap, his basketball maybe, a few other mementos of his early, carefree days.

He could envision Ruel boarding a bus, a train, maybe even some flashy jet if he had any cash left from Zero's various drawing accounts. He would have one small suitcase in hand. The same cardboard one he'd carried out of Cheney that day. Not the ideal outcome maybe, but better than the alternatives, given Ruel, given the general state of personal and public corruption. All the slick mouthings to the contrary, people were dispatched to prison to get them out of sight. Well, Ruel would be out of sight, no longer offending the local sensibilities with his unmanageable presence, and that seemed at least as useful as shipping him back to Cheney for a few thousand more meals on steel trays and another round of piety and uplift, administered by the same people who, if they hadn't ruined Ruel in their previous tries, hadn't done him much good either. If there was a logic behind trying to help our least successful citizens by committing them to our least successful institutions, Justin was hard put to discover it.

He didn't feel particularly eager to pass along the news to Olivia, at least not tonight. It wasn't only that he'd have to admit she'd been right all along—her favorite turning out, although dead, to be true-blue; while his, although still very much alive, showed himself a first-rate flop. He didn't want to give Olivia any more jolts tonight, good or bad. She'd had enough for one day.

She would learn soon enough anyhow, and might even find some comfort in Ruel's guilt, never having been one of his great fans. He was being unfair. Olivia took no joy in anyone's guilt. Only innocence pleased her. She wanted everyone to be innocent —especially Sylvester maybe, but everyone else too.

Even Zeronski. She wanted Zero to play the gentle blue-eyed aristocrat that her family saw as the natural role for a man of wealth and power, and wasn't so much offended by the aura of evil she imagined to be surrounding Zero as she was by his fall from grace, his failure to embody the kind of urbane benevolence that her theology so solemnly required of him.

Zero, of course, would be disappointed at the news. He had as much staked on Sylvester's guilt as Olivia did on his innocence. Zero would therefore decide that even if Ruel did it, it was only because Sylvester must have urged him on, or tricked him into it.

Justin wished that Zero had, just this once, gone too far, not only hiring Ruel to keep an eye on Sylvester but actually paying him to plant the bomb too, in order to frame Sylvester. He wished that just this once Zero had shown himself to be as purely debased as your every instinct told you he was capable of being.

He further wished, as long as he was at it, that Ruel had minded his own business and done something reasonable and intelligent for a change.

He could see Ruel getting off that bus, or train, or plane, suitcase dangling at the end of one long arm. He'd step off lean and hard but still awkward, full of jagged unresolved energies, like a kid stretched out overnight and still surprised by his height, by the amazing length of his strides, gazing around at the strange setting, the unfriendly faces, trying to get his bearings, blinking, as wide-eyed as a cow in a chute.

No big deal. Just one more wiped-out kid. Just one more crazy man loose in America.

He walked back toward the center of things, still looking for the riot. It would have at least got everybody up and moving, restoring their sense of community, revitalizing those dormant instincts for protest and survival. But the streets were quiet. Only the cops in their purring cruisers, and the cops strolling about watchfully on foot, disturbed the silence—and of course the cops weren't really disturbing the silence; they were keeping it. The paralysis and vacancy of the streets gave you an inkling of how smooth and easy that final peace would be, that ultimate state of domestic tranquillity. It was enough to make you yearn for the good old days when everyone was ready to charge the barricades at the drop of a slogan. Jesus: a guy like Sylvester, the apple of their collective eye and the best thing they had going for them, first accused of a bomb he had nothing to do with and then cut down by a couple of white cops: the whole West Side would have gone up in flames.

What had happened since then? Maybe everybody had lost his nerve. Or the cops and the National Guard had finally proved, once and for all, that they had more firepower, more troops, more discipline, more determination. Or everybody was bored. Or no one believed anymore that he could make a difference. Or everybody was tired. Or no one trusted simplicity anymore, and a revolution needed issues simple enough to squeeze onto a placard. Or everybody was confused. Or ripeness really *was* all, and the world at the moment was lying fallow. Or everybody was home worrying about Number One. Or no one believed good was that good anymore, or bad that bad; everything had turned draggy and mediocre, and not worth bothering about. Or everybody had found, or lost, the true religion.

Maybe people had finally discovered that everything, when you got right down to it, was one way or another a matter of politics, and at the same time discovered that politics, when you got right down to it, was a godawful bore.

There. He'd managed; he had enough to keep him feeling crummy for at least a week.

The first phone booth he came to had the coin slot jammed with gum. The second, a block further on, seemed to be working. The phone rang only once before Olivia picked it up. She sounded very calm.

"Where are you?" she asked. "I hear you're down there walking the streets."

"I am. But it's pretty quiet."

"I thought you had a riot on your hands."

"It isn't a riot."

"What is it? The Darktown Strutters' Ball?"

"Everybody's safe at home. No one's roaming around."

"Have the police been making trouble?"

"No. They've been good. Everybody's been good."

"They weren't too good this afternoon." She paused. "What happened there?"

"Either Sylvester went at them and they blew their cool, or else they started roughing him up and then he went at them, and *then* they blew their cool."

"Zero was out to get him. You know that."

He frowned, hunched over in the booth, leaning one shoulder against the glass wall. "Zero had nothing to do with Sylvester getting killed."

"You don't believe that."

"I'm afraid I do."

"How do you stand on virgin birth? What about life on distant planets?"

"I don't like this either, you know."

"Okay," she said. "I'm sorry." And then: "I guess you heard about the new clinic. Zero's grand gesture."

"I heard."

"He doesn't deserve that. After all this, he's going to end up playing the fucking hero." She paused. "What about Ruel? Have they got him yet?"

"No," Justin said.

"They're after him, you know."

"He's leaving. He's getting away."

"Are you sure?"

"Yes," Justin said.

"That's what I wanted to talk to you about. I told him this afternoon to get away, but it was right after I heard about Sylvester, right after I saw what happened. I must've sounded crazy, and was afraid he wasn't listening."

"I guess maybe he was," Justin said.

"No," Olivia said. "But that's all right. As long as he listened to you."

"I just hope he makes it," Justin said.

"Do they have a warrant or something out for him?"

"If they don't, they soon will."

"He better move fast," Olivia said.

"That's what I told him," Justin said.

He approached three officers standing together near a corner, a lieutenant and two patrolmen. They straightened up aggressively, then the lieutenant smiled and stepped forward and even, God bless him, saluted. The chief must have warned every cop on the force, showing them mug shots: *Now be nice to this son of a bitch, you hear?*

"Everything all right, Mr. Gage?"

"Oh yes. Everything's fine."

"Around here too. Not a murmur."

Justin stopped to chat. They were in a jovial mood; the magnanimous conquerors, floating on a cloud.

It happened so quickly then, and so unexpectedly after a long night of dreary trudging, that no one, not even the cops, had time to react. About eight black kids burst around the corner yelling and flailing away with what could have been clubs. But then Justin was struck on the shoulder and saw the white slash, felt the soft thudding numbness: nylon stockings, stuffed with powdered chalk. Jesus Christ!—chalk-filled stockings! Halloween! All they needed were goblin and ghost masks, crepe paper witch capes. Hadn't anybody ever told them about their own weapons and symbols, their own cabalistic mysteries? *Where the hell am I?* he wanted to shout. *What is the country, O watchman? What the century?*

Only one officer was rash enough, or alert enough, to slap his holster. Justin reached out to stop him, but the lieutenant saved him the trouble: "No!"

They watched the scattering kids, stockings streaming behind like fluorescent banners.

Justin laughed, brushing his shoulder. He laughed and shook his head as the chalk powder—that familiar dryness in your nostrils!—puffed into small white clouds, and the cops, after a moment of indecision, started slapping at their sleeves too, their shoulders, chuckling genially at the white puffs rising from their braided uniforms.

Justin decided to call it a night, and headed home.

In the theater of the inner eye, you could play everything out full blast because nobody else ever got to see the show.

When Ruel jumped from the bed to bolt for the door, Justin would rise to stop him. Enraged, Ruel would swing at him, and Justin, absolved by having been struck first, would have himself one hell of a good time beating the shit out of him.

That's what kept you coming back: In the theater of the inner eye you could take your joy unrestrained, and not have to worry about all the infinite and nagging niceties.

IX.

Jerome

THE AMETHYST GALLERY. Jerome had passed it downtown on occasion, bright pictures in the window, a stylish place. He wasn't surprised to see Olivia Cowan flourishing in business: a crisp young woman like that, with a fine head on her shoulders.

He climbed the flight of stairs to the apartment over the gallery. It'd been a long and rattling day, and now with the night upon him he was beginning to wear down, and had to blink to clear his eyes, and remember to keep his shoulders straight. He listened at the door. He wouldn't intrude if she had callers. He heard no voices, and knocked.

She must have leaped a foot, clattering and bumping. "Who is it? Who's there?"

My God, he thought, what have I done?

He heard a click from the miniature porthole in the door. He removed his hat and smiled, feeling a trifle foolish: posing for a portrait. "Jerome Tinney," he announced to the aperture. "Remember?" He waited for another click. "I thought I might be of service."

After a moment she pulled back the door, and shocked him with her appearance. She was dressed as exquisitely as ever in a long skirt and handsome white sweater, but the delicate coloring was gone from the high cheeks, and the bleakness of her expression had benumbed those porcelain-fine features. Only the stately carriage remained, her head still high.

He realized she was staring back. Had he too changed since their last meeting? It'd be no wonder, with bombs going off under him and lively boys swept away in their prime.

"What happened to your hair?"

"My hair?" Jerome said. Good grief—was it that bad? Had Budd been out to humiliate him? "We weren't finished . . . ," he stammered. "I went back and he—"

She shrugged, the numbness returning. "What do you want?"

"I realized how bad you must be feeling," he said.

She waited.

"And of course," Jerome went on, fingering his hat in front of him, "if there's any way I can help . . ."

The poor woman looked desolate enough to droop flowers for miles around. Nonetheless, she nodded him inside and indicated an archway to the living room. A nice room, full of color, with bookshelves and pictures, ceramic knickknacks, some kind of Indian rug on the floor. A cigarette sent up a curl of smoke from an ashtray, next to an empty glass on the end table.

"Make yourself comfortable," she said, more in resignation, it seemed, than enthusiasm. "Everybody else is off enjoying the riot."

"Is there really a riot?"

"There's supposed to be. Down in the West Side."

"I didn't see any riot," Jerome said.

"Do you drink?"

"Sherry would be fine. Dry, if you have it."

She also fetched another drink for herself, then sat on the couch in silence.

"I didn't think it looked that bad," Jerome said.

"What? Oh. Your hair. It doesn't. I didn't mean to imply it did."

"No offense taken," Jerome said.

"You look fine," she said, meaning his clothes, his tie. She paused, lapsing back into that vast depression. She blinked at a thought. "You met Ruel the other day, didn't you?"

"This afternoon too, when I went back for my car. He seemed pretty shaken up over his friend."

"He's leaving," she said. "He's getting out while he can."

"Are the police after him?"

"Yes. They've already got Louise."

"The one with the orange hair? What for?"

"They're rounding up all of them, with Ruel at the top of the list."

"Where's he going?"

"Somewhere else. Anywhere else would be better." She paused, then continued in the same toneless voice. "I guess you heard about Sylvester."

"It was a terrible thing."

"The police were out to get him. There were people making sure the police were out to get him."

Jerome studied Olivia's face. Did she still believe Sylvester innocent? It seemed she might, and Jerome had no desire to disabuse her. She looked sad enough as it was.

"I went there," she said.

"Where?"

"The clinic. This afternoon. I saw what was left of him. The . . . body."

"You shouldn't have."

"I thought it'd be nice if someone did. It sounds so clean and neat when you just hear it. But when you see—what's the term? —the remains?—it makes a different impression."

Jerome said nothing, and Olivia again fell silent, staring lifelessly across the room. Something that had been hovering at the edges of Jerome's mind abruptly asserted itself: he would not be surprised if the woman were considering suicide. His knock at the door might even have interrupted her. She might right now be waiting only for him to leave.

It jolted you, a thought like that. He'd never known anyone

who'd done it, had no idea what the signs might be. Perhaps she'd been even closer to Sylvester than he'd suspected. Perhaps there'd been other shocks, other losses, that he had no inkling of.

He cleared his throat and swallowed. "Maybe we could talk," he suggested.

She gazed at him in mild surprise. "I thought we were talking."

"If something's bothering you, it's best to get it off your chest." He waited. "Don't be too proud to accept help." He tried a smile. "People have to lend each other a hand, after all. It's the American way."

She finished her drink and placed the glass down. She stared at it for a while, or maybe the ashtray next to it. "I have to leave," she said. "When you knocked, I was getting ready."

He nodded, not sure of his next move. He couldn't stop her from going, but hardly felt comfortable leaving her to her own devices.

She rose as if to go, then wavered, clenching her eyes shut.

Jerome jumped up to steady her. "Are you all right?"

She smiled wanly, nodding toward the empty glass. "I should have skipped the last one."

"It was my fault," Jerome assured her. "You were being polite."

"I'm not drunk," she said, and of course she wasn't. Just a bit woozy. The blood rushing to the head. Or from the head.

"You shouldn't be driving."

"I can drive."

"But you shouldn't."

"I'm just exhausted. Really. I didn't drink that much."

"Wherever you're going, it can wait."

"No."

"I'll drive you then," Jerome announced.

"You're being very sweet. But—"

"I insist," Jerome said. "I have nothing else to do. I'd be glad to oblige."

She hesitated. "I hate to take advantage of your kindness."

"My pleasure," Jerome insisted.

"We can take my car," Olivia said on the sidewalk in front of the gallery.

266

"Are you sure you have to go tonight?"

"Yes."

Jerome gingerly eased the glistening Jaguar out from the curb. "I don't know that I've ever handled anything this big." The power steering was awesome. One touch and the wheels leaped. And the brakes, at a breath, clamped down with lockjaw efficiency.

"I can drive if you'd rather," Olivia offered. "I feel much better now."

"No," he said. "That was the whole idea."

It was the automobile Jerome had followed two days before, when Sylvester was at the wheel. Was somebody now following them? Jerome glanced at the rear-view mirror, reassuring himself.

"Just take Pendleton Street all the way out," she said.

They passed within a block of Budd's barbershop, and Jerome caught a glimpse of the candy-stripe pole against the boarded-up window. Olivia also looked down the side street.

"That's where it happened," Jerome said, still awed, remembering the explosion.

"It's where I saw him," Olivia said quietly. You could talk quietly in the car, the engine no more than a hum, the springs like foam rubber.

"At the barbershop?"

"The clinic," she said. "Right after they killed him."

"Is it down there?"

"Next to the barbershop."

"I didn't realize they were that close," Jerome said. They passed a police car parked at an intersection. "Is this where the riot's supposed to be?"

"We could go down a side street and see."

"I'm not driving you into a riot," Jerome said.

They left the city and moved in purring, cushiony silence through the rolling hills.

"Where are we going?" Jerome asked.

"Zeronski's."

"Who?"

"Zero Wrecking." She seemed quite in control of herself, exhibiting once again that composure Jerome so much admired.

"I think I've seen the trucks," Jerome said.

It wasn't his standard routine, delivering women to assignations in silvery Jaguars. He couldn't resist imagining himself as Olivia's prize, the reason for her journey. He found the idea shamefully delicious—waiting alone somewhere, dressed to the hilt and sipping Courvoisier while a beautiful woman raced toward him through the romantic dark.

Hardly. You were relegated now to driving the car—not even knowing where you were heading—for those whose fires still burned as bright as the tiger's eye.

"Why are we going there?" he asked.

"So I can make him do something he doesn't want to do. There it is. Up on the ridge."

They were some miles from town, past the suburban tracts, and the lights on the ridge were set well back from the highway.

Jerome swung onto a small private road that curved through grassland before rising into a growth of trees. They circled the house on an oleander-lined driveway to get to the paved garage area. The house was all pieces, big pieces, chunky structures with glass walls and flat roofs and overhanging log beams, coming together as a closed circle, like the pioneer wagon trains at night, when everyone slept with one eye open, just in case.

A Negro in a chauffeur's uniform appeared to assist Olivia and Jerome from the Jaguar.

"It's you again," Olivia said with her first hint of cheer.

"Good evening, ma'am." He seemed to be putting on an English accent, but looked pretty classy in his black suit and tie and visored cap.

Inside, the house wasn't all that impressive. Neither was Zeronski, who greeted them in sandals and bathrobe. And not some fancy velveteen smoking jacket either. A bathrobe, pure and simple, a big roomy affair that came down to his ankles. He was an odd-looking fellow, with a big head that seemed sunk halfway into his chest. Froglike all around, with bulging eyes and pudgy torso and short legs. He wore his hair in a World War II crew cut, except that it stood out as much on the sides as on top. It could have been trimmed with a mixing bowl.

"This is Jerome Tinney," Olivia said.

Zeronski stared drearily at Jerome, the interloper, the bumptious tag-along ruining his planned tête-à-tête.

Jerome stared back until Zeronski nodded. "How do," Jerome said.

"You are welcome," Zeronski announced without much conviction. He had a soft furry voice, with a kind of deep-throated growl rumbling underneath it. He offered his hand as if they'd just signed a treaty, his bathrobe sleeve riding up to reveal a remarkably hairy wrist. Zeronski turned to Olivia, his head rotating slowly, his feet still planted: "My dear. How very honored . . . I am."

He had an accent: *vwery*, and the words came with a slight stickiness. He was far enough into his cups not to want to take any chances, either with a difficult phrase or a sudden movement. And it wasn't the kind of momentary wooziness that'd hit Olivia earlier, and that she now seemed well over. Zeronski had downed more than a couple of quick ones.

He led them into a large room, moving stiffly, each step a distinct undertaking. The glass wall offered a nice view of the East Bay lights in the distance. "Won't you have a seat?" he offered, taking the words one at a time.

A colored maid wheeled in a fancy liquor cart. She was young and saucy in her transparent blouse and dainty miniature skirt. One look and the mystery's gone.

"None for me," Jerome said.

"Go ahead," Olivia said. "Be a sport."

"A little sherry maybe. Dry, if you have it."

The girl had it. There were enough bottles on the bottom shelf to accommodate a troopship. She presented the drinks with a little curtsy, one knee dipping quickly, her tiny skirt flaring. Olivia took scotch. Zeronski got handed four fat fingers of Wild Turkey over a chink of ice, as casually as water.

The maid retired, leaving the cart behind.

"I'm glad you came," Zeronski said, sounding a bit slurry as he raised his glass to Olivia. "I understand . . . what an unfortunate day . . . this has been."

Olivia was cool and stiff. "Mr. Tinney, you know, was in the barbershop when the bomb went off."

Zeronski turned somberly to Jerome. Between sips, he held his glass on one thigh, staining a wet circle on the bathrobe. They were more than sips; he was making real headway.

"He was getting his hair cut," Olivia said.

Zeronski looked at Jerome's hair. He drank and spoke to Olivia. "I meant . . . the unfortunate death . . . this afternoon."

"Oh yes, " Olivia said, very precise but with a hard edge coming through. "That."

You could see something had been rubbed raw between the two of them; the knives were out. Olivia's expression was odd, though. She was making no bones about her lack of enthusiasm for the guy, yet seemed kind of awed by his presence, as if responding to something—God only knew what, as far as Jerome was concerned—that kept her just a bit off balance.

"I heard about it from Mr. Gage," Zeronski said slowly. He could have been dragging a weight along with each word. "As soon as I heard, I wanted to cry out: *Stop*. But it was too late. The boy was dead. The policeman—what? Injured, I understand. Already in the hospital. It was too late. *Stop,* I would have said. *Stop this tragedy*. But it was too late."

"Your trucks were there," Olivia said, straight as a schoolmarm in her chair.

"A contract. On this date. For this sum. I had no knowledge, none whatsoever. I am no longer active . . . in Zero Wrecking. An executive officer, totally trustworthy, had complete charge."

"Did he know about the clinic?"

"No one told him. The owners . . ."

"You owned it."

"I sold all interest . . . months ago."

"Because of Sylvester."

"Because I no longer desired . . . to own the building."

"Because of Sylvester."

"I had no obligation . . . to further his schemes. He scorned me. He would have destroyed everything. Laughed at everything."

"Why didn't they let him take the equipment out?"

"They were in a rush. They did not care. They had other things on their mind." Zeronski kept his short legs stretched down, his toes barely touching the floor. "Don't blame me . . . for their stupidity."

Olivia seemed unimpressed.

"Money," Zeronski said with sudden intensity. "That is the real explanation. Greed. Lust. Avarice. How many names do we need for the same sin? To fill the belly, feed the wild animal. To devour. To grab and grab." He stopped, breathing hoarsely.

"You despised him," Olivia said.

"He would not accept . . . friendship. The truth was nothing . . . to him. My motives, my achievements . . . nothing. Only his pretense . . . of innocence."

"You wanted to get rid of him."

Zeronski eyed her stonily. "I have never lifted a finger . . . against him. I know how you feel. You think tragedy needs intent. You think it results from design. But there was no intent, no design. Only impatience, greed, ineptitude. You do not like that explanation. You want more meaning in his death . . . more grandeur. But what we want . . . any of us . . . counts for nothing. Only the truth . . . counts." Olivia wasn't conceding an inch, and he shifted his gaze to Jerome.

"Those people . . . fools . . . would not last ten minutes . . . with me. Their only god . . . is money."

"You must have made a dollar or two in your day," Jerome said. He wasn't itching for a fight, especially since those two already had their hackles up, but it always annoyed him to hear the richest bozo in the crowd shrugging off the importance of money.

Zeronski took a rustling breath and peered into his empty glass, like a beady poker player. He raised his eyes. "We are all responsible. All of us . . . love money . . . too much. We lust . . . for excrement . . . and a boy dies." He exhaled abruptly, a puff of contempt. The veins swelled darkly beneath his crew cut. "People paint their faces . . . like Indians . . . with excrement."

"I didn't know the Indians did that," Jerome said.

Zeronski frowned, holding the expression for a moment.

"You wanted it," Olivia said, the sharpest she'd spoken.

"His death? No. I did not want his death."

"You did everything you could to get rid of the clinic, to make sure Sylvester—"

"No!" Zeronski protested. "That is not true!" He let out a tremendous sigh, calming himself. "You are not talking sense." He turned again to Jerome, looking for support. "I am willing to accept guilt. We all share that. But I did not wish the boy's death. If I am as guilty as the next person . . . am I not also as innocent?"

"I'm afraid whole gobs of this are going over my head," Jerome said, and jumped.

They all jumped, and Olivia cried out. Zeronski tried to look everywhere at once. It could have been a car backfiring, but seemed too loud, too sharp.

The door flew open and the chauffeur plunged into the room.

"What was that?" Zeronski demanded.

"I don't know," the man shouted back. "I thought—"

"Find out. Check outside."

The man dashed from the room.

Jerome became aware of the thumping palpitation in his chest. His scar, his little scratch, itched ferociously.

"What's going on?" Olivia said. "Who's shooting around here?"

"I'm sure everything's all right." Zeronski hardly seemed to believe his own words, those bulging eyes terrified now.

The chauffeur barged back in and hurried across the carpet, but not frantic anymore, looking pretty cool and dignified again, and the three of them sagged with relief.

A head taller than Zeronski, the chauffeur bent over to whisper. Zeronski listened rigidly. "Are you sure?" The fellow nodded. Zeronski closed his eyes briefly in resignation. "What about downtown?"

The man whispered again.

"All right," Zeronski said, and the man hurried from the room. Neither coming nor going did he so much as glance at Jerome or Olivia.

"A dog," Zeronski said thickly.

Olivia drew back in disgust. "You mean someone shot a dog?"

"The woods are full of wild dogs," Zeronski explained.

"Did they hit it?"

"Apparently," Zeronski said, lowering his eyes.

"Pretty quick on the trigger there," Jerome said.

Zeronski remained silent.

"Who's running around with a gun?" Jerome asked. "Your bodyguard?"

"My valet," Zeronski said. *Vvalet.*

272

"What's happening downtown?" Olivia asked. "Are they having their riot?"

"It is under control," Zeronski said. "There will be no riot." He looked up at the large window, his eyes steady, bulging like a frog's, and then methodically, turned full circle to gaze gravely at the smaller windows, the door.

Jerome frowned. Was the man worried about snipers? Was he afraid that Olivia wasn't the only friend of Sylvester's ready to blame him for everything? Did he envision waves of black ruffians storming in for blood revenge?

To be met by the equally black faces of his faithful servants, ready to defend their beloved master to the death?

The flurry of excitement hadn't exactly sobered Zeronski, but it might have edged him in that direction. The remedy was quick at hand, though, for the cute little maid pranced back to fix drinks for everyone, including another wallop for Zeronski. When she left, her starched skirt twitching over the saucy swing of her hips, Jerome watched, not really ogling but sort of wondering how she fit into things.

Zeronski noticed. "It is difficult for them to find proper employment," he said. "I hire them every chance I get."

Jerome must have looked puzzled.

"Blacks," Zeronski added, by way of explanation.

They were still standing and both Jerome and Zeronski turned to Olivia, who seemed ready to take care of whatever business had brought her there. She looked so determined, in fact, yet still so grief-stricken, that Jerome wondered if maybe he'd misread the signs earlier, and that it was Zeronski, not herself, who might be threatened by her despair. A startling image: Olivia coolly extracting a tiny polished pistol from her handbag and leveling it at the man, her hand steady, her eyes merciless. And who then would leap forward to save him? Jerome himself? The gun-toting *vwalet*, the chauffeur in his fancy uniform? Maybe Zeronski, at the last instant, would reveal himself a master of some exotic form of Japanese trickery, disarming Olivia in a flash of whirling acrobatics.

Did Zeronski also see danger signs in her face? It was possible, and Olivia seemed, in turn, aware of what they both thought they saw, for she said, quite abruptly: "I didn't come here to argue, about Sylvester or anything else. I came to ask you for something." She spoke rapidly, feeling a little funny, maybe, asking favors of a guy she'd been pretty sharp with up to that moment.

"I am at your service," Zeronski responded, with a somber dip of his head.

"Not for me. I wouldn't ask anything for myself."

Zeronski waited for her to go on. He nodded toward a chair but she shook her head and the three of them remained standing.

"Ruel called me tonight," she said, and then paused. "I didn't realize you two knew each other."

"We are . . . acquainted."

"He said he had one of your scholarships. I didn't know that."

"We do not publicize . . . the scholarships."

"He's leaving. He's getting away."

Zero said nothing.

"I offered to help," Olivia said, still speaking rapidly. It was a strain for her, and she had to force herself on. "I was glad he called. I've never been, I guess, his favorite person."

"That is unfortunate."

"He's frightened over what happened to Sylvester. You probably can't see that, and won't take my word for it. But you'll believe Justin, won't you? It was all Justin's idea. He's the one who told Ruel to get away."

"I respect Justin's judgment. I also . . . respect yours."

"Ruel's got nothing. He's never had anything. He needs help to start somewhere else or he'll end up worse off than ever. Will you do it? He's counting on you." Olivia hardly gave him time to answer before she went on, her voice wavering at first but regaining strength as she continued. "I saw him this afternoon—right after I came out from the clinic. That's when I think I really understood. Sylvester was lying up there with his face shot away, and the cops were already eying Ruel. They were all over the place, and you could just see what was going through their minds. One more troublemaker. One more wise guy. One more candidate for the junk pile."

Zeronski frowned darkly.

"He needs help," Olivia said. "He deserves it. He's never had a chance to be anything but everybody's whipping boy." She stared uncertainly at Zeronski.

A fleck of froth appeared at one corner of Zeronski's lips. "I will do . . . whatever you ask."

Olivia hesitated, still dubious, then seemed to sag, as if disappointed that it'd gone so easy.

Jerome found the whole business an eye opener. He'd never have figured any connection between Ruel, straight off the streets, and a man like Zeronski. It was even harder to believe Ruel would have the cheek to ask for a flat handout, and not even on his own, but sending Olivia Cowan to plead his case. Or that she'd do it, or that Zeronski, after the way the woman had lit into him from the word go, would shrug all that off and do exactly what she asked.

Of course Zeronski could afford it, could probably stake a kid like Ruel for months on spare change. Still, it seemed a generous act, and he deserved credit for it.

Zeronski had been steadily observing Olivia's face. "You seem surprised . . . that I am willing . . . to help." He finished off his drink and stared into the empty glass, clutching it in both hands at his stomach. Then he raised his eyes to Olivia. "Did Ruel explain . . . why he does not share your . . . distrust . . . of me?"

Olivia's face hardened. "He said Sylvester did it."

Zeronski showed no surprise.

"Did what?" Jerome said.

"The bomb," Olivia said.

"Oh?" Jerome said. "You know."

"Yes," Olivia said.

"I didn't want to say anything," Jerome said. "I just found out myself—that he did it—from his lawyer."

Olivia shrugged irritably. "Justin was sure it was Sylvester from the beginning."

"I wasn't," Jerome said. "I wanted to believe in him."

"I can't condemn him," Olivia said, hardly a whisper. "It was wrong and terrible and he shouldn't have done it. But I can't condemn him."

"A man was killed," Jerome said.

"I'm not going to hate him. I'm not going to play God."

"It's best, at any rate," Zeronski said heavily, "that we all know the truth."

You could see how much the admission of Sylvester's guilt had cost Olivia. But the poet was right: too deep for tears. She held her composure, her eyes steady. "Sylvester would have done anything to protect the clinic. He felt threatened in a way none of us ever have. He knew how easily he could be destroyed. And he was right. They killed him, with hardly any fuss at all. That kinky little nightmare he kept having came true. They got him in a corner and blew his head off."

Zeronski had been listening impassively. The three of them were still standing, and when Olivia seemed finished he stepped forward, testing himself with each movement. She eyed him defiantly, but nonetheless he reached forth and took one of her hands, a solemn gesture, and held it sandwiched between his. He remained slightly bent toward her, his robe almost to his ankles, and looked at her in silence. "It is not . . . in your heart," he said finally, "to hate. You are . . . too good . . . in your heart."

His manner was almost cloying. You'd have thought he was playing the continental lover, sparking the local duchess.

Olivia didn't respond, leaving them in something of a standoff, their hands touching, their eyes meeting, and neither apparently willing to go further or pull back. But then Zeronski, with the room in a kind of hush, removed his right hand, still clutching her hand with his left, and with a concentration that seemed to increase the hush, very deliberately walked his fingers up her forearm, pushing her sleeve ahead as he went. His fingertips brushed her bare skin as lightly as a feather. He stopped at her elbow, and for a long time stared moonishly into her eyes. Then without a word he dropped his arms, like weights, to his sides.

Jerome sighed in relief. He'd felt like a peeping Tom, not sure if Zeronski was going to end up falling to one knee or ripping Olivia's clothes off. Her look was just as puzzling: it could have been either tenderness or suppressed rage.

What was it about these people? Did every kindness have to mask an assault, every charitable urge become a threat in disguise? You'd think they'd want to straighten that out, for their own benefit, and decide where one thing started and another left off.

276

Zeronski turned from Olivia. He looked spent, and headed, naturally, for the liquor cart. "Would anyone care . . . to join me?" He gestured again toward the couch, the chairs.

"We should go," Olivia said.

Zeronski refilled his glass and helped himself, as they watched, to a long slow swallow. His left eye had begun to droop and seemed to be gradually closing while the other, bulging glossily, remained wide open. "You know how much," he said to Olivia, "I have tried to help those people."

Olivia's mouth tightened. "I can't congratulate you. I can't manage that."

"I am not interested . . . in praise . . . in self-glorification." He broke up the word carefully, syllable by syllable. "Even the collection . . . that you have worked on . . . the art. It is not for me. Soon . . . it will be announced. It will all . . . be for others."

Olivia seemed unimpressed "And then you'll be able to tear everything down, build whatever you want."

"No. I only want . . . to help."

"It's a trade-off. You get your project and the people tossed out on the street get your charity."

"You insist . . . on distorting everything. I've worked all my life . . . to help others. I have known prejudice . . . and hatred. I have known . . . homelessness . . . despair. But always . . . I have dreamed . . . of helping others . . . rise . . . from the ashes. . . ."

For all the feeling he put into his words, Zeronski still looked ready to doze off on the spot, with one eye closed now and the other fading fast.

Olivia nodded to Jerome: she was ready to go.

Zeronski stared at them blearily, as if trying to remember what he'd been talking about.

"If you want to give something to Ruel, I'll take it to him. You'll trust me to do that, won't you?"

"Of course . . . I trust you."

Zeronski took a step forward, a real effort, and then paused to make sure he had his balance. Satisfied, he reached into the pocket of his robe and pulled out a white envelope. He looked at it, turned it over once, and handed it to Olivia.

The guy'd had it ready and waiting all along.

"You son of a bitch," Olivia said. "You prick."

Zeronski didn't even blink. "Ruel called," he explained, "and said you'd be coming."

They drove past Zeronski tottering in the driveway, clutching his glass. He wouldn't have made it outside, wouldn't be standing, if the grenadier-like chauffeur weren't holding him up, all the time looking pretty smug about it.

It was always like that with servants, one reason Jerome had never indulged in any. Sooner or later you found yourself being treated like a child by the very people you kept fed and clothed.

All the way down the hill to the highway Jerome looked for a dog's flung body along the road, blood matting its dirt-brown fur. He did not see it, and so was left with his own imaginings: a blasted carcass tossed into the woods like an old sack, carrion now for turkey buzzards.

Olivia was seething over the way Zeronski had toyed with her, letting her go on pleading her case long after he'd already decided to help Ruel out. She stared silently out at the darkness as they purred along the highway in the Jaguar. Thinking about God knows what. Maybe the variety and spice of her acquaintances: Sylvester to Zeronski to Ruel; mix and match indeed: the only cheery one blasting barbershops to bits; the only one with a dollar to his name a boozer in a bathrobe; and the surliest of the bunch now in line for the big handout, his hearty send-off to greener pastures.

"Why couldn't Ruel do his own running around?" Jerome asked.

Olivia turned from the window. "He doesn't trust Zero. He didn't want to put himself in his hands."

"But he tipped him off about you coming."

"Maybe he was afraid I couldn't handle Zero without help."

"Is that Zeronski's game? Giving it away now that he's piled up his first million or so?"

"He doles out enough, I guess, one way or the other. But he always manages to get what he wants out of it."

"You're certainly down on the man."

"What do you think of him?"

"Nothing special," Jerome said. "Another money grubber who can't hold his liquor." He waited a moment, then said: "You did pretty well tonight, keeping it polite, considering your feelings about the man."

"I've been polite too long to people like that. Maybe we all have."

"What about the scholarship Zeronski mentioned?"

Olivia didn't respond right away. "Ruel's been going to the university."

"That's hard to picture. Ruel in a classroom."

"He was trying," Olivia said.

"And Zeronski helped there too. And he's helping now, with whatever's in that envelope."

Olivia didn't seem to want to talk about it.

"Aren't you curious?" Jerome asked. "I wouldn't want to peek, of course, but suppose it's just pieces of yesterday's newspaper, cut to size."

Olivia thought it over. "He wouldn't do that."

"I'm not suggesting he would."

They reached the outskirts of the city, coming down off the foothills where the highway funneled into Pendleton Street.

"We have to call," Olivia said. "He gave me a number."

Jerome swung into a Safeway parking lot, the store closed, the lot empty, and stopped in front of the lighted phone booth. "You got a dime?" he asked as Olivia reached for the door.

She hesitated. "I don't think so."

Jerome fished one out for her.

"Thank you." She went to the booth and pulled the glass door shut behind her.

That's the way it was. Millionaires, tycoons, owners of Jaguars: they could float a hundred grand on credit but never had change for a phone call.

Olivia apparently got through, and was talking to somebody. Jerome couldn't help but admire the woman's generosity, and her spunk too. Sylvester dead only hours, and here she was doing her best to help someone else.

She returned to the car.

"Where is he?" Jerome asked.

"He'll be at the café across from the store front." She seemed, if possible, even more deflated than before.

"What is it? What's the matter?"

"He doesn't want me to come," she said quietly. "He wants you to bring it."

"Wait a minute now."

"He's really frightened. He doesn't trust anybody anymore."

"Not even you?"

"It's not just that. He's right: It'll be more conspicuous with two of us. But if you don't want to, I'll go alone."

"No, you won't," Jerome told her. You could see how bad she felt about it, a guy like Ruel suddenly cutting her off like that, whatever his reasons. "He's not worth half the trouble he's causing," Jerome said. "I don't like any part of this."

"I'll take it then."

"You will not. They're having a riot. There's cops all over the place."

"No. It's quiet."

"Because of the cops. Why on earth does he want to meet there?"

"He said you'd been there with him. He said you'd know the place."

"Can you call him back?"

"He's already left. He's on his way."

"He doesn't have a usable brain in his whole body," Jerome said.

He pulled back onto Pendleton and headed toward the West Side. "Should I take you home first?"

"We pass right by the Mayfair; I'll wait in their lounge."

Jerome stopped in front of the hotel marquee, and Olivia handed him the envelope. The flap had been opened, and was held closed now with a paper clip.

"I didn't peek," she said.

"What'd you do? Up the ante?"

She was silent a moment. "Not by that much."

It was a pretty hefty wad now from the feel of it, Olivia's money probably all small bills. Who'd break a hundred, even a fifty, for someone like Ruel?

"You don't have to say anything. Just hand it to him."

"I have nothing to say," Jerome assured her.

He watched her stride up to the gilt and glass entrance, those elegant legs flashing, her head high. A fine carriage. It was a pleasure for that brief moment just to observe her walking.

Then everything else came back, with a vengeance. He made a face, stretching his mouth back, and stomped on the gas.

He saw his first patrol car when he turned off Pendleton and headed down a side street of wretched brownstones and frame houses so run-down you'd swear they were tilting. He passed another squad car, then came upon a pair of foot patrolmen. One stepped into the street to flag down Jerome but changed his mind and let him pass.

It was the Jaguar, he decided. You hardly ever found rioters driving silver Jaguars.

The streets seemed quiet enough and Jerome saw no damage to speak of, although a couple of street lamps had been knocked out, and he passed one man, a janitor maybe, out alone in the gloom of night, patiently applying a big push broom to a scattering of garbage in front of an apartment house. An older man, and just from the way he moved you knew he'd seen worse messes, smelled worse smells; it wouldn't be long before he'd have the soup cans and crumpled milk cartons and the rest of the slop back inside those corrugated barrels, the sidewalk clean again, maybe hosed down, and that'd be the end of it. Not a man, maybe, who founded dynasties or furthered causes, but one you could count on to help out in a storm, to see that the horses were fed, the children taught their table manners; and thus admirable, ankle-deep in garbage.

And around here somewhere the man who cultivated that mythical pomegranate tree in his front yard, attracting people from miles around in blossom time.

As he turned the corner Jerome noticed first that the café—their meeting place—was closed for the night; then that the store front across the street had a black star-shaped hole in its whitewashed plate-glass window, big enough to march a horse through; and then that three cops were stationed near the storefront door. Ruel, naturally, was nowhere to be seen.

It vexed him. The whole business vexed him.

He drove by the cops, neither too fast nor too slow, keeping his eyes straight ahead. They watched closely but made no move to stop him, and he proceeded slowly down the block. He had no idea where to search for the boy, nor much inclination to do so. For all he knew, Ruel had taken one look at the police and was already gone. Or already taken off in a paddy wagon.

Whatever, Ruel would just have to fend for himself. Jerome had done his best and was ready to forget the whole business and rejoin Olivia for a nightcap, and at least end the day on a civilized note.

He spotted him in a tavern doorway. The place was locked shut, its windows protected behind iron grillwork, and it was too dark to see much of the person in the wedge-shaped entrance-way jutting out at the corner, but there was no mistaking the height.

"Damn," Jerome muttered. He hit the brake and immediately realized it was a mistake, with the cops only half a block behind and probably still watching. He turned the corner out of their sight, made sure there were no police on that block, and pulled to the curb about thirty feet beyond the tavern entrance.

He turned off the motor and lights and squirmed around on the leather seat to peer back. Another mistake. Suppose Ruel wanted to dash to the car for a quick getaway?

Was that next—dodging the cops on a screeching chase through the city streets, bullets shattering the windshield as they careened around corners?

He craned his neck to watch the doorway, then slid across the seat to the passenger side and rolled down the window. All Ruel had to do was stroll casually past, hardly breaking stride, as Jerome held out the envelope for him, like a runner passing a baton. The cops around the corner wouldn't be able to see a thing. It'd take a second, and that'd be the end of it.

Only Ruel didn't come out.

Jerome waited some more and then, in a pique, climbed out. If the cops saw him, that'd be Ruel's problem. He relented enough in his annoyance, though, to close the car door softly and stay close to the building as he walked along the sidewalk.

"Get in," Ruel said. He grabbed Jerome's sleeve and yanked him into the doorway. "They're all over the goddamn place."

"I could have told you that," Jerome muttered. There was room for both of them in the wedge-shaped space, Jerome pressed against one side, Ruel against the other, as far back as they could go. "Here," Jerome said, thrusting the envelope at him. He wanted it over and done with.

Ruel hesitated, as if even now fearing a trick, a trap.

"There's always the Salvation Army," Jerome pointed out. "We could always give it to the Red Cross."

Ruel took the envelope. The doorway wasn't as dark as it seemed from the street, and Ruel studied the envelope in his hand. He removed the paper clip and toyed, with one long finger, at the unglued flap.

"Don't worry," Jerome told him. "No one took anything. No one even peeked."

"Did you open it?"

"No," Jerome said.

Ruel waited for him to go on.

"Miss Cowan opened it. She added to it. So it's not all from Zeronski."

Ruel turned away and hunched his shoulders to block Jerome's view. He looked in the envelope, then stuffed it in the back pocket of his jeans. He was wearing his red and white wool cap, the white glowing softly in the dark.

"You're welcome," Jerome said.

"Yeah," Ruel said. "Thanks."

"You could thank Miss Cowan too. And Mr. Zeronski."

"Sure," Ruel said. "Tell them all thanks."

"I'll leave now."

"Don't let them see you," Ruel said.

Jerome had half a mind to tell him what he thought of him, begging for handouts and taking advantage of Olivia Cowan to do his dirty work. Instead he said: "Are you planning to stay here all night?"

"The place is crawling with cops."

"You're not that easy to hide, you know. You can't just tuck yourself away in a corner."

"What the hell do you think, I wanna stand here?"

"I'm leaving," Jerome said.

"Good," Ruel said. "Go."

The fellow probably had more money stuffed in his back pocket than he'd seen in his life, all of it charity, handed to him on a platter, and still he wore his insolence like a badge, throwing the whole burden onto you to prove yourself worthy of even the smallest part of his attention, even the shallowest courtesy.

"You could go down this block," Jerome said. "I didn't see any cops down there."

"Well, I did. Whatd'ya think I'm doing in here? I seen cops down that block and I seen cops down this block."

"How'd you get this far?"

"Maybe from where you live it's far. From where I live it ain't so far."

It wasn't a sound that'd normally make you start, even on a night as quiet as this, but they both started. People were moving along the sidewalk, talking in whispers, even their footsteps whispery. They were coming from the direction of the Jaguar.

"Stay back," Ruel said.

"I am back," Jerome said.

They waited, pressed against the door. Jerome could smell the yeasty barroom odors.

Not cops, certainly, whose boots struck hard on the pavement, whose metal gear clinked and clanked at their cartridge belts. A band of tiptoeing rioters maybe, looking for something to burn.

The first figure strolled into view. A colored boy with a belt or whip or something dangling in one hand. Then six or seven more, all of good size, each wearing sneakers and carrying something that looked like an oversized slingshot.

"Hey!" one whispered loudly, grabbing another's arm and motioning to the doorway.

The kids crowded forward like spectators at a zoo, forming a rough semicircle to stare in at Jerome and Ruel hunched into their dark corners.

"Jesus K. Christ," one of the kids said.

"Beat it," Ruel said, hardly moving his lips.

"Bar closed for the night, gents. Booze all drunk up, I reckon."

"Beat it," Ruel said. "Get outta here."

"What in holy shit you dudes *doing* there?" another wanted to know.

"The cops are right down the goddamn block," Ruel said. He gestured angrily with his head, not moving otherwise. Jerome hadn't moved either, as if still trying to remain inconspicuous.

The kids all turned to look toward the store front.

"I don't see no cops," one of them said.

"They were just there," Ruel insisted.

"Maybe they off taking themselves a stroll or something."

"They'll be back any minute, for Christ sake."

This didn't seem to faze the kids. They appeared ready to take whatever came. Nor were they particularly threatening, but mostly just enjoying the spectacle of two grown men hiding in a doorway.

One of the fellows stepped closer for a better look, resting one foot on the little step. He wore a glistening silky red and black jacket and a soft black hat with a huge floppy brim. He studied Ruel first, then Jerome. "This ain't your turf now," he said, more in curiosity than anything else. "What you screwing around here for?"

"I live around here," Ruel said, growing angrier by the minute.

"Come on," the fellow said. "Who you shitting?"

"For Christ sake, I was *born* around here. I lived around here my whole goddamn *life*."

"Hey, now," the fellow said quietly, seeming to concede that it might be so, although he had his doubts. "You too?" he inquired of Jerome.

"No," Jerome said. He tried to make it sound casual: "I'm his friend."

The fellow looked back and forth between them, hunched in their corners. "That so now?"

"Those cops are coming back any minute," Ruel said. "This is no joke."

Again they all gazed toward the store front.

"Not yet," the kid announced with a smile.

"They're after me, for Christ sake."

"That the truth now?"

"They see me here and I'm dead," Ruel said. He hardly moved his lips, forcing the words between his teeth. "Is that what you want? You guys big buddies with the cops now?"

The kid raised one eyebrow, the whiteness of his eye expanding impressively. "We kin keep a secret. What they after you for?"

"I was a friend of Sylvester's."

"Who?"

"Childs, for Christ sake. Sylvester Childs. The guy that got wiped out this afternoon."

"Hey, man. We heard about that. That wasn't too good, was it?"

"You don't have to tell me," Ruel said. "I was his friend. I was his goddamn buddy."

The fellow mulled this over a bit and then turned again to Jerome. "You too?"

"I only met him that once," Jerome explained, "but I took to him right away."

"You don't say now?"

"Are you sure those cops ain't there?" Ruel demanded. He seemed ready to burst.

The kids looked calmly down the block.

"Don't see them," the fellow in the jacket said.

"What about the other ways?"

The kids looked down the other three streets. It was an odd sight, all those heads turning one way and another, but not in unison.

"No cops nowhere," the fellow said.

"I'm beating it," Ruel said.

"Where to?" the fellow asked, still intrigued.

Ruel didn't get the chance to answer. The other kids had been listening with some interest, but a bit of impatience had set in, and one of them playfully swatted the guy next to him with the oversized slingshot thing in his hand. He hit him on the shoulder, leaving a large white slash. The other kid naturally hit him right back, with all the mock rage that made their games such fun for kids, and so terrifying for adults. His blow left the same kind of white mark—and Jerome realized they were carrying chalk-filled nylons.

In an instant they were all whirling and flashing at each other, whooping it up at every hit.

Ruel leaped from the doorway to break away but either tripped or was tripped, Jerome couldn't tell, and went down in a fearful tumble of arms and legs. He was immediately set upon by the whole pack, gleefully shoving each other aside for a good shot.

It was like a clash of Ferris wheels, those flailing stockings, like half a dozen sparkling pinwheels in a cloud of billowing chalk dust. Ruel writhed violently from side to side on the ground trying to dodge the thudding stockings. He wasn't being hurt, but the shrieks of the kids made it sound like someone being beaten within an inch of his life.

Somehow Ruel got to his feet. Coughing and half-blinded, swinging wildly, he lurched in the direction of the store front, stumbling more than running. He was having an awful time, trying to fend off the blows and beat back the kids at the same time, moving in fitful bursts, the kids moving with him, encircling him as he went and keeping him off balance with their pummeling.

Jerome scampered from the doorway after them. "Hey," he cried. "Stop it. Leave him be."

Ruel kept moving down the block, ducking and staggering, the kids moving right with him.

"The cops!" Jerome shouted, feeling silly, like a kid again, ages ago on the streets of Boston. But two policemen were racing across the street at the corner.

No one seemed to hear. Ruel and the kids were practically in front of the broken window. Jerome burst into the circle, into the choking dust, taking the blows on his upraised arms but staggered by them nonetheless. "The cops!" he gasped, and pushed Ruel forward, out of the circle. He had no idea why he did it, or what he hoped to accomplish. The kids, he was sure, would scatter and run, leaving the two of them to face the police, or to run too. But the kids had grown so cocky, or maybe had such childlike enthusiasm for their game, that they amazed him by turning around, laughing and taunting, to challenge the oncoming cops by slapping their stockings against the pavement.

Ruel grabbed Jerome's shoulders and shoved him toward the window, almost sending him crashing into it, and pushed him through the jagged star-shaped hole. Jerome had to step up—and quickly, with Ruel coming right behind him—to get through the opening, climbing onto a ledge inside the window, and then down off it, stumbling, slipping and sliding on the broken glass.

Ruel came crashing down on top of him and shoved him toward the back of the room. They could see only dim shapes and bumped and stumbled as they went along. The place was a shambles.

"The back room," Ruel said, giving Jerome another shove.

They had to circle an overturned table. The floor was covered with scattered papers, making the footing as bad as it'd been up front on the glass.

Ruel found the door and sent Jerome through. He rushed in behind him and latched the door. It was even darker in there. It was absolutely dark. Some light had come through the big whitewashed window in the other room, but this one had no windows.

"What are you trying to do?" Jerome was puffing hard. Everything smelled of chalk and his throat burned. "What on earth are you locking yourself in a closet for?"

"Shut up."

"They must have seen us," Jerome said.

"Shut up. Lemme listen."

Jerome listened too. He couldn't tell if it had quieted down out there or just seemed so from where they were.

"We gotta get something against the door," Ruel said. Jerome heard him groping around in the dark. "There's a desk here. Over here. Give me a hand."

"What good will that do?"

"For Christ sake, give me a hand."

Jerome moved toward the voice. You couldn't see your hand in front of your nose; Jerome tried. There was simply no light. He reached ahead and touched Ruel.

"Get the other side. We'll shove it over."

Jerome felt his way along the desk, a thick wood slab, rough and splintery.

"Let's go," Ruel said.

Jerome heard and felt the other end move. He shoved his end, then shoved again. They took turns, grunting, until they had it against the door. Jerome was puffing. "Isn't there another door? Isn't there some way out?"

"No."

"They can break in," Jerome said. "They can shove the desk aside."

"Let them try."

"Look what happened to Sylvester."

"Shut up."

Jerome listened again.

Ruel must have been listening too. "Maybe they're gone," he said.

"I don't see why on earth you're carrying on like this."

It was a while before Ruel answered. "What the hell am I *supposed* to do?"

Jerome could hear not only Ruel's anger and frustration but also, for the first time, a kind of awesome confusion, the sheer hopelessness of someone who'd never really figured out what he was supposed to do.

"I don't know," Jerome said, suddenly flustered. "But not run. Not act as if you've done something."

Ruel's breath was loud. "You don't know what the hell you're talking about."

Jerome said nothing. Where did you start with someone who didn't know if he was coming or going, helping or hurting himself? "How long are we planning to stay here?" he asked finally. It was still quiet on the street.

"As long as I feel like it, okay?"

"All night?"

"Why? You got an appointment somewhere?"

"Do you want me to take a look outside?"

"No."

"You're only bringing the cops on, the way you're acting."

"Don't tell me about the cops, all right? If there's one thing I know, it's the goddamn cops."

"How's that? Jerome said. "Have you been in trouble?"

"I was born in trouble."

"That's not true," Jerome said.

"That's what you say."

"What kind of trouble?"

"What kind you want? What kind you interested in?"

It was unsettling, staring wide-eyed and not seeing anything. "Have you ever been in jail?" he asked.

"Shit," Ruel said.

"Have you?"

"You name it," Ruel said. "I been there."

Jerome felt an airiness beneath his ribs. He forced himself to go on. "What about Sylvester?"

"What about him?"

"Has he been in jail too? Is that why the cops were after him?"

"I been places that guy never even dreamed of."

"I thought Sylvester was an ex-con too."

"Who told you that?"

Jerome was struggling, but what sense could you make of things barricaded in a room where you couldn't even see your hand before your face? "The police told me," he said. "The detective down there."

"Told you what? That Sylvester was an ex-con?"

"That's what I thought he said."

"Well, you thought wrong. I'll tell you one thing about Sylvester. He knew how to take care of himself. He wasn't getting shafted by anybody."

"He got himself killed."

"Well, all right. Only maybe that's why. Because he wasn't gonna get sent away. He wasn't that dumb. I'm the guy who's dumb. I'm the guy that gets shafted."

Jerome had trouble finding his voice. "The cops are after you," he said.

"Jesus, man. What the hell have I been *telling* you?"

"For the bomb," Jerome said. "They said they were after an ex-con."

Ruel said nothing.

"They were talking about you, not Sylvester."

"They been talking about me ever since I was born. I'm their favorite topic of conversation."

"I was there," Jerome said. "I saw a man killed by that bomb."

Ruel was silent.

"For what?" Jerome said. "What were you hoping to accomplish?"

Ruel remained silent, and Jerome couldn't tell if he was listening at the door, or thinking over his answer, or ignoring him.

"I got tricked into this," Jerome said. "So did Miss Cowan. You tricked us all."

"I didn't trick anybody."

"She still thinks Sylvester blew that place up. So does that fellow out there, Zeronski. Everybody's scurrying around trying to help you because they think you're innocent."

"Sure," Ruel said.

"Why'd you do it?"

"C'mon."

"At least give me that much satisfaction. You almost killed me with that bomb. Why'd you do it?"

"I like the noise, all right? I like to watch those funny guys running around in their uniforms. What are you trying to give me? Why the hell do you do things? Why does anybody do things? What the hell's supposed to be so different about me?"

They heard a siren. It grew louder and was joined by another, from a different direction. The two sirens converged out front, pitching and wailing, then growled down to silence.

"They'll kill you," Jerome said. "It's as simple as that."

"Sure," Ruel said. "One two three."

"Are you planning to fight them off with your bare hands?"

"It ain't just bare hands," Ruel said.

Jerome hesitated. "Have you got a gun?"

"I got a knife, you wanna know what I got."

"Sylvester had a dental tool."

"I ain't Sylvester. Besides, I got something else. I got you."

"Me? What do you expect me to do?"

"Right now, just be quiet."

"Let me go out and say you'll give up."

"Just stay where you are."

"You don't have any choice."

"I got a choice," he said.

They could hear someone moving outside in the alley. Sylvester had led Jerome through that alley on their tour, hopping the fence with his dashiki billowing and then pausing, with a smile and a bow, to open the gate for him.

"They're surrounding the place," Jerome said.

Ruel said nothing. Then he said: "Here."

"What?"

"Take this."

"What?"

"Take it. Where are you?"

Jerome reached ahead. He felt Ruel's outstretched arm, hard and sinewy, then his huge hand, then the envelope.

"Stick it in your pocket," Ruel told him. "They'll think I robbed a goddamn bank."

Jerome stuffed the envelope in his wallet. "Let me go out and talk to them."

"No."

"It's better than getting shot."

"They're not gonna shoot a nice old man like you."

"What about yourself?"

"I'm thinking about myself."

Jerome wet his lips. He could still taste the chalk dust. "It won't work," he said.

"We'll see maybe."

"You're twice my size."

"I can scrunch down."

"If I'm in front of you, they'll get you from behind."

"They better take good aim then, and make sure they don't get the wrong guy."

Jerome could envision himself, rigid and stretched, splay-footed, one arm wrenched back, the metallic edge like a razor against his Adam's apple. "It'll never work," he said. "You'd be crazy to even try it."

"We'll see," Ruel said.

There was an enormous shattering of glass. It was like the barbershop all over again. More glass shattered, and more. It sounded as if they were knocking out the whole front window to look in, taking no chances. A flash of light sliced under the door and disappeared: the cops playing their lights around the front room to make sure it was empty. Ready to shoot, maybe, at the first thing that moved.

"They're coming," Jerome said.

"Let them."

Jerome listened to the boots on the wooden floor, crushing the glass underneath, metal gear clanking. Another flash of light appeared beneath the door and remained for a few seconds: the cops staring at the door, maybe nodding to each other. The steps proceeded deliberately across the floor until they were right outside.

"All right," a voice bellowed, so loud and close Jerome jumped half out of his skin. "Come on out."

Jerome backed off to the side wall, as quietly as he could. It took him out of the direct line of the door, and farther from Ruel. Would he have a chance of dodging Ruel if it came to that? Scurrying from corner to corner in the pitch-black room?

"Are you coming out, or are we coming in?"

"He doesn't have a gun," Jerome shouted. "He's only got a knife. Don't shoot."

The silence seemed to reverberate. Ruel didn't move and neither did the cops. Jerome wondered if he'd actually yelled or just imagined it. His whole body was clenched. If someone touched him he'd have collapsed on the spot.

"Say you're coming out," he told Ruel. "Tell them you're giving up."

Ruel said nothing.

"They'll kill you if you try anything."

"Are you coming?" the cops demanded.

There was a long silence.

"Tell them yes," Jerome said. "Use your head."

"Yeah," Ruel said, but hardly loud enough to be heard through the door.

"What?" the cop called in.

"Yeah," Ruel said louder. "I'm coming."

There was another silence. "We'll have a light on you. Come out with your hands up."

"All right," Ruel yelled back.

The slice of light reappeared under the door and remained.

"Don't try to trick them," Jerome said.

Ruel said nothing. Jerome could hear him struggling with the desk.

"Do exactly what they say," Jerome told him.

Ruel moved the desk, scraping it noisily on the floor. "I'm coming," he called out.

"Keep your hands up. Don't try anything."

Jerome could see Ruel's feet as two interruptions in the line of light under the door. Ruel didn't move. He didn't move for a long time, and Jerome waited, brittle as a statue, knowing that Ruel could still grab him, could still press that knife to his stretched throat.

The door opened with a fantastic flash of light, as astonishing as a phosphorus flare, and so shattering that it could have been an explosion. It could have been a dozen guns firing at once. Jerome wheeled to the wall to cover his eyes and in that instant could envision Ruel's body like a blood-stained rag on the floor.

He opened his eyes, blinking in that still brilliant glare, to see Ruel with his long arms stretched overhead, his hat gone, his clothing chalked over, but still standing in that careless athlete's slouch; not straightening up for anyone, not even a posse of armed policemen.

"All right," a cop said, and Ruel stepped forward as if it were the commonest thing in the world, surrendering to the police.

Which showed, maybe, that Ruel had more sense than one might have imagined. Or that all Sylvester needed was somebody there with him, in the dental clinic, to inform the cops that he had no gun, that they need not shoot, the person's very presence serving to keep the cops from that temptation. Would they have shot Ruel if no one were around to witness it?

Ruel remained sullen and close-lipped, seeming in his own way as detached as the cops themselves until he was shouldered into a squad car and whisked away.

"That's right," the sergeant told Jerome. "The bomb in the barbershop."

"I was there," Jerome said. "I know all about it."

Which was a mistake, and just complicated things, since the cops were having trouble figuring out what to do with him anyway. They wanted to know what had brought him into the West Side at this time of night and what, in particular, he was doing with Ruel.

"We were afraid," the sergeant said, "he'd use you as a shield or something."

"What would you have done in that case?"

"Picked him off," the sergeant said.

"Maybe he realized that," Jerome said. "Or just didn't want to put me in that kind of danger."

"I'm not so sure about that."

"I'm not either," Jerome said. "I just mention it as a possibility."

"Could we kind of clear up now what you were doing here?"

"I'm a law-abiding citizen," Jerome pointed out. "I've never even gotten a traffic ticket."

"No one's accusing you of anything, Mr. Tinney. We'd just like to know what was going on."

"Mr. Amicus will understand," Jerome said. "We've already talked this whole thing over, at some length."

"We'll understand too, if you'll just tell us."

"It's pretty complicated."

"We'll try real hard to follow."

Jerome took a breath. "I thought the other fellow, Sylvester, did it. I thought this fellow, Ruel, was innocent, although deep down I guess I really thought the other fellow was too. But a mutual friend, who also thought he was innocent, but was afraid the cops thought he was guilty, asked me to see if I could help out. I didn't want to, in all honesty, because I didn't have a very good feeling about him, although I never really suspected he did it. Anyhow, we were just standing on the corner when all these kids came by, carrying nylon stockings filled with chalk dust."

The sergeant sucked thoughtfully on his lower lip.

"Here comes Amicus," one of the cops said.

And there he was, stepping out of a regular sedan, not a police car, but with one of those thick coiled antennas on the back.

"You work long hours," Jerome said.

"Only for the glory," Amicus said, touching the brim of his hat, his face as stony as ever. "The pay's lousy."

Jerome explained all over again, Amicus listening patiently on the sidewalk in front of the smashed-out window, the sergeant and four or five other cops listening too, a few paces back.

"When I get to your age," Amicus said when Jerome finished, "I figure on just settling down to watch the ball games on TV."

"I was never a great sports fan," Jerome said.

"Who was the friend who asked you to come?"

Jerome paused. "Olivia Cowan."

Amicus pulled back one side of his mouth.

"You may have seen her car around the corner," Jerome said. "The Jaguar."

"You're driving her car?"

"She was concerned about Ruel. She still thinks he's innocent."

"Where is she now?"

"Waiting for me at the Mayfair. I thought maybe, after a day like this, I'd treat the woman to a nightcap."

Amicus raised an eyebrow.

"Would you care to join us?"

"Maybe another time."

"She's a lovely woman," Jerome said.

"Lovely."

"Can I go now?"

"You're as free as the breeze."

Jerome paused. "I ought to appologize for some of the things I said. You people did your job. You got your man."

"We try our best," Amicus said.

"But Sylvester's dead."

"Nobody's perfect," Amicus said.

They had their nightcap. It'd been a strange feeling, pausing at the steps leading down into the lounge, making a few final swipes at the remaining smudges of chalk on his jacket, searching for Olivia in the dim greenish light and then seeing her, alone at a small table: tall and elegant, her head high, a beautiful woman forlornly fingering a long-stemmed glass. An image, maybe, that would stay with you.

He was surprised at how calmly he could recount what had happened, and at how calmly she listened, not interrupting, not reacting at all. The woman was drained, it was as simple as that. Even the news that Ruel, not Sylvester, had planted the bomb failed to bring any response.

It was understandable. How much satisfaction could she find in Sylvester's innocence, pitted against the fact of his death? And the prospect of Ruel being tossed back into a prison cell, no matter what you felt about the boy, hardly called for rejoicing. The one boy so easy to like, the other so hard, and both brought down, both written off. With Sylvester you'd had some inkling of what his final flowering might have been. Not so Ruel. Whatever promise he might have possessed, he'd done his best to hide it. But he must have had something to offer, and you wished you could have gotten at least a glimpse of it, a hint. You wished that you could have seen him just once the way you imagined him: on a basketball court, full of easy grace, with a kind of boyish enthusiasm, outleaping all the others with the tremendous spring of those legs, a thing of awe as he moved, that smile you'd never known maybe showing itself at last, broad enough to warm your heart.

"Maybe he shouldn't have given up," Olivia said when Jerome described how easily, at the end, Ruel had walked into their arms. "Maybe Sylvester had the right idea."

"You don't believe that."

"I guess not," she admitted.

He could see what was troubling her. It troubled him too. Hard as it was to live without answers—without being able to say, *This is it; this is what happened*—it was just as hard to live with them.

Of course she still saw things her own way, and maybe found some solace in that. She remained convinced that Zeronski was behind it all, Sylvester's death and the bomb too, now certain that the man had either tricked or bought off Ruel, and that he would, as sure as night followed day, escape untouched.

Jerome didn't argue. If it wasn't the truth, it served as such, and she had as much right as the next person to seek comfort in her own constructions.

"What about this?" Jerome said finally, placing the envelope on the table.

Olivia looked at it a long time. "Did you mention it to the police?"

"No."

"What should we do with it?"

"Give it back, I guess," Jerome said.

"I don't want anything back."

"The fellow out there may."

"He won't miss it."

"That's not the point," Jerome said.

"Maybe we should burn it."

"We could get Ruel a lawyer with it."

"Ruel will have a lawyer."

"We could give it to charity. Whatever you want. It's not up to me."

"Why not just scatter it from a rooftop? That'd be a kind of charity."

"Better than burning it," Jerome said.

Olivia toyed with her glass and then said, without looking up: "Sylvester's mother."

"Fine with me," Jerome said. "But not tonight."

"No," she said. "Not tonight."

"Good," Jerome said. The Courvoisier had just about done him in.

On the way back to the gallery they passed the street that led to the barbershop and the clinic, and Olivia again turned to gaze in that direction.

"I warned Sylvester," she said. "He should have gotten away while he had the chance." After a moment's silence she added: "I warned Ruel too."

"No one warned the schoolteacher," Jerome said. "No one told him to stay home that morning and skip his haircut."

"No one told you either, and you came through all right."

"It was just a scratch," Jerome said.

"How'd you manage? What's your secret?"

"Luck, I guess, as far as the bomb was concerned."

"Have you been lucky all your life?"

"Too soon to say."

"Thank you for everything," she told him on the sidewalk in front of the gallery. "You've been awfully sweet, and I appreciate it." She offered him her hand, cool and gentle, and once again Jerome felt that small delicate *flip* in his chest, the years melting like snow. She offered her cheek, and Jerome gave her a peck.

"The high point of the whole week," he said, hoping to cut her forlornness with a little cheer.

"Your first kiss?" she asked with a smile. A brave smile, pale and fluttering.

"The first was just yesterday," Jerome said. "Nineteen-twelve, I think it was."

"Will you get home all right?"

"Of course," he insisted.

But it was hard sledding at that hour, and exhaustion hit him like a hammer. Heart and lungs, a gaggle of workable organs and a pair of willing legs: that's all you had, your one ticket to the game, and he was grateful at least to have survived another round against the calendar and the clock with nothing worse to show for it than a fat pink worm over his ribs. It was something, after all, to push the elevator button and not have the whole building blow up in your face.

He would feel better in the morning. Braced and cross-braced, the newest kid on the block again, twirling a stick. Without any of the easy winners maybe, but not fool enough, not by a longshot, to start playing fast and loose with the kinds of truth that had gotten him this far.